The
Monkey Wrench
Gang

BOOKS BY EDWARD ABBEY

The Brave Cowboy

Desert Solitaire

Fire on the Mountain

Black Sun

The Monkey Wrench Gang

Hayduke Lives!

Good News

The Fool's Progress

Abbey's Road

Down the River

Beyond the Wall

One Life at a Time, Please

The Journey Home

The Hidden Canyon

edward abbey

The
Monkey Wrench
Gang

HARPER**PERENNIAL** ● MODERN**CLASSICS**

NEW YORK ● LONDON ● TORONTO ● SYDNEY

HARPER**PERENNIAL** ● MODERN**CLASSICS**

P.S.™ is a trademark of HarperCollins Publishers.

THE MONKEY WRENCH GANG. Copyright © 1975, 1985 by Edward Abbey. Introduction copyright © 2000 by Douglas Brinkley. All rights reserved. Printed in the United States of America. No part of this book may be used or reproduced in any manner whatsoever without written permission except in the case of brief quotations embodied in critical articles and reviews. For information address HarperCollins Publishers, 10 East 53rd Street, New York, NY 10022.

HarperCollins books may be purchased for educational, business, or sales promotional use. For information please write: Special Markets Department, HarperCollins Publishers, 10 East 53rd Street, New York, NY 10022.

First Perennial Classics edition published 2000.
Reissued in Harper Perennial Modern Classics 2006.

Library of Congress Cataloging-in-Publication data is available upon request.

ISBN-10: 0-06-112976-3 (reissue)
ISBN-13: 978-0-06-112976-6 (reissue)

08 09 10 RRD 10 9 8 7 6

This book, though fictional in form, is based strictly on historical fact. Everything in it is real or actually happened. And it all began just one year from today.

E. A.
Wolf Hole, Arizona

IN MEMORIAM: *Ned Ludd*

. . . a lunatic living about 1779, who in a fit of rage smashed up two frames belonging to a Leicestershire "stockinger."
—*The Oxford Universal Dictionary*

Down with all kings but King Ludd.
—Byron

CONTENTS

x   Contents

. . . but oh my desert
yours is the only death I cannot bear.
—Richard Shelton

Resist much. Obey little.
—Walt Whitman

Now. Or never.
—Thoreau

sabotage . . . *n.* [Fr. < *sabot,* wooden shoe + −AGE: from damage done to machinery by sabots] . . . .

—*Webster's New World Dictionary*

INTRODUCTION
by Douglas Brinkley

> Give me silence, water, hope.
> Give me struggle, iron, volcanoes.
> —PABLO NERUDA

Strange to think of him now hiding out in the mysterious canyons of the Colorado Plateau like some solitary prospector from a B. Traven novel. Trim, leathery, and artfully disheveled, complete with scraggly, unfashionable beard, for more than thirty years Edward Abbey presented himself as the literary watchdog of the arid American West, writing eight novels, dozens of travelogues, and hundreds of essays, all aimed at the heart of the industrial complex President Dwight D. Eisenhower had warned about in his surprisingly frank farewell address of January 17, 1961. Abbey's motto came from Walt Whitman—"resist much, obey little"—and he was delighted that everything from the FBI to the Sierra Club derided him as a "desert anarchist." Blessed with a wicked sense of humor and penchant for pranksterism, Abbey carefully cultivated his ever-changing role as a stubborn provocateur, be it in the guise of a river rat, a learned scholar, a gun-toting curmudgeon, or a committed ecologist, personae he shuffled at whim, the only apparent constant being the sarcasm he did so with. But he also was always a disciplined writer, even while playing the robust outdoorsman obsessed with stopping the pillage of the American West. "We can have wilderness without freedom," Abbey often said. "We can have wilderness without human life at all; but we cannot have freedom without wilderness."

And he believed it. Throughout the Cold War era, no writer went further to defend the West's natural places from strip-mining, speed-logging, power plants, oil companies, concrete dams, bombing ranges, and strip malls than the sardonic Edward Abbey. Saguaro cacti were sacred to Abbey, not utility poles. His entire adult life was devoted to stopping the "Californicating" of the Four Corners states he considered home—Arizona, Colorado, New Mexico, and Utah. Abbey was labeled the "Thoreau of the West" by novelist Larry McMurtry in an article in the *Washington Post,* a squib that remains the best shorthand description of this unorthodox yet meticulous literary craftsman. Abbey rejected out of hand the notion that he was a "nature writer" along the lines of John McPhee or Annie Dillard, even if the untamed wilderness did serve as his lifelong muse; instead he fancied himself an old-fashioned American moralist, a Mencken-esque maverick who kowtowed to no one in his quest to expose others' treachery, hypocrisy, and greed. It was the "moral duty" of a writer, Abbey insisted, to act as social critic of one's country and culture, and as such to speak for the voiceless. And so he did, especially in the memorable jeremiad with which he launched America's "ecodefense" movement and rattled the cages of both Big Industry and Big Government: his 1975 novel *The Monkey Wrench Gang,* here reprinted as a Perennial Classic on the twenty-fifth anniversary of its first publication.

Abbey was born to the task he would set himself on January 29, 1927, in Home, Pennsylvania. As an adolescent, he became disgusted with the big lumber companies' wanton destruction of the pristine Appalachian woodlands where he grew up hunting squirrels, collecting rocks, and studying plants with the budding fervor of William Bartram, in what he called these "glens of mystery and shamanism." Abbey fantasized that he was Natty Bumpo hiking the Adirondacks or Johnny Appleseed planting seeds in the Ohio River Valley. His father, Paul Revere Abbey, was a hardscrabble farmer and occasional coal miner who revered the radical leaders of the Industrial Workers of the

World, or "Wobblies," as they were popularly known, such as "Big Bill" Haywood and Joe Hill. The entire Abbey clan, in fact, was steeped in American folklore of the Daniel Boone variety: a deep love of the untrammeled frontier and an obsessive mistrust of Washington, D.C. Young Edward inherited from his father an uncouth and ornery disposition to take on the establishment with relish, and head-on: "Sentiment without action," Abbey always said, "is the ruin of the soul."

In the summer of 1944, the seventeen-year-old left Pennsylvania to seek the America he had heard about in Woody Guthrie songs and Carl Sandburg poems. He hitchhiked to Seattle, tramped down the Pacific Coast to San Francisco, ventured inland to the sequoia forests of Yosemite, then boxcarred down through the San Joaquin Valley, making his meager keep picking fruit or working in canneries along the way. His hobo holiday of storybook adventure and intoxicating freedom lost its allure only once, when he was arrested for vagrancy in Flagstaff, Arizona, and tossed into jail like the common drunkards already there. It only added to a coming-of-age experience Jack London would have approved of.

The glories of the American West captivated the young Edward Abbey. He stopped transfixed before the salmon-pink rangelands of Navajo County spreading out in front of him at sundown, at ancient sandstone cliffs, slick rock canyons, creosote bushes, hungry javelinas, Hopi arroyos, dusty cantinas, ash-throated flycatchers, turkey buzzards, loping coyotes, worn-edged arrowheads, and all the other wonders of the surreal region others mistook for barren. To Abbey, the Sonoran Desert and Death Valley were equally gorgeous dreamlands where an unrelenting vermillion sun bleached the bones of dead cattle a blinding white. "There is no shortage of water in the desert but exactly the right amount," Abbey would write later, "a perfect ratio of water to rock, of water to sand, ensuring that wide, free, open, generous spacing among plants and animals, homes and towns and cities, which makes the arid west so different from any other part of the nation. There is no lack of water here, unless you try to establish a city where no city should be." In this forsaken, naked paradise,

Abbey felt at peace. When he saw the great Colorado River tracing its ancient path near Needles, California, bringing its life-sustaining waters to the driest desert, Abbey wrote, "For the first time, I felt I was getting close to the West of my deepest imaginings, the place where the tangible and the mythical became the same."

Shortly thereafter, the wanderer of the canyons was drafted into the U.S. Army and spent the last year of World War II serving in Italy. Upon returning home he headed straight for the Land of Enchantment in the form of the University of New Mexico, where he earned a B.A. in philosophy in 1951 and an M.A. in 1956, the latter on a thesis titled "Anarchy and the Morality of Violence," in which he concluded that anarchism wasn't really about military might, as the Bolshevik Revolution had been, but about opposition to, as Leo Tolstoy had put it, "the organized violence of the state."

A self-styled flute-playing bum wandering his way through coffeehouses and university circles, Abbey was winked at as Albuquerque's take on the ancient Greek cynic Diogenes, who allegedly abandoned all his possessions to live in a barrel and beg for his keep. Along the same lines, Abbey took to passionately denouncing the spoilers of the West: greedy developers, cattle ranchers, strip-mining outfits, and the Federal Bureau of Land Management. In response, the FBI began monitoring Abbey for possible communist activities—and continued its surveillance of him for the next thirty-seven years, eventually concluding that he was just a particularly stubborn and individualistic pacifist.

In 1954 Abbey published his first novel, *Jonathan Troy,* the story of a nineteen-year-old anarchist who alienates everyone he encounters, while building the narrative theme that machines were ruining America. Over the next ten years Abbey published six more books, including *The Brave Cowboy* (1956)—the tale of a barbed-wire-cutting maverick engaged in his own war with the U.S. government's livestock grazing policy, which was made into the 1962 Kirk Douglas movie *Lonely Are the Brave*—and *Desert Solitaire* (1968), a first-person meditation based on the two seasons Abbey spent as a ranger at Utah's Arches National Monument, which the *New York Times* called "a passionately felt, deeply poetic book." Abbey, in fact, wrote these books while working on and off for the U.S. Forest Service and the National Park Service over nearly two decades. "For most of these years," he recalled, "I was living right around the official poverty line. . . . I pounded in survey stakes before I ever got the notion to pull them out."

Like Cervantes' Don Quixote tilting at windmills, Abbey became notorious in the American Southwest for ransacking construction sites, denouncing ranchers as "welfare parasites," and shocking Easterners with his harsh conservationist prose. Unlike more conventional advocates of the burgeoning environmental movement of the early 1970s, however, the mischievous Abbey also flaunted his wildly contradictory impulses, with acts such as roaring through the streets of Tucson in a vintage red Cadillac convertible with a plastic geranium stuck in the hood ornament and the radio blaring Mozart, Brahms, or Waylon Jennings. As a professional nose-tweaker, the bane of Abbey's existence, the purpose of his antigrowth prose and outlaw posture, was to rage against the machine, to become the most ferocious defender of the American West since John Muir.

The windmill Abbey wanted to tear down most was the Glen Canyon Dam, constructed in 1962 just sixty miles north of the Grand Canyon, a 792,000-ton hydraulic monstrosity that had cost U.S. taxpayers $750 million to build. This concrete colossus had stemmed the natural flow of the Colorado River, desecrating the steep walls of the magnificent Glen Canyon that Abbey imagined grander than all the cathedrals in Europe. Gone forever in the dam's building were groves of cottonwood and thickets of redbud, wolves' dens and eagles' nests, natural sandstone spires and ancient archaeological sites. In their place man made Lake Powell, a reservoir with an 1,800-mile shoreline that Abbey dubbed "the blue death." Glen Canyon Dam was a pork-barrel project ostensibly built to provide Los Angeles, Las Vegas, and Phoenix with electric power at low cost; in fact, it was an engineering abomination that destroyed an entire ecosystem. Even the dam's conservative godfather—Arizona Republican Senator Barry

Goldwater—would eventually admit that its construction had been a terrible mistake.

It was with a bellyful of bile over Glen Canyon Dam that Abbey began writing *The Monkey Wrench Gang* in the early 1970s, putting black humor, theater gimmicks, and clever characterizations together to form what would become a lasting cult classic. Drawing on facets of real people he knew of, Abbey created an inspired cast of anti-heroes: George Washington Hayduke, a former Green Beret medic in Vietnam who loved bombs, booze, and the great outdoors almost as much as he hated developers; Doc Sarvis, a rich Albuquerque heart specialist whose hobby was burning billboards; Bonnie Abbzug, a preternaturally sexy, sharp-tongued, and endearing Jewish exile from the Bronx; and Seldom Seen Smith, a Mormon riverboat guide and watermelon rancher with three contented wives. In what *Newsweek* approvingly reviewed as an "ecological caper," this gaggle of good-time anarchists mobilize themselves SWAT-like to harass power companies and logging conglomerates. Like their hero Ned Ludd—an early nineteenth-century British weaver who provoked his countrymen to save their jobs by sabotaging machinery in the early days of the Industrial Revolution, and to whom Abbey dedicated the novel—the Monkey Wrenchers develop into a charismatic clique of econuisances who pour Karo syrup into bulldozers' fuel tanks, snip barbed-wire fences, and try to blow up a coal train all in preparation for their real objective: dynamiting Glen Canyon Dam to bits. Their battle cry is "Keep it like it was."

The Monkey Wrench Gang is far more than just a controversial book—it is revolutionary, anarchic, seditious, and, in the wrong hands, dangerous. Although Abbey claimed it was just a work of fiction written to "entertain and amuse," the novel was swiftly embraced by ecoactivists frustrated with the timid approaches of mainstream environmental groups like the Sierra Club and the Audubon Society. To the radical-minded, Abbey's picaresque novel was a call to action, with the passion of Seldom Seen Smith when he knelt in the middle of Glen Canyon Dam and prayed: "Dear old God, you know and I know what it was like here, before them bastards from Washington moved in and ruined it all. You remember the river, how fat and golden it was in June, when the big runoff come down from the Rockies? . . . Remember that crick that come down through Bridge Canyon and Forbidden Canyon, how green and cool and clear it was? . . . Remember the cataracts in Forty-Mile Canyon? Well, they flooded out about half of them too. And part of the Escalante's gone now. . . . Listen, are you listenin' to me? There's somethin' you can do for me, God. How about a little old *pre*-cision-type earthquake right under this dam?"

Critic Donn Rawlings downplayed *The Monkey Wrench Gang* as a madcap tale of "symbolic aggression," but to many shocked readers it was an irresponsible blueprint for terrorism akin to the white supremacist *Turner Diaries* that supposedly sparked the 1995 bombing of the Murrah Federal Building in Oklahoma City. When asked if he was really advocating blowing up a dam, Abbey said, "No," but added that "if someone else wanted to do it, I'd be there holding a flashlight." Failing to see his humor, Abbey's detractors ignored an important point: lovable pranksters in his novel kill only machines, not people, unlike the truly violent protagonists of such fictional works as Anthony Burgess's *A Clockwork Orange* and Hubert Selby Jr.'s *Last Exit to Brooklyn*.

Astute reviewers saw *The Monkey Wrench Gang* for what it was: a wildly satiric, clever, postmodern pulp Western that lampooned everything from the Lone Ranger to John Wayne to the women's movement. No one claimed it a fictional masterwork—it isn't—but like Harriet Beecher Stowe's *Uncle Tom's Cabin* and Upton Sinclair's *The Jungle,* it was a rousing wake-up call, this time on behalf of endangered species and old-growth redwoods. Abbey wanted to return to a time when the American West was unmarred by industry and the ravages of so-called "progress." To him, anarchy was just democracy in action, and his book's ecoraiders were just bold American patriots like those who participated in the Boston Tea Party or fought alongside Ethan Allen and his Green Mountain Boys. Following this tradition, Abbey's fictional Monkey Wrenchers considered themselves justified in resorting to whatever means they found necessary to defend the

Four Corners region from "deskbound executives" with their "hearts in a safe deposit box and their eyes hypnotized by calculators." It was civil disobedience in the grand tradition of Thoreau. After all, in *A Week on the Concord and Merrimack Rivers* (1849), Thoreau surprised readers by advocating the use of violence against a dam: "I for one am with thee, and who knows what may avail a crowbar against Billerica dam."

After its publication *The Monkey Wrench Gang* took on a life of its own. By the early 1980s many grassroots environmentalists, like Abbey's gang, had come to feel betrayed by large organizations such as the Sierra Club, which had secretly negotiated the future of Glen Canyon in closed-door meetings with the U.S. Bureau of Reclamation during the Kennedy administration. Then, a real-life deal had been struck under which the bureau agreed to cancel its plans to build a dam in Dinosaur National Monument in Utah and Colorado in exchange for allowing one to be built in Glen Canyon. Disillusioned with the political process, a new, militant group of ecoanarchists calling themselves Earth First! adopted Abbey as their guru, *The Monkey Wrench Gang* as their bible, and George Washington Hayduke's credo—"Always pull up survey stakes anywhere you find them"—as their own.

Earth First! rankled the public and even other environmentalists from the start. The group announced itself in 1981 by unfurling a hundred-yard-long black plastic streamer designed to look like a deep crack down the face of Glen Canyon Dam—a scene taken straight from the opening pages of *The Monkey Wrench Gang*. It was a harmless, guerrilla-theater stunt, but the U.S. government chose to interpret it instead as a dangerous act by a new soft-core ecoterrorist group, setting off a swirl of controversy: the political right denounced Earth First! out of hand, while the left chuckled at its Yippieish antics. A 1991 *Los Angeles Times* headline summed up the dueling perceptions: "Terrorists or Saviors?"

Many applauded the group's bold antics, which ranged from blocking the paths of bulldozers in Nevada to sitting in trees slated for clear-cutting in California to burying salt in dirt airstrips in Idaho so that deer and elk would dig them up beyond usefulness. Arrested in Wyoming, jailed in Montana, and beaten in Oregon, the Earth First!ers made Sierra Clubbers look like Junior Leaguers on a do-gooder field trip. Abbey's volatile Hayduke—modeled after his real-life chum Doug Peacock, who after serving in Vietnam opted to live among the grizzly bears in Yellowstone National Park—became Earth First!'s avatar, a fearless eco-David slinging rocks at the mechanized Goliaths. David Foreman—one of the Earth First! founders who helped unfurl the phony crack down Glen Canyon—wrote an Abbeyesque sabotage primer titled *Eco-Defense: A Field Guide to Monkey Wrenching*.

As might be expected, the FBI had continued monitoring these latter-day Luddites, infiltrating the group, collecting 1,200 hours of tape-recorded conversations among its members and arresting a number of them for spiking trees, cutting power lines, or destroying bull-dozers. Abbey never joined Earth First!, refusing to take responsibility for its high-profile vandalism. Yet he took pride in this new generation of Monkey Wrenchers, and befriended some of their leaders, at whose request he occasionally contributed brief bursts of wisdom to the Earth First! newspaper. "Enjoy yourself," he instructed its readers in one such piece. "Keep your brain in your head and your head firmly attached to your body, the body active and alive, and I promise you one sweet victory over our enemies."

Twenty-five years after its initial publication, some 700,000 paperbacks of *The Monkey Wrench Gang* have been sold, even though Abbey—who died in 1989 at age sixty-two—made the *New Yorker* and *Paris Review* crowds uncomfortable. He called the revered Tom Wolfe a "faggoty fascist fop" and the sainted John Updike a boring armchair purveyor of "suburban soap operas," yet his diehard fans included such well-known writers as Joan Didion, Wendell Berry, Thomas Pynchon, Cormac McCarthy, Peter Matthiessen, Hunter S. Thompson, Larry McMurtry, and Thomas McGuane. The late Wallace Stegner, in fact, proclaimed that Abbey presented the "stinger of a scorpion" and was the "most effective publicist of the West's curious desire to rape itself since Bernard DeVoto."

The American Southwest has produced other fine writers—Mary

Austin, Oliver LaFarge, and Barbara Kingsolver come to mind—but none has piqued readers' imaginations to the same extent as Edward Abbey. And in his twentieth and last book—*Hayduke Lives!*, a posthumous sequel to *The Monkey Wrench Gang*—Abbey has the last word: "Anyone who takes this book seriously will be shot. Anyone who does not take it seriously will be buried alive by a Mitsubishi bulldozer."

In *Epitaph for a Desert Anarchist: The Life and Legacy of Edward Abbey,* journalist James Bishop Jr. recounts a letter that William Butler Yeats once wrote to Oscar Wilde stating that he "envied those men who become mythological while still living." *The Monkey Wrench Gang* transformed Abbey from being an exquisite chronicler of Utah's canyonlands to a full-fledged folk figure, the literary equivalent of a "Green" Jesse James. Even in death mystery surrounded Abbey, and in radical environmental circles many believe he is still alive. Scrawled on bathroom walls and campground bulletin boards throughout the West the phrase "Abbey Lives!" abounds.

It is my prediction that in the coming years both the legend of Edward Abbey and *The Monkey Wrench Gang* will grow in popularity as the environmental movement swells in numbers, Detroit automakers launch a "Clean Revolution" by phasing out the internal combustion engine in favor of hydrogen fuel cells, and the U.S. government tears down dams like Glen Canyon that should never have been built. Like Rachel Carson's *Silent Spring*, Abbey's notorious novel will be savored because of its proactive defense of nature in an era of dangerous hyperindustrialism. To Abbey, *The Monkey Wrench Gang*, however, was more in line with Tom Paine's *Common Sense*. It was written to be read in sawdust taverns and isolated cabins, on hiking trails and in humming factories. Abbey never cared whether it was deemed a work of art by the *New York Times* or Alfred Kazin—it was made to jar the soul—and even his most severe critics must grant that, at least in that regard, *The Monkey Wrench Gang* was a whopping success.

Douglas Brinkley is Director of the Eisenhower Center for American Studies and Professor of History at the University of New Orleans.

The
Monkey Wrench
Gang

PROLOGUE

❧❧

The Aftermath

When a new bridge between two sovereign states of the United States has been completed, it is time for speech. For flags, bands and electronically amplified techno-industrial rhetoric. For the public address.

The people are waiting. The bridge, bedecked with bunting, streamers and Day-Glo banners, is ready. All wait for the official opening, the final oration, the slash of ribbon, the advancing limousines. No matter that in actual fact the bridge has already known heavy commercial use for six months.

Long files of automobiles stand at the approaches, strung out for a mile to the north and south and monitored by state police on motorcycles, sullen, heavy men creaking with leather, stiff in riot helmet, badge, gun, Mace, club, radio. The proud tough sensitive flunkies of the rich and powerful. Armed and dangerous.

The people wait. Sweltering in the glare, roasting in their cars bright as beetles under the soft roar of the sun. That desert sun of Utah-Arizona, the infernal flaming plasmic meatball in the sky. Five thousand people yawning in their cars, intimidated by the cops and bored to acedia by the chant of the politicians. Their squalling kids fight in the back seats, Frigid Queen ice cream drooling down chins and elbows, pooling Jackson Pollock schmierkunst on the monovalent radicals of the Vinylite seat covers. All endure though none can bear to listen to the high-decibel racket pouring from the public-address system.

The bridge itself is a simple, elegant and compact arch of steel, concrete as a statement of fact, bearing on its back the incidental ribbon of asphalt, a walkway, railings, security lights. Four hundred feet long, it spans a gorge seven hundred feet deep: Glen Canyon. Flowing through the bottom of the gorge is the tame and domesticated Colorado River, released from the bowels of the adjacent Glen Canyon Dam. Formerly a golden-red, as the name implies, the river now runs cold, clear and green, the color of the glacier water.

Great river—greater dam. Seen from the bridge the dam presents a gray sheer concave face of concrete aggregate, impacable and mute. A gravity dam, eight hundred thousand tons of solidarity, countersunk in the sandstone Navajo formation, fifty million years emplaced, of the bedrock and canyon walls. A plug, a block, a fat wedge, the dam diverts through penstocks and turbines the force of the puzzled river.

What was once a mighty river. Now a ghost. Spirits of sea gulls and pelicans wing above the desiccated delta a thousand miles to seaward. Spirits of beaver nose upstream through the silt-gold surface. Great blue herons once descended, light as mosquitoes, long legs dangling, to the sandbars. Wood ibis croaked in the cottonwood. Deer walked the canyon shores. Snowy egrets in the tamarisk, plumes waving in the river breeze. . . .

The people wait. The speech goes on, many round mouths, one speech, and hardly a word intelligible. There seem to be spooks in the circuitry. The loudspeakers, black as charcoal, flaring from mounts on the gooseneck lampposts thirty feet above the roadway, are bellowing like Martians. A hash of sense, the squeak and gibber of technetronic poltergeists, strangled phrase and filbrillated paragraph, boom forth with the hollow roar, all the same, of AUTHORITY—

. . . this proud state of Utah [*bleeeeeeep!*] glad to have this opportunity [*ronk!*] take part in opening of this magnificent bridge [*bleeeeeeet!*] joining us to great state of Arizona, fastest growing [*yiiiiiiiiiiiinnnnnnnnnng!*] to help promote and assure continued growth and economic [*rawk! yawk! yiiiinnnng! niiiinnnnnng!*] could give me more pleasure, Governor, than this significant occasion [*rawnk!*] of our two states [*blonk!*] by that great dam. . . .

Waiting, waiting. Far back in the line of cars, beyond reach of speech and out of sight of cop, a horn honks. And honks again. The sound of one horn, honking. A patrolman turns on his Harley hog, scowling, and cruises down the line. The honking stops.

The Indians also watch and wait. Gathered on an open hillside above the highway, on the reservation side of the river, an informal congregation of Ute, Paiute, Hopi and Navajo lounge about among their brand-new pickup trucks. The men and women drink Tokay, the swarms of children Pepsi-Cola, all munching on mayonnaise and Kleenex sandwiches of Wonder, Rainbo and Holsum Bread. Our noble red brethren eyeball the ceremony at the bridge, but their ears and hearts are with Merle Haggard, Johnny Paycheck and Tammy Wynette blaring from truck radios out of Station K-A-O-S— *Kaos!*—in Flagstaff, Arizona.

The citizens wait; the official voices drone on and on into the mikes, through the haunted wiring, out of the addled speakers. Thousands huddled in their idling automobiles, each yearning to be free and first across the arch of steel, that weightless-looking bridge which spans so gracefully the canyon gulf, the airy emptiness where swallows skate and plane.

Seven hundred feet down. It is difficult to fully grasp the meaning of such a fall. The river moves so far below, churning among its rocks, that the roar comes up sounding like a sigh. A breath of wind carries the sigh away.

The bridge stands clear and empty except for the cluster of notables at the center, the important people gathered around the microphones and a symbolic barrier of red, white and blue ribbon stretched across the bridge from rail to rail. The black Cadillacs are parked at either end of the bridge. Beyond the official cars, wooden barricades and motorcycle patrolmen keep the masses at bay.

Far beyond the dam, the reservoir, the river and the bridge, the town of Page, the highway, the Indians, the people and their leaders, stretches the rosy desert. Hot out there, under the fierce July sun—the temperature at ground level must be close to 150 degrees Fahrenheit. All sensible creatures are shaded up or waiting out the day in cool burrows under the surface. No humans live in that pink wasteland. There is nothing to stay the eye from roving farther and farther, across league after league of rock and sand to the vertical façades of butte, mesa and plateau forming the skyline fifty miles away. Nothing grows out there but scattered clumps of blackbrush and cactus, with here and there a scrubby, twisted, anguished-looking juniper. And a little scurf pea, a little snakeweed. Nothing more. Nothing moves but one pale whirlwind, a tottering little tornado of dust which lurches into a stone pillar and collapses. Nothing observes the mishap but a vulture hovering on the thermals three thousand feet above.

The buzzard, if anyone were looking, appears to be alone in the immensity of the sky. But he is not. Beyond the range of even the sharpest human eyes but perceptible to one another, other vultures wait, soaring lazily on the air. If one descends, spotting below something dead or dying, the others come from all directions, out of nowhere, and gather with bowed heads and hooded eyes around the body of the loved one.

Back to the bridge: The united high-school marching bands of Kanab, Utah, and Page, Arizona, wilted but willing, now perform a spirited rendition of "Shall We Gather at the River?" followed by "The Stars and Stripes Forever." Pause. Discreet applause, whistles, cheers. The weary multitude senses that the end is near, the bridge about to be opened. The governors of Arizona and Utah, cheerful bulky men in cowboy hats and pointy-toe boots, come forward again. Each brandishes a pair of giant golden scissors, flashing in the sunlight. Superfluous flashbulbs pop, TV cameras record history in the making. As they advance a workman dashes from among the onlookers, scuttles to the barrier ribbon and makes some kind of slight but doubtless important last-minute adjustment. He wears a yellow hard hat decorated with the emblematic decals of his class—American flag, skull and crossbones, the Iron Cross. Across the back of his filthy coveralls, in vivid lettering, is stitched the legend AMERICA: LOVE IT OR

LEAVE IT ALONE. Completing his task, he retires quickly back to the obscurity of the crowd where he belongs.

Climactic moment. The throng prepares to unloose a cheer or two. Drivers scramble into their cars. The sound of racing engines: motors revved, tachs up.

Final words. Quiet, please.

"Go ahead, old buddy. Cut the damn thing."

"Me?"

"Both together, please."

"I thought you said . . ."

"Okay, I gotcha. Stand back. Like this?"

Most of the crowd along the highway had only a poor view of what happened next. But the Indians up on the hillside saw it all clearly. Grandstand seats. They saw the puff of smoke, black, which issued from the ends of the cut ribbon. They saw the flurry of sparks which followed as the ribbon burned, like a fuse, across the bridge. And when the dignitaries hastily backed off the Indians saw the general eruption of unprogrammed fireworks which pursued them. From under the draperies of bunting came an outburst of Roman candles, flaming Catherine wheels, Chinese firecrackers and cherry bombs. As the bridge was cleared from end to end a rash of fireworks blazed up along the walkways. Rockets shot into the air and exploded, Silver Salutes, aerial bombs and M-80s blasted off. Whirling dervishes of smoke and fire took off and flew, strings of firecrackers leaped through the air like smoking whips, snapping and popping, lashing at the governors' heels. The crowd cheered, thinking this the high point of the ceremonies.

But it was not. Not the highest high point. Suddenly the center of the bridge rose up, as if punched from beneath, and broke in two along a jagged zigzag line. Through this absurd fissure, crooked as lightning, a sheet of red flame streamed skyward, followed at once by the sound of a great cough, a thunderous shuddering high-explosive cough that shook the monolithic sandstone of the canyon walls. The bridge parted like a flower, its separate divisions no longer joined by any physical bond. Fragments and sections began to fold, sag, sink and fall, relaxing into the abyss. Loose objects—gilded scissors, a monkey wrench, a couple of empty Cadillacs—slid down the appalling gradient of the depressed roadway and launched themselves, turning slowly, into space. They took a long time going down and when they finally smashed on the rock and river far below, the sound of the impact, arriving much later, was barely heard by even the most attentive.

The bridge was gone. The wrinkled fragments at either end still clinging to their foundations in the bedrock dangled toward each other like pendant fingers, suggesting the thought but lacking the will to touch. As the compact plume of dust resulting from the catastrophe expanded upward over the rimrock, slabs of asphalt and cement and shreds and shards of steel and rebar continued to fall, in contrary motion from the sky, splashing seven hundred feet below into the stained but unhurried river.

On the Utah side of the canyon, a governor, a highway commissioner and two high-ranking officers of the Department of Public Safety strode through the crowd toward their remaining limousines. Stern-faced and furious, they conferred as they walked.

"This is their last stunt, Governor, I promise you."

"Seems to me I heard that promise before, Crumbo."

"I wasn't on the case before, sir."

"So what. What're you doing now?"

"We're on their tail, sir. We have a good idea who they are, how they operate and what they're planning next."

"But not where they are."

"No sir, not at the moment. But we're closing in."

"And just what the hell are they planning next?"

"You won't believe me."

"Try me."

Colonel Crumbo points a finger to the immediate east. Indicating *that thing*.

"The dam?"

"Yes sir."

"Not the dam."

"Yes sir, we have reason to think so."

"*Not* Glen Canyon *Dam!*"

"I know it sounds crazy. But that's what they're after."

Meanwhile, up in the sky, the lone visible vulture spirals in lazy circles higher and higher, contemplating the peaceful scene below. He looks down on the perfect dam. He sees downstream from the dam the living river and above it the blue impoundment, that placid reservoir where, like waterbugs, the cabin cruisers play. He sees, at this very moment, a pair of water skiers with tangled towlines about to drown beneath the waters. He sees the glint of metal and glass on the asphalt trail where endless jammed files of steaming automobiles creep home to Kanab, Page, Tuba City, Panguitch and points beyond. He notes in passing the dark gorge of the master canyon, the shattered stubs of a bridge, the tall yellow pillar of smoke and dust still rising, slowly, from the depths of the chasm.

Like a solitary smoke signal, like the silent symbol of calamity, like one huge inaudible and astonishing exclamation point signifying *surprise!* the dust plume hangs above the fruitless plain, pointing upward to heaven and downward to the scene of the primal split, the loss of connections, the place where not only space but time itself has come unglued. Has lapsed. Elapsed. Relapsed. Prolapsed. And then collapsed.

Under the vulture's eye. Meaning nothing, nothing to eat. Under that ultimate farthest eye, the glimmer of plasma down the west, so far beyond all consequence of dust and blue, the same. . . .

1

Origins I: A. K. Sarvis, M.D.

Dr. Sarvis with his bald mottled dome and savage visage, grim and noble as Sibelius, was out night-riding on a routine neighborhood beautification project, burning billboards along the highway—U.S. 66, later to be devoured by the superstate's interstate autobahn. His procedure was simple, surgically deft. With a five-gallon can of gasoline he sloshed about the legs and support members of the selected target, then applied a match. Everyone should have a hobby.

In the lurid glare which followed he could be seen shambling back to the Lincoln Continental Mark IV parked nearby, empty gas can banging on his insouciant shanks. A tall and ponderous man, shaggy as a bear, he cast a most impressive shadow in the light of the flames, across the arid scene of broken whiskey bottles, prickly pear and buckhorn cholla, worn-out tires and strips of retread. In the fire's glare his little red eyes burned with a fierce red fire of their own, matching the candescent coal of the cigar in his teeth—three smoldering and fanatic red bulbs glowing through the dark. He paused to admire his work:

HOWDY PARDNER
WELCOME TO ALBUQUERQUE, NEW MEXICO
HUB OF THE LAND OF ENCHANTMENT

Headlights swept across him from the passing traffic. Derisive horns bellowed as sallow pimply youths with undescended testicles drove by in stripped-down zonked-up Mustangs, Impalas, Stringrays and Beetles, each with a lush-lashed truelove wedged hard overlapping-pelvis-style on the driver's lap, so that seen from the back through the rear window in silhouette against oncoming headlights the car appeared to be "operated" by a single occupant with—anomaly—two heads; other lovers screamed past jammed butt to groin on the buddy seats of 880-cc chopped Kawasaki motorbikes with cherry-bomb exhaust tubes—like hara-kiri, kamikaze, karate and the creeping kudzu vine, a gift from the friendly people who gave us (remember?) Pearl Harbor—which, blasting sparks and chips of cylinder wall, roared shattering like spastic technical demons through the once-wide stillness of Southwestern night.

No one ever stopped. Except the Highway Patrol arriving promptly fifteen minutes late, radioing the report of an inexplicable billboard fire to a casually scornful dispatcher at headquarters, then ejecting self from vehicle, extinguisher in gloved hand, to ply the flames for a while with little limp gushes of liquid sodium hydrochloride ("wetter than water" because it adheres better, like soapsuds) to the pyre. Futile if gallant efforts. Dehydrated by months, sometimes years of desert winds and thirsty desert air, the pine and paper of the noblest most magnificent of billboards yearned in every molecule for quick combustion, wrapped itself in fire with the mad lust, the rapt intensity, of lovers fecundating. All-cleansing fire, all-purifying flame, before which the asbestos-hearted plutonic pyromaniac can only genuflect and pray.

Doc Sarvis by this time had descended the crumbly bank of the roadside under a billowing glare from his handiwork, dumped his gas can into trunk of car, slammed the lid—where a bright and silver caduceus glisters in the firelight—and slumped down in the front seat beside his driver.

"Next?" she says.

He flipped away his cigar butt, out the open window into the ditch—the trace of burning arc remains for a moment in the night, a retinal afterglow with rainbow-style trajectory, its terminal spatter of sparks the pot of gold—and unwrapped another Marsh-Wheeling, his famous surgeon's hand revealing not a twitch or tremor.

"Let's work the west side," he says.

The big car glided forward with murmurous motor, wheels crunching tin cans and plastic picnic plates on the berm, packed bearings sliding in the servile grease, the pistons, bathed in oil, slipping up and down in the firm but gentle grasp of cylinders, connecting rods to crankshaft, crankshaft to drive shaft through differential's scrotal housing via axle, all power to the wheels.

They progressed. That is to say, they advanced, in thoughtful silence, toward the jittery neon, the spastic anapestic rock, the apoplectic roll of Saturday night in Albuquerque, New Mexico. (To be an American for one Saturday night downtown you'd sell your immortal soul.) Down Glassy Gulch they drove toward the twenty-story towers of finance burning like blocks of radium under the illuminated smog.

"Abbzug."

"Doc?"

"I love you, Abbzug."

"I know, Doc."

Past a lit-up funeral parlor in territorial burnt-adobe brick: Strong-Thorne Mortuary—"Oh Death Where Is Thy Sting?" Dive! Beneath the overpass of the Sante Fe (Holy Faith) Railroad—"Go Santa Fe All the Way."

"Ah," sighed the doctor, "I like this. I like this. . . ."

"Yeah, but it interferes with my driving if you don't mind."

"El Mano Negro strikes again."

"Yeah, Doc, okay, but you're gonna get us in a wreck and my mother will sue."

"True," he says, "but it's worth it."

Beyond the prewar motels of stucco and Spanish tile at the city's western fringe, they drove out on a long low bridge.

"Stop here."

She stopped the car. Doc Sarvis gazed down at the river, the Rio

Grande, great river of New Mexico, its dark and complicated waters shining with cloud-reflected city light.

"My river," he says.

"Our river."

"Our river."

"Let's take that river trip."

"Soon, soon." He held up a finger. "Listen. . . ."

They listened. The river was mumbling something down below, something like a message: Come flow with me, Doctor, through the deserts of New Mexico, down through the canyons of Big Bend and on to the sea the Gulf the Caribbean, down where those young sireens weave their seaweed garlands for your hairless head, O Doc. Are you there? Doc?

"Drive on, Bonnie. This river aggravates my melancholia."

"Not to mention your self-pity."

"My sense of *déjà vu*."

"Yeah."

"*Mein Weltschmerz.*"

"Your *Welt-schmaltz*. You love it."

"Well. . . ." He pulled out the lighter. "As to that, who can say?"

"Oh, Doc." Watching the river, driving on, watching the road, she patted his knee. "Don't think about all that anymore."

Doc nodded, holding the red coil to his cigar. The glow of the lighter, the soft lights of the instrument panel, gave to his large and bony, bald but bearded head a hard-worn dignity. He looked like Jean Sibelius with eyebrows and whiskers, in the full vigor of his fruitful forties. Sibelius lived for ninety-two years. Doc had forty-two and a half to go.

Abbzug loved him. Not much, perhaps, but enough. She was a tough piece out of the Bronx but could be sweet as *apfelstrudel* when necessary. That classic Abbzug voice might rasp on the nerves at times, when her mood was querulous, but kisses or candy or con could usually mellow the harshest of her urban tones. Her tongue though adder-sharp was sweet (he thought) as Mogen David all the same.

His mother also loved him. Of course his mother had no choice. That's what she was paid for.

His wife had loved him, more than he deserved, more than realism required. Given sufficient time she might have outgrown it. The children were all grown up and a continent away.

Doc's nicer patients liked him but didn't always pay their bills. He had a few friends, some poker-playing cronies on the Democratic County Committee, some drinking companions from the Medical Arts Clinic, a couple of neighbors in the Heights. No one close. His few close friends were always sent away, it seemed, returning rarely, the bonds of their affection no stronger than the web of correspondence, which frays and fades.

He was therefore proud and grateful to have a nurse and buddy like Ms. Bonnie Abbzug at his side, this night, as the black automobile rose westward under the rosy smog-glow of the city's personal atmosphere, beyond the last of the Texaco, Arco and Gulf stations, past the final Wagon Wheel Bar, into the open desert. High on the western mesa near burnt-out volcanoes, under the blazing, dazzling, starry sky, they stopped among the undefended billboards at the highway's side. Time to choose another target.

Doc Sarvis and Bonnie Abbzug looked them over. So many, all so innocent and vulnerable, ranged along the roadway in serried ranks, clamoring for the eye. Hard to choose. Should it be the military?

THE MARINE CORPS
BUILDS MEN

Why don't it build women? Bonnie asked. Or how about the truckers' editorial?

IF TRUCKS STOP
AMERICA STOPS

Don't threaten *me*, you sons of bitches. He checked out the political:

WHAT'S WRONG WITH BEING RIGHT?
JOIN THE JOHN BIRCH SOCIETY!

But preferred the apolitical:

HAVE A NICE DAY
WE'RE ALL IN THIS TOGETHER

Dr. Sarvis loved them all, but sensed a certain futility in his hobby. He carried on these days more from habit than conviction. There was a higher destiny calling to him and Ms. Abbzug. That beckoning finger in his dreams.

"Bonnie—?"

"Well?"

"What do you say?"

"You might as well knock over one more, Doc. We drove all this way. You won't be happy if you don't."

"Good girl. Which one shall it be?"

Bonnie pointed. "I like that one."

Doc said, "Exactly." He climbed out of the car and stumbled to the back, through the tin-can tumbleweed community of the roadside ecology. He opened the trunk lid and removed, from among the golf clubs, the spare tire, the chain saw, the case of spray paint, the tire tools, the empty gas can, another gasoline can, full. Doc closed the lid. Across the length of his rear bumper a luminous sticker proclaimed in glowing red, white and blue, I AM PROUD TO BE AN ARMENIAN!

Doc's car carried other hex signs—he was indeed a decalcomaniac—to ward off evil: the M.D.'s caduceus, American flag decals in each corner of the rear window, a gold-fringed flag dangling from the radio aerial, in one corner of the windshield a sticker which read "Member of A.B.L.E.—Americans for Better Law Enforcement," and in the other corner the blue eagle of the National Rifle Association with the traditional adage, "Register Communists, Not Guns."

Taking no chances, looking both ways, severe and sober as a judge, carrying his matches and his can of gasoline, Dr. Sarvis marched through the weeds, the broken bottles, the rags and beer cans of the ditch, all that tragic and abandoned trivia of the American road, and climbed the cutbank toward the object of his fierymania:

WONDER ENRICHED BREAD
HELPS BUILD STRONG BODIES
12 WAYS

Liars!

While down below his Bonnie waited at the wheel of the Lincoln, her engines running, ready for getaway. The trucks and cars howled by on the highway and their lights shone briefly on the girl's face, her violet eyes, her smile, and on Doc's other bumper sticker, the one that confronted the future: GOD BLESS AMERICA. LET'S SAVE SOME OF IT.

2

❧

Origins II: George W. Hayduke

George Washington Hayduke, Vietnam, Special Forces, had a grudge. After two years in the jungle delivering Montagnard babies and dodging helicopters (for those boys up there fired their tumbling dumdums at thirty rounds per second at anything that moved: chickens, water buffalo, rice farmers, newspaper reporters, lost Americans, Green Beret medics—whatever breathed) and another year as a prisoner of the Vietcong, he returned to the American Southwest he had been remembering only to find it no longer what he remembered, no longer the clear and classical desert, the pellucid sky he roamed in dreams. Someone or something was changing things.

The city of Tucson from which he came, to which he returned, was ringed now with a circle of Titan ICBM bases. The open desert was being scraped bare of all vegetation, all life, by giant D-9 bulldozers reminding him of the Rome plows leveling Vietnam. These machine-made wastes grew up in tumbleweed and real-estate development, a squalid plague of future slums constructed of green two-by-fours, dry-wall fiberboard and prefab roofs that blew off in the first good wind. This in the home of free creatures: horned toads, desert rats, Gila monsters and coyotes. Even the sky, that dome of delirious blue which he once had thought was out of reach, was becoming a dump for the gaseous garbage of the copper smelters, the filth that Kennecott, Anaconda, Phelps-Dodge and American Smelting & Refining Co. were pumping through stacks into the public sky. A smudge of poisoned air overhung his homeland.

Hayduke smelled something foul in all this. A smoldering bitterness warmed his heart and nerves; the slow fires of anger kept his cockles warm, his hackles rising. Hayduke *burned*. And he was not a patient man.

After a month with his parents, he raced off to a girl at Laguna Beach. Found, fought and lost her. He returned to the desert, heading north by east for the canyon country, the Arizona Strip and the wild lands beyond. There was one place he had to see and brood upon awhile before he could know what he had to do.

He had in mind Lee's Ferry, the Colorado River, the Grand Canyon.

Hayduke rumbled up the asphalt trail in his new secondhand jeep, one eye on the road and the other itching with hay fever; he was allergic to tumbleweed, that exotic vegetable from the steppes of Mongolia. He had bought the jeep, a sandstorm-blasted sun-bleached blue, in San Diego from a team of car dealers named Square Deal Andy and Top Dollar Johnny. The fuel pump had given out first, near Brawley, and at Yuma, limping off the freeway with a flat, he discovered that Square Deal had sold him (for only $2795, it's true) a jeep without a jack. Small problems: he liked this machine; he was pleased with the handy extras—roll bars, auxiliary gas tank, mag rims and wide-tread tires, the Warn hubs and the Warn winch with 150-foot cable, the gimbal-mounted beer-can holder screwed to the dash, the free and natural paint job.

The desert eased his vague anger. Near the dirt road which turned off the highway and led east for ten miles to the volcanic ramparts of the Kofa Mountains, he stopped, well away from the traffic, and made himself a picnic lunch. He sat on warm rock in the blazing spring sun, eating pickle and cheese and ham in onion roll, washing it down with beer, and opened himself through pore and nerve ends to the sweet stillness of the Arizona desert. He gazed about and found that he still remembered most of the scrubby little trees: the mesquite (great fuel for cooking and heating, beans for hard times, shade for survival), the green-barked paloverde with its leafless stems (the chlorophyll is in the bark), the subtle smoke tree floating like a mirage down in the sandy wash.

Hayduke proceeded. The hot fury of the wind at 65 mph whistled past his open window, strummed his sleeve, kissed his ear as he drove on and on, northeast toward the high country, the good country, God's country, Hayduke's country, by God. And it better stay that way. Or by God there'll be trouble.

Twenty-five years old, Hayduke is a short, broad, burly fellow, well-muscled, built like a wrestler. The face is hairy, very hairy, with a wide mouth and good teeth, big cheekbones and a thick shock of blue-black hair. A bit of Shawnee blood back in there, maybe, somewhere, way back in the gene pool. His hands are large and powerful, pale white under the black hair; he's been in the jungle and then in the hospital for a long time.

He drank another beer as he drove along. Two and a half six-packs to Lee's Ferry. Out there in the open Southwest, he and his friends measured highway distances in per-capita six-packs of beer. L.A. to Phoenix, four six-packs; Tucson to Flagstaff, three six-packs; Phoenix to New York, thirty-five six-packs. (Time is relative, said Heraclitus a long time ago, and distance a function of velocity. Since the ultimate goal of transport technology is the annihilation of space, the compression of all Being into one pure point, it follows that six-packs help. Speed is the ultimate drug and rockets run on alcohol. Hayduke had formulated this theory all by himself.)

He felt and shared in the exhilaration of the sun, the rush of alcohol through the bloodstream, the satisfaction in his jeep running full and cool and properly, tooling up the pike toward the red cliffs of the canyon country, the purple mesas, the cliff-rose and the blue birds. All the readings of his complicated nervous system indicated trouble. But then they always did. He was happy.

There was a special camp of the Special Forces. There was a special sign that hung, along with the Confederate flags, from the entrance gateway to the special camp. The sign said:

> If you kill for money you're a mercenary.
> If you kill for pleasure you're a sadist.
> If you do both you're a Green Beret.
>
> WELCOME

Into the high country. The mountains of Flagstaff loomed ahead, the high peaks dappled with snow. Smoke from the lumber mills drifted gray-blue across the green coniferous haze of the Coconino National Forest, the great green woodland belt of northern Arizona. Through his open window came the chill clear air, the odor of resin, the smell of woodsmoke. The sky above the mountains was untouched by a single cloud, like the dark blue of infinite desire.

Hayduke smiled, flexing his nostrils (isometric yoga), popping the top from another can of Schlitz, cruising into Flag, pop. 26,000, elev. 6900, and remembered a Flagstaff cop he had always meant to get. Unjust arrest, a night in the tank with twenty puking Navajos. Something festering in one corner of his mind for three years, an unscratched itch.

Just for the hell of it, he thought, why not now? He was free. He had nothing better to do. Why not now as ever? He stopped for gas at a self-service station, filled tank, checked oil, then checked a phone book and found the name and address he wanted. He had no difficulty remembering that name: the nameplate on the tunic, like the badge, like the flag pins on the lapels, stood before Hayduke's mind's eye as vividly as if it had all happened the night before.

He ate supper in a dark café, then drove to the address and parked his jeep half a block away and waited. Evening, the brief Southwestern twilight; streetlights flickered on. He waited for night, watching the front of the house. Waiting, he reviewed procedures, inventoried the weapons in his possession, in the jeep, illegally concealed, available for use: one Buck knife, the Special, honed to the keenness of a razor's edge; one .357 magnum revolver, loaded except for an empty firing chamber; one small VC steel crossbow with broadhead darts, made of wrecked American helicopter, souvenir of Dak To (*Hoa binh!*); one Winchester carbine Model 94, the classic deer rifle, packed in a saddle scabbard; one AK 47 (another souvenir) with two banana clips taped together, loaded; and the basic item, backbone of his arsenal, a staple for any well-equipped death kit, the Remington .30-.06 bolt-action target rifle with Bausch & Lomb 3×–9× variable scope, accurate enough to pick off Gook, Greek or your brother's ear at five hundred yards (high velocity, flat trajectory, etc.). Plus reloading kit, powder, caps, bullets, salvaged casings, the works. Like so many American men, Hayduke loved guns, the touch of oil, the acrid smell of burnt powder, the taste of brass, bright copper alloys, good cutlery, all things well made and deadly.

Though still a lover of chipmunks, robins and girls, he had also learned like others to acquire a taste for methodical, comprehensive and precisely gauged destruction. Coupled in his case with a passion for equity (statistically rare), and the conservative instinct to keep things not as they are but as they should be (even rarer); to keep it like it was.

("Girls?" the sergeant had said. "They're all the same in the dark. Who gives a shit about girls; you ought to see my *gun collection!*" Some sergeant, that one, after the accident, awkwardly lumpy in his black body bag, shipped home in a wooden overcoat, like 55,000 others.)

Sitting in the dark, waiting, Hayduke proposed and discarded a number of options. First, no murder; the punishment shall fit the crime. The crime, in this case, was injustice. The officer, Hall by name, had arrested and booked him for public drunkenness, which constituted false arrest; Hayduke had not been drunk. What he had done, at three o'clock in the morning one block from his hotel, was stop to watch Hall the cop and a nonuniformed companion interrogate a passing Indian. Hall, not accustomed to being overseen by an unknown civilian, came charging across the street, annoyed, nervous, agitated, demanding instant identification. His manner got Hayduke's back up at once. "What for?" he said, hands in pockets. "Take your hands out of your pockets," the cop commanded. "What for?" said

Hayduke. Hall's hand had trembled on the butt of his gun; he was a young, neurotic, insecure policeman. The second man waited in the police car, observing, a shotgun held upright between his knees. Hayduke had not failed to notice the shotgun. Reluctantly, he drew his empty hands from his pockets. Hall grabbed him by the neck, hustled him across the street, slammed him against the patrol car, frisked him, smelled the beer on his breath. Hayduke spent the next twelve hours on a wooden bench in the city drunk tank, the one white man in a groaning chorus of sick Navajos. Somehow it rankled.

Of course I can't kill him, Hayduke thought. All I want to do is punch him around a little, give his orthodontist some work. Dislocate a rib, perhaps. Ruin his evening; nothing drastic or irreparable. The problem is, shall I identify myself? Shall I remind him of our previous and all-too-brief acquaintance? Or leave him lying on the sidewalk wondering who the hell and what the hell was that all about?

He felt certain that Hall would not be able to recall his identity. How could a cop who picked up a dozen drunks, vagrants and loiterers every night possibly remember short, swart, obscure and undistinguished George Hayduke, who had, besides, changed considerably in the meanwhile, grown heavier, bigger and hairier?

A patrol car, Flagstaff City Police, approached slowly, lights dimmed, and stopped in front of Hall's house. Good. One man in the car. Very good. The man got out. He wore plain clothes, not the uniform. Hayduke watched him through the gloom from half a block away, uncertain. The man walked to the door of the house and entered without pausing to knock. Got to be Hall. Or else a one-man raid. More lights went on inside the house.

Hayduke put his revolver into his belt, got out of the jeep, put on a coat to conceal the gun and walked past Hall's house. Curtains drawn and blinds down; he could see nothing of the interior. The motor of the patrol car was running. Hayduke tried the car door: unlocked. He walked around the corner of the block, under the trees and streetlights, and down a graveled alleyway that led behind the row of houses. Dogs barked among the garbage cans, clothesline poles, children's play swings. Counting doors, he saw, through a kitchen window, the man he was looking for. Still young, quite handsome, all Irish. Hall the cop was drinking a cup of coffee with one hand and patting his wife's rump with the other. She looked pleased; he looked distracted. Typical domestic scene. Hayduke's iron heart melted slightly, around the edges.

There was little time. He found an unfenced yard between houses and hurried back to the street. The patrol car was still there, motor running. At any moment Hall would put down that cup of coffee and come out, the malingering bastard. Hayduke slipped behind the wheel of the car and without turning on the headlights eased it quietly down the street toward the first corner. The single green eye of the police Motorola glowed from the dark under the dashboard, the speaker conveying a steady traffic of calm male voices discussing blood, wreckage, disaster. Head-on collision on Mountain Street. All the better for Hayduke; the routine tragedy gave him perhaps another minute before Hall could spread the alarm. Turning the corner and bearing south for Main and the tracks of the Santa Fe Railroad, he braced for the assault. Hall would certainly have a police radio transmitter in his home. Meanwhile Hayduke made his plans. Things not to do tonight. He decided first not to attempt to crash the patrol car into the lobby of City Hall. Second. . . .

He passed a police car going in the opposite direction. The officer at the wheel gave him a wave; Hayduke waved back. A few pedestrians on the street watched him go by. He glanced at the rearview mirror. The other police car had stopped at an intersection, waiting for a red light.

There was a pause in the radio traffic. Then Hall's voice: "All units, 10-99. All units, 10-99. Car Twelve, 10-35, 10-35. Repeat: all units, 10-99. Car Twelve, 10-35. Acknowledge, please. KB-34 remote."

Good control, thought Hayduke. How could he forget that voice? That Irish cool controlled hysteria. Good God but he hates me now! Hates somebody, anyway.

There was a clash of static on the radio as several voices attempted to answer at once. All went silent. One voice came through loud and clear.

"KB-5, KB-6."

"KB-5."

"We saw Car Twelve a minute ago, going south on Second Street between Federal and Mountain."

"Ten-four, KB-6. All mobile units except Car Four proceed to downtown area immediately; 10-99, 10-99, Car Twelve. KB-34, KB-5."

Hayduke grinned. They're calling Hall. Now he's on the spot.

"KB-34, KB-5. Answer please."

"KB-34."

"Ten-nine?"

"Ten-two?"

"Ten-nine?"

"What?"

"Where the hell are you, Hall?"

"KB-34 remote."

"So who's driving Car Twelve?"

"I don't know."

Hayduke picked up the microphone, pressed the transmitter button and said, "I am, you shitkickers. Just having a little fun in your little two-bit town, okay? KB-34, over."

"Ten-four," the dispatcher said. There was a pause. "Who is this speaking, please?"

Hayduke thought for a moment. "Rudolf," he said. "That's who."

Another pause. "KB-5, this is KB-6."

"Go ahead."

"We have subject under visual. Still headed south."

"Ten-four. Prepare to intercept."

"Ten-four."

"Ten-four, shit," said Hayduke into the microphone. "You'll have to catch me first, you bullet-headed motherfuckers." He regretted, for a moment, that there was not some way he could receive and hear his own broadcasts. Of course it was all being recorded on tape at the police base station. He thought for a moment of something called voice prints, the audible analogue to fingerprints. Maybe he *would* hear his broadcasts, later, after all. In an Arizona courtroom. With solemn jury joining. God damn their eyes.

The radio voice: "Subject is warned that all radio broadcasts are monitored by the Federal Communications Commission and that abuse or misuse of police transmission systems is a Federal offense."

"Fuck the Federal Communications Commission. Fuck you, too, Flagstaff fuzz. I piss on you all from a considerable height."

Grinning in the dark, speeding quietly through near-empty streets, he waited for a response. There was none. Then he realized that he was still clutching the mike, squeezing the transmitter button, and that as long as he did so he was shutting down the entire channel. He dropped the microphone and concentrated on his driving. The radio traffic resumed, the steady exchange of calm, tough, laconic masculine voices. Tell you what, he thought, let's drive it up the tracks. Santa Fe Railroad only a block ahead. Sirens behind, destruction ahead.

Red lights blinked at the crossing. The warning bell clanged. Hayduke slowed the car. Train approaching. The wooden barricades were swinging down. He passed beneath the near one and jammed on the power brakes, stopping the car dead in the middle of the crossing. He looked both ways and saw through the roaring dark the brilliant rotating light of an advancing locomotive, felt the thunder of the iron wheels, heard the bray of the diesel's air horn. At the same moment he heard the howl of sirens, saw the blue flasher lights racing toward him, less than two blocks away, in his rear.

Hayduke abandoned Hall's car there in the crux of the crossing. Before leaving, however, he grabbed a shotgun, a riot helmet and a six-batteried flashlight, carrying them off into the night. As he hustled away from the scene of his crime, arms full and heart beating with joy, he heard—beneath the screech of brakes, the bellow of klaxons—one solid metallic crash, deeply satisfying, richly prolonged.

He looked over his shoulder. The head locomotive, air brakes groaning, backed up by three extra power units and the weight and momentum of a 125-car freight train, rolled down the rails, pushing at its iron nose the hulk of the patrol car, grinding iron on steel in a shower of sparks. The car rolled once; the gas tank ruptured, exploded into saffron and violet flame, a sliding bonfire which illuminated, as it advanced, a string of boxcars on a siding, the backside of the Montezuma Hotel (Rooms $2 up), some telegraph poles, a billboard (Welcome to Flagstaff Heart of the Scenic North) and the obsolete, forgotten, antique water tower of the Atchison, Topeka & Santa Fe, Flagstaff Depot.

Clutching his prizes, Hayduke jogged through inky alleyways, outflanking the iron, the law, the police cars shrieking through the city like maddened hornets, reached the safety of his jeep and drove away, out of the city into the velvet dark, untouched.

He slept well that night, out in the piney woods near Sunset Crater, twenty miles to the northeast, snug in his broad-shouldered mummy bag, his goosedown sack, light as a feather, warm as the womb. Under the diamond blaze of Orion, the shimmer of the Seven Sisters, while shooting stars trailed languid flames through the troposphere. The sweetness of it. The satisfaction of a job well done. He dreamt of home. Wherever that is. Of silken thighs. Wherever they may lead. Of a tree greener than thought in a canyon red as iron.

Rising before the sun, in the silver-blue dawn, he made coffee on his tiny Primus stove. "Chemicals! Chemicals! I need chemicals!" he chanted, Hayduke's morning mantra. Through the lonesome pines he saw an orb of plasmic hydrogen, too bright to face, come up suddenly over the wrinkled ridges of the Painted Desert. A cool flute music floated out of nowhere: the hermit thrush.

Hit the road, George. Northward. He gassed up at his favorite gas station, the Sacred Mountain Trading Post, signed the petitions (Save Black Mesa; Stop the Strip Miners) and bought RED POWER THINK HOPI stickers for his bumpers, which he plastered over the former owner's sloganeering:

☺ HAVE A NICE DAY SCHMUCK ☺

Down from the sacred mountain into the rosy dawn he rolled, into the basin of the Little Colorado River, the pastel pink and chocolate brown and umbrous buff of the Painted Desert. Land of the petrified log. Land of the glaucomous Indian. Land of handwoven vegetable-dyed rugs, sand-cast silver concho belts and overloaded welfare case loads. Land of the former dinosaur. Land of the modern dinosaur. Land of the power-line pylon marching league on league in lockstep like 120-foot outer-space monsters across the desert plains.

Hayduke frowning as he opens the first official six-pack of the day (one and a half to Lee's Ferry). He hadn't remembered so many power lines. They stride across the horizon in multicolumn grandeur, looped together by the swoop and gleam of high-voltage cables charged with energy from Glen Canyon Dam, from the Navajo Power Plant, from the Four Corners and Shiprock plants, bound south and westward to the burgeoning Southwest and California. The blazing cities feed on the defenseless interior.

Tossing his empty beer can out the window, Hayduke races north, through the Indian country. A blighted land, crisscrossed with new power lines, sky smudged with smoke from power plants, the mountains strip-mined, the range grazed to death, eroding away. Slum villages of cinder-block huts and tarpaper shacks line the highway—the tribe is spreading, fruitful as a culture bouillon: from 9500 in 1890 to 125,000 today. Fecundity! Prosperity! Sweet wine and suicide, of thee we sing.

The real trouble with the goddamned Indians, reflected Hayduke, is that they are no better than the rest of us. The real trouble is that the Indians are just as stupid and greedy and cowardly and dull as us white folks.

Thinking this, he opens his second beer. Gray Mountain Trading Post comes into view, tired Indians resting against the sunny side of the wall. A squaw in traditional velveteen blouse squats by the men, lifting her long and voluminous skirts to piss upon the dust. She is grinning, the men laughing.

Approaching Grand Canyon Junction.

Traffic obstructs his impatient advance. In front of him a little lady with blue hair peers through her steering wheel at the highway, her head barely showing above the dashboard. What's she doing here? Little old man beside her. Indiana plates on their Oldsmobile. Mom and Pop out seeing the country. Driving at a safe and prudent 45 mph. Hayduke snarls. Move it, lady, or get it the fuck off the road. My God, makes you wonder how they ever got the thing backed out of the garage and pointed west.

Junction Trading Post two miles ahead. Stopping there once for a beer, he'd overheard the manager confide to a clerk, as he showed him a handwoven Navajo blanket, "Paid forty dollars for this. Squaw was going to a Sing and wanted some money right away; we'll sell it for two hundred and fifty."

The road still sank before him, descending into the valley of the Little Colorado River and the Painted Desert. From seven thousand feet at the summit of the pass to three thousand at the river. He glanced at the altimeter mounted on his dash. The instrument agreed. Here's the turnoff to South Rim, Grand Canyon. Even now, in May, the tourist traffic seemed heavy: a steady stream of steel, glass, plastic and aluminum issued from the junction, most of it turning south toward Flagstaff but some turning the other way, north to Utah and Colorado.

My way, he thought, they're going my way; they can't do that. Gotta remove that bridge. Soon. Them bridges. Soon. All of them. Soon. They're driving their tin cars into the holy land. They can't do that; it ain't legal. There's a law against it. A higher law.

Well you're doing it too, he reminded himself. Yeah, but I'm on important business. Besides, I'm an elitist. Anyway, the road's here now, might as well use it. I paid my taxes too; I'd be a fool to get out and walk and let all them other tourists blow their foul exhaust gases in my face, wouldn't I? Wouldn't I? Yes I would. But if I wanted to walk—and I will when the time comes—why, I'd walk all the way from here to Hudson Bay and back. And will.

Hayduke forged straight ahead at maximum cruising speed, in

high range, hubs free, bearing steadily north-northwest past The Gap and Cedar Ridge (gaining altitude again) toward the Echo Cliffs, Shinumo Altar, Marble Canyon, the Vermilion Cliffs and the river. The Colorado. *The* river. Until, topping a long and final grade, he gained a view—at last—of the country he was headed for, the heartland of his heart, spread out before and beyond him exactly as he'd dreamed it all, for three years, lost in the jungle war.

He proceeded almost cautiously (for him) down the long and winding grade toward the river, twenty miles by road and four thousand feet of descent. Had to live at least one more hour. Marble Canyon gaped below, a black crevasse like an earthquake's yawn zigzagging across the dun-colored desert. The Echo Cliffs ranged northeastward toward a dark notch in the sandstone monolith where the Colorado rolled out from the depths of the plateau. North and west of the notch rose the Paria Plateau, little known, where nobody lives, and the thirty-mile-long Vermilion Cliffs.

Hayduke, rejoicing, scarfing up more beer, concluding his Flagstaff six-pack, wheels down to the river on the narrow road at a safe and sane 70 per, bellowing some incoherent song into the face of the wind. He was indeed a menace to other drivers but justified himself in this way: If you don't drink, don't drive. If you drink, drive like hell. Why? Because freedom, not safety, is the highest good. Because the public roads should be wide open to all—children on tricycles, little old ladies in Eisenhower Plymouths, homicidal lesbians driving forty-ton Mack tractor-trailers. Let us have *no* favorites, no licenses, no goddamn rules for the road. Let every freeway be a free-for-all.

Happy as a pig in shit, that's Hayduke coming home. Hairpin curves at the bridge approach: SLOW: 15 MPH. Tires squealing like cats in rut, he hangs a four-wheel drift around the first curve. Another. Scream of rubber, stink of hot brake drums. The bridge appears. He brakes hard, gearing down, doing the heel-and-toe dance on brake, clutch, gas pedal.

NO STOPPING ON BRIDGE, the sign says. He stops in the middle of the bridge. Shuts off engine. Listens for a moment to the silence, to the sigh from four hundred feet below of the rolling river.

Hayduke climbs out of the jeep, walks to the rail of the bridge and peers down. The Colorado, third longest river in America, murmurs past its sandy shores, swirls around fallen rocks, streams seaward under the limestone walls of Marble Canyon. Upstream, beyond the bend, lies the site of Lee's Ferry, rendered obsolete by the bridge on which Hayduke stands. Downstream, fifty miles away by water, is the river entrance to the Grand Canyon. On his left, north and west, the Vermilion Cliffs shine pink as watermelon in the light of the setting sun, headland after headland of perpendicular sandstone; each rock profile wears a mysterious, solemn, inhuman nobility.

The bladder aches. The highway is silent and deserted. Maybe the world has already ended. Time to tap a kidney, release that beverage. Hayduke unzips and sends a four-hundred-foot arc of filtered Schlitz pouring down through space to the master stream below. No sacrilege—only a quiet jubilation. Bats flicker in the shadows of the canyon. A great blue heron flaps upriver. You're among friends now, George.

Forgetting to rezip and leaving the jeep in the empty roadway, he walks to the end of the bridge and climbs a knoll on the canyon rim, a high point overlooking the desert. He goes down on his knees and takes up a pinch of red sand. Eats it. (Good for the craw. Rich in iron. Good for the gizzard.) Standing again he faces the river, the soaring cliffs, the sky, the flaming mass of the sun going down like a ship beyond a shoal of clouds. Hayduke's cock, limp, wrinkled, forgotten, dangles from his open fly, leaking a little. He spreads his legs solidly on the rock and lifts his arms wide to the sky, palms up. A great and solemn joy flows through bone, blood, nerve and tissue, through every cell of his body. He raises his head, takes a deep breath—

The heron in the canyon, a bighorn ram on the cliff above, one lean coyote on the rim across the river hear the sound of a howl, the song of a wolf, rise in the twilight stillness and spread through the emptiness of the desert evening. One long and prolonged, deep and dangerous, wild archaic howl, rising and rising and rising on the quiet air.

3

❧❧

Origins III:
Seldom Seen Smith

Born by chance into membership in the Church of Jesus Christ of Latter-Day Saints (Mormons), Smith was on lifetime sabbatical from his religion. He was a jack Mormon. A jack Mormon is to a decent Mormon what a jackrabbit is to a cottontail. His connections to the founding father of his church can be traced in the world's biggest genealogical library in Salt Lake City. Like some of his forebears Smith practiced plural marriage. He had a wife in Cedar City, Utah, a second in Bountiful, Utah, and a third in Green River, Utah—each an easy day's drive from the next. His legal name was Joseph Fielding Smith (after a nephew of the martyred founder), but his wives had given him the name Seldom Seen, which carried.

On the same day that George Hayduke was driving up from Flagstaff to Lee's Ferry, Seldom Seen Smith was driving from Cedar City (Kathy's) after the previous night in Bountiful (Sheila's), on his way to the same destination. En route he stopped at a warehouse in Kanab to pick up his equipment for a float trip through Grand Canyon: three ten-man neoprene rafts, cargo rig, oars, waterproof bags and war-surplus ammo cans, tents, tarpaulin, rope, many many other things, and an assistant boatman to help man the oars. He learned that his boatman had already taken off, apparently, for the launching point at Lee's Ferry. Smith also needed a driver, somebody to shuttle his truck from Lee's Ferry to Temple Bar on Lake Mead, where the canyon trip would end. He found her, by prearrangement, among the other river groupies hanging around the warehouse of Grand Canyon Expeditions. Loading everything but the girl into the back of his truck, he went on, bound for Lee's Ferry by way of Page.

They drove eastward through the standard Utah tableau of perfect sky, mountains, red-rock mesas, white-rock plateaus and old volcanic extrusions—Millie's Nipple, for example, visible from the highway thirty miles east of Kanab. Very few have stood on the tip of Mollie's Nipple: Major John Wesley Powell, for one; Seldom Seen Smith for another. That blue dome in the southeast, fifty miles away by line of sight, is Navajo Mountain. One of earth's holy places, God's navel, *om* and omphalos, sacred to shamans, witches, wizards, suncrazed crackpots from mystic shrines like Keet Seel, Dot Klish, Tuba City and Cambridge, Massachusetts.

Between Kanab, Utah, and Page, Arizona, a distance of seventy miles, there is no town, no human habitation whatsoever, except one ramshackle assemblage of tarpaper shacks and cinder-block containers called Glen Canyon City. Glen Canyon City is built on hope and fantasy: as a sign at the only store says, "Fourty Million $Dollar Power Plant To Be Buildt Twelve Miles From Here Soon."

Smith and his friend did not pause at Glen Canyon City. Nobody pauses at Glen Canyon City. Someday it may become, as its founders hope and its inhabitants dream, a hive of industry and avarice, but at present one must report the facts: Glen Canyon City (NO DUMPING) rots and rusts at the side of the road like a burned-out Volkswagen forgotten in a weedy lot to atrophy, unmourned, into the alkaline Utah earth. Many pass but no one pauses. Smith and girl friend shot by like bees in flight, honey-bound.

"What was that?" she said.

"Glen Canyon City."

"No, I mean *that*." Pointing back.

He looked in the mirror. "That there was Glen Canyon City."

They passed the Wahweap Marina turnoff. Miles away down the

long slope of sand, slickrock, blackbrush, Indian ricegrass and prickly pear they could see a cluster of buildings, a house-trailer compound, roads, docks and clusters of boats on the blue bay of the lake. Lake Powell, Jewel of the Colorado, 180 miles of reservoir walled in by bare rock.

The blue death, Smith called it. Like Hayduke his heart was full of a healthy hatred. Because Smith remembered something different. He remembered the golden river flowing to the sea. He remembered canyons called Hidden Passage and Salvation and Last Chance and Forbidden and Twilight and many many more, some that never had a name. He remembered the strange great amphitheaters called Music Temple and Cathedral in the Desert. All these things now lay beneath the dead water of the reservoir, slowly disappearing under layers of descending silt. How could he forget? He had seen too much.

Now they came, amidst an increasing flow of automobile and truck traffic, to the bridge and Glen Canyon Dam. Smith parked his truck in front of the Senator Carl Hayden Memorial Building. He and his friend got out and walked along the rail to the center of the bridge.

Seven hundred feet below streamed what was left of the original river, the greenish waters that emerged, through intake, penstock, turbine and tunnel, from the powerhouse at the base of the dam. Thickets of power cables, each strand as big around as a man's arm, climbed the canyon walls on steel towers, merged in a maze of transformer stations, then splayed out toward the south and west—toward Albuquerque, Babylon, Phoenix, Gomorrah, Los Angeles, Sodom, Las Vegas, Nineveh, Tucson, the cities of the plain.

Upriver from the bridge stood the dam, a glissade of featureless concrete sweeping seven hundred feet down in a concave façade from the dam's rim to the green-grass lawn on the roof of the power plant below.

They stared at it. The dam demanded attention. It was a magnificent mass of cement. Vital statistics: 792,000 tons of concrete aggregate; cost $750 million and the lives of sixteen (16) workmen. Four years in the making, prime contractor Morrison-Knudsen, Inc., sponsored by U.S. Bureau of Reclamation, courtesy of U.S. taxpayers.

"It's too big," she said.

"That's right, honey," he said. "And that's why."

"You can't."

"There's a way."

"Like what?"

"I don't know. But there's got to be a way."

They were looking at only the downstream face and topside surface of the dam. That topside, wide enough for four Euclid trucks, was the narrowest part of the dam. From the top it widened downward, forming an inverted wedge to block the Colorado. Behind the dam the blue waters gleamed, reflecting the blank sky, the fiery eye of day, and scores of powerboats sped round and round, dragging water skiers. Far-off whine of motors, shouts of joy. . . .

"Like how?" she said.

"Who you workin' for?" he said.

"You."

"Okay, think of something."

"We could pray."

"Pray?" said Smith. "Now there's one thing I ain't tried. Let's pray for a little *pre*-cision earthquake right here." And Smith went down on his knees, there on the cement walkway of the bridge, bowed his head, closed his eyes, clapped hands together palm to palm, prayerwise, and prayed. At least his lips were moving. Praying, in broad daylight, with the tourists driving by and walking about taking photographs. Someone aimed a camera at Smith. A park rangerette in uniform turned her head his way, frowning.

"Seldom," the girl murmured, embarrassed, "you're making a public spectacle."

"Pretend you don't know me," he whispered. "And get ready to run. The earth is gonna start buckin' any second now."

He returned to his solemn mumble.

"Dear old God," he prayed, "you know and I know what it was like here, before them bastards from Washington moved in and ruined it all. You remember the river, how fat and golden it was in June, when the big runoff come down from the Rockies? Remember the deer on the sandbars and the blue herons in the willows and the catfish so big and tasty and how they'd bite on spoiled salami? Remember that crick that come down through Bridge Canyon and Forbidden Canyon, how green and cool and clear it was? God, it's enough to make a man sick. Say, you recall old Woody Edgell up at Hite and the old ferry he used to run across the river? That crazy contraption of his hangin' on cables; remember that damn thing? Remember the cataracts in Forty-Mile Canyon? Well, they flooded out about half of them too. And part of the Escalante's gone now—Davis Gulch, Willow Canyon, Gregory Natural Bridge, Ten-Mile. Listen, are you listenin' to me? There's somethin' you can do for me, God. How about a little old *pre*-cision-type earthquake right under this dam? Okay? Any time. Right now for instance would suit me fine."

He waited a moment. The rangerette, looking unhappy, was coming toward them.

"Seldom, the guard's coming."

Smith concluded his prayer. "Okay, God, I see you don't want to do it just now. Well, all right, suit yourself, you're the boss, but we ain't got a hell of a lot of time. Make it pretty soon, goddammit. A-men."

"Sir!"

Smith got up off his knees, smiling at the rangerette. "Ma'am?"

"I'm sorry, sir, but you can't pray here. This is a public place."

"That's true."

"United States Government property."

"Yes ma'am."

"We have thirteen churches in Page if you wish to worship in the church of your choice."

"Yes, ma'am. Do they have a Paiute church?"

"A what?"

"I'm a Paiute. A pie-eyed Paiute." He winked at his truck driver.

"Seldom," she said, "let's get out of here."

They drove from the bridge up to the grade to the neat green government town of Page. A few miles to the southeast stood the eight-hundred-foot smokestacks of the coal-burning Navajo Power

Plant, named in honor of the Indians whose lungs the plant was treating with sulfur dioxide, hydrogen sulfide, nitrous oxide, carbon monoxide, sulfuric acid, fly ash and other forms of particulate matter.

Smith and friend lunched at Mom's Café, then went to the Big Pig supermarket for an hour of serious shopping. He had to buy food for himself, his boatman and four customers for fourteen days.

Seldom Seen Smith was in the river-running business. The back-country business. He was a professional guide, wilderness outfitter, boatman and packer. His capital equipment consisted basically of such items as rubber boats, kayaks, life jackets, mountain tents, outboard motors, pack saddles, topographic maps, waterproof duffel bags, signal mirrors, climbing ropes, snakebite kits, 150-proof rum, fly rods and sleeping bags. And a pickup and a $2\frac{1}{2}$-ton truck, each with this legend on magnetic decals affixed to the doors: BACK OF BEYOND EXPEDITIONS, Jos. Smith, Prop., Hite, Utah.

(Twenty fathoms under in a milky green light the spectral cabins, the skeleton cottonwoods, the ghostly gas pumps of Hite, Utah, glow dimly through the underwater mist, outlines and edges softened by the cumulative blur of slowly settling silt. Hite has been submerged by Lake Powell for many years now, but Smith will not grant recognition to alien powers.)

The tangible assets were incidental. His basic capital was stored in head and nerves, a substantial body of special knowledge, special skills and special attitudes. Ask Smith, he'll tell you: Hite, Utah, will rise again.

His gross income last year was $64,521.95. Total expenses, *not* including any wages or salary for himself, ran to $44,010.05. Net income, $20,511.90. Hardly adequate for an honest jack Mormon, his three wives, three households and five children. Poverty level. But they managed. Smith thought he lived a good life. His only complaint was that the U.S. Government, the Utah State Highway Department and a consortium of oil companies, mining companies and public utilities were trying to destroy his livelihood, put him out of business and obstruct the view.

Smith and his driver bought $685 worth of food, Smith paying in warm soiled cash (he didn't believe in banks), loaded it all in the truck and headed out of town for the rendezvous at Lee's Ferry, into the westerly wind across the sandy red-rock wastelands of Indian country.

WELCOME TO NAVAJOLAND the billboards say. And, on the reverse side, GOOD-BYE COME AGAIN.

And the wind blows, the dust clouds darken the desert blue, pale sand and red dust drift across the asphalt trails and tumbleweeds fill the arroyos. Good-bye, come again.

The road curves through a dynamited notch in the Echo Cliffs and from there down twelve hundred feet to the junction at Bitter Springs. Smith paused as he always did at the summit of the pass to get out of the truck and contemplate the world beyond and below. He had gazed upon this scene a hundred times in his life so far; he knew that he might have only a hundred more.

The girl came and stood beside him. He slipped an arm around her. They pressed together side by side, staring out and down at the hazy grandeur.

Smith was a lanky man, lean as a rake, awkward to handle. His arms were long and wiry, his hands large, his feet big, flat and solid. He had a nose like a beak, a big Adam's apple, ears like the handles on a jug, sun-bleached hair like a rat's nest, and a wide and generous grin. Despite his thirty-five years he still managed to look, much of the time, like an adolescent. The steady eyes, though, revealed a man inside.

They went down into the lower desert, turned north at Bitter Springs and followed Hayduke spoor and Hayduke sign (empty beer cans on the shoulder of the road) to the gorge, around a jeep parked on the bridge and on toward Lee's Ferry. They stopped at a turnoff for a look at the river and what was left of the old crossing.

Not much. The riverside campgrounds had been obliterated by a gravel quarry. In order to administrate, protect and make the charm, beauty and history of Lee's Ferry easily accessible to the motorized public, the Park Service had established not only a new paved road and the gravel quarry but also a ranger station, a paved campground, a hundred-foot-high pink water tower, a power line, a paved picnic area, a motor pool with cyclone fence, an official garbage dump and a boat-launching ramp covered with steel matting. The area had been turned over to the administration of the National Park Service in order to protect it from vandalism and commercial exploitation.

"Suppose your prayer is answered," the girl was saying in the silence. "Suppose you have your earthquake at the dam. What happens to all the people here?"

"That there dam," Smith replied, "is twelve miles upriver through the crookedest twelve miles of canyon you ever seen. It'd take the water an hour to get here."

"They'd still drown."

"I'd warn 'em by telephone."

"Suppose God answers your prayer in the middle of the night. Suppose everybody at the dam is killed and there isn't anybody left alive up there to give warning. Then what?"

"I ain't responsible for an act of God, honey."

"It's your prayer."

Smith grinned. "It's His earthquake." And he held up a harkening finger. "What's that?"

They listened. The cliffs towered above. The silent evening flowed around them. Below, hidden deep in its dark gorge, the brawling river moved among rocks in complicated ways toward its climax in the Grand Canyon.

"I don't hear anything but the river," she said.

"No, listen. . . ."

Far off, echoing from the cliffs, a rising then descending supernatural wail, full of mourning—or was it exultation?

"A coyote?" she offered.

"No. . . ."

"Wolf?"

"Yeah. . . ."

"I never heard of wolves around here before."

He smiled. "That's right," he said. "That's absolutely right.

There ain't supposed to be no wolves in these parts anymore. They ain't supposed to be here."

"Are you sure it's a wolf?"

"Yup." He paused, listening again. Only the river sounded now, down below. "But it's a kind of unusual wolf."

"What do you mean?"

"I mean it's one of them two-legged-type wolves."

She stared at him. "You mean human?"

"More or less," Smith said.

They drove on, past the ranger station, past the pink water tower, across the Paria River to the launching ramp on the muddy banks of the Colorado. Here Smith parked his truck, tailgate toward the river, and began unloading his boats. The girl helped him. They dragged the three inflatable boats from the truck bed, unfolded them and spread them out on the sand. Smith took a socket wrench from his toolbox, removed a spark plug from the engine block and screwed in an adapter on the head of an air hose. He started the motor, which inflated the boats. He and the girl pulled the boats into the water, leaving the bows resting on the shore, and tied them on long lines to the nearest willow tree.

The sun went down. Sloshing about in cutoff jeans, they shivered a little when a cool breeze began to come down the canyon, off the cold green river.

"Let's fix something to eat before it gets completely dark," the girl said.

"You bet, honey."

Smith fiddled with his field glasses, looking for something he thought he had seen moving on a distant promontory above the gorge. He found his target. Adjusting the focus, he made out, a mile away through the haze of twilight, the shape of a blue jeep half concealed beneath a pedestal rock. He saw the flicker of a small campfire. A thing moved at the edge of the field. He turned the glasses slightly and saw the figure of a man, short and hairy and broad and naked. The naked man held a can of beer in one hand; with the other hand he held field glasses to his eyes, just like Smith. He was looking directly at Smith.

The two men studied each other for a while through 7 × 35 binocular lenses, which do not blink. Smith raised his hand in a cautious wave. The other man raised his can of beer as an answering salute.

"What are you looking at?" the girl asked.

"Some kind of skinned tourist."

"Let me see." He gave her the glasses. She looked. "My God, he's naked," she said. "He's waving it at me."

"Lee's Ferry is gone to hell," Smith said, rummaging in their supplies. "You can't argue that. Where'd we put that goddanged Coleman stove?"

"That guy looks familiar."

"All naked men look familiar, honey. Now sit down here and let's see what we can find to eat in this mess."

They sat on ammo boxes and cooked and ate their simple supper. The Colorado River rolled past. From downstream came the steady roar of the rapids where a tributary stream, the Paria, has been unloading its rocks for a number of centuries in the path of the river. There was a smell of mud on the air, of fish, of willow and cottonwood. Good smells, rotten and rank, down through the heart of the desert.

They were not alone. Occasional motor traffic buzzed by on the road a hundred yards away: tourists, boaters, anglers bound for the marina a short distance beyond.

The small and solitary campfire on the far-off headland to the west had flickered out. In the gloom that way Smith could see no sign of friend or enemy. He retreated into the bushes to urinate, staring at the gleam of the darkened river, thinking of nothing much. His mind was still. Tonight he and his friend would sleep on the shore by the boats and gear. Tomorrow morning, while he rigged the boats for the voyage down the river, the girl would drive back to Page to pick up the paying passengers scheduled to arrive by air, from Albuquerque, at eleven.

New customers for Back of Beyond. A Dr. Alexander K. Sarvis, M.D. And one Miss—or Mrs.?—or Mr.?—B. Abbzug.

4

Origins IV: Ms. B. Abbzug

No relation to the Senator, she always said. Which was mostly true. Her first name was Bonnie and she came from the Bronx, not Brooklyn. Furthermore, she was half Wasp (white anglo sexy Protestant); her mother's maiden name was McComb. That strain perhaps accounted for the copper glints in Ms. Abbzug's long, rich, molasses-colored hair, draped in glossy splendor from crown of head to swell of rump. Abbzug was twenty-eight years old. A dancer by training, she had first come to the Southwest seven years earlier, member of a college troupe. She fell in love—at first sight—with mountains and desert, deserted her troupe in Albuquerque and continued at the university there, graduating with honors and distinction into the world of unemployment offices, food stamps and basement apartments. She worked as a waitress, as a teller trainee in a bank, as a go-go dancer, as a receptionist in doctors' offices. First for a psychiatrist named Evilsizer, then for a urologist named Glasscock, then for a general surgeon named Sarvis.

Sarvis was the best of a sorry lot. She had stayed with him and after three years was still with him in the multiple capacities of office clerk, nurse-aide and chauffeur (he was incapable of driving a car in city traffic, though perfectly at home with scalpel and forceps slashing

about in another man's gallbladder or excising a chalazion from someone's inner eyelid). When the doctor's wife died in a meaningless accident—plane crash during takeoff from O'Hare Field—she watched
him stumble like a sleepwalker through office, ward and eight days
until he turned to her with a question. In his eyes. He was twenty-
one years older than she. His children were grown up and gone.

Ms. Abbzug offered him what consolation she could, which was
much, but refused the offer of marriage that followed a year after the
accident.

She preferred (she said) the relative independence (she thought)
of female bachelorhood. Though she often stayed with the doctor in
his home and accompanied him on his travels, she also retained her
own quarters, in a humbler part of Albuquerque. Her "quarters" was
a hemisphere of petrified polyurethane supported by a geodetic frame
of cheap aluminum, the whole resting like an overgrown and pallid
fungus on a lot with tomato patch in the wrong or southwestern sec-
tor of the city.

The interior of Abbzug's dome glittered like the heart of a
geode, with dangling silvery mobiles and electric lanterns made of
multiperforated No. 8 tin cans hanging from the ceiling, and crystalline clusters of mirrors and baubles attached at random to the curved
interior. On sunny days the translucent single wall admitted a general
glow, filling her inner space with pleasure. Beside her princess-size
water bed stood a bookshelf loaded with the teenybopper intellectual's standard library of the period: the collected works of J. R. R. Tol-
kien, Carlos Castaneda, Hermann Hesse, Richard Brautigan, *The
Whole Earth Catalog*, the *I Ching*, *The Old Farmer's Almanack* and
The Tibetan Book of the Dead. Spiders crawled upon the wisdom of
Fritz Perls and Prof. Richard ("Baba Ram Dass") Alpert, Ph.D. Lonesome earwigs explored the irrational knots of R. D. Laing. Silverfish
ate their way through the cold sludge of R. Buckminster Fuller. She
never opened any of them anymore.

The brightest thing in Abbzug's dome was a brain. She was too
wise to linger long with any fad, though she tested them all. With an
intelligence too fine to be violated by ideas, she had learned that she

was searching not for self-transformation (she liked herself) but for something good *to do*.

Dr. Sarvis detested geodesic domes. Too much of the American countryside, he thought, was being encysted with these giant sunken golf balls. He despised them as fungoid, abstract, alien and inorganic structures, symptom and symbol of the Plastic Plague, the Age of Junk. But he loved Bonnie Abbzug despite her dome. The loose and partial relationship which was all she would give him he accepted with gratitude. Not only was it much better than nothing but in many ways it was much better than everything.

Likewise, she thought. The fabric, she said, of our social structure is being unraveled by too many desperately interdependent people. Agreed, said Dr. Sarvis; our only hope is catastrophe. So they lingered together, the small dark arrogant slip of a girl and the huge pink paunchy bear of a man, for weeks, months, a year. . . . Periodically he repeated his marriage proposal, as much for form's sake as out of love. Is one more important than the other? And regularly she turned him down, firmly and tenderly, with open arms, with prolonged kisses, with her mild and moderate love.

Love me little, love me long. . . .

Other men were such obscene idiots. The doctor was an aging adolescent but he was kind and generous and he needed her and when he was with her he was really there, with her. Most of the time. It seemed to her that he withheld nothing. When he *was* with her.

For two years she had lived and loved, off and on, with Dr. Sarvis. There was this tendency simply to drift. Millions were doing it. It irritated Abbzug a bit that she, with her degree in French, her good healthy strong young body, her restless and irritable mind, was fulfilling no function more demanding than that of office flunky and lonely widower's part-time mistress. And yet, when she thought about it, what did she really want to do? Or be? She had given up dancing—*the dance*—because it was too demanding, because it required an almost total devotion which she was unwilling to give. The cruelest art. She could certainly never go back to the night world of the cabaret, where all those vice squad detectives, claims adjusters and fraternity boys sat in the murk with their blues, their beers, their limp lusts, straining their eyeballs, ruining their eyesight for a glimpse of her crotch.

What then? The maternal instinct seemed to be failing to function so far as she was concerned, except for her role as mother to the doctor. Playing mother to a man old enough to be her father. The generation gap, or vice versa? The cradle robber? Who's a cradle robber? I'm the cradle robber; he's in his second childhood.

She had built most of the dome herself, buying assistance only for the plumbing and wiring. The night before she moved into the thing she held a ceremony, a consecration of the house, a "chant." She and her friends formed a circle round a small and burning coal-oil lamp. They twisted their long, awkward American legs into overhand knots—the lotus posture. Then the six middle-class college-educated Americans sitting under an inflated twenty-first-century marshmallow of plastic foam intoned a series of antique Oriental chants which had long ago been abandoned by educated people in the nations of their origin.

"*Om,*" they chanted. "*Ommmmmmmmmmmmmmmmmmmmmm- mmm. Om mani padma ommmmmmmmmmmmmmmmmmmmm. . . .*"

Or as Doc Sarvis liked to say, "*Om* sweet *om:* be it ever so humble . . ." and he hung a needlework sampler on the curvispatial wall: *God Bless Our Happy Dome.*

But he seldom entered there. When she was not with him, at his place or on their frequent travels, she lived alone in her fungus. Alone with her cat, tending her potted plants, her tomato patch in the backyard, playing her recorder, dusting her unread and unreadable books, brushing her marvelous hair, meditating, exercising, lifting her lovely and longing face toward the inaudible chant of the sun, she drifted through her time, through space, through all the concatenate cells of her unfolding self. Where to now, Abbzug? You're twenty-eight and a half years old, Abbzug.

For diversion she joined the good doctor on his nighttime highway beautification projects, assisting him in the beginning as driver and lookout. When they tired of fire she learned to hold her own at one end of a crosscut saw. She learned how to swing an ax and how to notch the upright posts of a billboard so as to fell it in any desired direction.

When the doctor acquired a lightweight McCulloch chain saw she learned how to operate that too, how to start it, how to oil and refuel it, how to adjust the chain when it became too tight or too loose. With this handy tool they were able to accomplish much more work in limited time although it did raise the ecological question, whatever that meant, of noise and air pollution, the excessive consumption of metal and energy. Endless ramifications. . . .

"No," the doctor said. "Forget all that. Our duty is to destroy billboards."

They proceeded, furtive figures in the night, the sinister black Lincoln with the silvery caduceus on the license tag, the big car parked with motor running on obscure side roads near major highways, the huge man, the short woman, climbing fences, shuffling through the weeds lugging their chain saw and fuel can. They became familiar shapes and smells to the ground squirrels and hoot owls, a major and irritating mystery to the outdoor advertising agencies and the Special Investigation Squad of the Bernalillo County sheriff's department.

Somebody had to do it.

The local press spoke first of meaningless vandalism. Later, for a time, reports of such incidents were suppressed on the theory that publicity might only encourage the vandals. But as the advertising men, the highway patrolmen and the county sheriffs became aware of the repetition of these attacks on private property and the singularity of the targets, comment arose.

Pictures and stories began to appear in the Albuquerque *Journal,* the Santa Fe *New Mexican,* the Taos *News,* the Belen *Bugle.* The Bernalillo County Sheriff denied a report that he had assigned a full-time detective detail to the problem. The outdoor advertising executives, interviewed and quoted, spoke of "common criminals."

Anonymous letters appeared in the mail of city and county officials, all claiming credit for the crimes. The newspaper stories mentioned "organized bands of environmental activists," a phrase soon shortened to the much handier and more dramatic "eco-raiders." The county attorneys warned that the perpetrators of these illegal acts, when caught, would be prosecuted to the fullest extent of the law. Nasty letters, pro and con, appeared in the Letters-to-the-Editor columns.

Doc Sarvis chuckled within his mask, stitching up a stranger's yellow belly. The kid smiled as she read the papers by the evening fire. It was like celebrating Hallowe'en all year round. It was something to do. For the first time in years Ms. Abbzug felt the emotion called delight in her cold Bronx heart. She was learning anew the solid satisfaction of good work properly done.

The billboard men schemed, measured costs, drafted new designs, ordered new materials. There was talk of electrifying the uprights, of set guns, of armed watchmen, of rewards to vigilantes. But the billboards followed the highways for hundreds of miles across New Mexico. Where and when the criminals would attack next no one could guess; you'd need a guard for every billboard. There was a phased changeover to steel. The extra costs, of course, could be passed on to the consumers.

One night they went out, Bonnie and Doc, far to the north of the city, to level a target they had chosen weeks earlier. They parked the car out of sight of the highway, on a turnoff, and walked the half mile back to their objective. The usual precautions. As usual he carried the chain saw, she led the way (she had better night vision). They stumbled through the dark, using no other light than that of the stars, following the right-of-way fence. Traffic hissed by on the four-lane freeway, frantic and fast as always, following private tunnels of light through the darkness, oblivious to all but the need to make haste, to get there, somewhere, wherever.

Bonnie and Doc ignored the fanatic engines, disregarded the human minds and bodies hurtling by, paid them no attention at all; why should they? They were working.

They came to the target. It looked the same as before.

MOUNTAIN VIEW RANCHETTE ESTATES
TOMORROW'S NEW WAY OF LIVING TODAY!
Horizon Land & Development Corp.

"Beautiful," she said, leaning against the panting Doc.

"Beautiful," he agreed. After resting a moment he put down his McCulloch, knelt, turned on the switch, set the choke, grasped the throttle and gave a good pull on the starter cord. The snappy little motor buzzed into life; the wicked chain danced forward in its groove. He stood up, the machine vibrating in his hands, eager for destruction. He pushed the oiler button, revved the engine and stepped to the nearest upright post of the billboard.

"Wait," Bonnie said. She was leaning against the center post, tapping it with her knuckles. "Wait a minute."

He didn't hear her. Squeezing the throttle, he set the blade against the post. The saw bounced off with a shriek of steel, a spray of sparks. Doc was dumbfounded for a moment, unable to accept what he saw and heard. Then he shut off the motor.

A blessed quiet in the night. Faces pale in the gloom, they stared at each other.

"Doc," she said, "I told you to wait."

"Steel," he said. Wonderingly he passed a hand over the post, bonged on it with his big fist.

"That's what it is."

They waited. They thought.

After a pause she said, "You know what I want for my birthday?"

"What?"

"I want an acetylene torch. With safety goggles."

"When?"

"Tomorrow."

"Tomorrow's not your birthday."

"So?"

The very next night they were back, same place, same sign, this time adequately equipped. The torch functioned perfectly, the intense blue flame licking silently and furiously at the steel, making an ugly red-hot wound. But in the dark the glare seemed dangerously conspicuous. Doc lowered the torch to the base of the center post, down where it emerged from the stony desert ground, down among the tumbleweed and rabbit brush. Even then the light of the flame seemed much too bold. Bonnie squatted down and opened her coat wide, trying to shield the flame from sight of the passing traffic. Nobody seemed to notice. Nobody stopped. The heedless autos, the bellowing trucks, all swept past with vicious hiss of rubber, mad roar of engines, rushing into the black oblivion of the night. Maybe nobody cared.

The torch was deadly but it was slow. The molecules of steel released their bonds with one another most painfully, reluctantly, loath to part. The red wound widened slowly, slowly, even though, as expected, the post was hollow.

The torch was slow but it was deadly. Doc and the girl worked steadily, one relieving the other from time to time. Patience, patience. The heavy-gauge alloy yielded to the flame. Progress became discernible. Obvious. Conclusive.

Doc shut off the torch, removed the goggles, wiped his sweating brow. The welcome darkness closed around them.

"She'll go now," he said.

The center post was cut all the way through. The outer posts were each cut more than two thirds through. The great sign rested mostly on its own weight, precariously balanced. A south breeze would make it totter. A child could push it over. Within its gravitational time-space continuum, the billboard's destiny was predetermined, beyond appeal. The arc of its return to earth could have been computed to within a tolerance of three millimeters.

They savored the moment. The intrinsic virtues of free and worthy enterprise. The ghost of Sam Gompers smiled upon their labors.

"Push it over," he said.

"You," she said. "You did most of the work."

"It's your birthday."

Bonnie placed her small brown hands against the lower edge of the sign, above her head, barely within her reach, and leaned. The billboard—some five tons of steel, wood, paint, bolts and nuts—gave a little groan of protest and began to heel over. A rush of air, then the thundering collision of billboard with earth, the boom of metal, the rack and wrench of ruptured bolts, a mushroom cloud of dust, nothing more. The indifferent traffic raced by, unseeing, uncaring, untouched.

They celebrated at the revolving Skyroom Grill.

"I want a Thanksgiving dinner," she said.

"It's not Thanksgiving."

"If I want a Thanksgiving dinner it's *got* to be Thanksgiving."

"That sounds logical."

"Call the waiter."

"He won't believe us."

"We'll try to reason with him."

They reasoned. Food appeared, and wine. They ate, he poured, they drank, the hour slouched by into eternity. Doc spoke.

"Abbzug," the doctor said, "I love you."

"How much?"

"Too much."

"That's not enough."

Charlie Ray or Ray Charles or somebody at the ivories, playing "Love Gets in Your Eyes," pianissimo. The circular room, ten stories above the ground, revolved at 0.5 kilometer per hour. All the night lights of Greater Albuquerque New Mex. pop. 300,000 souls lay about them below, the kingdom of neon, electric gardens of babylonic splendor surrounded by the bleak, black, slovenly wilderness that never would shape up. Where the lean and hungry coyote skulked, unwilling to extinct. The skunk. The snake. The bug. The worm.

"Marry me," he said.

"What for?"

"I don't know. I like ceremony."

"Why spoil a perfectly good relationship?"

"I'm a lonely old middle-aged meatcutter. I require security. I like the idea of commitment."

"That's what they do to crazy people. Are you crazy, Doc?"

"I don't know."

"Let's go to bed. I'm tired."

"Will you still love me when I'm old?" he asked, filling her glass again with ruby-red La Tache. "Will you still love me when I'm old and bald and fat and impotent?"

"You're already old, bald, fat and impotent."

"But rich. Don't forget that. Would you still love me if I were poor?"

"Hardly."

"A whiskery wreck of a wino, puttering about in garbage cans on South First Street, barked at by small rabid dogs, hounded by *les fuzz?*"

"No."

"No?" He took her hand, the left one, which she had left lying on the table. Silver and turquoise glittered richly on her slender wrist. They liked Indian jewelry. They smiled at each other, in the unsteady candlelight in a large round room that turned, on tracks, round and slowly round above the city of tomorrow today.

Good old Doc. She was familiar with each bump on his bulbous head, every freckle on his sunburned dome, each and every wrinkle on that map of nearly fifty years they had agreed to designate—jointly—as Doc Sarvis's face. She understood his longing well enough. She helped him all she could.

They went home, back to Doc's old pile of F. L. Wright rock in the foothills. Doc went upstairs. She placed a stack of records (her own) on the spindle of the turntable of the quadraphonic record player (his). Through the four speakers came the heavy beat, the electronic throb, the stylized voices of four young degenerates united in song: some band—the Konks, the Scarabs, the Hateful Dead, the Green Crotch—which grossed about two million a year.

Doc came down in his bathrobe. "Are you playing that goddamned imitation-Negro music again?"

"I like it."

"That slave music?"

"Some people like it."

"Who?"

"Everybody I know except you."

"Hard on the plants, you know. Kills geraniums."

"Oh, God. All right." She groaned and changed the program.

They went to bed. From below rose the genteel, discreet and melancholy sounds of Mozart.

"You're too old for that kind of noise," he was saying. "Those teen tunes. That bubble-gum music. You're a grown-up girl now."

"Well I like it."

"After I go to work in the morning, okay? You can play it all day then if you want to, okay?"

"It's your house, Doc."

"It's yours too. But we must consider the potted plants."

Through the open French doors of the bedroom, beyond the second-story terrace, miles away down the sloping plain of the desert, they could see the glow of the great city. Airplanes circled softly, inaudible, above the metropolitan radiance, quiet as fireflies in the distance. Tall searchlights stalked through the velvet dark probing the clouds.

His hands were upon her. She stirred sleepily in his arms, waiting. They "made" love, for quite some time.

"Used to do this all night," Doc said. "Now it takes me all night to do it."

"You're a slow comer," she said, "but you get there."

They rested for a while. "How about a river trip?" he said.

"You've been promising that for months."

"This time I mean it."

"When?"

"Very soon."

"What made you think of that?"

"I hear the call of the river."

"That's the toilet," she said. "The valve is stuck again."

She was a walker too, that girl. In lug-soled boots, army shirt, short pants and bush ranger's hat, she marched along, alone, through Albuquerque's only mountains, the pink Sandia range, or tramped about over the volcanoes west of town. She didn't own a car but on her ten-speed bicycle sometimes pedaled all the fifty miles north to Santa Fe, pack on her narrow back, and from there up into the real mountains, the Sangre de Cristo (Blood of Christ) Mountains, to the end of the pavement, and hiked on to the peaks—Baldy, Truchas, Wheeler—camping alone for two or three nights at a time, while black bear snuffled about her midget tent and mountain lions screamed.

She searched. She hunted. She fasted on the mesa rim, waiting for a vision, and fasted some more, and after a time God appeared incarnate on a platter as a roasted squab with white paper booties on His little drumsticks.

Doc kept muttering about the river. About the Grand Canyon. About a place called Lee's Ferry and a riverman named Seldom S. Smith.

"Any time," she said.

Meanwhile they cut down, burned up, defaced and mutilated billboards.

"Kid stuff," the good doctor complained. "We are meant for finer things. Did you know, my dear, that we have the biggest strip mine in the United States, up near Shiprock? Right here in New Mexico the Land of Enchantment? Have you thought about where all that smog is coming from that blankets the whole bloody Rio Grande valley? Paul Horgan's 'great river,' channelized, subsidized, salinized, trickling into cotton fields under the sulfur skies of New Mexico? Did you know that a consortium of power companies and government agencies are conspiring to open more strip mines and build even more coal-burning power plants in the same four-corners area where all that filth is coming from now? Together with more roads, power lines, railways and pipelines? All in what was once semi-virginal wilderness and still is the most spectacular landscape in the forty-eight contiguous bloody states? Did you know that?"

"I was once a semi-virgin," she said.

"Did you know that other power companies and the same government agencies are planning even bigger things for the Wyoming-

Montana area? Strip mines bigger than any that have devastated Appalachia? Have you thought about the nukes? Breeder reactors? Strontium, plutonium? Did you know that the oil companies are preparing
to disembowel vast areas of Utah and Colorado to recover the oil in
oil shale? Are you aware of what the big logging companies are doing
to our national forests? Of what the Corps of Engineers and the Bureau of Reclamation are doing to our streams and rivers? The rangers
and game managers to our wildlife? Do you realize what the land
developers are doing to what's left of our open spaces? Do you know
that Albuquerque–Santa Fe–Taos will soon become one big strip city?
The same for Tucson–Phoenix? Seattle to Portland? San Diego to
Santa Barbara? Miami to Saint Augustine? Baltimore to Boston? Fort
Worth to—"

"They're way ahead of you," she said. "Don't panic, Doc."

"Panic?" he said. "Pandemonium? Pan shall rise again, my dear.
The great god Pan."

"Nietzsche said God is dead."

"I'm talking about Pan. *My* God."

"God is dead."

"My God is alive and kicking. Sorry about yours."

"I'm bored," she said. "Amuse me."

"How about a trip down the river?"

"What river?"

"Down *the* river through God's Gulch on a rubber boat with
handsome hairy sweaty boatmen waiting on you hand and mouth?"

Bonnie shrugged. "So what're we waiting for?"

5

The Wooden Shoe Conspiracy

There was this bum on the beach.

Fiercely bearded, short, squat, malevolent, his motor vehicle loaded with dangerous weapons: this bum. Did nothing; said nothing; stared.

They ignored him.

Smith's assistant boatman did not appear. Never did appear. Smith rigged his boat alone, chewing on jerky. He sent his girl friend to Page with the truck to pick up the passengers arriving that morning by air.

The bum watched. (As soon as the work was completed he would probably ask for a job.)

Flight 96 was late, as usual. Finally it emerged from a cloudbank, growled overhead, banked and turned and landed into the wind on the strictly limited Page runway—limited at one end by a high-tension power line and at the other end by a three-hundred-foot cliff. The aircraft itself was a bimotored jet-prop job with an antiquarian look; it might have been built in 1929 (the year of the crash) and seemed to have been repainted several times since, in the manner of a used car touched up for sale on the corner lot. (Square Deal Andy's. Top Dollar Johnny's.) Somebody had painted it recently with one thick coat of yellow, which failed, however, to quite conceal the underlying coat of green. Little round glass ports lined the sides of the craft, through which the white faces of passengers could be seen, peering out, crossing themselves, their lips moving.

The plane turned from the runway and lumbered onto the apron of the strip. The engines smoked and grumbled and backfired but provided enough power to bring the plane almost to the loading zone. There the engines died and the plane stopped. The airport ticket agent, flight traffic controller, manager, and baggage handler removed his ear protectors and climbed down from the open-air control tower, buttoning his fly.

Black fumes hovered about the plane's starboard engine. From the interior came little ticking noises; a hatch was opened and lowered by hand crank, transforming itself into a gangway. The stewardess appeared in the opening.

Flight 96 discharged two passengers.

First to alight was a woman. She was young, handsome, with an arrogant air; her dark shining hair hung below her waist. She wore this and that, not much, including a short skirt which revealed tanned and excellent legs.

The cowboys, Indians, Mormon missionaries, Government officials and other undesirables lounging about the terminal stared with hungry eyes. The city of Page, Arizona, pop. 1400, includes 800 men and sometimes three or four good-looking women.

Behind the young woman came the man, of middle age, though his piebald beard and steel-rimmed spectacles may have made him look older than he really was. His nose, irregular, very large, cheerily refulgent, shone like a polished tomato under the bright white light of the desert sun. A stogie in his teeth. Well dressed, he looked like a professor. Blinking, he put on a straw hat, which helped, and came tramping up to the terminal door beside the woman. He towered over the girl at his side. Nevertheless everybody present, including the women, stared at the girl.

No doubt about it. Under a wide-brimmed straw hat, wearing

huge black opaque sunglasses, she looked like Garbo. The old Garbo. Young Garbo.

Smith's girl friend greeted them. The big man took her hand, which vanished within the clasp of his enormous paw. But his grasp was precise, gentle and firm. The surgeon.

"Right," he said. "I'm Dr. Sarvis. This is Bonnie." His voice seemed strangely soft, low, melancholy, issuing from so grand (or gross) an organism.

"Miss Abbzug?"

"Miz Abbzug."

"Call her Bonnie."

Into the truck, duffel bags and sleeping bags in back. They whipped out of Page past the thirteen churches of Jesus Row, through the official government slums and the construction workers' trailer-house slums and out of town into the traditional pastoral slums of Navajoland. Sick horses loitered along the highway looking for something to eat: newspapers, Kleenex, beer cans, anything more or less degradable. The doctor talked with Seldom's driver; Ms. Abbzug remained aloof and mostly silent.

"What utterly ghastly country," she said once. "Who lives here?"

"The Indians," Doc said.

"It's too good for them."

Down through Dynamite Notch to Bitter Springs to Marble Canyon and under the paranoid gargoyled battlements of the Jurassic Age to Lee's Ferry, into the hot-muck green-willow smell of the river. The hot sun roared down through a sky blue as the Virgin's cloak, emphasizing with its extravagant light the harsh perfection of the cliffs, the triumphant river, the preparations for a great voyage.

A second round of introductions.

"Dr. Sarvis, Miz Abbzug, Seldom Seen Smith. . . ."

"Pleased to meet you, sir; you too, ma'am. This here's George Hayduke. Behind the bush. He's gonna be number-two nigger this trip. Say something, George."

The bum behind the beard growled something unintelligible. He crunched an empty beer can in his hand, lobbed the wreckage toward a nearby garbage can, missed. Hayduke was now wearing ragged shorts and a leather hat. His eyes were red. He smelled of sweat, salt, mud, stale beer. Dr. Sarvis, erect and dignified, his beard smartly trimmed, regarded Hayduke with reservations. It was people like Hayduke who gave beards a bad name.

Smith, looking at them all with his happy grin, seemed pleased with his crew and passengers. Especially with Miz Abbzug, at whom he tried hard not to stare. But she was something, she was something. Smith felt, down below, belowdecks, that faint but unmistakable itching and twitching of scrotal hair which is the sure praeludium to love. Venereal as a valentine, it could have no other meaning.

About that time the remainder of the passenger list arrived by car: two secretaries from San Diego, old friends of Smith, repeaters, who had been with him on many river trips before. The party was complete. After a lunch of tinned snacks, cheese, crackers, beer and soda pop, they got under way. Still no regular assistant boatman; Hayduke had himself a job.

Sullen and silent, he coiled the bow line in nautical trim, gave the boat a shove from shore and rolled on board. The boat floated into the current of the river. Three ten-man rubber rafts lashed snug together side by side, a triple rig, it made a ponderous and awkward-looking craft but just right for rocks and rapids. The passengers sat in the middle; Hayduke and Smith, as oarsmen, stood or sat on each side. Smith's truck driver waved good-bye from shore, looking wistful. They would not see her again for fourteen days.

The wooden oars creaked in the oarlocks; the vessel advanced with the current, which would carry it along at an average of four to five miles an hour through most of the canyon, much faster in the rapids. Not as in a rowboat but facing forward, like gondoliers, pushing (not pulling) on the oars, Hayduke and Smith confronted the gleaming river, the sound of fast water around the first bend. Smith stuck a stick of jerky in his teeth.

Back-lit by the afternoon sun, the rolling waters shone like hammered metal, like bronze lamé, each facet reflecting mirror-fashion the blaze in the sky. While glowing dumbly in the east, above the red canyon walls, the new moon hung in the wine-dark firmament like a pale antiphonal response to the glory of the sun. New moon in the afternoon, fanatic sun ahead. A bird whistled in the willows.

Down the river!

Hayduke knew nothing about river-running. Smith knew he knew nothing. It didn't matter too much, so long as the passengers didn't find out right away. What did matter to Smith was Hayduke's broad and powerful back, his gorilla arms, the short strong legs. The kid would learn all he had to learn quick enough.

They approached the riffles of the Paria, under the bluff where the park rangers lived. Tourists watched them from the new metallic campground on the hill. Smith stood up to get a better view of the rocks and rough water immediately ahead. Nothing much, a minor rapid, Grade 1 on the boatman's scale. The green river curled around a few fangs of limestone, the sleek smooth waters purling foam. A toneless roar, what acousticians call "white noise," vibrated on the air.

As prearranged, Hayduke and Smith turned the boat 90 degrees and bore sideways (this foolish craft was wider than long) onto the glassy tongue of the little rapid. They slipped through with barely a splash. Through the tail of the turmoil they rode into the confluence, where the Paria (in flood) mixed its gray greasy bentonite waters with the clear green of the dammed Colorado. From 12 mph their speed slowed to four or five again.

Hayduke relaxed, grinning. Wiped the water from his beard and eyebrows. Why, hell's fuck, he thought, that's nothing. Why shit I'm just a natural riverman.

They passed beneath Marble Canyon Bridge. From above looking down the height had not seemed so great; there was no standard for scale. But from the river looking up they realized the meaning of a vertical four hundred feet: about thirty-five skyscraper stories from here to there. The automobile creeping across the bridge looked like a toy; the tourists standing about on the observation point were insect size.

The bridge moved away behind them, vanished beyond the turning of the canyon walls. They were now well into Marble Gorge, also known as Marble Canyon, sixty miles of river three thousand feet below the level of the land, leading into the Grand Canyon at the mouth of the Little Colorado River.

Seldom Seen Smith as usual was fondling memories. He remembered the real Colorado, before damnation, when the river flowed unchained and unchanneled in the joyous floods of May and June, swollen with snow melt. Boulders crunching and clacking and grumbling, tumbling along the river's bedrock bed, the noise like that of grinding molars in a giant jaw. That was a river.

Still, even so, not all was lost. The beaded light of afternoon slanted down beyond the canyon walls, whiskey-gold on rock and tree, a silent benison from the flawless sky, free from your friendly solar system. Cut off, then reappearing, the pale elided wafer of the new moon followed after. A good spirit, a faery queen, watching over them.

Again the white roar. Another rapids coming. Smith gave the order to fasten life jackets. They turned another corner. The noise swelled alarmingly, and down the canyon where all now stared they saw rocks like teeth rising through a white rim of foam. The river apparently went underground at that point; from boat level nothing of it could be seen beyond the rapids.

"Badger Crick Rapids," Smith announced. Again he stood up. Grade 3, nothing serious. All the same he wanted a good look before diving in. He stood and read the river as others might read the symbols on a score, the blips on a radarscope, or signs of coming weather in cloud formations far away. He looked for the fat swell that meant hidden fang of stone, the choppy stretch of wavelets signifying rocks and shallow water, the shadow on the river that told of a gravel bar six inches under the surface, the hook and snag of submerged logs that could gash the bottom of his rubber boats. He followed with his eye the flecks of foam gliding steadily down the mainstream, the almost invisible ripples and eddies on the river's flanks.

Smith read the river, the ladies reading him. He was not aware

of how comic and heroic he looked, the Colorado man, long and lean
and brown as the river used to be, leaning forward on his oar, squinting into the sun, the strong and uncorrupted teeth shining in the
customary grin, the macho bulge at the fly of his ancient Levi's, the
big ears out and alert. Rapids closing in.

"Everybody down," Smith orders. "Grab rope."

In a frantic clamor of tumbled water, the mass of the river crashes
upon the rubble of rock fanning out from the mouth of a side canyon—Badger. The deep and toneless vibration all around, a mist of
spray floating on the air, little rainbows suspended in the sunlight.

Again they swing the craft about. Smith heaves mightily on his
oar, taking the bow, and steers the boat straight onto the tongue of
the rapids, the oil-smooth surge of the main current pouring like a
torrent into the heart of the uproar. No need to cheat on this, a minor
rapid; he'll give his customers a thrill, their money's worth, what they
paid for.

A wave eight feet high looms above Smith, crouched in the bow.
The wave stands there, waiting, does not move. (On the river, unlike
the sea, the water moves; the waves remain in place.) The front end
of the boat climbs the wave, pushed up by momentum and the weight
behind. Smith hangs on to the lines. The tripartite boat almost folds
back upon itself, then bends over the wave and slides down into the
trough beyond, the middle and third parts following in like fashion.
A wet and shining boulder stands dead ahead, directly in their course.
The boat pauses before it. A ton of water, recoiling from the rock,
crashes into the boat. Everyone is instantly soaked. The women
scream with delight; even Doc Sarvis laughs. Smith hauls on his oar;
the boat rolls off the boulder and careens like a roller coaster over the
waves in the tail of the rapids, then slows in the steadier water below.
Smith looks back. He has lost an oarsman. Where George Hayduke
should have been the unmanned oar swings loosely in its lock.

There he comes. Hayduke in his orange life jacket bobs down
the billows, grinning with ferocious determination, knees up under
his chin, the fetal pose, using his feet and legs as shock absorbers,

caroming off the rock. Instinctive and correct response. Has lost his hat. Makes no sound. . . .

In the calmer water below the rapid they dragged him back aboard.

"Where you been?" Smith said.

Grinning, sputtering, Hayduke shook his head, popped the water from his ears and managed to look both fierce and sheepish. "Fucking river," he muttered.

"You got to grab a line," Smith said.

"I was holding onto the fucking oar. Jammed it on a rock and it hit me in the stomach." Nervously he pawed his tangled mass of soaked hair. His hat, an old leather sombrero from Sonora, was floating on the waves, about to go down for the third time. They retrieved it with an oar.

The river bore them calmly on, through the plateau, into the Precambrian mantle of the earth, toward the lowlands, the delta and the Sea of Cortez, seven hundred miles away.

"Soap Crick Rapids next," Smith said. And sure enough, they heard again the tumult of river and stone in conflict. Around the next bend.

"This is ridiculous," Abbzug said privately to Doc. They sat hunched hard together with a wet poncho spread over their laps and legs. She was beaming with pleasure. Water dripped from the brim of her exaggerated hat. The doctor's stogie burned bravely in the damp.

"Absolutely ridiculous," he said. "How do you like our boatmen?"

"Weird; the tall one looks like Ichabod Ignatz; the short one looks like a bandit out of some old Mack Sennett movie."

"Or Charon and Cerberus," Doc said. "But try not to laugh; our lives rest in their uncertain hands." And they laughed again.

All together now they plunged into another maelstrom, Grade 4 on the river runner's chart. More gnashing river, heaving waves, the clash of elementals, the pure and brainless fury of tons of irresistible water crashing down upon tons of immovable limestone. They felt the shock, they heard the roar, saw foam and spray and rainbows floating on the mist as they rode through chaos into the clear. The adrenaline of adventure, without the time for dread, buoyed them high on the waves.

This was the forty-fifth trip down the Grand for Smith, and so far as he could measure, its pleasure was not staled by repetition. But then no two river trips were ever quite alike. The river, the canyon, the desert world was always changing, from moment to moment, from miracle to miracle, within the firm reality of mother earth. River, rock, sun, blood, hunger, wings, joy—this is the real, Smith would have said, if he'd wanted to. If he felt like it. All the rest is androgynous theosophy. All the rest is transcendental transvestite transactional scientology or whatever the fad of the day, the vogue of the week. As Doc would've said, if Smith had asked him. Ask the hawk. Ask the hungry lion lunging at the starving doe. They know.

Thus reasoneth Smith. Only a small businessman, to be sure. Never even went to college.

In the grand stillness between rapids, which was half the river and most of the time, Smith and Hayduke rested on their oars and let the song of a canyon wren—a clear glissando of semiquavers—mingle with the drip of waterdrops, the gurgle of eddies, the honk of herons, the rustle of lizards in the dust on shore. Between rapids, not silence but music and stillness. While the canyon walls rose slowly higher, 1000, 1500, 2000 feet, the river descending, and the shadows grew longer and the sun shy.

A chill from the depths crept over them.

"Time to make camp, folks," Smith announced, sculling for shore. Hayduke pitched in. Close ahead, on the right bank, lay a slope of sand, fringed by thickets of coppery willow and stands of tamarisk with lavender plumes nodding in the breeze. Again they heard the call of a canyon wren, a little bird with a big mouth. But musical, musical. And the far-off roar of still another rapids, that sound like the continuous applause of an immense and tireless multitude. The grunt and breath of two men laboring, oars scraping. The quiet talk of the first-class passengers.

"Dig the scene, Doc."

"No technical jargon, please. This is a holy place."

"Yeah but where's the Coke machine?"

"Please, I'm meditating."

The bow grated on gravel. Hayduke, general swamper, coiled line in hand, splashed through ankle-deep water and tethered the boat to a stout clump of willows. All came ashore. Hayduke and Seldom passed each passenger his/her river bag, the rubberized dunnage, the little ammo boxes containing personal items. The passengers wandered off, Doc and Bonnie in one direction, the two women from San Diego in another.

Smith paused for a moment to watch the retreating figure of Ms. Abbzug.

"Now, ain't she something?" he said. "Ain't she *really* something?" He closed one eye, as if sighting down a rifle barrel. "Now that little girl is a real honey. Finger-lickin' good."

"Cunt is cunt," said George Hayduke, philosopher, not bothering to look. "Do we unload all this stuff now?"

"Most of it. Lemme show you."

They wrestled with the heavy baggage, the big ammo boxes full of food, the ice chest, the wooden box holding Seldom's cooking pots, frypans, Dutch oven, grills, other hardware, and lugged it all onto the beach. Smith outlined an area on the sand as his kitchen where he set up the cookstove, his folding table, his pantry, the bar, the black olives and fried baby clams. He chipped off little chunks of ice for all the begging cups that would soon appear and poured a spot of rum for Hayduke and himself. The passengers were still back in the bushes, changing into dry clothing, fortifying themselves in private for the cool of the evening.

"Here's to you, boatman," Smith said.

"Hoa binh," said Hayduke.

Smith built a fire of charcoal, peeled the butcher paper from the standard first-night entree—huge floppy steaks—and stacked them near the grill. Hayduke prepared the salad and, as he did so, chased the rum with his tenth can of beer since lunch.

"That stuff'll give you kidney stones," Smith said.

"Bullshit."

"Kidney stones. I oughta know."

"I been drinking beer all my life."

"How old are you?"

"Twenty-five."

"Kidney stones," Smith said. "In about ten more years."

"Bullshit."

The passengers, dry and refurbished, came straggling in one at a time, the doctor first. He placed his tin cup on the bar, installed one miniature iceberg and poured himself a double shot from his bottle of Wild Turkey.

"It is a beauteous evening, calm and free," he announced.

"That's true," Smith said.

"The holy time is quiet as a nun."

"You said a mouthful, Doctor."

"Call me Doc."

"Okay, Doc."

"Cheers."

"Same to you, Doc,"

There was some further discussion of the ambience. Then of other matters. The girl came up, Abbzug, wearing long pants and a shaggy sweater. She had shed the big hat but even in twilight still wore the sunglasses. She gave a touch of tone to Marble Gorge.

Meanwhile the doctor was saying, "The reason there are so many people on the river these days is because there are too many people everywhere else."

Bonnie shivered, slipping into the crook of his left arm. "Why don't we build a fire?" she said.

"The wilderness once offered men a plausible way of life," the doctor said. "Now it functions as a psychiatric refuge. Soon there will be no wilderness." He sipped at his bourbon and ice. "Soon there will be no place to go. Then the madness becomes universal." Another thought. "And the universe goes mad."

"We will," Smith said to Abbzug. "After supper."

"Call me Bonnie."

"Miss Bonnie."

"Miz Bonnie," she corrected him.

"Jesus fucking Christ," muttered Hayduke nearby, overhearing, and he snapped the cap from another can of Coors.

Abbzug cast a cold eye on Hayduke's face, or what could be seen of it behind the black bangs and the bushy beard. An oaf, she thought. All hairiness is bestial, Arthur Schopenhauer thought. Hayduke caught her look, scowled. She turned back to the others.

"We are caught," continued the good doctor, "in the iron treads of a technological juggernaut. A mindless machine. With a breeder reactor for a heart."

"You said a mouthful, Doc," says Seldom Seen Smith. He started on the steaks, laying them tenderly on the grill, above the glowing coals.

"A planetary industrialism"—the doctor ranted on—"growing like a cancer. Growth for the sake of growth. Power for the sake of power. I think I'll have another bit of ice here." (*Clank!*) "Have a touch of this, Captain Smith, it'll gladden your heart, gild your liver and flower like a rose down in the compost of your bowels."

"Don't mind if I do, Doc." But Smith wanted to know how a *machine* could "grow." Doc explained; it wasn't easy.

Smith's two repeaters from San Diego emerged from the bushes, smiling; they had unrolled his sleeping bag between their own. One young woman carried a bottle. Something about a river trip always seems to promote the consumption of potable drugs. Except for Abbzug, who sucked from time to time on a little hand-rolled Zig-Zag cigarette pinched between her fastidious fingers. There was the smell of some kind of burning hemp in the air around her head. (Give a girl enough rope and she'll smoke it.) The odor reminded Hayduke of dark days and darker nights. Muttering, he set the table, buffet-style, with the salad, the sourdough bread, corn on the cob, a stack of paper plates. Smith turned the steaks. Doc explained the world.

Hog-nosed bats flickered through the evening making radar noises, gulping bugs. Downriver the rapids waited, gnashing their teeth in a steady sullen uproar. High on the canyon rim a rock slipped or was dislodged by something, gave up its purchase anyway, and tumbled down from parapet to parapet, lost in the embrace of gravity, into the alchemy of change, one fragment in the universal flux, and crashed like a bomb into the river. Doc paused in mid-monologue; all listened for a moment to the dying reverberations.

"Grab a plate," said Smith to his customers, "and load up." There was no hesitation; he served the steaks. Last in line and disdaining a plate, Hayduke held out his G.I. canteen cup. Smith draped a giant steak over the cup, covering not only the cup but Hayduke's hand, wrist and forearm.

"Eat," said Smith.

"Sweet holy motherfuck," said his boatman, reverently.

Smith kindled a campfire, now that his passengers and help were feeding, with driftwood from the beach. Then he heaped a plate for himself.

All eyes turned toward the fire as the darkness of the canyon gathered around them. Little blue and green flames licked and lapped at the river wood—sculptured chunks of yellow pine from the high country a hundred miles away, juniper, pinyon pine, cottonwood, well-polished sticks of redbud, hackberry and ash. Following the sparks upward they saw the stars turning on in staggered sequence—emeralds, sapphires, rubies, diamonds and opals scattered about the sky in a puzzling, random distribution. Far beyond those galloping galaxies, or perhaps all too present to be seen, lurked God. The gaseous vertebrate.

Supper finished, Smith brought out his musical instruments and played for the assembled company. He played his harmonica—what the vulgar call a "mouth organ"—his Jew's harp, or what the B'nai B'rith calls a "mouth harp," and his kazoo, which last, however, added little to anyone's musical enrichment.

Smith and the doctor passed around the firewater. Abbzug, who did not as a rule drink booze, opened her medicine pouch, removed a Tampax tube, took out some weed and rolled a second little brown cigarette twisted shut at one end. She lit up and passed it around, but no one cared to smoke with her except a reluctant Hayduke and his memories.

"The pot revolution is over?" she said.

"All over," Doc said. "Marijuana was never more than an active placebo anyway."

"What nonsense."

"An oral pacifier for colicky adolescents."

"What utter rubbish."

The conversation lagged. The two young women from San Diego (a suburb of Tijuana) sang a song called "Dead Skunk in the Middle of the Road."

The entertainment palled. Fatigue like gravitation pulled at limbs and eyelids. As they had come so they departed, first Abbzug, then the two women from San Diego. The ladies first. Not because they were the weaker sex—they were not—but simply because they had more sense. Men on an outing feel obliged to stay up drinking to the vile and bilious end, jabbering, mumbling and maundering through the blear, to end up finally on hands and knees, puking on innocent sand, befouling God's sweet earth. The manly tradition.

The three men hunched closer to the shrinking fire. The cold night crawled up their backs. They passed Smith's bottle round and around. Then Doc's bottle. Smith, Hayduke, Sarvis. The captain, the bum and the leech. Three wizards on a dead limb. A crafty intimacy crept upon them.

"You know, gentlemen," the doctor said. "You know what I think we ought to do. . . ."

Hayduke had been complaining about the new power lines he'd seen the day before on the desert. Smith had been moaning about the dam again, that dam which had plugged up Glen Canyon, the heart of his river, the river of his heart.

"You know what we ought to do," the doctor said. "We ought to blow that dam to shitaree." (A bit of Hayduke's foul tongue had loosened his own.)

"How?" said Hayduke.

"That ain't legal," Smith said.

"You prayed for an earthquake, you said."

"Yeah, but there ain't no law agin that."

"You were praying with malicious intent."

"That's true. I pray that way all the time."

"Bent on mischief and the destruction of government property."

"That's right, Doc."

"That's a felony."

"It ain't just a misdemeanor?"

"It's a felony."

"How?" said Hayduke.

"How what?"

"How do we blow up the dam?"

"Which dam?"

"Any dam."

"Now you're talking," Smith said. "But Glen Canyon Dam first. I claim that one first."

"I don't know," the doctor said. "You're the demolitions expert."

"I can take out a bridge for you," Hayduke said, "if you get me enough dynamite. But I don't know about Glen Canyon Dam. We'd need an atom bomb for that one."

"I been thinking about that dam for a long time," Smith said. "And I got a plan. We get three jumbo-size houseboats and some dolphins—"

"Hold it!" Doc said, holding up a big paw. A moment of silence. He looked around, into the darkness beyond the firelight. "Who knows what ears those shadows have."

They looked. The flames of their little campfire cast a hesitant illumination upon the bush, the boat half grounded on the sandy beach, the rocks and pebbles, the pulse of the river. The women, all asleep, could not be seen.

"There ain't nobody here but us bombers," Smith said.

"Who can be sure? The State may have its sensors anywhere."

"Naw," Hayduke said. "They're not bugging the canyons. Not

yet anyhow. But who says we have to start with dams? There's plenty of other work to do."

"Good work," the doctor said. "Good, wholesome, constructive work."

"I hate that dam," Smith said. "That dam flooded the most beautiful canyon in the world."

"We know," Hayduke said. "We feel the same way you do. But let's think about easier things first. I'd like to knock down some of them power lines they're stringing across the desert. And those new tin bridges up by Hite. And the goddamned road-building they're doing all over the canyon country. We could put in a good year just taking the fucking goddamned bulldozers apart."

"Hear, hear," the doctor said. "And don't forget the billboards. And the strip mines. And the pipelines. And the new railroad from Black Mesa to Page. And the coal-burning power plants. And the copper smelters. And the uranium mines. And the nuclear power plants. And the computer centers. And the land and cattle companies. And the wildlife poisoners. And the people who throw beer cans along the highways."

"I throw beer cans along the fucking highways," Hayduke said. "Why the fuck shouldn't I throw fucking beer cans along the fucking highways?"

"Now, now. Don't be so defensive."

"Hell," Smith said, "I do it too. Any road I wasn't consulted about that I don't like, I litter. It's my religion."

"Right," Hayduke said. "Litter the shit out of them."

"Well now," the doctor said. "I hadn't thought about that. Stockpile the stuff along the highways. Throw it out the window. Well . . . why not?"

"Doc," said Hayduke, "it's liberation."

The night. The stars. The river. Dr. Sarvis told his comrades about a great Englishman named Ned. Ned Ludd. They called him a lunatic but he saw the enemy clearly. Saw what was coming and acted directly. And about the wooden shoes, *les sabots*. The spanner in the works. Monkey business. The rebellion of the meek. Little old ladies in oaken clogs.

"Do we know what we're doing and why?"

"No."

"Do we care?"

"We'll work it out as we go along. Let our practice form our doctrine, thus assuring precise theoretical coherence."

The river in its measureless sublimity rolled softly by, whispering of time. Which heals, they say, all. But does it? The stars looked kindly down. A lie. A wind in the willows suggested sleep. And nightmares. Smith pushed more drift pine into the fire, and a scorpion, dormant in a crack deep in the wood, was horribly awakened, too late. No one noticed the mute agony. Deep in the solemn canyon, under the fiery stars, peace reigned generally.

"We need a guide," the doctor said.

"I know the country," Smith said.

"We need a professional killer."

"That's me," Hayduke said. "Murder's my specialty."

"Every man has his weakness." Pause. "Mine," added Doc, "is Baskin-Robbins girls."

"Hold on here," Smith said, "I ain't going along with that kind of talk."

"Not people, Captain," the doctor said. "We're talking about bulldozers. Power shovels. Draglines. Earthmovers."

"Machines," said Hayduke.

A pause in the planning, again.

"Are you certain this canyon is not bugged?" the doctor asked. "I have the feeling that others are listening in to every word we say."

"I know that feeling," Hayduke said, "but that's not what I'm thinking about right now. I'm thinking—"

"What are you thinking about?"

"I'm thinking: Why the fuck should we trust *each other*? I never even met you two guys before today."

Silence. The three men stared into the fire. The oversize surgeon. The elongated riverman. The brute from the Green Berets. A sigh.

They looked at each other. And one thought: What the hell. And one thought: They look honest to me. And one thought: Men are not the enemy. Nor women either. Nor little children.

Not in sequence but in unison, as one, they smiled. At each other. The bottle made its penultimate round.

"What the hell," Smith said, "we're only talkin'."

6

The Raid at Comb Wash

Their preparations were thorough.

First, at Captain Smith's suggestion, they cached supplies at various points all over their projected field of operations: the canyon country, southeast Utah and northern Arizona. The stores consisted of (1) food: tinned goods, dried meats, fruits, beans, powdered milk, sealed drinking water; (2) field equipment: medical kits, tarps and ponchos, fire starters, topographical maps, moleskin and Rip-Stop, sleeping bags, canteens, hunting and fishing equipment, cooking gear, rope, tape, nylon cord; and (3) the basic ingredients: monkey wrenches, wrecking bars, heavy-duty wirecutters, bolt cutters, trenching tools, siphon hoses, sugars and syrups, oil and petrol, steel wedges, blasting caps, detonating cord, safety fuse, cap crimpers, fuse lighters and adequate quantities of Du Pont Straight and Du Pont Red Cross Extra. Most of the work was carried out by Smith and Hayduke. Sometimes they were assisted by the doctor and Ms. Abbzug, flying up from Albuquerque. Hayduke objected, for a while, to the presence of the girl.

"No fucking girls," he hollered. "This is man's work."

"Don't talk like a pig," said Bonnie.

"Here now, here now," the doctor said. "Peace."

"I thought we were gonna keep the cell down to three men," Hayduke insisted. "No girls."

"I'm no girl," Bonnie said. "I'm a grown-up woman. I'm twenty-eight and a half years old."

Seldom Seen Smith stood somewhat aside, smiling, rubbing the blond furze on his long jaw.

"We agreed on only three people," Hayduke said.

"I know," the doctor said, "and I'm sorry. But I want Bonnie with us. Whither I goest Bonnie goeth. Or vice versa. I don't function very well without her."

"What kind of a man are you?"

"Dependent."

Hayduke turned to Smith. "What do you say?"

"Well," he said, "you know, I kinda like this little girl. I think it's kinda nice to have her around. I say let's keep her with us."

"Then she has to take the blood oath."

"I'm not a child," said Bonnie, "and I refuse to take any blood oaths or play any little-boy games. You'll just have to trust me. If you don't I'll turn you all in to the Bureau of Land Management."

"She's got us by the balls," Smith said.

"And no vulgarity either," she said.

"Testicles," he said.

"Grab 'em by the testicles, and their hearts and minds will follow," the doctor said.

"I don't like it," Hayduke said.

"Tough," Bonnie said. "You're outvoted three to one."

"I don't like it."

"Peace," the doctor said. "I assure you she'll be very useful."

The doctor had the last word. After all, it was he who would be financing the campaign. He was the angel. Avenging angel. Hayduke knew it. And the expense was great. Ninety dollars for a decent sleeping bag. Forty dollars for a good pair of boots. Even the price of pinto beans had gone up to 89 cents a pound. By far the biggest expense, however, was not supplies but simply transportation over the immense, rugged and intricate expanses of the Southwest, with gasoline selling at 49 to 55 cents per gallon and a new truck tire (six-ply heavy duty) at least $55. Plus the air fare for the doctor and his Bonnie—$42.45 each, one way, Albuquerque to Page.

Many of these expenditures could be itemized as business expenses, tax deductible, by Smith (Back of Beyond Expeditions), but even so the initial outlay was heavy. The good doctor provided the cash, which Smith seldom had available, and wrote most of the checks. Explosives, of course, were tax write-offs; Doc would list them on his IRS return as ranch improvement costs—for the little 225-acre tax shelter he owned out in the Manzano Mountains east of Albuquerque—and as assessment work on a cluster of mining claims he also held, in the same area.

"Gloves!" Hayduke demanded. "Gloves! No fucking monkey business without gloves!"

So Doc bought everyone in the crew three pair each of top-quality buckskin gloves.

"Sno-Seal!" (For boots.)

He bought Sno-Seal.

"Sidearms!"

"No."

"Guns!"

"No."

"Peanut butter!" said Bonnie.

"Guns *and* peanut butter!" Hayduke roared.

"Peanut butter, yes. Guns, no."

"We gotta defend our fucking selves."

"No guns." Doc could be stubborn.

"Them fuckers'll be shooting at us!"

"No violence."

"We gotta shoot back."

"No bloodshed." The doctor stood fast.

Again Hayduke was outvoted, again by a vote of three to one. So for the time being he kept his own weapons concealed, as best he could, and carried only the revolver hidden in the inner pocket of his pack.

Doc bought six cases of Deaf Smith organic peanut butter, an unblanched, unhydrogenated product manufactured from sun-dried peanuts grown on composted soil without benefit of herbicides, pesticides or county agents. Seldom Seen Smith (no relation) and Hayduke distributed the peanut butter strategically about the Colorado Plateau, a jar here, a jar there, all the way from Onion Creek to Pakoon Spring, from Pucker Pass to Tin Cup Mesa, from Tavaputs, Utah, to Moenkopi, Arizona. Rich brown peanut butter.

Once, early in the campaign, filling their fuel tanks at a gas station, Doc was about to pay with his credit card. Hayduke pulled him aside. No credit cards, he said.

No credit cards?

No fucking credit cards; you want to leave a fucking documented trail one mile wide with your fucking signature on it everywhere we go?

I see, said Doc. Of course. Pay cash, let the credit go. Nor heed the rumble of a distant drum.

Nor did they actually steal, buy or use explosives, at first. Hayduke urged their use immediately, energetically and massively, but the other three opposed him. The doctor was afraid of dynamite; it suggested anarchy, and anarchy is not the answer. Abbzug pointed out that any type of fireworks was illegal in all the Southwestern states; she had also heard that blasting caps could cause cervical cancer. The doctor reminded Hayduke that the use of explosives for illegal (however constructive) purposes was a felony, as well as being a Federal offense where bridges and highways were concerned, whereas simply pouring a little Karo syrup into the fuel tank and sand or emery powder into the oil intake of a dump truck was merely a harmless misdemeanor, hardly more than a Hallowe'en prank.

It became a question of subtle, sophisticated harassment techniques versus blatant and outrageous industrial sabotage. Hayduke favored the blatant, the outrageous. The others the other. Outvoted as usual, Hayduke fumed but consoled himself with the reflection that things would get thicker as operations proceeded. For every action a bigger reaction. From one damn thing to another worse. After all, he was a veteran of Vietnam. He knew how the system worked. Time, lapsing and collapsing from day to day, advanced on his side.

Each cache of provisions was made with scrupulous care. All edible, potable or otherwise perishable or destructible items were placed in metal footlockers. Tools were sharpened, oiled, sheathed or cased and wrapped in canvas. Everything was buried, if possible, or well covered with rocks and brush. The sites were camouflaged and tracks swept away with broom or bough. No cache was considered satisfactory until it passed inspection by both Hayduke and Smith, senior military advisers to the—the Foxpack? Sixpack? Wilderness Avengers? Wooden Shoe Mob? They couldn't even agree on a name for themselves. Peanut Butter Cabal? Raiders of the Purple Sage? Young Americans for Freedom? Woman's Christian Temperance Union? Couldn't agree. Who's in charge here? We're all in charge here, Bonnie says. Nobody's in charge here, says Doc. Lousy way to run a fucking revolution, Hayduke complained; he suffered from a faint authoritarian streak, ex-Sgt. Geo. Wash. Hayduke.

"Peace, please, *pax vobiscum,*" Doc said. But his own excitement was growing too. Look what happened, for example, at the fifty-million-dollar new University Medical Center, in one of the new Bauhaus million-dollar classroom buildings. The building smelled of raw cement. The windows, long and narrow and few, looked like gunports in a pillbox. The air-conditioning system was of the very latest design. When Dr. Sarvis entered the classroom where he was to give a lecture one day—"Industrial Pollution & Respiratory Illness"—he found the room overheated, the air stale. The students seemed sleepier than usual, but unconcerned.

Need some air in here, the doctor grumbled. A student shrugged. The rest were nodding—not in agreement but in slumber. Doc went to the nearest window and tried to open it. But how? There didn't seem to be any sort of hinge, sash, latch, catch, crank or handle. How do you open this window? he asked the nearest student. Don't know, sir, the student said. Another said, You can't open it; this's an air-conditioned building. Suppose we need air? the doctor asked, calm and reasonable. You're not supposed to open the windows in an air-conditioned building, the student said. It screws up the system. I see, Doc said; but we need fresh air. (Outside, below, in the sunshine, little birds were singing in the forsythia, fornicating in the hydrangea.) What do we do? he asked. I guess you could complain to the Administration, another student said, a remark always good for a laugh. I see, said Dr. Sarvis. Still calm and reasonable, he walked to the steel-framed desk by the blackboard, picked up the steel-legged chair waiting behind the desk and, holding it by seat and back, punched out the window glass. All of it. Thoroughly. The students watched in quiet approval and when he was finished gave him a sitting ovation. Doc brushed his hands. We'll skip rollcall today, he said.

One fine day in early June, bearing west from Blanding, Utah, on their way to cache more goods, the gang paused at the summit of Comb Ridge for a look at the world below. They were riding four abreast in the wide cab of Seldom's 4 × 4 pickup truck. It was lunchtime. He pulled off the dusty road—Utah State Road 95—and turned south on a jeep track that followed close to the rim. Comb Ridge is a great monocline, rising gradually on the east side, dropping off at an angle close to 90 degrees on the west side. The drop-off from the rim is about five hundred feet straight down, with another three hundred feet or more of steeply sloping talus below the cliff. Like many other canyons, mesas and monoclines in southeast Utah, Comb Ridge forms a serious barrier to east-west land travel. Or it used to. God meant it to.

Smith pulled the truck up onto a shelf of slickrock within twenty feet of the rim and stopped. Everybody got out, gratefully, and walked close to the edge. The sun stood high in the clouds; the air was still and warm. Flowers grew from cracks in the rock—globe mallow, crownbeard, gilia, rock cress—and flowering shrubs—cliff-rose, Apache plume, chamisa, others. Doc was delighted.

"Look," he said, "*Arabis pulchra. Fallugia paradoxa. Cowania mexicana*, by God."

"What's this?" Bonnie said, pointing to little purplish things in the shade of a pinyon pine.

"Pedicularis centranthera."

"Yeah, okay, but what is it?"

"What is it?" Doc paused. "What it is, no man knows, but men call it . . . wood betony."

"Don't be a wise-ass."

"Also known as lousewort. A child came to me saying, 'What is the lousewort?' And I said, 'Perhaps it is the handkerchief of the Lord.' "

"Nobody loves a wise-ass."

"I know," he admitted.

Smith and Hayduke stood on the brink of five hundred feet of naked gravity. That yawning abyss which calls men to sleep. But they were looking not down at death but southward at life, or at least at a turmoil of dust and activity. Whine of motors, snort and growl of distant diesels.

"The new road," Smith explained.

"Uh huh." Hayduke raised his field glasses and studied the scene, some three miles off. "Big operation," he mumbled. "Euclids, D-Nines, haulers, scrapers, loaders, backhoes, drills, tankers. What a beautiful fucking layout."

Doc and Bonnie came up, flowers in their hair. Far off south in the dust, sunlight flashed on glass, on bright steel.

"What's going on down there?" Doc said.

"That's the new road they're working on," Smith said.

"What's wrong with the old road?"

"The old road is too old," Smith explained. "It crawls up and down hills and goes in and out of draws and works around the head of canyons and it ain't paved and it generally takes too long to get anywhere. This new road will save folks ten minutes from Blanding to Natural Bridges."

"It's a county road?" Doc asked.

"It's built for the benefit of certain companies that operate in this county, but it's not a county road, it's a state road. It's to help out the poor fellas that own the uranium mines and the truck fleets and the marinas on Lake Powell, that's what it's for. They gotta eat too."

"I see," said Doc. "Let me have a look, George."

Hayduke passed the field glasses to the doctor, who took a long look, puffing on his Marsh-Wheeling.

"Busy busy busy," he said. He returned the glasses to Hayduke. "Men, we have work to do tonight."

"Me too," Bonnie said.

"You too."

One thin scream came floating down, like a feather, from the silver-clouded sky. Hawk. Redtail, solitaire, one hawk passing far above the red reef, above the waves of Triassic sandstone, with a live snake clutched in its talons. The snake wriggled, casually, as it was borne away to a different world. Lunchtime.

After a little something themselves the gang got back in Smith's truck and drove two miles closer, over the rock and through the brush, in low range and four-wheel drive, to a high point overlooking the project more directly. Smith parked the truck in the shade of the largest pinyon pine available, which was not big enough to effectively conceal it.

Netting, Hayduke thought; we need camouflage netting. He made a note in his notebook.

Now the three men and the girl worked their way to the rim again, to the edge of the big drop-off. Out of habit Hayduke led the way, crawling forward on hands and knees, then on his belly the last few yards to their observation point. Were such precautions necessary? Probably not, so early in their game; the Enemy, after all, was not aware yet that Hayduke & Co. existed. The Enemy, in fact, still fondly imagined that he enjoyed the favor of the American public, with no exceptions.

Incorrect. They lay on their stomachs on the warm sandstone, under the soft and pearly sky, and peered down seven hundred vertical feet and half a mile by line of sight to where the iron dinosaurs romped and roared in their pit of sand. There was love in neither head nor heart of Abbzug, Hayduke, Smith and Sarvis. No sympathy. But considerable involuntary admiration for all that power, all that controlled and directed superhuman force.

Their vantage point gave them a view of the heart, not the whole, of the project. The surveying crews, far ahead of the big machines, had finished weeks earlier, but evidence of their work remained: the Day-Glo ribbon, shocking pink, that waved from the boughs of juniper trees, the beribboned stakes planted in the earth marking center line and shoulder of the coming road, the steel pins hammered into the ground as reference points.

What Hayduke and friends could and did see were several of the many phases of a road-building project that follow the survey. To the far west, on the rise beyond Comb Wash, they saw bulldozers clearing the right-of-way. In forested areas the clearing job would require a crew of loggers with chain saws, but here in southeast Utah, on the plateau, the little pinyon pines and junipers offered no resistance to the bulldozers. The crawler-tractors pushed them all over with nonchalant ease and shoved them aside, smashed and bleeding, into heaps of brush, where they would be left to die and decompose. No one knows precisely how sentient is a pinyon pine, for example, or to what degree such woody organisms can feel pain or fear, and in any case the road builders had more important things to worry about, but this much is clearly established as scientific fact: a living tree, once uprooted, takes many days to wholly die.

Behind the first wave of bulldozers came a second, blading off the soil and ripping up loose stone down to the bedrock. Since this was a cut-and-fill operation it was necessary to blast away the bedrock down to the grade level specified by the highway engineers. Watching from their comfortable grandstand bleachers, the four onlookers saw drill rigs crawl on self-propelled tracks to the blasting site, followed by tractors towing air compressors. Locked in position and linked to the compressors, the drill steel bit into the rock with screaming teconite bits, star-shaped and carbide-tipped. Powdered stone floated on the air as the engines roared. Resonant vibrations shuddered through the bone structure of the earth. More mute suffering. The drill rigs moved on over the hill to the next site.

The demolition team arrived. Charges were lowered into the bore holes, gently tamped and stemmed, and wired to an electrical circuit. The watchers on the rim heard the chief blaster's warning whistle, saw the crew move off to a safe distance, saw the spout of smoke and heard the thunder as the blaster fired his shot. More bull-dozers, loaders and giant trucks moved in to shovel up and haul away the debris.

Down in the center of the wash below the ridge the scrapers, the earthmovers and the dump trucks with eighty-ton beds unloaded their loads, building up the fill as the machines beyond were deepening the cut. Cut and fill, cut and fill, all afternoon the work went on. The object in mind was a modern high-speed highway for the convenience of the trucking industry, with grades no greater than 8 percent. That was the immediate object. The ideal lay still farther on. The engineer's dream is a model of perfect sphericity, the planet Earth with all irregu-larities removed, highways merely painted on a surface smooth as glass. Of course the engineers still have a long way to go but they are patient tireless little fellows; they keep hustling on, like termites in a territorium. It's steady work, and their only natural enemies, they believe, are mechanical breakdown or "down time" for the equip-ment, and labor troubles, and bad weather, and sometimes faulty preparation by the geologists and surveyors.

The one enemy the contractor would not and did not think of was the band of four idealists stretched out on their stomachs on a rock under the desert sky.

Down below the metal monsters roared, bouncing on rubber through the cut in the ridge, dumping their loads and thundering up the hill for more. The green beasts of Bucyrus, the yellow brutes of Caterpillar, snorting like dragons, puffing black smoke into the yellow dust.

The sun slipped three degrees westward, beyond the clouds, be-yond the silver sky. The watchers on the ridge munched on jerky, sipped from their canteens. The heat began to slacken off. There was talk of supper, but no one had much appetite. There was talk of getting ready for the evening program. The iron machines still rolled in the wash below, but it seemed to be getting close to quitting time.

"The main thing we have to watch for," Hayduke said, "is a night watchman. They just might keep some fucker out here at night. Maybe with a dog. Then we'll have problems."

"There won't be any watchman," Smith said. "Not all night, anyhow."

"What makes you so sure?"

"It's the way they do things around here; we're out in the country. Nobody lives out here. It's fifteen miles from Blanding. This here project is three miles off the old road, which hardly nobody drives at night anyhow. They don't expect any trouble."

"Maybe some of them are camping out here," Hayduke said.

"Naw," Smith said. "They don't do that kind of thing either. These boys work like dogs all day long; they wanta get back to town in the evening. They like their civilized comforts. They ain't campers. These here construction workers don't think nothing of driving fifty miles to work every morning. They're all crazy as bedbugs. I worked in these outfits myself."

Doc and Hayduke, armed with the field glasses, kept watch. Smith and Bonnie crawled down from the ridge, keeping out of sight, until they were below the skyline. Then they walked to the truck, set up the campstove and began preparing a meal for the crew. The doctor and Hayduke, poor cooks, made good dishwashers. All four were qualified eaters, but only Bonnie and Smith cared enough about food to cook it with decency.

Smith was right; the construction workers departed all together long before sundown. Leaving their equipment lined up along the right-of-way, nose to tail, like a herd of iron elephants, or simply *in situ,* where quitting time found them, the operators straggled back in small groups to their transport vehicles. Far above, Doc and Hayduke could hear their voices, the laughter, the rattle of lunch buckets. The carryalls and pickups driven by men at the eastern end of the job came down through the big notch to meet the equipment operators. The men climbed in; the trucks turned and ground uphill through the dust, into the notch again and out of sight. For some time there was the fading sound of motors, a cloud of dust rising above the pinyon and juniper; then that too was gone. A tanker truck appeared, full of diesel fuel, groaning down the grade toward the machines, and proceeded from one to the next, the driver and his helper filling the fuel tanks of each, topping them off. Finished, the tanker turned and followed the others back through the evening toward the distant glow of town, somewhere beyond the eastward bulge of the plateau.

Now the stillness was complete. The watchers on the rim, eating their suppers from tin plates, heard the croon of a mourning dove far down the wash. They heard the hoot of an owl, the cries of little birds retiring to sleep in the dusty cottonwoods. The great golden light of the setting sun streamed across the sky, glowing upon the clouds and the mountains. Almost all the country within their view was roadless, uninhabited, a wilderness. They meant to keep it that way. They sure meant to try. *Keep it like it was.*

The sun went down.

Tactics, materials, tools, gear.

Hayduke was reading off his checklist. "Gloves! Everybody got his gloves? Put 'em on now. Anybody goes fucking around down there without gloves I'll chop his hand off."

"You haven't washed the dishes yet," Bonnie said.

"Hard hat! Everybody got his hard hat?" He looked around at the crew. "You—put that thing on your head."

"It doesn't fit," she said.

"Make it fit. Somebody show her how to adjust the headband. Jesus Christ." Looking back at his list. "Bolt cutters!" Hayduke brandished his own, a 24-inch pair of cross-levered steel jaws for cutting bolts, rods, wire, most anything up to half an inch in diameter. The rest of the party were equipped with fencing pliers, good enough for most purposes.

"Now, you lookouts," he went on, addressing Bonnie and Doc. "Do you know your signals?"

"One short and a long for warning, take cover," Doc said, holding up his metal whistle. "One short and two longs for all clear,

resume operations. Three longs for distress, come help. Four longs
for . . . what are four longs for?"

"Four longs mean work completed, am returning to camp,"
Bonnie said. "And one long means acknowledgment, message re-
ceived."

"Don't much like them tin whistles," Smith said. "We need
something more natural. More eco-logical. Owl hoots, maybe. Anybody hears them tin whistles will know there's two-legged animals
slinkin' around. Lemme show you how to hoot like a owl."

Training time. Hands cupped and close, one little opening between thumbs, shape the lips, blow. Blow from the belly, down deep;
the call will float through canyons, across mountainsides, all the way
down in the valley. Hayduke showed Dr. Sarvis; Smith showed Abbzug, personally, holding her hands in the necessary way, blowing into
them, letting her blow into his. She picked it up quickly, the doctor
not so fast. They rehearsed the signals. For a while the twilight seemed
full of great horned owls, talking. Finally they were ready. Hayduke
returned to his checklist.

"Okay, gloves, hats, wire cutters, signals, Now: Karo syrup, four
quarts each. Matches. Flashlights—be careful with those: keep the
light close to your work, don't swing it around, shut it off when
you're moving. Maybe we should work out light signals? Naw, later.
Water. Jerky. Hammer, screwdriver, cold chisel—okay, I got them.
What else?"

"We're all set," Smith said. "Let's get a move on."

They shouldered their packs. Hayduke's pack, with most of the
hardware in it, weighed twice as much as anyone else's. He didn't
care. Seldom Seen Smith led the way through the sundown gloom.
The others followed in single file. Hayduke at the rear. There was no
trail, no path. Smith picked the most economic route among the
scrubby trees, around the bayonet leaves of the yucca and the very
hairy prickly pear, across the little sandy washes below the crest of the
ridge. As much as possible he led them on the rock, leaving no tracks.

They were headed south by the stars, south by the evening
breeze, toward a rising Scorpio sprawled out fourteen galactic worlds

wide across the southern sky. Owls hooted from the pygmy forest. The saboteurs hooted back.

Smith circumvented an anthill, a huge symmetric arcologium of sand surrounded by a circular area denuded of any vestige of vegetation. The dome home of the harvester ants. Smith went around and so did Bonnie but Doc stumbled straight into it, stirring up the formicary. The big red ants swarmed out looking for trouble; one of them bit Doc on the calf. He stopped, turned and dismantled the anthill with a series of vigorous kicks.

"Thus I refute R. Buckminster Fuller," he growled. "Thus do I refute Paolo Soleri, B. F. Skinner and the late Walter Gropius."

"How late was he?" Smith asked.

"Doc hates ants," Bonnie explained. "And they hate him."

"The anthill," said Doc, "is sign, symbol and symptom of what we are about out here, stumbling through the gloaming like so many stumblebums. I mean it is the model in microcosm of what we must find a way to oppose and halt. The anthill, like the Fullerian foam fungus, is the mark of social disease. Anthills abound where overgrazing prevails. The plastic dome follows the plague of runaway industrialism, prefigures technological tyranny and reveals the true quality of our lives, which sinks in inverse ratio to the growth of the Gross National Product. End of mini-lecture by Dr. Sarvis."

"Good," Bonnie said.

"Amen," said Smith.

The evening gave way to night, a dense violet solution of starlight and darkness mixed with energy, each rock and shrub and tree and scarp outlined by an aura of silent radiation. Smith led the conspirators along the contour of the terrain until they came to the brink of something, an edge, a verge, beyond which stood nothing tangible. This was not the rim of the monocline, however, but the edge of the big man-made cut *through* the monocline. Below in the gloom those with sufficient night vision could see the broad new roadway and the dark forms of machines, two hundred feet down.

Smith and friends proceeded along this new drop-off until they reached a point where it was possible to scramble down to the crushed rock and heavy dust of the roadbed. Looking northeast, toward Blanding, they saw this pale raw freeway leading straight across the desert, through the scrub forest and out of sight in the darkness. No lights were visible, only the faint glow of the town fifteen miles away. In the opposite direction the roadbed curved down between the walls of the cut, sinking out of view toward the wash. They walked into the cut.

The first thing they encountered, on the shoulder of the road-bed, were survey stakes. Hayduke pulled them up and tossed them into the brush.

"Always pull up survey stakes," he said. "Anywhere you find them. Always. That's the first goddamned general order in the monkey wrench business. Always pull up survey stakes."

They walked deeper into the cut to where it was possible, looking down and west, to make out though dimly the bottom of Comb Wash, the fill area, the scattered earth-moving equipment. Here they stopped for further consultation.

"We want our first lookout here," Hayduke said.

"Doc or Bonnie?"

"I want to wreck something," Bonnie said. "I don't want to sit here in the dark making owl noises."

"I'll stay here," Doc said.

Once more they rehearsed signals. All in order. Doc made himself comfortable on the operator's seat of a giant compactor machine. He toyed with the controls. "Stiff," he said, "but it's transportation."

"Why don't we start with this fucker right here?" Hayduke said, meaning Doc's machine. "Just for the practice."

Why not? Packs were opened, tools and flashlights brought out. While Doc stood watch above them his three comrades entertained themselves cutting up the wiring, fuel lines, control link rods and hydraulic hoses of the machine, a beautiful new 27-ton tandem-drummed yellow Hyster C-450A, Caterpillar 330 HP diesel engine, sheepsfoot rollers, manufacturer's suggested retail price only $29,500 FOB Saginaw, Michigan. One of the best. A dreamboat.

They worked happily. Hard hats clinked and clanked against the steel. Lines and rods snapped apart with the rich *spang!* and solid *clunk!* of metal severed under tension. Doc lit another stogie. Smith wiped a drop of oil from his eyelid. The sharp smell of hydraulic fluid floated on the air, mixing uneasily with the aroma of Doc's smoke. Running oil pattered on the dust. There was another sound, far away, as of a motor. They paused. Doc stared into the dark. Nothing. The noise faded.

"All's clear," he said. "Carry on, lads."

When everything was cut which they could reach and cut, Hayduke pulled the dipstick from the engine block—to check the oil? not exactly—and poured a handful of fine sand into the crankcase. Too slow. He unscrewed the oil-filler cap, took chisel and hammer and punched a hole through the oil strainer and poured in more sand. Smith removed the fuel-tank cap and emptied four quart bottles of sweet Karo syrup into the fuel tank. Injected into the cylinders, that sugar would form a solid coat of carbon on cylinder walls and piston rings. The engine should seize up like a block of iron, when they got it running. If they could get it running.

What else? Abbzug, Smith and Hayduke stood back a little and stared at the quiet hulk of the machine. All were impressed by what they had done. The murder of a machine. Deicide. All of them, even Hayduke, a little awed by the enormity of their crime. By the sacrilege of it.

"Let's slash the seat," said Bonnie.

"That's vandalism," Doc said. "I'm against vandalism. Slashing seats is petty-bourgeois."

"So okay, okay," Bonnie said. "Let's get on to the next item."

"Then we'll all meet back here?" Doc said.

"It's the only way back up on the ridge," Smith said.

"But if there's any shit," Hayduke said, "don't wait for us. We'll meet at the truck."

"I couldn't find my way back there if my life depended on it," Doc said. "Not in the dark."

Smith scratched his long jaw. "Well, Doc," he said, "if there's any kind of trouble maybe you better just hightail it up on the bank there, above the road, and wait for us. Don't forget the hoot owl. We'll find you that way."

They left him there in the dark, perched on the seat of the maimed and poisoned compactor. The one red eye of his cigar watched them depart. The plan was for Bonnie to stand watch at the far west end of the project, alone, while Hayduke and Smith worked on the equipment down in the wash. She murmured against them.

"You ain't afraid of the dark, are you?" Smith asked.

"Of course I'm afraid of the dark."

"You afraid to be alone?"

"Of course I'm afraid to be alone."

"You mean you don't want to be lookout?"

"I'll be lookout."

"No place for women," Hayduke muttered.

"You shut up," she said. "Am I complaining? I'll be lookout. So shut up before I take your jaw off."

The dark seemed warm, comfortable, secure to Hayduke. He liked it. The Enemy, if he appeared, would come loudly announced with roar of engines, blaze of flares, an Operation Rolling Thunder of shells and bombs, just as in Vietnam. So Hayduke assumed. For the night and the wilderness belong to *us*. This is Indian country. Our country. Or so he assumed.

Downhill, maybe a mile, in one great switchback, the roadway descended through the gap to the built-up fill across the floor of Comb Wash. They soon reached the first group of machines—the earthmovers, the big trucks, the landscape architects.

Bonnie was about to go on by herself. Smith took her arm for a moment. "You stay close, honey," he told her, "only concentrate on looking and listening; let me and George do the hard work. Take the hard hat off so you can hear better. Okay?"

"Well," she agreed, "for the moment." But she wanted a bigger share of the action later. He agreed. Share and share alike. He showed her where to find the steps that led to the open cab of an 85-ton Euclid mountain mover. She sat up there, like a lookout in a crow's nest, while he and Hayduke went to work.

Busywork. Cutting and snipping, snapping and wrenching. They crawled all over a Caterpillar D-9A, world's greatest bulldozer, the idol of all highwaymen. Put so much sand in the crankcase that Hayduke couldn't get the dipstick reinserted all the way. He trimmed it short with the rod-and-bolt cutter. Made it fit. Sand in the oil intake. He climbed into the cab, tried to turn the fuel-tank cap. Wouldn't turn. Taking hammer and chisel he broke it loose, unscrewed it, poured four quarts of good high-energy Karo into the diesel fuel. Replaced the cap. Sat in the driver's seat and played for a minute with the switches and levers.

"You know what would be fun?" he said to Smith, who was down below hacking through a hydraulic hose.

"What's that, George?"

"Get this fucker started, take it up to the top of the ridge and run it over the rim."

"That there'd take us near half the night, George."

"Sure would be fun."

"We can't get it started anyhow."

"Why not?"

"There ain't no rotor arm in the magneto. I looked. They usually take out the rotor arm when they leave these beasts out on the road."

"Yeah?" Hayduke takes notebook and pencil from his shirt pocket, turns on his flashlight, makes notation: *Rotor arms.* "You know something else that would be fun?"

Smith, busy nullifying all physical bond between cylinder heads and fuel injection lines, says, "What?"

"We could knock a pin out of each tread. Then when the thing moved it would run right off its own fucking tracks. That would really piss them."

"George, this here tractor ain't gonna move at all for a spell. It ain't a-goin' *nowheres.*"

"For a spell."

"That's what I said."

"That's the trouble."

Hayduke climbed down from the cab and came close to Smith,

there in the black light of the stars, doing his humble chores, the pinpoint of his flashlight beam fixed on a set screw in an engine block the weight of three Volkswagen buses. The yellow Caterpillar, enormous in the dark, looms over the two men with the indifference of a god, submitting without a twitch of its enameled skin to their malicious ministrations. The down payment on this piece of equipment comes to around $30,000. What were the men worth? In any rational chemico-psycho-physical analysis? In a nation of two hundred and ten million (210,000,000) bodies? Getting cheaper by the day, as mass production lowers the unit cost?

"That's the trouble," he said again. "All this wire cutting is only going to slow them down, not stop them. Godfuckingdammit, Seldom, we're wasting our time."

"What's the matter, George?"

"We're wasting our time."

"What do you mean?"

"I mean we ought to really blast this motherfucker. This one and all the others. I mean set them on fire. Burn them up."

"That there's arson."

"For chrissake, what's the difference? You think what we're doing now is much nicer? You know damn well if old Morrison-Knudsen was out here now with his goons he'd be happy to see us all shot dead."

"They ain't gonna be too happy about this, you're right there. They ain't gonna understand us too good."

"They'll understand us. They'll hate our fucking guts."

"They won't understand why we're doin' this, George. That's what I mean. I mean we're gonna be misunderstood."

"No, we're not gonna be misunderstood. We're gonna be hated."

"Maybe we should explain."

"Maybe we should do it right. None of this petty fucking around."

Smith was silent.

"Let's *destroy* this fucker."

"I don't know," Smith said.

"I mean roast it in its own grease. I just happen to have a little siphon hose here in my pack. Like I just happen to have some matches. I mean we just siphon some of that fuel out of the tank and we just sort of slosh it around over the engine and cab and then we just sort of toss a match at it. Let God do the rest."

"Yeah, I guess He would," Smith agreed. "If God meant this here bulldozer to live He wouldn't of filled its tank with diesel fuel. Now would He of? But George, what about Doc?"

"What about him? Since when is he the boss?"

"He's the one bankrolling this here operation. We need him."

"We need his money."

"Well, all right, put it this way: I like old Doc. And I like that little old lady of his too. And I think all four of us got to stick together. And I think we can't do anything that all four of us ain't agreed to do beforehand. Think about it that way, George."

"Is that the end of the sermon?"

"That's the end of the sermon."

Now Hayduke was silent for a while. They worked. Hayduke thought. After a minute he said, "You know something, Seldom? I guess you're right."

"I thought I was wrong once," Seldom said, "but I found out later I was mistaken."

They finished with the D-9A. The siphon hose and the matches remained inside Hayduke's pack. For the time being. Having done all they could to sand, jam, gum, mutilate and humiliate the first bull-dozer, they went on to the next, the girl with them. Smith put his arm around her.

"Miss Bonnie," he says, "how do you like the night shift?"

"Too peaceful. When's my turn to wreck something?"

"We need you to look out."

"I'm bored."

"Don't you worry about that none, honey. We're gonna have enough excitement pretty soon to last you and me for the rest of our lives. If we live that long. How you think old Doc is doing back there all by his lonesome?"

"He's all right. He lives inside his head most of the time anyway."

Another giant machine looms out of the darkness before them. A hauler; they chop it up. Then the next. Bonnie watches from her post in the cab of a nearby earthmover. Next! The men go on.

"If only we could start up the motors on these sombitches," Hayduke said. "We could drain the oil out, let the motors run and walk away. They'd take care of themselves and we'd be finished a lot faster."

"That'd do it," Smith allowed. "Drain the oil and let the engines run. They'd seize up tighter'n a bull's asshole in fly time. They never would get them buggers prised open."

"We could give each one a try anyhow." And acting on his words, Hayduke climbed to the controls of a big bulldozer. "How do you start this mother?"

"I'll show you if we find one ready to go."

"How about a hot wire? Maybe we could start it that way. Bypass the ignition."

"Not a caterpillar tractor. This ain't no car, George, you know. This is a D-Eight. This here's heavy-duty industrial equipment; this ain't the old Farmall back home."

"Well, I'm ready for driving lessons anytime."

Hayduke climbed down from the operator's seat. They worked on the patient, sifting handfuls of fine Triassic sand into the crankcase, cutting up the wiring, the fuel lines, the hydraulic hoses to fore and aft attachments, dumping Karo into the fuel tanks. Why Karo instead of plain sugar? Smith wanted to know. Pours better, Hayduke explained; mixes easier with the diesel, doesn't jam up in strainers. You sure about that? No.

Hayduke crawled under the bulldozer to find the drain plug in the oil pan. He found it, through an opening in the armored skid plate, but needed a big wrench to crack it loose. They tried the tool-box in the cab. Locked. Hayduke broke the lock with his cold chisel and hammer. Inside they found a few simple and massive instruments: an iron spanner three feet long; a variety of giant end wrenches; a sledgehammer; a wooden-handled monkey wrench; nuts, bolts, friction tape, wire.

Hayduke took the spanner, which looked like the right size, and crawled again underneath the tractor. He struggled for a while with the plug, finally broke it loose and let out the oil. The great machine began to bleed; its lifeblood drained out with pulsing throbs, onto the dust and sand. When it was all gone he replaced the plug. Why? Force of habit—thought he was changing the oil in his jeep.

Hayduke surfaced, smeared with dust, grease, oil, rubbing a bruised knuckle. "Shit," he said, "I don't know."

"What's the matter?"

"Are we doing this job right? That's what I don't know. Now the operator gets on this thing in the morning, tries to start it up, nothing happens. So the first thing he sees is all the wiring cut, all the fuel lines cut. So putting sand in the crankcase, draining the oil, isn't going to do any good till they get the motor to run. But when they fix all the wiring and lines they're gonna be checking other things too. Like the oil level, naturally. Then they find the sand. Then they see somebody's drained the oil. I'm thinking if we really want to do this monkey wrench business right, maybe we should hide our work. I mean keep it simple and sophisticated."

"Well, George, you was the one wanted to set these things on fire about a minute ago."

"Yeah. Now I'm thinking the other way."

"Well, it's too late. We already showed our hand here. We might as well go on like we started."

"Now think about it a minute, Seldom. They'll all get here about the same time tomorrow morning. Everybody starts up the engine on his piece of equipment, or tries to. Some'll discover right away that we cut up the wiring. I mean on the machines we already cut. But look, on the others, if we let the wiring alone, let the fuel lines alone, so they can start the engines, then the sand and the Karo will really do some good. I mean they'll have a chance to do the work we want them to do: ruin the engines. What do you think about that?"

They leaned side by side against the steel track of the Cat, gazing at each other through the soft starlight.

"I kind of wish we had figured all this out before," Smith said. "We ain't got all night."

"Why don't we have all night?"

"Because I reckon we ought to be fifty miles away from here come morning. That's why."

"Not me," Hayduke said. "I'm going to hang around and watch what happens. I want that personal fucking satisfaction."

A hoot owl hooted from the earthmover up ahead. "What's going on back there?" Bonnie called. "You think this is a picnic or something?"

"Okay," Smith said, "let's keep it kinda simple. Let's put these here cutters away for a while and just work on the oil and fuel systems. God knows we got plenty of sand here. About ten thousand square miles of it." Agreed.

They went on, quickly and methodically now, from machine to machine, pouring sand into each crankcase and down every opening which led to moving parts. When they had used up all their Karo syrup, they dumped sand into the fuel tanks, as an extra measure.

All the way, into the night, Hayduke, Smith, they worked their way to the end of the line. Now one, now the other, would relieve Bonnie at the lookout post so that she too could participate fully in field operations. Teamwork, that's what made America great: teamwork and initiative, that's what made America what it is today. They worked over the Cats, they operated on the earthmovers, they gave the treatment to the Schramm air compressors the Hyster compactors the Massey crawler-loaders the Joy Ram track drills the Dart D-600 wheel loaders not overlooking one lone John Deere 690-A excavator backhoe, and that was about all for the night; that was about enough; old Morrison-Knudsen had plenty of equipment all right but somebody was due for headaches in the morning when the sun came up and engines were fired up and all those little particles of sand, corrosive as powdered emery, began to wreak earth's vengeance on the cylinder walls of the despoilers of the desert.

When they reached the terminus of the cut-and-fill site, high on the folded earth across the wash from Comb Ridge, and had thoroughly sand-packed the last piece of road-building equipment, they sat down on a juniper log to rest. Seldom Seen, reckoning by the starts, estimated the time at 2 A.M. Hayduke guessed it was only 11:30. He wanted to go on, following the surveyors, and remove all the stakes, pins and flagging that he knew was waiting out there, in the dark, in the semi-virgin wilds beyond. But Abbzug had a better idea; instead of destroying the survey crew's signs, she suggested, why not relocate them all in such a manner as to lead the right-of-way in a grand loop back to the starting point? Or lead it to the brink of, say, Muley Point, where the contractors would confront a twelve-hundred-foot vertical drop-off down to the goosenecks of the San Juan River.

"Don't give them any ideas," Hayduke said. "They'd just want to build another goddamned bridge."

"Them survey markings go on west for twenty miles," Smith said. He was against both plans.

"So what do we do?" says Bonnie.

"I'd like to crawl into the sack," Smith said. "Get some sleep."

"I like that idea myself."

"But the night is young," Hayduke said.

"George," says Smith, "we can't do everything in one night. We got to get Doc and get back to the truck and haul ass. We don't want to be around here in the morning."

"They can't prove a thing."

"That's what Pretty-Boy Floyd said. That's what Baby-Face Nelson said and John Dillinger and Butch Cassidy and that other fella, what's his name—?"

"Jesus," Hayduke growls.

"Yeah, Jesus Christ. That's what they all said and look what happened to them. Nailed."

"This is our first big night," Hayduke said. "We ought to do as much work as we can. We're not likely to get more easy operations like this. Next time they'll have locks on everything. Maybe booby traps. And watchmen with guns, shortwave radios, dogs."

Poor Hayduke: won all his arguments but lost his immortal soul. He had to yield.

They marched back the way they'd come, past the quiet, spayed, medicated machinery. Those doomed dinosaurs of iron, waiting patiently through the remainder of the night for buggering morning's rosy-fingered denouement. The agony of cylinder rings, jammed by a swollen piston, may be like other modes of sodomy a crime against nature in the eyes of *deus ex machina;* who can say?

A hoot owl called from what seemed far away, east in the pitch-black shadows of the dynamite notch. One short and a long, then a pause, one short and a long repeated. Warning cry.

"Doc's on the job," Smith said. "That there's Doc a-talkin' to us."

The men and the girl stood still in the dark, listening hard, trying to see. The warning call was repeated, twice more. The lonesome hoot owl, speaking.

Listening. Nervous crickets chirred in the dry grass under the cottonwoods. A few doves stirred in the boughs.

They heard, faint but growing, the mutter of a motor. Then they saw, beyond the notch, the swing of headlight beams. A vehicle appeared, two blazing eyes, grinding down the grade in low gear.

"Okay," says Hayduke, "off the roadway. Watch out for a spotlight. And if there's any shit we scatter."

Understood. Caught in the middle of the big fill, there was nowhere to go but over the side. They slid down the loose rock to the jumble of boulders at the bottom. There, nursing abrasions, they took cover.

The truck came down the roadway, moved slowly by, went as far as it could and stopped among the machines huddled at the far end of the fill. There it paused for five minutes, engine still, lights turned off. The man inside the truck, sitting with windows open, sipped coffee from a thermos jug and listened to the night. He switched on his left-hand spotlight and played the beam over the roadbed and the machinery. So far as he could see, all was well. He started the engine, turned back the way he had come, passed the listeners fifty feet below, drove on up the grade through the notch and disappeared.

Hayduke slipped his revolver back into his rucksack, blew his nose through his fingers and scrambled up the talus to the top of the roadway. Smith and Abbzug emerged from the dark.

"Next time dogs," says Hayduke. "Then gunners in helicopters. Then the napalm. Then the B-52s."

They walked through the dark, up the long grade into the eastern cut. Listening for the bearded goggled great bald owl to sound.

"I don't think it's quite like that," Smith was saying. "They're people too, like us. We got to remember that, George. If we forget we'll get just like them and then where are we?"

"They're not like us," Hayduke said. "They're different. They come from the moon. They'll spend a million dollars to burn one gook to death."

"Well, I got a brother-in-law in the U.S. Air Force. And he's a sergeant. I took a general's family down the river once. Them folks are more or less human, George, just like us."

"Did you meet the general?"

"No, but his wife, she was sweet as country pie."

Hayduke silent, smiling grimly in the dark. The heavy pack on his back, overloaded with water and weapons and hardware, felt good, solid, real, meant business. He felt potent as a pistol, dangerous as dynamite, tough and mean and hard and full of love for his fellowman. And for his fellow woman, too, e.g., Abbzug there, goddamn her, in her goddamned tight jeans and that shaggy baggy sweater which failed nevertheless to quite fully conceal the rhythmic swing, back and forth, of her unconstrained fucking mammaries. Christ, he thought, I need work. Work!

They found Doc sitting on a rock at the edge of the cutbank, smoking the apparently inextinguishable and interminable stogie. "Well?" he says.

"Well now," Smith says, "I'd say I reckon we done our best."

"The war has begun," says Hayduke.

The stars looked down. Preliminary premonitions of the old moon already modifying the eastern reaches. There was no wind, no sound but the vast transpiration, thinned to a whisper by distance, of the mountain forest, of sagebrush and juniper and pinyon pine spread out over a hundred miles of semi-arid plateau. The world hesitated, waiting for something. At the rising of the moon.

7

Hayduke's Night March

Hayduke awoke before sunrise, feeling the familiar pang of aloneness. The others were gone. He crawled out of the goosedown sack and stumbled into the brush, checking the color of his urine as it streamed out, smoking warm, upon the cold red sand. Hayduke the medic didn't quite like that shade of yellow. Jesus fucking Christ, he thought, maybe I am crystallizing a bit of a urethral calculus up there in the old kidney. How many six-packs from here to the hospital?

He shambled about for a while, stiff and sore from last night, blear-eyed and groggy, rubbing his hairy belly. A roll of fat had recently appeared there, magically. Sloth and bloat, bloat and sloth, they'll ruin a man quicker than women. Women? Damn her. He could not quite force the image from his mind's eye. He worked hard at not thinking about her. Failed. Unsummoned, unwanted, unwelcome, the joyprong rose as always, perpendicular to the imagined field of reference, a mind of its own but no conscience. He . . . ignored it.

Pause.

No sound yet from the wash below the rim. Hayduke gathered a double handful of dead sticks, built a little squaw fire, filled the pot with water and set it on the flames. The sun-cured juniper burned with clear smokeless intensity, hot and bright.

He was camped in a sandy basin below the crest of the ridge, surrounded by juniper and pinyon pine, out of sight of all but the birds. Nearby were tire tracks in the sand, where Seldom Seen Smith had turned his truck around last night, as the old moon came up.

Waiting for his water to boil, Hayduke tore a bough from the nearest juniper and swept away the tire tracks to where they disappeared onto the sandstone. Returning, he distributed pine needles over the disturbed sand. Hard to hide anything in this goddamned desert. The desert speaks with many tongues, some forked.

The others had given him an argument last night about this separation. Hayduke had insisted. He wanted to see the results of the work, if any worth seeing. And he meant to walk the rest of the right-of-way, all the way to the next road junction, and see what he could do to undo the surveyors' work. There comes a time in a man's life when he has to pull up stakes. Has to light out. Has to stop straddling, and start cutting, fence.

He fixed and consumed his humble breakfast: tea with powdered milk; Hayduke's Munchies, a private Granola mix; beef jerky; an orange. Sufficient. Squatting close to the fire, he sipped his tea. Chemicals: his mind cleared.

In the big backpack under the head of his sleeping bag he carried enough dried food for ten days. Plus a gallon of water; he'd find more on the way. Would have to. And topo maps, snakebite kit, halazone tablets, knife, rain poncho, spare socks, signal mirror, fire starter, flashlight, parka, binoculars, so forth, and the revolver and fifty rounds of ammo. Life was returning.

Hayduke finished his morning tea and repaired to the shelter of a juniper. He dug a hole, squatted again and shat. He checked his stool: structurally perfect. This was going to be a good day. He wiped himself with the rough green scales of a juniper twig, Navajo style, filled the hole with sand and camouflaged it with twigs. Returning to the fire, which had also been built in a hole in the sand, he covered and concealed it as he had the other.

He cleaned his dishes—the cup and little blackened pot—and packed them, along with all his other gear except field glasses and one canteen, into his backpack. He was now prepared for quick departure. He carried the pack, glasses and canteen to the slickrock close to the rim and set them on the ground, concealed by a pinyon pine. Taking the juniper-bough broom which he had used earlier, he obliterated his tracks and all other signs of the camp as he walked backward to the sandstone which extended for many miles along the crest of Comb Ridge.

All chores completed, he took glasses and canteen and crawled to his lookout point on the rim. There in the shade of a flowering cliff rose he lay down on his belly and waited. The cliff rose smelled like orange blossoms. The stone was already warm.

Going to be a hot day. The sun turned in a cloudless sky. The air was still except for a steady flow of warm air rising over the rim where Hayduke waited. He judged the time at seven by the sun.

Presently the pickups appeared, lurching down the roadway to the work site, stopping, discharging passengers, returning. Watching through his field glasses, Hayduke saw the workmen spread out, swinging their lunch buckets, hard hats shining in the morning sunlight, and clamber aboard their vehicles. There was further movement, a blast of diesel smoke here and yonder. Some machines started; others did not, or would not, or never would. Hayduke watched with satisfaction. He knew what the operators didn't: they were all in trouble.

You don't lift the hood of a Caterpillar tractor. There is no hood. You walk forward over the steel cleats of the track and hunker down for a look at the power plant. What you see, if your name is Wilbur S. Schnitz this bright morning at Comb Wash, Utah, is a fuel line leading into empty air, a cluster of ignition leads snipped clean in two, cylinder injection heads hammered off, linkage rods cut, air and oil filters gone, hoses severed and dripping fluid. What you do not see is the sand in the crankcsae, the syrup in the fuel tank.

Or say your name is J. Robert ("Jaybob") Hartung and you're on your back looking up into the underparts of the engine of your GMC Terex 40-ton hauler (which Abbzug had got to), what you see dangling in your face and dripping in your eye is a festoon of muti-lated hydraulic hoses and seeping fuel lines.

All up and down the line, from east to west of the project site, the story was the same. All systems mangled, half the equipment down already and the rest doomed. Gnawing on his breakfast jerky, wrig-gling his toes with pleasure, Hayduke watched through field glasses the disarray below.

The sun rose higher, invading his shade. He was getting bored anyhow. He decided to put some distance between himself and the potential lynch mob down in Comb Wash. For all he knew or could see there might already be a squad of tractor lovers and heavy-equipment freaks trudging up the slope on the east, following the tracks which he and his friends might have left—could not have helped but leave—the night before.

He crawled backward from the verge, not rising to his feet until he was safely below the skyline. Among the trees, he took a deep drink from his canteen—no use nursing the water when the body needs it now—put it into a side pocket of his pack, shouldered the pack and marched off to the north, away from the highway project, toward the old road. The plan was to slip across Comb Wash and down the other side, on the west, to intersect the highway right-of-way. Five miles? Ten miles? He didn't know.

Hayduke took pains, as he walked, to stay on the sandstone. Making no pictures, leaving no tracks. Where it was necessary to cross intervals of sand or dirt he turned and walked backward, for confu-sion's sake, reversing his trail.

Most of the way he was able to walk on bare rock, on the smooth, slightly rolling surface of a stratum of sedimentary sandstone, Wingate formation. Good solid well-knit stone, deposited, cemented and petri-fied some twenty-five million years ago, according to the fantasies of the geomorphologists.

He was not aware of being followed. Once, however, when he heard an airplane droning toward him, he stepped quickly beneath the nearest tree and squatted there, *not looking up*, until the airplane passed beyond and out of sight and sound. Then he went on.

Hot motherfucking day, thinks Hayduke, wiping the sweat from his nose, wringing the sweat from his thick eyebrows, feeling the sweat trickle from armpits down over ribs. But it felt good to be marching again; the hot dry clean air smelled good to him; he liked the picture of far-off mesas shimmering under heat waves, the glare of sunlight on red stone, the murmur of stillness in his ears.

He marched north over the boulevard of sandstone, among the junipers and pinyon pines oozing their chewy gum, in reverse across the sand flats and—almost!—into a nest of needle-tipped yucca blades: Spanish bayonet. Maneuvering around that hazard, trying to get more authentic-looking weight on the heel, he back-walked to the comfort of the slickrock and, facing forward again beneath the ambiguous shelter of the sky, advanced.

For some time. Then stopped in the shade, removed the Stone—his oversize pack—and drank more water. Only two quarts left.

The sun hung noon high. When he came within sight of the old road, the original dirt road from Blanding to Hite, he picked out a juniper shading a comfortable slab of stone and laid himself down, pillowing his head on the pack frame, and fell asleep.

He slept for three hours, not without dreams, through the heat of the afternoon.

He might have slept longer, for he was certainly very tired, but thirst, a dry throat and parched tongue, kept him uncomfortable, and when a truck went by on the road, groaning in low gear down the long steep grade to the wash, he woke up.

The first thing he did was drink a half quart of water. He ate some jerky, stayed in the shade and waited for dark. When it came, he hoisted the great pack to his back and started down the road, through an old "dugway" in the ridge. Unless he walked clear around the head of Comb Wash, a detour of thirty miles, there was no other way to descend from the ridge into the wash and reach the other side. To rappel down the cliff he would have needed a rope a thousand feet long.

Walking down the road offered few places to hide, in case of traffic, but nobody appeared. The road was as empty as it must have been half a century before. When he came to the wash he filled his canteens in the lukewarm stream, popped a purifying tablet in each and carried on.

He reached the summit of the plateau beyond Comb Wash, left the old road and headed south, guiding himself by the stars. The going was rough, rocky, over a highly irregular surface cut up by draws, gullies and ravines, some of them tending west, others east back to Comb Wash. Hayduke tried to follow the divide between the two drainage systems—not easy in the dark, in a piece of back country where he had never set foot before.

He guessed he had already walked ten miles that day, most of it up and down, all of it with a sixty-pound pack on his back. He was tired again. Worried that he might cross the highway right-of-way in the dark, where it consisted of nothing but a survey route, without seeing it, he decided to stop and wait for the dawn. He found a level spot open to the east, kicked a few stones away, unrolled his sleeping bag and slept the sleep of the just—the just plain tired.

The cool twilight of dawn. Jaybirds crying in the pinyon pines. A band of pearl and ivory spread across the east. . . .

Hayduke awoke.

A quick breakfast. Repacking. Off again. He walked down the sandstone ledges, around the heads of a dozen arid watercourses, to the highway right-of-way.

Survey stakes in the ground. Pink flagging like ribbons dangled from the branches of trees. Taller stakes made of lathing, also with ribbons, were set out at one-hundred-yard intervals. Limbs had been lopped off trees to provide the surveyor with a clear line of sight and to make way for the survey crew's jeep. The tracks, coming and going, were plain on the ground.

The view was about the same in both directions. He was too far west to see any part of the construction project. Nor did he hear any sound of machinery in action: only the stillness, the breeze among the junipers, the call of a mourning dove.

Hayduke waited for an hour or so in the shade of a pinyon pine near the right-of-way, making sure that none of the enemy were stalking about in the area. He heard nobody. When the sun flared above the horizon he went to work.

First he concealed his pack. Then he walked east toward the project site, removing as he went every stake, lath and ribbon on the north shoulder of the right-of-way. Returning, he would clean up the south side.

He topped a rise and came within sight of the man-made notch in Comb Ridge, the big fill below. Hayduke found a good vantage point and put the field glasses to his eyes.

As expected, repairs were under way on part of the equipment. All up and down the line he saw busy men crawling over, under, in and out of their master machines, replacing fuel lines, soldering cut rods, splicing wiring, clamping on new hydraulic hoses. Had they also discovered the punched-through oil strainers, the sand on the dipsticks, the syrup in the fuel tanks? No way of telling, from where he lay. But many of the machines were both idle and unattended; they had a hopeless, abandoned look.

Hayduke was tempted for a moment by the notion of walking down to the work site and asking for a job. If you were serious about this wooden-shoe business, he tells himself, you'd get a haircut, shave off the beard, take a shower, put on some clean work clothes and get a job, some kind of a job, any kind of a job, with the construction company itself. Then—bore from within, like the noble cutworm.

These whims faded when he spotted, through the glasses, a pair of armed men in uniform—guns, boots, shoulder patches, badges, the tight shirts with the three sharp creases ironed up the back. He watched them with interest.

We should have left them a clue to fasten their attention on, he thought. Like a "Free Jimmy Hoffa" button. Or "Think Hopi" or "Winos for Peace." He tried to think of something new, something cryptic, a prophylactic conundrum not too clever, not too obvious, but inviting. But couldn't, Hayduke being more destructive than bright. He hung the binoculars on his neck and took a drink from the canteen. Would soon have to start worrying about water again.

He got up and went back along the south side of the right-of-way, paralleling his former route, and pulled up the stakes and threw them off in the brush, as he had done before, and plucked the ribbons from the branches and stuffed them down gopher holes, whistling softly as he worked.

He retrieved his backpack and continued, plodding through the scrub, doing his job as before with this difference: now he zigzagged back and forth across the right-of-way, working both sides of the street, clearing it completely on a one-way trip.

Tired, hot, thirsty. The midges danced their molecular dance in the air, in the scattered shade of the trees, bit Hayduke on the earlobe, tried to crawl into his eyes and inside his shirt collar. He brushed them aside, ignored them, trudged onward. The sun turned higher, beaming down on Hayduke's hard head, on George Hayduke's strong back. "A back," his captain once had said, proudly, "that any pack would fit." He marched on, snatching off ribbon, yanking up stakes and not forgetting to keep both eyeballs skinned for trouble, an ear cocked for danger.

The jeep tracks veered away, northward, over the rock and through the bush. But the stakes and flagging went straight ahead. Hayduke followed the survey, a patient, resolute, sweating man doing his job.

He arrived, abruptly, at the stony rim of another canyon. A modest abyss; the wall of the canyon dropped two hundred feet to the talus of rubble below. The opposite wall of the canyon was four hundred feet away, and there the stakes and staves and Day-Glo flags continued merrily on to the northwest. This canyon, then, was going to be bridged.

It was only a small and little-known canyon, to be sure, with a tiny stream coursing down its bed, meandering in lazy bights over the sand, lolling in pools under the acid-green leafery of the cottonwoods, falling over lip of stone into basin below, barely enough water even in spring to sustain a resident population of spotted toads, red-winged dragonflies, a snake or two, a few canyon wrens, nothing special. A nice canyon but not a great canyon. And yet Hayduke he demurred;

he didn't want a bridge here, ever; he liked this little canyon, which he had never seen before, the name of which he didn't even know, quite well enough as it was. He saw no need for a bridge.

Hayduke knelt and wrote a message in the sand to all highway construction contractors: "Go home."

After some thought he added: "No fucking bridge, please."

To which, after further thought, he signed his secret name: "Rudolf the Red."

After a moment he crossed that out and wrote: "Crazy Horse." Best not identify oneself exactly.

Forewarned. Well, so be it. He'd be back, Hayduke would, with or without the rest of the crew, properly armed next time, i.e., with a *sabot* big enough to lever a bridge from its foundations.

He walked north along the rim toward the head of the canyon, looking for a place to cross. Might save miles of walking if he could find one.

He did. Pinyon pines and junipers on the rim, contoured terraces below, the canyon floor not so far away—150 instead of 200 feet. Hayduke took his rope out of the pack—120 feet of quarter-inch laid nylon—uncoiled it and looped it around the base of a tree. Steadying himself with the left hand, controlling the free ends of the rope with his right, he leaned backward over the edge of the rim and hung there for a moment, enjoying the sensation of gravity neutralized, then swiftly rappeled to the ledge below.

A second rappel lowered him to within scrambling distance of the canyon floor. He lined his pack to the ground with the rope, dropped the rope and climbed down through a chimney to the sandy alluvium at the base of the wall.

He refilled his four canteens at the stream, where it purled through sculptured grooves in the pink bedrock of the canyon. He took a good drink and rested for a while in the shade, dozing. The sun moved; the light and heat crept upon him. He awoke, took another drink, hoisted the pack to his back and climbed a high talus slope through a break in the west rim of the canyon. The final pitch, above the slope, was steep, tricky, twenty feet high. He took off the

pack, tied the rope to it and climbed to the rim, one end of the rope
in his belt. He drew up the pack, rested again, then marched south
along the canyon rim to regain the project right-of-way.

Through the afternoon he continued *his* project toward the
northwest, into the sun, nullifying in one day the patient, skilled,
month-long work of four men. All afternoon and into the evening he
plodded along, back and forth, pulling up stakes, removing ribbons.
Aircraft passed overhead, miles above, trailing vapor plumes across the
sky, not concerned with Hayduke or his work. Only the birds watched
him, the pinyon jays, a mountain bluebird, a hawk, the patient buzzards. Once he startled a herd of deer—six, seven, eight does, three
spotted fawns—and watched them bound off into the brush. He blundered into a bunch of cattle and they rose reluctantly at his approach,
half wild, half tame, hoisting hind ends and then foreparts from the
shady ground, and trotted away. This wilderness at least would support pastoral man for a long time to come.

When the cities are gone, he thought, and all the ruckus has died
away, when sunflowers push up through the concrete and asphalt of
the forgotten interstate freeways, when the Kremlin and the Pentagon
are turned into nursing homes for generals, presidents and other such
shitheads, when the glass-aluminum skyscraper tombs of Phoenix Arizona barely show above the sand dunes, why then, why then, why
then by God maybe free men and wild women on horses, free women
and wild men, can roam the sagebrush canyonlands in freedom—
goddammit!—herding the feral cattle into box canyons, and gorge on
bloody meat and bleeding fucking internal organs, and dance all night
to the music of fiddles! banjos! steel guitars! by the light of a reborn
moon!—by God, yes! Until, he reflected soberly, and bitterly, and
sadly, until the next age of ice and iron comes down, and the engineers and the farmers and the general motherfuckers come back again.

Thus George Hayduke's fantasy. Did he believe in the cyclical
theory of history? Or the linear theory? You'd find it hard to pin him
down in these matters; he wavered and wobbled and waffled from one
position to another, from time to time; what the fuck who gives a shit
he would say if pressed, and grab the tab snap the cap from another

can of Bud, buddy, pop the top, Pappy, from another can of Schlitz. Floating his teeth, gassing his guts, bloating his bladder with beer. Hopeless case.

Sundown: a gory primal sunset lay splattered like pizza pie across the west. Hayduke stuck another wad of jerky in his teeth and dogged on until he could no longer see the flagging on the trees and darkness compelled him to call it a day. He had worked from dawn to dusk or, as his old man used to say, "from can't see to can't see."

He must have walked twenty miles this day. At least the ache in his limbs, the swell of his feet, made it seem so. He ate his supper of Hayduke Granola and crawled into the sack, deep in the bush, he believed, dead to the world of care.

Hayduke slept late into the next morning, roused at last by the roar of a car or truck rushing past nearby. He staggered up to find himself within fifty yards of a road. For a minute he didn't know where he was. He rubbed his eyes, pulled on pants and boots, skulked through the trees to within sight of a road junction. He read the signs: LAKE POWELL 62; BLANDING 40; NATURAL BRIDGES NATIONAL MONUMENT 10; HALL'S CROSSING 45.

Good. Almost home.

He pulled out the last few stakes, removed the last few ribbons, slipped across the road and took off through the scrub forest cross-country toward Natural Bridges. Within that relative sanctuary, following Armstrong Canyon and the trail from Owachomo Natural Bridge, he would find the gang waiting, he hoped, hidden in the crowds of tourist and camper, at the official, designated, national monument campground. That had been the plan, and Hayduke was twenty-four hours ahead of schedule.

He buried the final handful of stakes and ribbon under a rock, adjusted the pack and marched boldly forward into the trees. He carried no compass but relied on topo maps, his infallible sense of direction and his overweening self-confidence. Justified. By four o'clock that afternoon he was sitting on the tailgate of Smith's truck slurping beer, gobbling an Abbzug-constructed ham sandwich and exchanging stories with the crew—Hayduke, Sarvis, Abbzug & Smith: it could have been a brokerage firm.

"Gentlemen and lady," Doc was saying, "this is only the beginning. Greater things wait ahead. The future lies before us, spread-eagled like a coronary upon the dunghill of Destiny."

"Doc," says Smith, "you said a mouthful."

"We need dynamite," Hayduke mumbles through his sandwich. "Thermite, carbon tet, magnesium filings. . . .

While Abbzug, aloof and lovely in the background, smiles her sardonic smile.

"Talk, talk, talk," she says. "That's all I ever hear. Talk, talk, talk."

8

Hayduke and Smith at Play

Campground, Natural Bridges National Monument.

"Can I borrow your bolt cutters?"

The man seemed pleasant enough, a suntanned gentleman in slacks and polo shirt and canvas shoes.

"We don't have any bolt cutters," Abbzug said.

He ignored her, talking to Smith. "Having a little trouble." He nodded his head back toward another campsite, where a pickup truck and camper trailer were parked. California license tags.

"Well," Smith said.

"We don't have any bolt cutters," Abbzug said again.

"I see you're a professional outfitter," the man said, still talking to Smith. He gestured toward Smith's truck. "Thought you might have a set of tools with you."

BACK OF BEYOND EXPEDITIONS HITE UTAH all across the door panels on big red magnetic decals.

"Yeah, but no bolt cutters," Abbzug said.

"Maybe heavy-duty wire cutters?"

"Well sir," says Smith, "we could loan you—"

"A set of pliers," Abbzug said.

"—a set of pliers."

"I have pliers. Need something bigger."

"Try the ranger's office," Abbzug said.

"Yes?" He finally condescended to speak directly to her, as if he hadn't been inspecting her all the time anyway from the corners of his eyes. "I'll do that." He finally walked away, through the junipers and pinyon pines, to his own outfit.

"Persistent cuss," Smith said.

"Nosy, I'd say," she said. "You see the way he was looking at me? The swine. I ought to give him a knuckle sandwich."

Smith was thinking about his decals. "Guess we don't need no more advertising." He peeled them off.

Hayduke and Dr. Sarvis returned from their walk in the woods. They had been preparing a shopping list for the next series of punitive raids, scheduled to begin ten days from today. Paranoid as always, Hayduke preferred the discussion held well away from the public campground.

Dr. Sarvis, chewing on his cigar, read over the list: rotor arms, iron oxide flakes, Du Pont Red Cross Extra, Number 50 blasting machine, fuse lighters, good things like that.

Doc slipped the paper into his shirt pocket. "I'm not sure I approve of this," he said.

"You want to take out that bridge or just play funny games?"

"I'm not sure."

"Make up your mind."

"I can't get all this stuff up here in a plane."

"You sure as hell can."

"Not on a commercial flight. Do you realize what you have to go through to get on a plane these days?"

"Charter a plane, Doc, charter a plane."

"You think I'm a rich bastard, don't you?"

"I never met a poor doctor yet, Doc. Better yet, *buy* us a fucking plane."

"I can't even drive a car."

"Let Bonnie take flying lessons."

"You're full of ideas today."

"It's a beautiful day, right? A motherfucking beautiful day."

The doctor laid his arm across Hayduke's broad back and squeezed that musclebound shoulder. "George," he said, "try to have a little patience. Just a little."

"Patience, shit."

"George, we don't know exactly what we're doing. If constructive vandalism turns destructive, what then? Perhaps we'll be doing more harm than good. There are some who say if you attack the system you only make it stronger."

"Yeah—and if you don't attack it, it strip-mines the mountains, dams all the rivers, paves over the desert and puts you in jail anyway."

"You and me."

"Not me. They'll never put me in one of their jails. I'm not the type, Doc. I'll die first. And take about ten of them with me. Not me, Doc."

They entered the campsite, joining the girl and Seldom Seen. Lunchtime. The sultry air of a clouded noon pressed down on them. Hayduke opened another can of beer. He was always opening another can of beer. And always pissing.

"How about some more poker?" Smith said to Dr. Sarvis. "Beat the heat."

Doc expelled a cloud of cigar smoke. "If you like."

"Don't you ever learn?" Hayduke said. "That grizzled fart has cleaned us out twice now."

"I learn but seems like I always forget," Smith said.

"No more poker games," Abbzug harshly butted in. "We have to go. If I don't get this so-called surgeon back to Albuquerque tomorrow we're going to have malpractice suits on our heads and that means no more money and higher insurance premiums and no more fun and games with you two clowns up here in the enchanted wilderness."

She was right, as usual. They broke camp promptly and hustled down the road, the four jammed hip to hip in the cab of Smith's truck. The bed of the truck, canopied by an aluminum shell, carried their camping gear, their food supplies and Smith's toolbox, icebox and other staples of his profession.

The plan was to drive Doc and Bonnie to the landing strip at Fry Canyon, where they were to meet a small private plane which would take them to Farmington, New Mexico, in time to catch the evening flight to Albuquerque. Roundabout, expensive and tiresome but still much better, from Dr. Sarvis's point of view, than commuting that awful span of bulging desert—some four hundred miles—on the four wheels of his Continental.

Hayduke and Smith would then go on to what once was the river, now the upper arm of Lake Powell, to reconnoiter the next objective: three new bridges. On the day following, Smith had to drive on to Hanksville to rendezvous with a group of his client backpackers for a five-day tour of Utah's Henry Mountains, last-discovered and last-named U.S. mountain range.

And Hayduke? Didn't know. He might go with Smith, or he might go wandering off on his own for a while. The old jeep, loaded with all his valuables, had been left a week earlier in a parking lot at Wahweap Marina near Page, close to the ultimate, final, unspoken, impossible objective, Smith's favorite fantasy, the dam. Glen Canyon Dam. *The* dam.

How Hayduke was to get his jeep back or himself back to his jeep he didn't know at this point. He could always walk it if necessary—200 miles? 300?—up and down and in and out of God's finest canyon wilderness. He could borrow one of Smith's little rubber boats, inflate it and paddle down the 150 miles of stagnant Lake Powell. Or he could wait for Smith to drive him down there.

The beauty of his situation was, for Hayduke, that he felt he could be let off anytime, anywhere, in the middle of nowhere, with his backpack, a gallon of water, a few relevant topo maps, three days' food supply, and he'd make it, survive and thrive, on his own, man. (All that fresh beef wandering around on the range; all that venison on the hoof down in the box canyons; all those sweet-water springs under the lucent cottonwoods a convenient day's march one from the next.)

So he thought. So he felt. The sensation of freedom was exhilarating, though tinged with a shade of loneliness, a touch of sorrow. The old dream of total independence, beholden to no man and no woman, floated above his days like smoke from a pipe dream, like a silver cloud with a dark lining. For even Hayduke sensed, when he faced the thing directly, that the total loner would go insane. Was insane. Somewhere in the depths of solitude, beyond wildness and freedom, lay the trap of madness. Even the vulture, that red-necked black-winged anarchist, most indolent and arrogant of all the desert's creatures, even the vulture at evening likes to gather with his kin and swap a few stories, the flock of them roosting on the highest branches of the deadest tree in the neighborhood, all hunched down and wrapped up in their black-wing robes, cackling together like a convocation of scheming priests. Even the vulture—fantastic thought—goes through the nesting fit, mates for a time, broods on a clutch of vulture eggs, produces young.

Captain Smith & Crew, rolling merrily down the road, left the Monument turnoff at the junction with Utah 95. Here they saw a string of four-wheel-drive vehicles—CJ-5s, Scouts, Blazers, Broncos, elaborately equipped with spotlights, hard tops, gun racks (loaded), winches, wide-rim wheels, shortwave radios, chrome-plated hubcaps, the works—parked in a file at the side of the road. Each vehicle bore on its door panel identical decalcomania, a bold insigne complete with eagle, shield and scroll:

SAN JUAN COUNTY
SEARCH & RESCUE TEAM
BLANDING, UTAH

A group of Search and Rescuers squatted in the shade with Coke, Pepsi, 7-Up clutched in hairy hands. (These men are regular churchgoers.) A few were scuffling about in the brush, along the now unflagged and unstaked survey route of the projected right-of-way. One of them hailed Smith. He was obliged to stop.

The hailer came toward them. "Hey there," he bellows cheerily, "if it ain't old Cohab Smith. Ol' Seldom Seen hisself. How you doin', Smith?"

Smith, letting the motor idle, answered, "Just fine, Bishop Love. Fine as a frog's hair. What're you doin' out this neck of the woods?"

The man, huge as Dr. Sarvis, lumbered up to the door of the truck, laid his big red hands on the frame of the open window and smiled in. He looked like a rancher: a mouthful of powerful, horselike yellow teeth, a leather-skinned face half shaded by a big hat, the regulation snap-button shirt. He squinted beyond Smith at the three passengers in the gloom of the cab. (The light outside was dazzling.) "How you folks today?"

The doctor nodded; Bonnie gave her receptionist's frigid smile; Hayduke dozed. Smith offered no introductions. Bishop Love turned his attention back to Smith.

"Seldom," he says, "haven't seen you around these parts for some time. How's everything?"

"Can't holler." Smith nods toward his passengers. "Making a living and paying my tithe."

"Payin' your tithe, are you? That ain't what I hear." The bishop laughed to show he was only kidding.

"I pay mine to IRS, which is more'n I hear you do, Bishop."

The bishop glanced around; the smile grew broader. "Now don't you start no rumors. Besides"—he winked—"that income tax is socialistic and against the Constitution and a sin against man and God, you know that." Pause. Smith raced the engine for a moment. Love's wandering eyes came back. "Listen, we're lookin' for somebody. There's a man afoot out here somewhere makin' a public nuisance of hisself. We think he might be lost."

"What's he look like?"

"Wears about size ten or eleven boots. Vibram lug soles."

"That ain't much of a description, Bishop."

"I know it. It's all we got. You seen him?"

"No."

"Didn't think so. Well, we'll find him pretty quick." Pause. Again Smith raced the engine. "Now you take care yerself, Seldom, and listen, next time you come through Blanding you stop and see me, understand? We got some things to talk about."

"I'll see you, Bishop."

"Good boy." The bishop grabbed Smith's shoulder, gave it a vigorous shake, then withdrew from the truck window. Smith drove away.

"Old friend of yours?" Bonnie said.

"Nope."

"Old enemy?"

"Yep. Old Love he ain't got much use for me."

"Why'd you call him Bishop?"

"He's a bishop in the church."

"That man is a *bishop*? In the *church*?"

"L.D.S. The Mormon church. We got more bishops than we got saints." Smith grinned. "Why hell, honey, I'd be a bishop myself by now if I'd kept my nose clean and stayed out of Short Crick and Cohabitation Canyon."

"All right, come on," Bonnie said, "talk American."

Hayduke, who'd only been feigning sleep, put in his two cents. "He means if he hadn't been following his cock all over Utah and Arizona he'd have a bishop-prick of his own."

"Nobody was talking to you, garbage mouth."

"I know it."

"Then shut up."

"Sure."

"That's about it," Smith said. "What George said."

"So what's a search and rescue team doing on that road project?"

"They work pretty close with the county sheriff's department. What you might call a posse. They're mostly a bunch of businessmen who like to play vigilante in their spare time. They don't mean no harm. Every fall they bring a few California deer hunters in outa the blizzard. Every summer they bring a few dehydrated Boy Scouts up out of Grand Gulch. They try to do good. It's their hobby."

"When I see somebody coming to do *me* good," Hayduke said, "I reach for my revolver."

"When I hear the word culture," Dr. Sarvis said, "I reach for my checkbook."

"That's neither here nor there," Bonnie said. "Let's try to keep our thoughts in clear logical order." She and her mates stared ahead through the windshield at the red panorama beyond, the blue cliffs, the pale canyons, the angular silhouette of Woodenshoe Butte against the northwest horizon. "What I want to know now," she continued, "is who is this Bishop Love and why does he hate your guts, Captain Smith, and should I or should I not put a hex on him?"

"The name is Seldom," he said, "and old Love hates me because last time we locked horns he's the one got throwed. You don't wanna hear about it."

"Probably not," Bonnie said. "So what happened?"

The truck rambled down the red-dust Utah country road, wandering a bit on the ruts and rocks. "Think maybe the front end's a little outa line," Smith says.

"So what happened?" Bonnie says.

"Just a little difference of opinion which cost old Love about a million dollars. He wanted a forty-nine-year lease on a section of state land overlooking Lake Powell. Had in mind some kind of tourist development: summer homes, shopping center, airfield and so on. There was a hearing in Salt Lake, and me and some friends talked the Land Commission into blocking the deal. Took a lot of talking but we convinced 'em Love's project was a fraud, which it was, and he ain't forgiven me yet. We've had differences like that before, him and me, several times."

"I thought he was a bishop."

"Well that's on Sundays and Wednesday church-study nights only. Rest of the time he's neck deep in real estate, uranium, cattle, oil, gas, tourism, most anything that smells like money. That man can hear a dollar bill drop on a shag rug. Now he's running for the state legislature. We got plenty like him in Utah. They run things. They run things as best they can for God and Jesus, and what them two don't want why fellas like Bishop Love pick up. They say it's a mighty convenient arrangement all around. Jesus Saves at eight and a half percent compounded daily, and when they make that last deposit they go straight to heaven. Them and all the ancestors they can dig out of the genealogical libraries. It's enough to make a man want to live forever."

"Tell them Hayduke's back," Hayduke said. "That'll calm them down." He tossed his beer can out the window. And opened another. Bonnie studied him.

"I thought we were only going to litter paved roads," she said. "This is not a paved road, in case your eyes are too bloodshot to notice."

"Fuck off." He tossed the little metal tab out the window.

"That's a brilliant retort you've worked out, Hayduke," she said. "Really brilliant. A real flash of wit for all occasions."

"Fuck off."

"Touché. Doc, are you going to sit there like a lump of lard and let that hairy swine insult me?"

"Well . . . yes," Doc said, after due consideration.

"You better. I'm a full-grown woman, and I can take care of myself."

Hayduke, by the window, gazed out at the scenery, that routine canyon country landscape—grandiose, desolate, shamelessly spectacular. Among those faraway buttes and pinnacles, rosy red against the sky, lay the promise of something intimate—the intimate in the remote. A secret and a revelation. Later, he thought, we'll get into all that.

They came to Fry Canyon, which consists of a slot in the bedrock ten feet wide and fifty feet deep, crossed by an old wooden bridge; a cinder-block warehouse, which functions as Fry Canyon's store, gas station, post office and 3.2 social center; and a bulldozed airstrip, cobbled with rocks, stippled with cow dung, on which waited one Cessna four-seater—Fry Canyon Airport.

Smith drove past the limp wind sock dangling from a pole straight to the wing of the aircraft and stopped. As he unloaded passengers and baggage, the pilot came out of the store drinking Coke from a can. Within five minutes all kisses (Smith and Bonnie), handshakes, embraces and farewells were completed and Dr. Sarvis and Ms. Abbzug, airborne once again, were winging their course southeast toward New Mexico and home.

Hayduke and Smith restocked the beer chest and drove on, sunward, downward, riverward, upwind, into the red-rock rimrock country of the Colorado River, heart of the heart of the American West. Where the wind always blows and nothing grows but stunted juniper on the edge of a canyon, scattered blackbrush, scrubby cactus. After the winter rains, if any, and again after the summer rains, if any, there will be a brief flourish of flowers, ephemeral things. The average annual rainfall comes to five inches. It is the kind of land to cause horror and repugnance in the heart of the dirt farmer, stock raiser, land developer. There is no water; there is no soil; there is no grass; there are no trees except a few brave cottonwoods deep in the canyons. Nothing but skeleton rock, the skin of sand and dust, the silence, the space, the mountains beyond.

Hayduke and Smith, jouncing down into the red desert, passed without stopping (for Smith could not bear the memories) the turnoff to the old road which formerly had led to the hamlet of Hite (not to be confused with Hite Marina). Hite, once home for Seldom Seen and still official headquarters of his business, now lies underwater.

They drove on, coming presently to the new bridge that spanned the gorge of White Canyon, the first of the three new bridges in the area. Three bridges to cross one river?

Consult the map. When Glen Canyon Dam plugged the Colorado, the waters backed up over Hite, over the ferry and into thirty miles of canyon upstream from the ferry. The best place to bridge the river (now Lake Powell) was upstream at Narrow Canyon. In order to reach the Narrow Canyon bridge site it was necessary to bridge White Canyon on the east and Dirty Devil Canyon on the west. Thus, three bridges.

Hayduke and Smith stopped to inspect the White Canyon bridge. This, like the other two, was of arch construction and massive proportion, meant to last. The very bolt heads in the cross members were the size of a man's fist.

George Hayduke crawled about for a few minutes underneath the abutments, where nomads already, despite the newness of the bridge, had left their signatures with spray paint on the pale concrete and their dung, dried and shriveled, in the dust. He came up shaking his head.

"Don't know," he says, "don't know. It's one big mother-fucker."

"The middle one's bigger," says Smith.

They stared down over the railing at the meandering trickle, two hundred feet below, of White Canyon's intermittent, strictly seasonal stream. Their beer cans sailed light as Dixie cups into the gloom of the gorge. The first flood of the summer would flush them, along with all other such detritus, down to the storage reservoir, Lake Powell, where all upstream garbage found a fitting resting-place.

On to the middle bridge.

They were descending, going down, yet so vast is the scale of things here, so complex the terrain, that neither river nor central canyon become visible until the traveler is almost on the rim of the canyon.

They saw the bridge first, a high lovely twin arch rising in silvery steel well above the level of its roadway. Then they could see the stratified walls of Narrow Canyon. Smith parked his truck; they got out and walked onto the bridge.

The first thing they noticed was that the river was no longer there. Somebody had removed the Colorado River. This was old news to Smith, but to Hayduke, who knew of it only by hearsay, the discovery that the river was indeed gone came as a jolt. Instead of a river he looked down on a motionless body of murky green effluent, dead, stagnant, dull, a scum of oil floating on the surface. On the canyon walls a coating of dried silt and mineral salts, like a bathtub ring, recorded high-water mark. Lake Powell: storage pond, silt trap, evaporation tank and garbage dispose-all, a 180-mile-long incipient sewage lagoon.

They stared down. A few dead fish floated belly up on the oily surface among the orange peels and picnic plates. One waterlogged tree, a hazard to navigation, hung suspended in the static medium. The smell of decay, faint but unmistakable, rose four hundred and fifty feet to their nostrils. Somewhere below that still surface, down where the cloudy silt was settling out, the drowned cottonwoods must yet be standing, their dead branches thick with algae, their ancient knees laden with mud. Somewhere under the heavy burden of water going nowhere, under the silence, the old rocks of the river channel waited for the promised resurrection. Promised by whom? Promised by Capt. Joseph "Seldom Seen" Smith; by Sgt. George Washington Hayduke; by Dr. Sarvis and Ms. Bonnie Abbzug, that's whom.

But how?

Hayduke climbed down the rocks and inspected the foundations of the bridge: very concrete. Abutments sunk deep into the sandstone wall of the canyon, huge I beams bolted together with bolts the size of a man's arm, nuts big as dinner plates. If a man had a wrench with a 14-inch head, thinks Hayduke, and a handle like a 20-foot crowbar, he might get some leverage on those nuts.

They drove on to the third bridge, over the now-submerged mouth of the Dirty Devil River. On the way they passed an unmarked dirt road, the jeep trail leading north toward the Maze, Land of Standing Rocks, the Fins, Lizard Rock and Land's End. No-man's land. Smith knew it well.

The third bridge, like the others, was of arch construction, all steel and concrete, built to bear the weight of forty-ton haulers loaded with carnotite, pitchblende, bentonite, bituminous coal, diatomaceous earth, sulfuric acid, Schlumberger's drill mud, copper ore, oil shale, sand tar, whatever might yet be extracted from the wilderness.

"We're going to need a carload of H.E.," says George Hayduke. "Not like them old wooden truss and trestle bridges over in 'Nam."

"Well, hell, who says we have to blow all three?" Smith says. "If we take out any one it will cut the road."

"Symmetry," says Hayduke. "A nice neat job on all three would be more appreciated. I don't know. Let's think about it. Do you see what I see?"

Leaning on the rail of the Dirty Devil bridge, they looked south to Hite Marina, where a few cabin cruisers floated at their moorings, and at something more interesting closer by, the Hite airstrip, which appeared to be undergoing expansion. They saw a quarter mile of cleared land, a pickup truck, a wheeled loader, a dump truck and, coming to a halt, a Caterpillar D-7 bulldozer. The airstrip was laid out north and south on a flat bench of land below the road, above the reservoir; one edge of the airstrip was no more than fifty feet from the rim of the bench, with a vertical drop-off of 300 feet to the dark green waters of Lake Powell.

"I see it," Smith said at last, reluctantly.

Even as they watched, the dozer operator was getting off the machine, getting into the pickup and driving down to the marina. Lunchtime again.

"Seldom," says Hayduke, "that guy shut off the engine but he sure as hell didn't remove anything."

"No?"

"Absolutely not."

"Well . . ."

"Seldom, I want you to give me a lesson in equipment operation."

"Not here."

"Right here."

"Not in broad daylight."

"Why not?"

Smith seeks an excuse. "Not with them motorboaters hangin' around the marina."

"They couldn't care less. We'll have our hard hats and your pickup truck, and people will think we're construction workers."

"You ain't supposed to make a big wake near the boat docks."

"It'll make one fine helluva splash, won't it?"

"We can't do it."

"It's a matter of honor."

Smith thinking, reflecting, meditating. Finally the deep creases shifted position, his leathery face relaxed into a smile.

"One thing first," he says.

"What's that?"

"We take the license plates off my truck."

Done.

"Let's go," says Smith.

The road wound about the heads of side canyons, rose, descended, rose again to the mesa above the marina. They turned off and drove out on the airstrip. Nobody around. Down at the marina, half a mile away, a few tourists, anglers and boaters lounged in the shade. The Cat operator's pickup stood parked in front of the café. Heat waves shimmered above the walls of red rock. Except for the purr of a motorboat far down the lake, the world was silent, drugged with heat.

Smith drove straight to the side of the bulldozer, a middle-aged dust-covered iron beast. He shut off his engine and stared at Hayduke.

"I'm ready," says Hayduke.

They put on their hard hats and got out.

"First we start the starting engine, right?" Hayduke says. "To warm up the diesel engine, right?"

"Wrong. It's warmed up for us already. First we check the controls to make sure the tractor is in correct starting position."

Smith climbed into the operator's seat, facing an array of levers and pedals. "This," he said, "is the flywheel clutch lever. Disengage." He pushed it forward. "This here is the speed selector lever. Put in neutral."

Hayduke watched closely, memorizing each detail. "That's the throttle," he said.

"That's right. This is the forward and reverse lever. It should be in neutral too. This is the governor control lever. Push forward all the way. Now we apply the right steering brake"—Smith stepped on the right pedal—"and we lock it in position." He flipped forward a small lever on the floorboards. "Now—"

"So everything's in neutral and the brake is locked and it can't go anywhere?"

"That's right. Now"—Smith got out of the seat and moved to

the port side of the engine—"now we start the starting engine. The new tractors are a lot simpler, they don't need a starting engine, but you'll find plenty of these old ones still around. These big tractors will last for fifty years if they're taken good care of. Now this here little lever is called the transmission control lever. It goes in HIGH SPEED position for starting. This is the compression release lever; we put it in START position. Now we disengage the starting-engine clutch with this handle here." He pushed the lever in toward the diesel block.

"Oh, Jesus," mutters Hayduke.

"Yep, it's a little complicated. Now . . . where was I? Now we open the fuel valve by unscrewing this little valve, right . . . here. Now we pull out the choke. Now we set the idling latch in position. Now we turn on the switch."

"That's the ignition switch for the starting engine?"

"Yep." Smith turned on the switch. Sound of a positive click. Nothing else.

"Nothing happened," Hayduke says.

"Oh, I reckon something happened," Smith said. "We closed a circuit. Now if this was a fairly old-model tractor the next thing you'd have to do is get the crank and crank up the engine. But this model has an electric starter. Let's see if she works." Smith put his hand on a lever under the clutch handle and pushed it back. The engine growled, turned over, caught fire. Smith released the starter lever, adjusted the choke; the engine ran smoothly.

"That's only the gasoline engine," Hayduke said. "We still have to get the diesel started, right?"

"That's right, George. Anybody coming?"

Hayduke climbed to the driver's seat. "Nobody in sight."

"All right." The starting engine was warm; Smith closed the choke. The engine throbbed at a comfortable idling speed. "Okay, now we grab these two levers here." Hayduke watching again, all attention. "This upper one is the pinion control and the lower one is the clutch control. Now we push the clutch lever all the way in"—toward the diesel engine block—"and pull the pinion lever all the way out. Now we move the idle latch to let the starting engine run at full speed. Now we engage the starting-engine clutch." He pulled the clutch lever out. The engine slowed, almost stalled, then picked up speed. He moved the compression release lever to RUN position. "Now the starting engine is cranking the diesel engine against compression," Smith said, shouting above the roar of the meshing motors. "It'll start right off."

Hayduke nodded but was no longer sure he followed it all. The tractor was making a great noise; black smoke jetted up, making the hinged lid dance on top of the exhaust stack.

"Now the diesel is running," Smith shouted, looking at the exhaust smoke with approval. He came back to the operator's seat, beside Hayduke. "So now we give it more speed. Pull the governor back to half speed. Now we're about ready to go," he shouted. "So we shut off the starting engine."

He moved forward again and disengaged the starting engine clutch, closed the fuel valve, shut off the ignition switch and returned to Hayduke. They sat side by side on the wide leather-covered operator's seat.

"Now we're ready to drive this thing," he shouted, grinning at Hayduke. "You still interested or would you rather go drink a beer?"

"Let's go," Hayduke shouts back. He scanned the road and marina again for any sign of hostile activity. All seemed to be in order.

"Okay," shouted Smith. He pulled a lever, lifting the hydraulic dozer blade a foot off the ground. "Now we select our operating speed. We have five speeds forward, four in reverse. Since you're kind of a beginner and that cliff is only a hundred yards away we'll stick to the slowest speed for right now." The tractor faced toward the big drop-off. He shifted the speed selector from neutral into first, pulled the forward-and-reverse lever *back* to the *forward* position. Nothing happened.

"Nothing's happening," says Hayduke, nervous again.

"That's right and ain't supposed to neither," says Smith. "Keep your shirt on. Now we rev up the engine a bit." He pulled the throttle back to full speed. "Now we engage the flywheel clutch." He pulled the clutch lever back; the great tractor started to tremble as the transmission gears slid into meshing position. He pulled the clutch lever all the way back and snapped it over center. At once the tractor began to move—thirty-five tons of iron bearing east toward St. Louis, Mo., via Lake Powell and Narrow Canyon.

"I reckon I'll get off now," Smith said, standing up.

"Wait a minute," Hayduke shouts. "How do you steer it?"

"Steering too, huh? Okay, you use these two levers in the middle. These are steering clutch levers, one for each track. Pull back on the right lever and you disengage the clutch on the right side." He did as he said; the tractor began a ponderous turn to the right. "Pull back on the other for a left turn." He released the right lever, pulled back on the left; the tractor began a ponderous turn to the left. "To make a sharper turn you apply the steering clutch brakes." He stepped on first one then the other of the two steel pedals that rose from the floor panels. "You catch on?"

"I get it," shouted Hayduke happily. "Let me do it."

Smith got up, letting Hayduke take over. "You sure you understand the whole thing?" he said.

"Don't bother me, I'm busy," Hayduke shouted, big grin shining through his shaggy beard.

"All right." Smith stepped from the fender to the drawbar of the slow-moving machine and jumped lightly to the ground. "You be careful now," he shouted.

Hayduke didn't hear him. Playing with clutch levers and clutch brakes he wove a crazy course toward the loading machine at the side of the airstrip. At the rate of two miles per hour the bulldozer smashed into the loader, a great mass of metal colliding with a lesser mass. The loader yielded, sliding sideways over the ground. Hayduke steered toward the edge of the runway and the plunge beyond, pushing the loader ahead. He grinned ferociously. Dust clouds billowed above the grind, the crunch, the squeal and groan of steel under stress.

Smith got into his pickup and started the motor, ready to take off at the first hint of danger. Despite the uproar there seemed to be no sign of alarm in any quarter. The yellow pickup remained at the café. Down at the marina a boater refueled his runabout. Two boys fished for channel cat from the end of the dock. Tourists picked over trinkets in the curio shop. A pair of hawks soared high above the radiant cliffs. Peace. . . .

Standing at the controls Hayduke saw, beyond the clouds of dust, the edge of the mesa coming toward him. Beyond that edge, far below, lay the waters of Lake Powell, the surface wrinkled by the wake of a passing boat.

He thought of one final point.

"Hey!" he shouted back at Smith. "How do you stop this thing?"

Smith, leaning against the door of his truck, cupped his ears and shouted back, "What's that?"

"How do you stop this thing?" Hayduke bellowed.

"What?" bellowed Smith.

"HOW DO YOU STOP THIS THING?"

"CAN'T HEAR YOU. . . ."

The loader, pushed by the dozer blade, arrived at the verge, wheeled over, vanished. The bulldozer followed steadily, chuffing black smoke from the burnt metal of the exhaust stack. The steel treads kept firm grip on the sandstone ledge, propelling the machine forward into space. Hayduke jumped off. As the tipover point approached the tractor attempted (so it seemed) to save itself: one tread being more advanced into the air than the other, the tractor made a lurching half-turn to the right, trying to cling to the rim of the mesa and somehow regain solid footing. Useless: there was no remedy; the bulldozer went over, making one somersault, and fell, at minimal trajectory, toward the flat hard metallic-lustered face of the reservoir. As it fell the tracks kept turning, and the engine howled.

Hayduke crawled to the edge in time to see, first, the blurred form of the loading machine sinking into the depths and, second, a few details of the tractor as it crashed into the lake. The thunder of the impact resounded from the canyon walls with shuddering effect, like a sonic boom. The bulldozer sank into the darkness of the cold subsurface waters, its dim shape of Caterpillar yellow obliterated, after a second, by the flare of an underwater explosion. A galaxy of bubbles rose to the surface and popped. Sand and stone trickled for another minute from the cliff. That ceased; there was no further activity but the cautious advance of one motorboat across the dying ripples of the lake: some curious boatman drawn to the scene of calamity.

"Let's get out of here!" Smith called, as he noticed finally, down at the marina, the pickup truck pulling away from the café.

Hayduke stood up dripping dust and jogged toward Smith, a great grim grin on his face.

"Come on!" yelled Smith. Hayduke ran.

They pulled away as the yellow truck ascended the switchbacks leading from marina to road. Smith headed back the way they'd come, across the bridge over the Dirty Devil and on toward the Colorado, but braked hard and turned abruptly before they reached the center bridge, taking the jeep road north around a bend which concealed them from direct view of anyone passing on the highway.

Or did it? Not entirely, for a cloud of dust, like a giant rooster tail hovering in the air, revealed their passage up the dirt road.

Aware of the rising dust, Smith stopped his truck as soon as they were behind the rocks. He left the engine idling in case it became necessary to move on quickly.

They waited.

They heard the whine of the pursuing truck, the vicious hiss of rubber on asphalt as it rushed past on toward the east. They listened to the diminishing noise of its wheels, the gradual return of peace and stillness, harmony and joy.

9

Search and Rescue on the Job

Laughing, Hayduke and Smith slapped each other on the shoulder blades, hugged each other with delight, and opened up a fresh cold six-pack. Ah, that frosty glitter. Oh, that clean snap of the pop top.

"Hah!" roared Hayduke, feeling the first good rush course through his blood. "Goddamn but that was beautiful!" He jumped out of the truck and danced a sort of jig, a sort of tarantella, a kind of Hunkpapa Sioux peyote shuffle, in 2/4 time, around the truck. Smith started to follow but first, out of caution, climbed to the roof of the cab for another look-see. Who knew what the Enemy might be plotting at this very moment.

And he was right.

"George," he says, "stop your war dance for a minute and hand me them there Jap bi-noculars."

Hayduke passed up the glasses. Smith took a long and studious look to the east-northeast, above the humpback rock, straight toward that lovely bridge which rose, like an arc of silver, like a rainbow of steel, above Narrow Canyon and the temporarily plugged Colorado River. Hayduke, waiting, listened to the sounds of late afternoon. There didn't seem to be any. A troubling calm prevailed. Even the bird, the one bird that lived in Narrow Canyon, had shut his beak.

"Yeah, it's him," Smith said. "The horse's ass returns."

"Which one?"

"I mean my buddy Bishop Love. Good old J. Dudley. Him and his Search and Rescue Team."

"What are they doing?" A little more soberly now, Hayduke flips the tab from another can of Schlitz.

"They're all out there on the Colorado bridge talking with this guy in the yellow truck."

"What are the fuckers saying?"

"I can't read lips too good, but I can guess."

"Yeah?"

"Bishop Love is telling the other guy he didn't see no green pickup with no gray canopy come by on the highway. And the other guy is telling Bishop Love that that there green pickup sure as hell didn't double back on *him*. So the bishop is saying they must of turned off on that Maze jeep trail and that's where they are right now—and we ought to been out of here five minutes ago."

Smith jumped down from the cab roof and scrambled into the seat.

"C'mon, George."

Hayduke thinking. "I should've brought a rifle along."

"Get in!"

He got in. They took off, north into the sandstone jungle, at maximum possible speed on the rocky rutted axle-busting road: twenty miles per hour.

"Listen," says Hayduke, "they've got those V-Eight Chevy Blazers. Don't panic, but they're gonna catch us sure as shit. If they don't call in 104s first. With napalm."

"I know it," says Smith. "You got any more bright ideas?"

"Sure do. We stop them. We set a trap. What's ahead on this road? Any little wooden bridges we could burn? How about a pucker-pass setup we could block with a boulder?"

"Don't know."

"Think fast, Seldom. How about if I shoot some of those cows going across the road up there? Block the way. That might slow them down for a minute."

"You're the Green Beret, George, you think of something. We got about five minutes' head start on them and that's all. There ain't no little wooden bridges and there ain't no tight passes on this road for the next ten miles that I can recollect. And you ain't shootin' no cows."

Smith's truck bounced and rattled over the rocks, in and out of the ruts, across the deadly little gullies, braking, gearing down for a rush through sand and up the other side, gearing up for a sprint across a level stretch, then the rocks again, another gully. Everything loose in the cargo space—and that included cooking pots, iceboxes, shovels, tire irons, an outboard motor, Dutch oven, canteens, tow chain, pick, prise bar, canned goods—danced and dithered, reinforcing the clamor of the truck itself. To their rear a splendid tail of dust towered into the evening, hovering in the blaze of sunlight, each mote, beam and grain of desert earth enhaloed by the sun, enhanced by the albedo-reflectivity of the plateau walls. Visible for miles. A pillar of dust by day, a fire by night. A giveaway; but the dust also concealed.

The road was impossible; it now became even worse. Smith had to stop and get out to lock the hubs, shift into four-wheel drive. Hayduke got out too. He studied the terrain. About two miles behind he saw the dust plumes of the pursuing traffic: three Blazers and a yellow pickup pounding along, hot for action, lusting for the kill. (That's us.) How'd we get into this mess anyhow? Whose brilliant idea was this anyway?

On the east the elephant-backed sandstone humps and hollows sloped down toward the hidden gorge; on the west two-thousand-foot cliffs; ahead was the narrow benchland between them, on which the road meandered in its snakelike progress northward. Out of the red dust and auburn sand grew nothing but scrubby blackbrush a foot high, a few stunted junipers, a few tough yuccas on the dunes. No place to hide a truck.

"Let's go! Let's go!" Smith rushed back to the driver's seat.

Not even a side canyon in view. And if there was one, and they drove up into it, they'd find themselves in a dead end, boxed up. Anywhere they drove, unless they could reach slickrock, they'd leave a trail of tire tracks in the sand, crushing the brush, displacing stones. The naked desert is no place for little secrets.

Smith raced the engine. "Let's go, George."

Hayduke jumped back in. They roared down the high-centered road, bristly blackbrush and spiny prickly pear clawing at the truck along the greasy perineum of its General Motors crotch.

"George," Smith says, "I've got it figured out. There's a fence around the next bend. The road goes across an old wooden cattle guard. We could fire that."

"I'll pour, you light."

"Right," says Smith.

The fence appeared, stretching right-angled across the line of their advance, from cliff to canyon. An opening for the road was formed by a rack or grill of two-by-fours set on edge, resting on a pair of railway ties. Cattle guard. Wheels could cross; hoofed animals like sheep, cows and horses could not. There was a closed gate beside the cattle guard, through which livestock might be driven, but this, like most of the fenceline, was banked thick and solid with years' accumulation of windblown tumbleweeds. From a distance the fence resembled a hedgerow, brown and tangled.

The truck rumbled across the two-by-fours. Smith jammed on the brakes. Before the truck had stopped Hayduke was out, blinking in the dust, fumbling at a fuel can strapped in a racket on the side. Opening the can on the run, back to the cattle guard, he sloshed generous gouts of gasoline over the old timbers, the creosoted beams, the gateposts and—still running—along the ground under the mass of tumbleweeds, first to the west side then the east, as far as the fuel would reach. Running back to the truck he heard a *shooooom!* and the *snap! crackle! pop!* of tumbleweed exploding into fire. Here came Smith running toward him, a dark sweaty silhouette against the barricade of flames, under a mushroom roll of black rich evil smoke.

"Let's get out of here," he says.

They heard, already, the sound of the pursuit.

Smith drove, Hayduke looked back. He saw the flames, clear yellow in the sun, tangerine-colored in the shadow of the cliff, and a purple curtain of weed smoke leaning across the sky. On the far side, cut off, came the four pursuing vehicles. Slowing down, no doubt stopping—for who would be mad enough to drive a bright new $6500 Blazer fully equipped all extras (roll bar heavy-duty clutch auxiliary gas tank tape deck steel-belted radials twin spares spotlights altimeter tachometer tiltmeter chrome-plated Spalding winch factory air two-way radio whiptail antenna 385-cubic-inch displacement four-on-the-floor stick shift) through a wall of fire chasing evildoers in an old pickup on the basis of evidence at best no more than circumstantial?

Bishop Love, that's who. J. Dudley Love, Bishop of Blanding, Captain of Search and Rescue.

Here he comes that sonofabitch leaping through the flames over the fiery cattle guard, the shining Blazer apparently unharmed. But a fountain of sparks from the fall of a burning timber was enough to make the second driver halt for a moment; he turned eastward along the fenceline to outflank the fire, followed by the others.

"They're still coming."

"I see 'em." Smith stepped harder on the gas but the road was too rough for much more speed. "Did we gain on them?"

"All but the first."

"Now what?"

"Let me out, Seldom, leave me behind that rock up ahead. I'll pink their tires with my little hollow points here and run like hell and meet you later in Hanksville or someplace sexy."

"Let me think."

"Another beer?"

"I'm a-tryin' to think, George, lemme think. There's an old mine road up ahead, leads off to the west, and maybe it goes clear to the top of the mesa. Don't know for certain. If it don't we're sunk. If it does we'll lose 'em easy up there in the woods. But if it don't we're sunk."

Hayduke staring back. "They're gaining on us. If we don't get off this road we're sunk." He opened another beer.

"Then we'll try the other way."

They rounded the next bend in the cliffs and there ahead, sure enough, was a fork in the road, the right fork all rock and rut, pothole and washout—that's the main road, the arterial route—and the other somewhat the worse for neglect.

"Here we go," says Smith, turning sharp left.

Hayduke spilled his beer in his lap. "Oh, shit, I'm drunk already and I sure do apologize for the mess I got you into on this otherwise sound and peaceful afternoon, Captain Smith, and if you'll stop this fuckin' truck for a minute so I can get out, I'll take care"—Hayduke waving his magnum—"of that lovable old bishop of yours."

"Careful with that golblamed gun, George. We got a problem on our hands right now."

"You're absolutely right." Hayduke slid the revolver back into its pocket.

Smith's truck meantime was bucking and heaving in low gear 5 mph up this antique trail to the west, a trail about as old as the Federal Mining Act of 1872. It led in multiple switchbacks up the side of a talus slope, among a jumble of rocks and boulders under the foot of the plateau wall. The scenery was magnificent as usual but their situation precarious and exposed. The Enemy, only a few miles behind, out of sight but closing the gap, spurred on with extra vigor by the indignity of singed bottoms, scorched automotive coccyges, seared differential scrota, would soon come round the last bend in the trail and see them—Hayduke and Smith, Inc.—crawling slow and beetlelike up this improbable exit way.

The trail became still rougher; already in four-wheel drive, Smith transferred into low range. The truck ground upward at the rate of two miles per hour toward the possible haven above—if the road went that far. Haven, heaven, maybe salvation.

Carved out of rock by dynamite decades before, the road tended to slope down and outward—the wrong way. The truck leaned in sickening style far off plumb, away from footing and toward the void. Hayduke, on the outside, would never have a chance if the truck rolled over.

"Look here, Seldom," he says, "stop this truck, I want to get out."

"What for?"

"I'll take that bar out of the back and do a little road work. Slow down that Search and Rescue Team."

Smith considered. "You see them yet?"

"Not yet, but I see dust rising around the bend. The bishop is on the way."

Smith stopped. Hayduke fell out, clung to the truck, stumbled over the loose talus, opened the back and found the big iron prise bar. He came to the window on Smith's side.

Smith says, "Now what's the plan?"

"I'll lever some boulders into the road. You wait for me on top. Or as far as you can get. Hand me that heavy bluish item out of the back pocket of my pack."

"All right, I'll wait for you on top. Or not more'n a couple miles ahead. Hand you what?"

"The gun, the gun. No, don't stop, keep on going, the sun'll soon be down, I'm good for twenty miles in this nice weather. The gun and canteen. Drop off my pack at the top."

"No guns."

"If them Search and Rescue fuckers start shooting at me I'm gonna shoot back."

"No, George, we can't do that. You know the rule."

"Listen, I'm naked as a baby without that gun." He tried to reach it. Smith blocked his arm.

"Nope. Here's your canteen, George."

"All right. Jesus Christ. Get going. Here they come. See you in a little while."

Smith drove on. Hayduke took his iron bar and went to work on the nearest movable boulder. Down below and two miles away the four pursuing vehicles halted at the fork in the road. Insects emerged: men checking wheel tracks.

They'd be looking Hayduke's way in a second. Smith in his truck labored up the steep grade, engine whining in high rpm, cargo clattering in the steel bed. The noise flowed out, concentric waves of sound, toward the seekers under the plateau wall. There was no possibility of concealment.

Hayduke, shirtless, shoved a sandstone fulcrum against the rock he wanted to move, strained and levered. The boulder flopped onto the road, came to rest in the center of the way.

Let's try for something bigger. He dragged the bar upgrade toward a monster block of fallen cliff. After two minutes of struggle he succeeded: the boulder moved, turned, began to roll—to roll with a will all its own.

Hayduke slid down the bank, getting out of the way. The boulder rolled across the jeep trail, over the edge, and down the slope, bounding from obstacle to obstacle in a jackrabbit course toward some point of repose.

Pale faces in the shadows down yonder, looking up. But Hayduke, triumphant, was already searching for his next missile. Let them come. Let them try and come; he'd bombard their asses with a fusillade of boulders. The first rock came to a halt in the rubble at the slope's foot. He looked for the next.

The Team was coming. Four vehicles in motion, taking the left fork, the path seldom used, following Hayduke and Smith. Hayduke worked two more big rocks onto the roadway and took off for higher ground, carrying canteen in one hand, the heavy bar in the other. Heart pounding, chest laboring, his broad brown and hairy back shining under a film of sweat. Hard labor; he was not in the shape he should be. And barely beyond rifle range. That target point between his shoulder blades tingled with the old familiar cellular dread. He trotted along, searching out likely rocks. Found two more and paused long enough to hoist them off their bases and onto the roadway.

The sun dropped at last beyond the rim of the plateau. A shadow huge as the state of Connecticut crept across the heat-veiled land of rock, heart of the canyonlands. All action slowed to low-gear pace: Smith about two miles ahead, worried, anxious, looking for safety; Hayduke panting in the middle, dragging his twenty-pound cast-iron bar; Bishop Love and the Team, plus the Caterpillar operator in the yellow pickup, closing in from the rear. The Team was not stopped for long by any of Hayduke's rocks; the Caterpillar man also had a bar.

The chase proceeded, uphill, in slow motion, no shooting, some shouting, rather dull, until Hayduke reached a strategic position three switchbacks ahead and above, where he found what he'd been looking for.

It was a massive chunk of Navajo sandstone, in shape and size like a sarcophagus, nicely balanced on a natural pedestal. Breathing hard and sweating like a horse, Hayduke reached it, groped around for the best fulcrum, jammed the bar in place, put his weight on the free end, tested. The stone moved, ready to roll. He waited.

Above, out of sight, he heard Smith driving upward; a thousand feet below and three switchbacks down, the leading Blazer poked its nose around a corner. The bishop himself. In a moment the target would be in range.

All three Blazers came into view, groaning up the grade, the yellow pickup following. Hayduke pushed. The boulder creaked, tilted over, began to tumble. Though he knew he ought to run, Hayduke stayed to watch.

The boulder rolled down the talus, over the mass of debris, a clumsy but formidable object. It did not gain speed—the line of fall was not steep enough, the friction and interference too great—but it continued to descend, ponderous and single-minded as a steamroller, dislodging other big rocks as it blundered on, acquiring followers, outriders, satellites and acolytes, with the net result that not one rock but a herd of rocks came down to greet and meet the San Juan County Search and Rescue Team. (The Team, incidentally, was beyond the bounds of its proper jurisdiction, having passed the county line when it crossed the bridge over Narrow Canyon.)

The men below, stopped by another obstacle in the road, stared up the talus slope. Some took shelter behind their vehicles; others stood and dodged. Most of the rocks passed them safely by and nobody got hit. But the granddaddy rock, Hayduke's boulder, bounding straight ahead, smashed to a stop on the lead vehicle: Bishop Love's.

There was an anguished crunch of steel as the Blazer, squirting vital internal juices in all directions—oil, gas, grease, coolants, battery acids, brake fluids, windshield wash—sank and disappeared beneath the unspeakable impact, wheels spread-eagled, body crushed like a bug. The precious fluids seeped outward from the squashed remains, staining the roadway. The boulder remained in place, pinning down the carcass. At repose.

The pursuit was halted, at least by wheel; the boulder and the wreckage of Love's Blazer blocked the way of the others. Hayduke, delighted, looking down through the swirling haze of dust, saw the glint of gun metal, the flash of field glasses, the movement of men afoot.

Retreat seemed appropriate. Crouching on the inside of the road, dragging the bar, he jogged upward after the distant sounds of Smith's truck, choking with laughter all the way to the top of the mesa. Smith was waiting for him.

They sat on the rimrock, legs dangling over the edge of a 150-foot escarpment, and supervised from afar the retreat of the Search and Rescue Team. When all were gone they celebrated the victory with a pint of Jim Beam which Smith, that scandalous jack Mormon, just happened to have handy in his old kit bag. When that was half gone they cooked themselves a supper of bacon and beans. After dark they wended their way by starlight (headlights hooded to prevent aerial observation) along the rim of the Orange Cliffs, around the head of Happy Canyon, past Land's End and on to the junction with the Hanksville road.

By midnight they had reached Hanksville, half an hour later the Henry Mountains. Out in the woods somewhere they crashed for the night and slept the sleep of the just. The just plain satisfied.

10

Doc and Bonnie Go Shopping

G. B. Hartung & Sons, Mine & Engineering Supplies. Hartung's youngest boy loaded the Du Pont Straight and the Du Pont Red Cross Extra into the back of Doc's new Buick station wagon. Ten cases, waxed, sealed and stamped. Plus blaster, blasting caps, wire, safety fuse, crimping pliers and fuse lighters. A dramatic-looking cargo. Style. Class.

"Whatcha gonna do with all this, Doc?" the boy says.

"Monkey business," Doc says, signing the last of the Federal forms. "Out there on the ranch."

"Seriously."

"Pretty serious."

Abbzug scowled. "We have a mining claim," she said.

"Oh," the boy says.

"Thirty claims," Doc says.

"I hear gold is up to $180 an ounce over there in Europe. You're gonna develop your claims?"

"That's right," Doc said. "Now stick this in your mouth—I mean your pocket."

The boy glanced at the bill. "Hey, thanks a lot, Doc."

"Think nothing of it, young man."

"You come back again now, real soon."

"We will," Bonnie said. "Nosy little punk," she added as they drove away. "I was ready to bust him one in the mouth."

"Now now, he's only a kid."

"Only a kid. You see that awful pimply face? I bet he already has VD."

"That may well be. Half of them do in this state. And half of those have oral clap. We ought to staple a tag on every adolescent penis in New Mexico: 'Girls: Examine Carefully Before Inserting in Mouth.'"

"Don't be vulgar."

"Mouth organs," Doc rants on. "Spirochetes. Gonococci. *Treponema pallida.* Consider: *'Syphilis, sive Morbus Gallicus,'* a poem by one Girolamo Fracastoro, circa A.D. 1530. The hero of this metrical pastoral tragedy was a shepherd named—no kidding—Syphilis. Like many shepherds he conceived a passion for one of his flock, a ewe whose name I forget. I love ewe, anyway, said Syphilis, stuffing her hind legs into his buskins, then his pseudo-pod past her pudenda. Chancres followed quickly, then lesions. He died horribly thirty years later. Thus the origin of the common belief that syphilis began with a bang."

"I want a raise," Bonnie said.

Doc broke down into song:

> "I need no chancres to remind me
> I'm just a prisoner of lu-u-u-u-u-ve. . . ."

"You sound like you've got a chancre of the larynx."

"Throat cancer. Nothing to get alarmed about. When I was a young fella I wanted to be a sheepherder too. But I discovered I liked girls better."

"I want a transfer."

"I want a kiss."

"That'll cost you."

"How much?"

"A Baskin-Robbins ice cream cone, double-dip strawberry."

"Would you like to hear my most perverse secret sexual fantasy?"

"No."

"I want to bugger a Baskin-Robbins girl. While she's scooping out the last of the caramel nut fudge. *Before lunch.*"

"Doctor, you need a doctor."

"I need a drink. A drink a day keeps the shrink away. What's next on the list?"

"It's in your shirt pocket."

"Oh yes. Yes." Doc Sarvis scanned the paper. Bonnie guided the car through the heavy Albuquerque traffic. The smoke from his stogie streamed through the open window at his side, joining the general smog. "Rotor arms," he read, "Bosch and Eisemann, three each."

"We got those."

"Caltrops."

"We got 'em."

"Check. Powdered aluminum, ten pounds. Iron oxide flakes, ten pounds. Magnesium powder, barium peroxide, Ajax cleanser, Tampax—to the alchemist's."

"Don't know any."

"To the apothecary's shop. Down Paracelsus Way off Faustus Street just half a block from Zosimus Square, at the house of Theophrastus Bombastus von Hohenheim."

"Come on, Doc, talk American. We'll go to Walgreen's."

"Where they burnt poor Bruno on Saint Cecilia's Day."

"Skagg's Drug Store?"

They went to Skagg's, where the doctor prescribed himself a thermite suppository, then to a hardware store for the flaked and powdered metals plus ten gallons of kerosene. (For the billboard trade.) The station wagon was well loaded by now, reeking of chemicals. (Chemicals! Chemicals! sang Hayduke.) Doc bought a 20-by-30-foot camouflage net at Bob's Bargain Barn, together with other items on the list and other things they discovered they just had to have, like a flint-stick fire starter (for those rainy days), a pair of fire-engine-red elastic galluses to hold up Doc's baggy pants, a vast floppy new straw hat from Guatemala for Bonnie, and presents for Hayduke and Smith:

an insulated beer can holder and a Hohner chromatic harmonica. Doc covered their cargo with the camouflage net. Then to an engineering supplies and blueprint shop, where they bought certain key topographic maps.

"Is that everything?"

Reading the list and checking it twice. "That's it," Doc says. "Santa Claus is coming to town."

They retired from the heat and glare of the afternoon to the cool decadent gloom of a Naugahyde-padded bar. Even the walls were padded; it was like a good old-fashioned insane asylum. With Muzak. Candles flickered dimly inside little red globes. The bartender wore a red jacket and black bow tie. At four o'clock it was half filled with lawyers, architects, city-hall politicos. Exactly the kind of place that Bonnie most detested.

"What a depressing den this is," she said.

"Let's have a tall cool one and beat the rush home."

"You're not going home. You're due at the Medical Center at five."

"Right. Back to the butcher shop."

"Dr. Sarvis!" Her mock shock.

"Well sometimes that's the way I feel," he said apologetically. "Sometimes, dear girl, I wonder. . . ."

"Yes? Wonder what?"

The cocktail waitress came between them, wearing her barely there see-through flimsy, her barely anywhere expression. She too was weary of it all. She brought their drinks and floated away, Doc watching her depart. Those pale thighs I love.

"Yes?" said Bonnie.

They touched glasses. Doc peered into Bonnie's eyes.

"I love you," he lied. At the moment his mind was twenty feet elsewhere. Was a thousand miles elsewhere.

"So what else is new?"

"I hate those Yiddish locutions."

"I hate phony declarations of love."

"Phony?"

"Yes, phony. You weren't thinking about me when you said that. You were probably thinking—God only knows what you were thinking about. But it wasn't me."

"Good," he said. "Let's have a fight. What a lovely way to steady my nerves for a little meniscectomy."

"I'm glad I'm not your patient."

"Me too." He drank down half his gin and tonic. "All right, you're right. I said it pro forma. But it's true anyway. I do love you. I'd be one miserable and lonesome man without you around."

"Yeah, around. Somebody to keep your appointments straight and wash your stinking socks. Somebody to keep your foot out of your mouth and your head out of plastic bags. Somebody to chauffeur you around town and get your house cleaned up now and then and look good in the swimming pool."

"Let's get married," he said.

"That's your solution to everything."

"What's wrong with getting married?"

"I'm tired of being your flunky. You think I want to make it official?"

Doc Sarvis was a bit stymied by this one. He sipped cautiously at the remaining half of his gin and tonic. "Well then, damn it, what *do* you want?"

"I don't know."

"That's what I thought," he said. "So shut up."

"But I know what I don't want," she added.

"So does a pig, madam."

"So what's wrong with pigs? I like pigs."

"I think you're in love with George."

"Not *that* pig. No thanks."

"Smith? Old Seldom Seen, so-called?"

"Now that's a little more plausible. He's a sweet man. I like him. I think he really cares about women. But he seems to be pretty well married."

"Only three. You could be Wife Number Four."

"I think I'd rather have four husbands. And visit each once a month."

"You already have three lovers. Hayduke and Smith and poor Dr. Sarvis, M.D. Not to mention all those cats and chickens and high school dropouts and hippie degenerates that hang around that plastic igloo of yours down in Sick City."

"Those people are my friends. They are not what you would call lovers, though I don't suppose you can understand that."

"If their pricks are as limp as their spines I can understand why they're not lovers."

"You don't know anything about them."

"But I've seen them. All trying to look different in the same way. The androgynous anthropoids."

"All they want is a chance to follow their own life-style. They're trying to get back to something we all lost a long time ago."

"Wearing a headband doesn't make you an Indian. Looking like a weed doesn't make you organic."

"At least they don't do any harm. I think you're envious."

"I'm tired of people who don't do any harm. I'm tired of soft weak passive people who can't *do* anything or *make* anything. Except babies."

"You sound tired, Doc."

He hunched up his shoulders, scowled and did his George W. Hayduke imitation: "I don't like nobody," he snarled.

Bonnie smiled over her half-empty glass. "Let's get out of here. You're going to be late."

"Let's." He reached over and took her drink and finished it for her. They rose to go. "And one other thing."

"What?"

Doc pulled her close. "I love you anyway."

"That's what I really like," she said. "Ambivalent declarations of love."

"I'm also ambidextrous." He demonstrated.

"Oh, Doc . . . not here, for God's sake."

"How about . . . here? There?"

"Come *on!*" She dragged him out of the well-padded insane asylum up the steps to the sidewalk, into the scalding glare the mad roar the frantic rush of Albuquerque.

Off to the east beyond the towers of steel and glass and aluminum the mountains stood, the rough rock wall of the Sandias, transected now by an aerial tramway and topped with a spiky coronet of TV pylons. Where once bighorn sheep had patrolled the crags now the tourists played, the children potting birds with their BB guns. Westward on the bleak horizon the three volcanoes, quiescent for the time being, rose like warts, black, wrinkled, stubbed, against the haze of the afternoon.

In the parking lot he fondled her from gate to car.

"God you're horny today."

"I am a veritable unicorn of love."

She got him into the car, the bloated station wagon, jockeyed it out of their parking space and pointed it to the freeway. En route, involved with the traffic, she submitted to the caresses of his large and graceful hands, which were indeed as he had boasted each as dexterous as the other. When they reached the freeway, however, she pushed away his lower hand—the one between her thighs—and stepped on the gas.

"Not now," she said.

Doc withdrew his hand. He looked hurt.

"We'll be late," Bonnie said.

"It's only a meniscectomy," he said. "Not a cardiac arrest. What's a meniscus to come between lovers?"

She was silent.

"We are still lovers, aren't we?"

At the moment she wasn't sure. A vague oppression filled her mind, a sense of things absent, lost, yet to be found.

"We were lovers last night," he reminded her gently.

"Yes, Doc," she finally said.

He lit up another cigar. Through the first ragged shoal of smoke, expelled upon then folded over and reshaped by the contours of dashboard and windshield, he contemplated, soberly, the ramparts of the mountain beyond the smog-veiled sprawl of the city.

Bonnie put one hand on his knee for a moment, squeezed, then returned the hand to the wheel as she wove the big car skillfully in and out of the racing traffic, from lane to lane and back again, always keeping a cushion of space between her car and the fellow ahead. God damn him, why doesn't he move it or get it the hell off the road? As Hayduke would say, she thought. Doc was not going to be late but she was in a hurry. In a hurry, she realized, to be rid of him for a while.

Poor Doc; she felt, for a moment, immensely fond of him. Now that she was dropping him. Off.

He would not stay down for long. "Look at this traffic," he said. "Look at them, rolling along on their rubber tires in their two-ton entropy cars polluting the air we breathe, raping the earth to give their fat indolent rump-sprung American asses a free ride. Six percent of the world's population gulping down forty percent of the world's oil. Hogs!" he bellowed, shaking his huge fist at the passing motorists.

"What about us?" she said.

"That's who I'm talking about."

She dropped him off at the Medical Center, Neurosurgical Ward, staff entrance, then sped home via street, ramp and freeway to the "plastic igloo" in "Sick City." She would have to pick up the doctor again in five hours. I really should get that man a bicycle, she thought—but of course he wouldn't even know how to park it straight, let alone pedal it safely down a city street.

When she got home she was tense from the strain of the driving. She entered her dome and paused for a minute, looking about. All seemed in order, silent, in place, serene. *Om* sweet *om*. Her cat came up with a little whine and rubbed against her ankle, purring. She stroked him for a while, then lit a joss stick, put on her Ravi Shankar record—an evening raga—and sat down on the rug. She crossed her legs, lotus fashion, and gazed at the gleaming phonograph record as it revolved, thirty-three and a third revelations per minute, on the tireless slightly wobbling turntable. The sitar droned from the speakers, set wide and low in this room without corners. From her position on the floor the interior of the dome seemed spacious as a planetarium; the crystalline clusters on the high vault of ceiling glittered like stars. Through the polyurethane walls the late-afternoon sunlight, lucent and indirect, filled the dome with a soft, diffused and cocaine glow.

She closed her eyes, allowing the radiant light to diffuse her mind. The cat lay still between her legs. From outside, transmuted by the walls, she heard only a remote murmur, the pullulation of the city's restless hive. She closed off the sound gradually, concentrating on inner reality.

The city became unreal. Doc Sarvis peered at her still, though, from the periphery of her consciousness, like Kilroy over a fence, red nose and all. She stopped thinking about him; he became nil, null and void. The last vibrations of the freeway died in her nerves. Step by step she emptied and composed her mind, removing one by one all images stamped by the day—the shopping tour, the pimply adolescent, the strange cargo in Doc's station wagon, the way he had stared at the cocktail waitress's legs, the pointless talk, the drive to the hospital, his shambling bulk disappearing into those endless corridors of pain, the fur of the cat between her shaven calves, the sound of Shankar's sitar, the odor of the incense. All passed, faded, glided off into nothingness as she concentrated on her own, her secret, her private, her personal (cost $50) meditation word. . . .

But. A speck, an irritant, grew like a seed pearl in one corner of that cornerless consciousness. Eyes shut, nerves still, brain at rest, she saw nevertheless a thatch of sun-bleached hair, a pair of green bright jack-Mormon eyes, a nose like a buzzard's beak, beaming at her down telepathic microwaves. Behind the beak, off to one side, a finely reticulated pattern of dancing microdots resolved themselves into the image, transient but true, of a bearded bum with eyes like twin pissholes in a snowbank, confronting her.

Bonnie opened her eyes. The cat stirred lazily. She stared at the smooth-rotating record on the still-turning faintly cambered turntable—she heard the steady, languorous, mesmeric whine, twang, drone and singsong of Ravi Shankar and his Hindu zither, accompanied by the pitter-patter of little brown hands bouncing on the taut cowskin (*cow* skin?) of an Advaita-Vedantist shakti-yoga bongo drum. (Lo, the poor Hindu, he does the best he can do.)

Well, shee-it, thought Ms. Abbzug. Well Jesus jumping blue Christ, she thought. She got up. The cat writhed around her leg, purring. She kicked it, not too hard, into a pile of cushions. Holy motherfuck, Bonnie thought, I am bored. Am I bored! Her lips moved.

"I want some action," she said softly, into the quiet womb-dome.

There was no immediate reply.

Loudly, definitely, defiantly, she said, "It's time to get fucking back to work!"

11

Back to Work

It seemed wiser to leave Utah for a while. When Smith had completed his Henry Mountain trip, he and Hayduke sped west by night from Hanksville, around the west side of the mountains, and south down a dirt road along the Waterpocket Fold. Nobody lives there. They reached Burr Pass and climbed the switchbacks, fifteen hundred feet, to the top of the Fold. Halfway to the summit they found a defenseless Highway Dept. Bulldozer, Cat D-7, parked on the shoulder of the road. They paused for rest and refreshment.

It only took a few minutes. The work was developing into a smooth routine. While Smith stood watch from the top of the hill, Hayduke performed the drill perfected in Comb Wash, adding a last step: Siphon fuel from fuel tank into can; pour fuel over engine block, track carriage and operator's compartment; set machine on fire.

Smith didn't entirely approve of the last step. "That there's just likely to catch the eye of some sonofabitch up in the sky in an airy-plane," he complained.

He looked up; the kindly stars looked down. One space capsule jam-packed with astronauts and other filler material glided across the field of stars, entered earth's shadow and disappeared. One TWA jet-liner at 29,000 feet, L.A. to Chicago, passed across the southern sky, visible only by its running lights. No one else was mucking about this time of night. The nearest town was Boulder, Utah, pop. 150, thirty-five miles to the west. Nobody lived any nearer.

"Besides," Smith went on, "it don't do much good. All you're doing is burning the paint off."

"Well, shit," Hayduke gasped, too winded for debate. "Shit . . . whew! . . . I just like . . . hah! . . . to sort of . . . hah! . . . clean things up good." The pyromantic.

From within the fiery glow of the dying machine, a terminal case, came the muffled report of a small explosion. Followed by another. A fountain of sparks and gobs of burning grease lofted into the night.

Smith shrugged. "Let's get out of here."

They passed through the village of Boulder in the middle of the night. Sleepers stirred at the sound of the truck but no one saw them. They turned south and followed the ridge road between forks of the Escalante River, dropped down into the canyon, up the yonder side, among the pale domes—hundreds of feet high—of cross-bedded sandstone. The ancient dunes that turned to rock some years previous. Five miles east of the town of Escalante, Smith hung a left onto the Hole-in-the-Rock road.

"Where we going?"

"A shortcut to Glen Canyon City. We're gonna go up over the middle of the Kaiparowits Plateau."

"I didn't know there was any road up there."

"You might call it that."

The lights of drill-rig towers glimmered in the distance, far off across the uninhabited immensities of the Escalante benchlands. They passed, from time to time, familiar names on little metal signs at turn-offs along the road: Conoco, Arco, Texaco, Gulf, Exxon, Cities Service.

"The bastards are everywhere," Hayduke grumbled. "Let's go get those rigs."

"There's men out there a-workin'. Out there in the cold at four in the morning slaving away to provide us with oil and gas for this here truck so we can help sabotage the world planetary maggot-machine. Show a little gratitude."

The light of dawn found them rolling southeast under the façade of the Fifty Mile Cliffs. Hole-in-the-Rock was a dead end (for motor vehicles) but their route lay another way, up a connecting jeep trail over the plateau.

Hayduke spotted geophones along the road. "Stop!"

Smith stopped. Hayduke jumped out and tore the nearest geophone out of the dirt, along with the cable that connected it to a series. Geophones mean seismic exploration, the search for mineral deposits by means of analysis of vibration patterns—seismographs—in the subsurface rock, the vibrations created by explosive charges set off in the bottom of drill holes. Hayduke wrapped a loop of the cable around the rear bumper of the truck and got back in the cab.

"Okay." He opened a beer. "Christ, I'm hungry."

Smith drove forward. Behind them, as the cable tightened, the geophones began popping from the ground and scuttling along behind the truck, dancing in the dust. Dozens of them, expensive little instruments, ripped untimely from the earth. As they proceeded the truck yanked still more out of the ground, the whole lot.

"Soon as the sun comes up," Smith promised, "we'll fix some breakfast. Soon as we get out of the open and up in the woods."

They reached the jeep road and turned right, southward, toward the high cliffs. Hayduke saw something else. "Stop."

Reluctantly Smith stopped the truck. In the cold blue dawn they gazed across a half mile of sagebrush toward what seemed to be an unmanned drilling rig. No lights, no movement, no motor vehicles. Hayduke groped for the field glasses, found them and studied the scene.

"Seldom, there's nobody there. Nobody."

Smith looked eastward. The clouds that way were slowly turning salmon-pink. "George, we're right out in the open. If anybody comes . . ."

"Seldom, there's work to do."

"I don't like it too much here. We ain't got no cover *a*-tall."

"It's our duty."

"It's our first duty not to get ourselves strung up."

Hayduke reflected. That was true. There was truth in that statement. "But this is too beautiful to pass up. Look at that thing. A nice big jackknife oil rig and not an oilman in ten miles."

"They might come driving by most any time."

"Seldom, I *got* to do it. I'll get out here, walk over to it. You drive the truck on up into that canyon out of sight. Get breakfast started. Lots of coffee. I'll be with you in an hour."

"George—"

"I feel safer on foot anyhow. If anybody comes I hide in the sagebrush and wait for night. If I don't show up in, say, two hours, you go on up into the woods and wait for me there. Leave sign beside the road so I don't miss your turnoff. I'll take my pack."

"Well, George, goldammit . . ."

"Don't *worry*."

Hayduke got out and took his backpack containing food, water, tools, sleeping bag—all packed and ready—from the bed of the truck. From the rear bumper, looking back, he could see about half a mile and twenty thousand dollars' worth of geophones strung out in the dust, waiting for disposal.

"The geophones and that cable . . ." he said.

"I'll get rid of 'em," Smith said.

Hayduke took off through the waist-high brush. Smith drove away, dragging the oil company equipment up the road. A fine fog of dust rose into the air, floating like spun gold against the light.

Halfway to his objective Hayduke came upon the truck road leading to the drill rig. He broke into a jog, the backpack belted firmly to his hips. He was tired, hungry, overloaded with beer, sick in the stomach and light in the head, but adrenaline and excitement and a high and noble purpose kept him going.

The rig. Nobody there. He climbed the steel gangway to the drilling platform. Racks of six-inch steel pipe stood in one corner of the drill tower. The pipe tongs swung from their chains. The drill hole was empty, covered only by a steel lid which he lifted off. He looked down into the blackness of the casing. Some of these holes, he knew, went six miles into the earth's mantle, over 30,000 feet, deeper than Everest is high. He reached for the nearest loose object, a two-foot pipe wrench, and dropped it into the opening.

He bent his ear to the hole and listened. The falling wrench made a hissing noise, growing fainter as it rose in pitch toward the intensity of a scream. He imagined, involuntarily, a living creature falling down that awful pipe, feet first let us say, looking up at the dwindling point of light that meant hope and air and space and life. He did not hear or could not hear the wrench hit bottom.

Hayduke looked about for other missiles. He found wrenches, chains, drill bits, pipe fittings, nuts, bolts, crowbars, broken pipe and drill steel and dropped them all down the black hole. Whatever would fit, everything he could find, went whistling down the casing. He even took one of the hanging pipe tongs and tried to wrestle a length of drill pipe into the casing but that was too much for one man. Needed the tower man, on the little catwalk eighty feet above, to manage the other end.

Tired of dropping things, he turned his attention to the big Gardner-Denver diesel engines that powered the rotary drilling unit. He broke open the driller's toolbox, found the end wrench he needed, crawled on his back under the engines and turned the crankcase plug in each, draining the oil. Then he started the engines and let them run.

There was nothing much more he could do with his bare hands. If he had thermite he could burn the legs off the drill tower; if he had explosives he could blow it up. He had neither.

Hayduke left his signature in the sand: N E M O. He took a drink of water from his canteen and looked about. The desert world appeared empty of all human life but himself. Black-throated sparrows sang reedily in the sagebrush. The edge of the sun flamed at the rim of the Hole-in-the-Rock. Holy country; which is exactly why he had to do the work he had exactly done. Because somebody had to do it.

He walked toward the canyon and cliffs, angling toward the road that Smith had taken. (The drill-rig engines whined in the rear, dying.) As he walked he plucked sprigs of sagebrush and crushed the powdery leaves, silver-blue and gray-green, between his fingers. He loved the spicy fragrance of sage, that rare and troubling odor which evoked, in itself, the whole Southwestern world of canyon, mesa and mountainside, of charged sunlight and visionary vistas.

Okay big-foot, all right wise-ass, here's the jeep trail; now we're entering the vagina of the canyon into the womb of the plateau and where's our asshole buddy Seldom Smith?

The answer appeared around the bend after next: the tail-end geophone of a half-mile string of geophones, property of Standard Oil of California, lying in the dust and rocks. He gathered them up as he walked, following the string into a grove of jack pine to the truck. Nobody there. But the smell of cowboy coffee boiled to its rich embittered essence, the smell of frying bacon, gave away Smith's location.

"You forgot something," Hayduke said, dragging the immense tangle of cable and geophones into camp.

Smith rose from the fire. "Jesus Christ!" The bacon sizzles. The coffee smokes. "Plumb dumb forgot," he said.

They stashed the stuff in the lee of a boulder in the wash below, where the next flash flood would bury it all under tons of sand and gravel.

After breakfast, still feeling not quite immune from discovery and interrogation, they drove to the summit of the plateau, a rolling woodland of yellow pine and scrub oak, high and cool. They turned off the main road onto a dead-end side road (erasing their track with broom and bough) and lay down in the sunlight, on pine needles, indifferent to the busy ants, the scrabbling squirrels, the crested jays, the galaxies of midges dancing in the sunrays, and slept.

They rose at the crack of noon and lunched on longhorn cheese and crackers, washed down the gullet with a good cheap workingman's beer. Not Coors. On the road again, driving through the woods, they munched apples for dessert.

Hayduke, who had never been on the Kaiparowits Plateau before, who had never seen it except from below and across various canyon systems, was surprised to discover what a vast, forested, fragrant and lovely island of land it really is. However, protected only by that limber reed that supple straw that trembling twig the U.S. Department of the Interior, and coveted by several consortia of oil companies, power companies, coal companies, road builders and land developers, the Kaiparowits Plateau, like Black Mesa, like the high plains of Wyoming and Montana, faced the same attack which had devastated Appalachia.

Into other parts. The clouds passed, in phrases and paragraphs, like incomprehensible messages of troubling import, overhead across the forested ridges, above the unscaled cliffs, beyond the uninhabited fields of lonely mesas, followed by their faithful shadows flowing with effortless adaptation over each crack, crevice, crease and crag on the wrinkled skin of the Utahn earth.

"We're still in Utah?"

"That's right, pardner."

"Have another beer."

"Not till we cross that Arizona line."

The road clung to the spine of the ridge, sidewinding in sinuous loops toward the blue smokes of Smoky Mountain where deposits of coal, ignited by lightning some long-gone summer afternoon a thousand—ten thousand?—years before, smoldered beneath the surface of the mountain's shoulders.

There seemed to be no pursuit. But why should there be? They hadn't done anything wrong. So far they had done everything right.

Down on the alkali flats where only saltbush, cholla and snakeweed grew, they met a small herd of baldface cows ambling up to the higher country. Beef on the hoof, looking for trouble. What Smith liked to call "slow elk," regarding them with satisfaction as a reliable outdoor meat supply in hard times. How did they survive, these wasteland cattle? It was these cattle which had *created* the wasteland. Hayduke and Smith dallied several times to get out the old pliers and cut fence.

"You can't never go wrong cuttin' fence," Smith would say. "Especially sheep fence." (*Clunk!*) "But cow fence too. Any fence."

"Who invented barbed wire anyhow?" Hayduke asked. (*Plunk!*)

"It was a man named J. F. Glidden done it; took out his patent back in 1874."

An immediate success, that barbwire. Now the antelope die by the thousands, the bighorn sheep perish by the hundreds every winter from Alberta down to Arizona, because fencing cuts off their escape from blizzard and drought. And coyotes too, and golden eagles, and peasant soldiers on the coils of concertina wire, victims of the same fat evil the wide world over, hang dead on the barbed and tetanous steel.

"You can't never go wrong cuttin' fence," repeated Smith, warming to his task. (*Pling!*) "Always cut fence. That's the law west of the hundredth meridian. East of that don't matter none. Back there it's all lost anyhow. But west, cut fence." (*Plang!*)

They came to Glen Canyon City, pop. 45 counting dogs. The single store in town was closed and the hopeful sign now hung by one rusty nail to the doorjamb, swinging with the wind. It would soon fall. Only the café and a gasoline station remained open. Smith and Hayduke stopped to refuel.

"When you gonna get that forty-million-dollar power plant built, Pop?" Hayduke asked the old man at the pump. (Texaco, 55¢ per gallon; a rip-off at half the price.) The old man, lank of jaw and phlegmy-eyed, looked at him with distrust. Hayduke's shaggy beard full of wildlife, his wild hair, the greasy leather sombrero: enough to inspire suspicion in anyone.

"Don't exackly know yet," the old man says. "Them goldamn envirn-meddlers is a-holdin' things up."

"They won't let you degrade the quality of the fucking air, is that the trouble?"

"Why them ignorant sonsabitches. Why we got more air around here'n ary man can breathe." He waves one skinny arm at the sky. "Looky up there. More air'n you could shake your pecker at. How much you want?"

"Fill her up."

The old man wore his green and white pinstripe official Texaco uniform. An original, it appeared to have been last washed during the heavy rains of August 1972. He wore the red star of the Texas Com-

pany on the sleeve, and over the shirt pocket his name in red pip-
ing—*J. Calvin Garn*. (You can always tell a shithead by that initial
initial.) The pants drooped slack and baggy in the area of that part of
his frame where the buttocks would ordinarily be found, if you were
looking for them. Calvin seemed to have none. An old man, embittered, and no wonder—lacking hams. *You can trust your car to the
man who wears the star* but not if his ass has fallen off.

"Yeah, but maybe you oughta save some for all the people that
got to breathe that city air back east and out in California."

"Well I don't know about all that," the old man says. His
rheumy eyes leaked: gasoline fumes are getting to him. "This here's
ahr air and I reckon we know best what we want to do with it. We
don't like them outsiders from the Sahara Club tryin' to tell us what
we can do with ahr air."

"Okay, but look at it this way, Calvin. Keep your fucking air here
halfways clean and you can sell it to them city dudes by the jugful, like
pure-spring drinking water."

"We already think of that. There ain't enough money in it."

"You could put meters on their noses when they cross the state
line."

"We thunk of that but there ain't no money to it. There's the
shippin' costs and all them permits you gotta buy from the goldamn
state. You want the oil checked?"

They drove on to Wahweap Marina, across the line in Arizona,
where Hayduke had left his jeep weeks earlier. He decided now he
wanted it, especially the hardware inside. Getting it started, he followed Smith to the Glen Canyon Bridge. They parked, got out and
walked to the middle of the bridge to pray.

"Okay, God, I'm back," Seldom Seen began, on his knees, head
bowed. "It's me again, Smith, and I see you still ain't done nothing
about this here dam. Now you know as well as me that if them goddamn Government men get this dam filled up with water it's gonna
flood more canyons, suffocate more trees, drown more deer and generally ruin the neighborhood. Why that there water's gonna back right

up under Rainbow Bridge itself if you let them sonsabitches fill this dam. You gonna let them do that?"

Some tourists stopped to stare at Smith; one raised a camera. Hayduke, standing guard, put a hand on the pommel of his sheathed knife and glared. They went away. The rangerette did not appear.

"How about it, God?" Smith asked. He paused, cocking an eye upward to the sky where a procession of clouds in stately formation, like an armada of galleons, floated eastward on the prevailing winds, out of the sunrays of the west toward approaching night.

Again no immediate reply. Smith bowed his head and went on with his supplication, knees on the cold cement, the temple steeple of his brown hands pointing heavenward.

"All we need here, God, is one little *pre*-cision earthquake. Just one surgical strike. You can do it right now, right this very second; me and George here we don't mind, we'll go down with the bridge and all these innocent strangers come here from every state in the Union to admire this great work of man. How about it?"

No response, so far as eye, ear or any other sense could tell.

After another minute Smith stopped his useless Mormon mumbling and rose to his feet. He leaned on the parapet of the bridge beside Hayduke and stared at the concave immensity of the face of the dam.

After a period of meditation Hayduke spoke. "You know, Seldom," he says, "if we could just get into the heart of that motherfucker. . . ."

"That dam don't have a heart."

"Okay, if we could just get into the guts of it. If I got a haircut and a shave and put on a suit and necktie and a slide rule and a shiny new yellow hard hat like all the Reclamation engineers wear, why maybe—just maybe—I could get right down into the control center with a satchel full of good shit, TNT or something. . . ."

"You can't get in there, George. They got guards. They keep every door locked. You have to have a ID badge. They got to know you; the security is tight. And even if you made it all the way down in there, one little satchelful of dynamite ain't gonna do much good."

"I'm thinking of the control center. Maybe force our way in there. Open the diversion tunnels, let all the water out of the reservoir. Blow up the controls so they can't close the tunnels."

Smith smiled sadly. "That's a nice thought, George. But it ain't enough. They'd fill it again. Now what we really need is about three-four jumbo-size houseboats, the kind millionaires use, them sixty-five-footers. We pack them full of fertilizer and diesel fuel. Then we head down the lake toward the dam, slow and easy, in broad daylight, with your girl friend Miz Abbzug layin' around on deck in her black string bikini—"

"Yeah. The girl on the houseboat with the big tits."

"That's the idea. So it'll look natural. Then we sort of sidle up to that boom out there—you can see it from here—that's supposed to keep boats away from the dam, and we cut it. In broad daylight."

"How?"

"Goddammit, I don't know how. You're the Green Beret; cutting that boom is your job. Then we head the boats toward the dam, and when we're about the right distance we scuttle the boats and kind of let them sink down toward the base of the dam, still moving forward under the water with the momentum so they come to rest against the cement."

"And what about us? What about Bonnie and her black string bikini?"

"We'll be busy paddling our canoes to shore and unreeling the blasting wire as we go."

"In broad daylight."

"Make it two o'clock in the morning, on a stormy night. So we get ashore, we connect up the wire from all the houseboats to an electric blaster and we set off the charge."

"And the charge is tamped by a million tons of water."

"That's right, George. Good-bye and so long, Glen Canyon Dam. Welcome back Glen Canyon and the old Coloraddy River."

"Beautiful, Captain Smith."

"Thank you, George."

"It won't work."

"Prob'ly not."

They returned to their vehicles and charged up the hill to the Big Pig supermarket to replenish provisions. That done, meat and vegetables packed in ice chests, they checked in for a quick one at the nearest bar, feeling friendly, fun-loving and feisty. Nobody there but construction workers in hard hats, some truck drivers in sweaty T-shirts, a number of cowboys in salt-encrusted sombreros.

Hayduke gulped down the first shooter of Jim Beam and chased it with a schooner of Coors. Wiping his beard, he turned to face the crowd, his back to the bar, his buddy old Seldom Seen beside him facing the other way.

When the jukebox—Tennessee Ernie Ford, Engelbert Humperdinck, Hank Williams, Jr., Merle Haggard, Johnny Cash, Johnny Paycheck et al.—lapsed for a moment into silence, Hayduke spoke, addressing the patrons of the bar, loudly.

"Hello," he said. "My name's Hayduke. I'm a hippie."

Smith stiffened, staring at the mirror behind the bar.

A few of the cowboys, truck drivers and construction workers glanced at Hayduke, then returned to their quiet conversations. Hayduke ordered a second boilermaker. He drank it. When the jukebox paused between records he again spoke out. Clearly.

"My name's Hayduke," he roared, "and I'm a queer. I go barefoot in the summertime. My mother is a welfare chiseler and I want to tell you men I'm glad to be here. Because if it wasn't for men like you I'd have to work for a living myself. All *I* do is read dirty books, push dope and screw little girls."

Smith looked quickly around for the nearest exit.

Hayduke waited. There were a few smiles, a few quiet remarks, but no deep, sincere or meaningful response. The truck drivers, cowboys, construction workers, even the barmaid, each little clique in its private intercourse, ignored him. Him, George Washington Hayduke, queer hippie loudmouth.

"I was a sergeant in the Green Berets," he explained, "and I can bust the ass of any cocksucker in this room."

This announcement produced a few seconds of respectful silence, some chilly stares. Hayduke stared back, ready to go on. But again the jukebox interrupted, breaking the spell.

Smith clutched his arm. "Okay, George, you done fine. Now let's get out of here. Kind of quick."

"Well, shit," Hayduke complained. "Gotta piss first."

He turned, training his gaze on the little sign that said BULLS, next door to the COWS, found the doorknob and shut himself in the cubicle of uric light. The kidney-colored urinal yawned before him (sleepily) like a holy-water font. Pissing heartily—oh, that ecstatic release, that mystic discharge—he read the label on the two-bit vending machine bolted to the wall:

> Improve Your Personal Life!
> Embark on a *New Adventure!*
> with SAMOA!!!
> The Exotic New Prophylactic
> In Colors from the South Seas!
> Sunset Red, Midnight Black,
> Dawn Gold, Morning Blue,
> Siesta Green!
> New Freedom and Pleasure!
> Specially Lubricated!
> Colors Will Not Rub Off!
> (Help stamp out VD.)

Outside, in the sundown glare, through the roasting heat that floated in planes above the concrete and asphalt, Hayduke again complained.

Smith mollified. "It's that there *sex* revolution, George," he explained. "It's finally come to Page Arizona even. Now even them truck drivers and construction workers they can get some ass whenever they want."

"Well, shit."

"Now even cowboys can get laid."

"Shit. . . ."

"This is your car right here, George. This jeep. Don't climb in the window. Open the door."

"Door don't open." He climbed in through the window, stuck his awful head out. "I still don't like it," he said.

"That's the way it is, George. They just don't want to fight anymore. They're all saving their strength for the night shift."

"Yeah? Well, shit. Which way out of here?"

"Follow me."

"Maybe that's what *I* need."

"We'll see her tomorrow, George. Maybe we can get her to go swimming in some Navajo stockpond with her black string bikini."

"Who cares?" says Hayduke, philosopher and liar.

They shook hands once more, mountaineer's grip, heavy hand on hairy wrist in reciprocal union, integrated splice of bone, tendon, bloodline and muscle. Then off, up the street, Hayduke spinning the jeep in one complete circle on the supermarket lot before determining his course and launching south, after Smith, with a smart screech of rubber, the stylish burn of blistered asphalt.

Their way out of town led past Jesus Row, the crescent street where Page's thirteen churches stood ranged in cheek-to-cheek ecumenicism (all Christian, of course), unbroken by any check more secular than junked cars on vacant lots where drunk and abandoned Navajos lay half hidden among the weeds and shattered wine bottles.

Page, Arizona: thirteen churches, four bars. Any town with more churches than bars, that town's got a problem. That town is *asking* for trouble. And they're even trying to make Christians out of the Indians. As if the Indians weren't bad enough already.

Twenty miles from town they turned far off the highway to make camp for the night and cook their supper on the clean passionate fire of juniper coals. Alone out there on the golden plain of the Navajo desert, far from any house or hogan, they ate their beans under the soaring skywide flare of one of God's better Arizona sunsets.

Tomorrow to Betatakin for rendezvous with Doc and Bonnie. Then on to Black Mesa for a little chat with the Peabody Coal Company, the Black Mesa and Lake Powell Railroad. And then? They preferred not to speculate. They pissed, belched, farted, scratched, grunted, brushed their teeth, unrolled their bedrolls on the sandy ground and turned in for the night.

Smith was awakened past midnight, with Scorpio down and Orion rising, but muttered moans from the sack nearby. He lifted his head, peering through the starlight darkness, and saw Hayduke twitching, fumbling, heard him cry out.

"No! No! No!"

"Hey, George. . . ."

"No!"

"George. . . ."

"No! No!"

Trapped in nightmare, Hayduke trembled, moaned and fidgeted in his greasy army-surplus mummy bag. Smith, unable to reach him without crawling out of his own sack, threw a boot, hit Hayduke on the shoulder. Instantly the groaning stopped. Eyes adapting to the dim light, Smith saw the dull sheen on the barrel and cylinder of Hayduke's .357 magnum, suddenly produced from the sleeping bag. The muzzle turned toward him, seeking a target.

"George, it's me."

"Who's that?"

"Me, Smith."

"Who?"

"For chrissake, George, wake up."

Hayduke paused. "I'm awake."

"You was havin' a nightmare."

"I know."

"Put down that goddamned cannon."

"Somebody threw something."

"It was me. I tried to wake you up."

"Yeah. All right." Hayduke lowered the gun.

"Thought I was doing you a favor," Smith said.

"Yeah. Well, fuck."

"Go back to sleep."

"Yeah. Right. Only Seldom—don't wake me up that way again."

"Why not?"

"It's not safe."

"So how am I supposed to wake you up?" No immediate response from George Hayduke. "So what is the safe way?" Smith said.

Hayduke thought for a while. "There isn't any safe way."

"What?"

"There ain't any *safe* fucking way to wake me up."

"Okay," Smith said. "Next time I'll just bash you on the head with a rock."

Hayduke thought. "Yeah. That's the only safe way."

12

❧❧

The Kraken's Arm

*Reconnoitering the target, the fearless four drove down from the high-*lands of Betatakin, down from the juniper woodlands and sandstone humpbacks, to the highway at Black Mesa Junction. Ms. Abbzug at the wheel; she trusted no one else to drive Doc's extravagant new ($9955) Buick station wagon. (Some car, Doc, Smith had said. Doc shrugged: It's transportation.) They parked at the junction café—despite Bonnie's objections—for coffee and intellectual refreshment.

Abbzug thought it unwise to appear in a public place so close to the scene of their proposed project.

"We're criminals now," she says, "and we've got to start *acting* like criminals."

"That's right," Doc says, lighting up his second stogie of the day. "But George needs his chemicals."

"Shit," says Hayduke. "The main thing is just to do the fucking job and get the fuck out of here."

Bonnie stared at him across the sights of her nose and cigarette. She looked lovely that morning: fresh as a primrose, the large violet eyes bright with exuberance and good humor, her mane of hair fragrant and rich, brushed to the gloss of burnished chestnut, glowing with glints of Scots copper.

"Why," she said, impaling Hayduke the oaf on the beam of her laser stare, her casual scorn, "why is it"—blowing smoke rings into his hairy face—"that you can never speak a single complete English sentence without swearing?"

Smith laughed.

Hayduke, under the hair and sunburned hide, appeared to be blushing. His grin was awkward. "Well, shit," he said. "Fuck, I don't know. I guess . . . well, shit, if I can't swear I can't talk." A pause. "Can't hardly *think* if I can't swear."

"That's exactly what I thought," said Bonnie. "You're a verbal cripple. You use obscenities as a crutch. Obscenity is a crutch for crippled minds."

"Fuck," said Hayduke.

"Exactly."

"Fuck off."

"You see?"

"Now now," Doc said. "Peace. We have work to do, friends, and the morning is slipping by." He called the waitress, obtained the check, reached for his wallet and removed the credit card.

"Cash," muttered Hayduke. "Pay cash."

"Right," said Doc.

Outside, they made their way through throngs of hardworking genuine tourists and clusters of genuine nonworking Indians to the big black car with the California license tag. California? During the early morning, Hayduke and Bonnie had "borrowed" the front license plates from tourist automobiles from three different states and attached them (temporarily) to their own vehicles. Assuming, naturally, that the loss would not be noticed for hundreds of miles.

Bonnie driving, they went up the road to the rim of Black Mesa. From a vantage point near the road, armed with binoculars, they examined the layout of the coal transmission system.

To the east, beyond the rolling ridges on the mesa's surface, lay the ever-growing strip mines of the Peabody Coal Company. Four thousand acres, prime grazing land for sheep and cattle, had been eviscerated already; another forty thousand was under lease. (The les-

sor was the Navajo Nation, as represented by the Bureau of Indian
Affairs under the jurisdiction of the U.S. Government.) The coal was
being excavated by gigantic power shovels and dragline machines, the
largest equipped with 3600-cubic-foot buckets. The coal was trucked
a short distance to a processing depot, where it was sorted, washed
and stored, some of it loaded into a slurry line for a power plant near
Lake Mohave, Nevada, the rest onto a conveyor belt for transportation to storage towers at the railhead of the BM & LP railway, which
in turn hauled the coal eighty miles to the Navajo Power Plant near
the town of Page.

Smith and Hayduke, Abbzug and Sarvis were especially interested in the conveyor belt, which seemed to be the weakest link in the
system. It ran for nineteen miles from mine to railhead. For most of
this distance the conveyor was vulnerable, running close to the
ground, half concealed by juniper and pinyon pine, unguarded. At the
rim of the mesa it descended to the level of the highway, where it rose
again, over the highway and into the top of the four storage silos. The
belt ran on rollers, the entire apparatus powered electrically.

They sat and watched this mighty engine in motion, conveying
coal at the rate of 50,000 tons per day across the mesa and down to
the plain and up into the towers. Fifty thousand tons. Every day. For
thirty—forty—fifty years. All to feed the power plant at Page.

"I think," said Doc, "these people are serious."

"It ain't people," said Smith. "It's a mechanical animal."

"Now you've got it," Doc agreed. "We're not dealing with
human beings. We're up against the megamachine. A megalomaniacal
megamachine."

"No sweat," Hayduke said. "It's all rigged up for us. We'll use
that fucking conveyor to blow up the loading towers. Nothing could
be prettier. Look—it's so goddamned simple it makes me nervous.
We take our shit out in the woods there, close to the belt. We throw
it on the belt, light the fuse, cover it up with a little coal, let it ride up
over the road and into the tower. *Ka-blam!*"

"How do you time it?"

"That's the mathematical part. We have to figure out the speed of this thing, measure our distance from the towers, calculate how much fuse we need. Simple."

"Suppose," said Doc, "there's someone working up in those loading towers?"

"That's just a chance we'll fucking well have to take," Hayduke said.

"We'll who have to take?"

"All right, there won't be anybody up in that tower but we'll telephone the company anyway, give them maybe ten minutes to clear out. That's fair."

Silence. The slightest of zephyrs leaned upon the dried ricegrass at their feet. There was a smell on the air, a certain smell . . . a sharp metallic odor—

"I ain't sure about this," Smith said.

"I don't like it either," Hayduke said. "I'd a hell of a lot rather forget the whole thing and go fly fishing down on West Horse Creek. Let's forget Black Mesa. Let the coal company tear it up. Who cares if five years from now you can't see fifteen miles across the Grand Canyon because the air is so fucked up by these motherfucking new power plants? I'd rather be picking columbines up in the mountains above Telluride anyhow. Why the hell should we worry about it?"

"I know, but I don't like this here fooling around with explosives," Smith said. "Some folks are gonna get hurt."

"Nobody's gonna get hurt. Unless they start shooting at me."

"It's a felony and I reckon it's a Federal offense too, to blow things up. Ain't that right, Doc?"

"That is correct," Doc said. "Furthermore"—puffing steadily on his long Marsh-Wheeling, squinting through the smoke first at Hayduke then at Smith then at Hayduke—"it's unpopular. Bad public relations. Anarchy is not the answer."

"Doc's right," says Smith.

"Goddamn Mormon," Hayduke muttered. "Why don't you go back to B.Y.U. where you belong? You L.D.S. motherfucker. Latter-Day Shithead."

"You can't insult *my* religion," Smith said, grinning. "There just ain't no way to do it. Besides, what I mean is, I don't think it's a good idea. This here dynamite, I mean."

"It's dangerous," Doc said. "We may kill somebody. We may get ourselves killed. It's not good PR."

"They tried everything else," Hayduke grumbled. "They tried lawsuits, big fucking propaganda campaigns, politics."

"Who's they?"

"I mean the Hopi elders, the American Indian Movement, the Black Mesa Defense Committee, all the bleeding-heart types."

"Now hold your horses," Smith says. "I ain't saying we should quit. But I say I ain't sure we need that stuff you got in the back under them sleeping bags. I say we can de-rail the coal train with a couple of steel wedges. We can cut the fences, let the horses and sheep graze over the tracks. We can take Doc's McCulloch here and saw down the power-line poles along the railway. That'll stop it. It runs on electricity, don't it? We can saw down the power line to the strip mines; them big duckfooted ten-story draglines, they run on electricity too. Hauling those five-mile extension cords around. We can shoot a few holes in their transformers with old George's cannon, let the cooler leak out. We can throw a few logs in that conveyor belt here and there, jam it up good. I don't like dynamite. We don't need it."

"Let's take a vote," Hayduke said. "What do you say, Doc?"

"No voting," Doc said. "We're not going to have any tyranny of the majority in this organization. We proceed on the principle of unanimity. What we do we do all together or not at all. This is a brotherhood we have here, not a legislative assembly."

Hayduke looked to Bonnie for support. His last hope. Her steady eyes returned his gaze; she mashed out her cigarette, staring at him.

"I ain't saying I'm absolutely agin it," Smith went on, "I'm just saying I ain't sure."

"Shit," said Hayduke, turning back to Smith. "You're saying you're willing to commit crimes but you're not sure we should do the job right. That's what you're saying, Seldom."

"No, George, I'm saying we got to be careful about how we do it. We can't do it right if we do it wrong."

Hayduke shrugged wearily, disgusted with the argument. They listened to the steady rumble of the coal conveyor, the scream of traffic on the highway, the far-off rattle of the electrical railway. Eastward, ten miles away, the dust from the strip mines rose toward the sky, obscuring the morning sun behind an immense smudge of coal-gray and soil-brown particulates.

The pause threatened to become paralysis. So Bonnie spoke. "Men," she began, "such as you are—"

"Fucking Christ," growls Hayduke.

"—such as you are, we're in this together, for better or for worse. We've already done enough to get locked up for life if we ever got caught. Therefore I say let's get on with it. Let's use whatever we need—and whatever we have."

Smith smiled, a little sadly, at that rose-cheeked bright-eyed full-bosomed dish of delights, lost out here, forever exiled, from the far-away Bronx. With her snug-fitting blue jeans on today, those pants worn and shrunk and faded to a soft-as-flannel surface that clung like a second skin to each edible curve. Too much. The girls, thought Smith, oh them college girls, one day they wear their miniskirts and show us their groins, next day hip-huggers and show us their bellies. Goddamn, it's too much for a man to bear. Gotta get back to Bountiful. Cedar City. Green River. Back where my balls belong.

"Bonnie," he says, wrenching himself from reverie, "you mean dynamite?"

She blessed him with her sweetest smile. "Whatever you say."

Smith melted to slush. "Honey," he says, "I'm with *you* all the way. I'm all for Abbzug, A to Z."

"Okay, for chrissake," says the impatient Hayduke. "Now we're talking business. Doc?"

"Friends," says Doc, "I don't believe in majority rule. You know that. I don't believe in minority rule either. I am against all forms of government, including good government. I hold with the consensus of the community here. Whatever it may be. Wherever it may lead. So long as we follow our cardinal rule: no violence to human beings.

Note the *Verbesina enceliodes* in full bloom over there, underneath the *Juniperus osteosperma*."

"Which weed is that?" Bonnie says.

"You mean *J. monosperma*, Doc," Smith said. "Take another squint."

Doc Sarvis lowered his spectacles and took another squint. "Of course, of course. *Monosperma*. Quite right. The foliage not so bunchy. The berry large and brown."

"Let's get moving," says Hayduke, punching Bonnie, not too gently, on the shoulder.

They drove east through the scrub to have a look at the strip-mine operation. They rode in and out of washes, across more sage-brush flats, past Navajo hogans with their doorways, as per regulations, facing the morning sun; they passed through a flock of sheep attended by a small child on a horse, and on toward the cloud of dust against the light, the vast hurly-burly of great machines.

The first thing they saw were ridges of overturned earth—spoil banks in parallel formation, windrows of rock and inverted soil never again to nourish the roots of grass, bush or tree (within the likely lifetime of the sold-out, deceived and betrayed Navajo Nation).

The next thing they saw was a Euclid earthmover with cab twenty feet high bearing down on them, headlights glaring, stack belching black diesel fumes, air horn bellowing like a wounded dinosaur. At the wheel was a gut-jarred kidney-shook uprooted dirt farmer from Oklahoma or East Texas hanging for dear life to the power steering, staring at them through opaque sun goggles, a dirty respirator dangling from his neck. Bonnie took the big car off the road barely in time to save their lives.

Parking in the shade and concealment of a group of pinyon pines, the gang took a walk up the nearest knoll, armed with field glasses.

Their view from the knoll would be difficult to describe in any known terrestrial language. Bonnie thought of something like a Martian invasion, the War of the Worlds. Captain Smith was reminded of Kennecott's open-pit mine ("world's largest") near Magna, Utah. Dr. Sarvis thought of the plain of fire and of the oligarchs and oligopoly beyond: Peabody Coal only one arm of Anaconda Copper; Anaconda only a limb of United States Steel; U.S. Steel intertwined in incestuous embrace with the Pentagon, TVA, Standard Oil, General Dynamics, Dutch Shell, I. G. Farben-industrie; the whole conglomerated cartel spread out upon half the planet Earth like a global kraken, pantentacled, wall-eyed and parrot-beaked, its brain a bank of computer data centers, its blood the flow of money, its heart a radioactive dynamo, its language the technetronic monologue of number imprinted on magnetic tape.

But George Washington Hayduke, his thought was the clearest and simplest: Hayduke thought of Vietnam.

Peering through the dust, the uproar, the movement, they could make out a pit some two hundred feet deep, four hundred feet wide, a mile long, walled on one side by a seam of coal, where power shovels ten stories high, as Smith had said, gouged at the earth, ripped the fossil rock from its matrix of soil and sandstone, dumped it in ten-ton bites into the beds of haulers. Beyond the first machine, in a farther pit, they saw the top of a boom, the cables and pulley wheel of another alien invader at work, digging itself in deep, almost out of view. To the south they saw a third machine, bigger yet: it did not roll on wheels like a truck, or on endless treads like a tractor, but "walked," one foot at a time, toward its goal. The feet were a pair of steel base plates resembling pontoons, each as big as a boat, lifted first one, then the other, on eccentric gears, rotated forward, placed down and the cycle repeated. Waddling forward, ducklike, the enormous structure of powerhouse, control cabin, chassis, superstructure, crane, cables and ore bucket yawed from side to side. Like a factory walking. The machine was electrically powered; as it proceeded a separate crew of men handled its umbilicus the power line, an "extension cord" thick as a man's thigh through which throbbed the voltage driving the engines in the powerhouse—enough juice, its builders like to boast, to light a city of 90,000 humans. The cable crew, four men with truck, kept the line clear and also towed the transformer unit, mounted on an iron sledge, keeping pace with the dragline machine. Giant Earth Mover: the GEM of Arizona.

We are so small, thought Bonnie. They are so huge.

"What's that got to do with it?" Hayduke said, grinning at her, white fangs shining through the dust.

Why the brute has intuition, she thought, cheerfully surprised. Imagine. Him, intuition. Or did I say it aloud?

Back to the railway, through clouds of dust over the rolling road, they followed the stationary serpent with the peristaltic gut—the coal conveyor system, the endless belt. Hayduke watched every twist and turn, each wash, gully, gulch, ravine and draw, every copse of juniper and thicket of Gambel oak along the contraption's course, and made his plans.

The doctor was thinking: All this fantastic effort—giant machines, road networks, strip mines, conveyor belt, pipelines, slurry lines, loading towers, railway and electric train, hundred-million-dollar coal-burning power plant; ten thousand miles of high-tension towers and high-voltage power lines; the devastation of the landscape, the destruction of Indian homes and Indian grazing lands, Indian shrines and Indian burial grounds; the poisoning of the last big clean-air reservoir in the forty-eight contiguous United States, the exhaustion of precious water supplies—all that ball-breaking labor and all that backbreaking expense and all that heartbreaking insult to land and sky and human heart, for what? All that for what? Why, to light the lamps of Phoenix suburbs not yet built, to run the air conditioners of San Diego and Los Angeles, to illuminate shopping-center parking lots at two in the morning, to power aluminum plants, magnesium plants, vinyl-chloride factories and copper smelters, to charge the neon tubing that makes the meaning (all the meaning there is) of Las Vegas, Albuquerque, Tucson, Salt Lake City, the amalgamated *metropoli* of southern California, to keep alive that phosphorescent putrefying glory (all the glory there is left) called Down Town, Night Time, Wonderville, U.S.A.

They parked for a moment close to the railway line. The tracks curved off in a great arc across Navajoland toward the power plant at Page, seventy miles beyond the horizon. The rails, clamped to cement sleepers, were set on a roadbed of crushed traprock. Overhead hung a kind of high-voltage trolley line suspended from the crossarms of wooden poles. Power shovels, conveyor line, railway: each component of the system required electricity. No wonder (thought Bonnie) they had to build a whole new power plant to supply energy to the power plant which was the same power plant the power plant supplied—the wizardry of reclamation engineers!

"See what I mean?" Hayduke says. "Simple as shit. We place a charge here, a charge there, unreel a hundred yards of wire, set up the blaster, put Bonnie's little white hands on the plunger—"

"Don't talk about it," Doc said. "The sensors. . . ."

Summer tourists roared by only half a mile away in their two-ton trucks towing Airstream trailers, cabin cruisers on wheels, dune buggies, jeeps with magnum rims, or in Winnebagos with Kawasaki trail bikes bracketed astern, boats on top. . . . The foursome waved. Blue-haired ladies with slant-eyed sunglasses in sequined frames waved back, dentures gleaming.

Back at camp in Navajo National Monument, under the whispering pinyon pines, they spread out maps on the picnic table and made plans. Juniper flamed and flickered in the fireplace, keeping warm the coffeepot. Sweet and subtle fragrance of the wood, aroma of coffee, odor of something else: Hayduke smelled weed again.

He glared at Abbzug. "Throw that joint in the fire."

"You're drinking beer."

"I always drink beer. I have a high fucking tolerance for beer. It doesn't affect my judgment. Also, it's legal. All we need now is a pot bust. One of those rangers is liable to be around here any minute. You can smell that grass burning for half a mile."

Bonnie shrugged.

"Doc, don't you have any control over this woman? Make her throw that goddamned joint in the fire."

"All right all right all right already." Bonnie extinguished her little Zig-Zag on the tabletop and stashed the roach in a Tampax tube (junior size). "My God you're jumpy. What's the matter with you?"

"What's the matter with *you*?" Hayduke said.

Doc gazed thoughtfully into the evening woods. Smith pondered his fingernails. Bonnie looked down at the table.

"I'm scared," she said.

A moment of embarrassed silence.

"Well, shit, I'm scared too," Hayduke said. "That's why we got to be very very very careful."

"All right," said Dr. Sarvis. "Enough. Let's get on with the evening's program."

"Sun's going down," Smith said. "The old moon's gonna rise around midnight."

"That's the signal," Hayduke said.

Softly Doc began to sing, to the tune of "The Wearing of the Green":

> "Oh, I tell you, Sean O'Farrell,
> Get you ready quick and soon,
> For our pikes must be together
> At the rising of the moon. . . ."

"Right. Let's remember to put those blue lenses in the flashlights this time."

"What's that for?"

"Makes the flashlight beams blend with the moonlight. Not so conspicuous. Hand me that map, Doc."

Again they reviewed possible plans. Hayduke, wishing to make the most of their one clear advantage—surprise—urged what he called a Grand Slam: take out the railway, the coal train, the power shovels, the storage towers and the conveyor line all at once, all together, at the rising of the moon. Never again, he argued, a chance like this; hereafter the line will be watched and guarded, men with guns will patrol the roads, helicopters cut sign in the sky. Never again so shining an opportunity. The others demurred, advanced difficulties, suggested alternatives; Hayduke, ruthless, crushed them all.

"Look," he said, "it's simple. We mine the bridge over Kaibito Canyon. Abbzug doesn't have to sit out there by herself all night. Pressure-release mine: when the locomotive hits it—*blooeeee!* That takes out bridge, railroad and train all in one shot. Also probably the power line; if not, we get that fucker later with Doc's chain saw, like Seldom said. Meanwhile, back at the pits, I place satchel charges in the engine rooms of those draglines. *Ka-blam!* Out of commission for months. Down time, men. While I'm doing that, old Doc here and Abbzug and Smith, you guys are loading the conveyor belt with a case of Red Cross Extra and a five-minute fuse and sending it up to the towers. *Ka-rump!* Return to camp here. Stay a few days. Take the hiking tours, see Keet Seel, Betatakin. Then leave quietly. Don't attract attention. Watch out for state police disguised as Navajo hippies. Make sure you're clean. No goddamned weed in the car. Make like tourists. Abbzug, put on a dress for God's sake. Doc—well, we don't have to worry about Doc; even in bib overalls he'd look straight." (Doc frowned severely.) "Throw away that California tag. Smile sweetly at the nice cop if he stops you. Try to remember that the policeman is your friend. Be polite to the sonofabitch. We'll all meet again in a month, after the dust settles. Up in the canyon country. Important fucking work to do up there. Any questions?"

"All this violence," Doc said. "We are a law-abiding people."

"What's more American than violence?" Hayduke wanted to know. "Violence, it's as American as pizza pie."

"Chop suey," said Bonnie.

"Chile con carne."

"Bagels and lox."

"I don't like to handle dynamite," Smith said. "Who's gonna set the charge for the loading towers while you're nineteen miles east a-foolin' around with them draglines?"

"I'll fix the charge. All you and Doc have to do is load it on the belt and light the fuse. While Abbzug stands watch. Then get in the car and take off. You should be two miles away when the blast goes off, on your way back here. Just make sure that fuse is lit." Hayduke looked at them; the fire crackled quietly. Twilight again.

"George," says Doc, "you're *so* enthusiastic. You frighten me."

Hayduke grinned his barbarian grin, taking it as a compliment. "Scare myself," he said.

"Yes, and you didn't think of everything, either," Bonnie said. "How about this, Lawrence of Arizona: when—"

"Call me Rudolf the Red."

"—when do the trains run, Rudolf? How many men in the crew? What about them? And if a train hits that bridge before we carry out the rest of the plan, what then? There goes your element of surprise."

"I've done my homework. The loaded trains leave Black Mesa Junction twice a day, at 0600 hours and at 1800 hours. The dead-heads leave the Page depot at noon and midnight. So a train crosses some point on the tracks every six hours. Kaibito Canyon Bridge is about halfway between the two terminals. The loaded trains cross it sometime around 0800 and 2000 hours."

"Talk American."

"That's eight in the morning and eight in the evening. So we sit up there around eight, watch the loaded train go by and plant our mine. We have six hours before the deadhead coming back from Page hits it. We hustle back here, get everything ready, start the fireworks promptly at two in the morning, just about the time the empty train is crashing into the canyon. Three separate incidents at widely separate locations; the Feds will think it's an Indian uprising. In fact—"

"We'll blame it on the Indians," Doc said. "Everybody loves Indians, now they're domesticated. So we offer a bit of a clue here and there. Tokay bottles. Comic books. Peach brandy bottles. *Ya-ta-hay, BIA* sprayed on the bridge abutment. The media will play it up big and half a dozen Indian organizations will rush to claim the credit."

"You haven't answered all my questions," Bonnie said. "What about the men on the train?"

"Okay," says Hayduke. "Here's the part you pacifists will like best. Those coal trains are automated. There is no crew. There is nobody aboard."

A pause.

"You're quite sure of that?" Doc asks.

"I read the papers."

"You read this in a newspaper?"

"Listen, the company has been boasting about these trains for a year. Computerized. No human hand at the controls! World's first automated coal train!"

"Not even an observer on board?"

Hayduke hesitated. "Maybe they had an observer on the pilot runs," he said. "But not now. They've been operating these trains for a year without a hitch. Till we came along."

Pause.

"I don't like it," Smith said.

"Good Christ, do we have to go through all that again?"

Silence.

A poorwill began to chant, off in the gloom of the pinyon pines: *poor-will . . . poor-will . . . poor-will. . . .*

"You know what I wish," Bonnie said. "I wish I had a double-dip caramel-nut-fudge Baskin-Robbins ice cream cone right now."

"You know what I wish?" Dr. Sarvis said. "I wish—"

"Yeah yeah, we know," Bonnie said.

"Right. You guessed it. With braces on her teeth, bending over the French vanilla. Or the wild cherry."

"Nothing more predictable than a senile lecher. And so easy to recognize. Always forgetting to zip his fly."

A significant pause.

Three men, in the dark, under the picnic table, reached furtively toward the front of their pants. There followed the sound of one zipper zipping.

From the nearest occupied camping site, beyond three vacancies, came the sound clear and distinct of one ax chopping. And the bird: *poor-will. . . .*

"One other thing," says Bonnie, "and this is serious, men. And that is this: What in the fucking name of sweet motherfucking Christ is the use of blowing up a railroad bridge *and* a coal train if we're not going to be there to watch it happen? Hey? Answer me that one, you pointy-headed masterminds."

"Well put," says Dr. Sarvis.

13

Duologues

"Doc," says Seldom Seen Smith, *"what I want to know, confidentially,* is what exactly do you know about this here boy Hayduke?"

"No more than you."

"He talks rough, Doc. Wants to blow up damn near everything in sight. You think he might be one of them—what do you call 'em—agent prevaricators?"

Doc considered for a moment. "Seldom," he says, "we can trust George. He's honest." Doc paused again. "He talks the way he does because—well, because he is full of anger. George is warped but warped in the right way. We need him, Seldom."

Smith thought about these remarks. Then, embarrassed, he said, "Doc, I don't mind saying I kind of wonder about you too. You're older than the rest of us and a hell of a sight richer, and—you're a doctor. Doctors aren't supposed to act like you act."

Doc Sarvis's turn to reflect. Reflecting, he said, "Don't step on the *Cryptantha*. Spiny little bugger." He stooped for a better look. *"Arizonica?"*

"Arizonica," said Smith. They strolled on.

"But about your question: it's seeing too much insulted tissue under the microscope. All those primitive blood cells multiplying like a plague. Platelets eaten up. Young men and women in the flower of their youth, like Hayduke there, or Bonnie, bleeding to death without a wound. Acute leukemia on the rise. Lung cancer. I think the evil is in the food, in the noise, in the crowding, in the stress, in the water, in the air. I've seen too much of it, Seldom. And it's going to get a lot worse, if we let *them* carry out their plans. That's why."

"That's why you're here?"

"Precisely."

Hayduke to Abbzug: "What about Smith?"

"What about him?"

"Why is he always trying to throw a monkey wrench into my plans?"

"*Your* plans? What do you mean, *your* plans, you arrogant, pig-headed, self-centered schmuck. *Your* plans! What about the rest of us?"

"I'm not sure I trust him."

"So you don't trust him. All right, listen to me, Hayduke. He's the only decent person in this whole morbid crew. He's the *only* one *I* trust."

"What about Doc?"

"Doc is just a little boy. A complete *innocent*. He thinks he's on some kind of crusade."

Hayduke looked severe. "We are. What else is it? Why are you here, Bonnie?"

"That's the first time you ever called me by my first name."

"Bullshit."

"True. The first time."

"Well, shit, I'll try to be more careful in the future."

"Such as it is."

"Such as it fucking is."

"Still think we might be better off without that fucking girl."

"Are you crazy, George? She's the only thing makes this here goldang Communist foolery worth a grown-up man's time."

* * *

"They're both crazy, Doc."

"Now now."

"A pair of weirdos. Eccentrics. Misfits. Anachronisms. Screwballs!"

"Now now, they're good boys. A little odd but good. Captain Smith there, solid as a—stout and sturdy as a—ah, a—"

"Brick shithouse."

"Young George, all fire and passion, a good healthy psychopath."

"A Creature from the Sewage Lagoon."

"I know, I know, Bonnie. He's difficult. But we've got to be patient. We're probably the only friends he has."

"With him for a friend who needs an enema?"

"Well said. But we've got to help him understand we're not like the others."

"Yeah, I'm sure he's heard that before. And what about Captain Smith?"

"A good man. The best. Good sound American stock."

"You some kind of racist, maybe? He's a red-neck, a peasant, a Utah hillbilly."

"The best men come from the hills. Let me refine that statement: The best men, like the best wines, come from the hills."

"And a sexist, too. Where do the best women come from?"

"From God."

"Oh, shit!"

"From the Bronx. I don't know—from the bedroom and the kitchen, maybe. Who knows? Who cares? I'm tired of that ancient squabble."

"You'd better get used to it, man. We're going to be around for a while."

"Bonnie, my tough little nut, I'm glad to hear that. Better the cold and bitter world with woman than Paradise without her. Roll over."

"That's exactly what I mean."

"Roll over."

"Go to hell. Roll over yourself."

"The ass-man cometh."

"The ass-man can go take a flying leap at the moon."

"Now, Bonnie. . . ."

"Doc, you've got to change your ways."

"You mean there's another way?"

"No, that's not what I mean. Don't you ever listen to me?"

"All the time."

"What did I say?"

"Same thing you always say."

"I see. Doc, there's something I'd better tell you."

"I don't think I want to hear it."

"Seldom, you're a good fucking cook. But for chrissake do we have to have beans with every fucking meal?"

"Them beans they're basic, George. You rather have shit on a shingle? You shut up now and eat your beans."

"When they going to invent a fartless bean?"

"They're workin' on it."

"But they have everything. They have the organization and the control and the communications and the army and the police and the secret police. They have the big machines. They have the law and drugs and jails and courts and judges and prisons. They are so huge. We are so small."

"Dinosaurs. Cast-iron dinosaurs. They ain't got a fucking chance against us."

"Four of us. Four million of them, counting the Air Force. That's a contest?"

"Bonnie, you think we're alone? I'll bet—listen, I'll bet right this very minute there's guys out in the dark doing the same kind of work we're doing. All over the country, little bunches of guys in twos and threes, fighting back."

"You're talking about a well-organized national movement."

"No I'm not. No organization at all. None of us knowing anything about any other little bunch. That's why they can't stop us."

"Why don't we ever hear about it?"

"Because it's *suppressed,* that's why; they don't want the word to get around."

"The ex-Green Beret. How do we know you're not a stool pigeon, Hayduke?"

"You don't."

"Are you?"

"Maybe."

"How do you know I'm not one?"

"I've studied you."

"Suppose you're wrong?"

"That's what this knife is for."

"Would you like to kiss me?"

"Fuck yes!"

"Well?"

"Yeah?"

"What are you waiting for?"

"Well . . . shit. You're Doc's woman."

"Like hell I am. I'm my *own* woman."

"Yeah? Well, I don't know."

"Well *I* know. Now kiss me, you ugly bastard."

"Yeah? I guess not."

"Why not?"

"Have to talk to Doc about it first."

"You can go to hell, George."

"I've been there before."

"You're a coward."

"I'm a coward."

"You had your chance, Hayduke, and you blew it. Now sweat."

"Sweat? I never sweated over any woman in my life. I never knew a woman that was worth the trouble. There are some fucking things more important than women, you know."

"If it weren't for women you wouldn't even *exist.*"

"I didn't say they weren't useful. I said there are some things more important. Like guns. Like a good torque wrench. Like a winch that works."

"Good God, a whole nest of them. I'm surrounded by idiots. All three of them would-be cowboys. Nineteenth-century pigs. Eighteenth-century anachronisms. Seventeenth-century misfits. Absolutely unhip. Out of it, nowhere, just simply nowhere. You're obsolete, Hayduke."

"Like a decent valve job. Like a decent—well, I mean, like drawing trips to a pair. Like—"

"Unhip. Unhip. An old man at twenty-five."

"—like a good coon dog. Like a cabin in the woods where a man can piss off the front porch—wait a minute—where a man can piss off the front porch anytime he by God fucking well feels like it!" He stopped, unable to think of any more withering similes.

Abbzug smiled her specialty, the scornful smile.

"History has passed you by, Hayduke." With a fling of her wonderful hair she turned her back on him. Crushed and silent, he watched her walk away.

Later, crawling into his greasy fartsack under the blinking fiery stars, he thought (too late) of the right rejoinder: Today's hip is tomorrow's hype, kid.

14

Working on the Railroad

Hayduke stumbling around in the dark, blue light glimmering. "All right now, everybody up, everybody up. Drop your cocks and grab your socks. Off your ass and on your feet. . . ."

The old moon low in the west

Good God, the man *is* mad, she thought. He really *is* a psychopath.

"What time is it?" somebody mumbled—Doc, buried in his bag.

"Four by the stars," Hayduke growled. "Up, up, up. Only one hour till dawn."

She rolled over and opened her eyes. Saw Captain Smith bending above the Coleman stove, heard the encouraging sizzle of country sausage, smelled the heartening smell of cowboy coffee.

Hayduke, steaming mug in hand, was nudging Dr. Sarvis in the ribs with the toe of his iron-toed climbing boot. "Come on, Doc, get your ass in gear."

"You let him alone," she said. "I'll wake him."

Bonnie crawled out of her own sack, pulled on jeans and boots, went to the doctor close by. Wrapped in the cozy luxury of his goosedown bag (which could be zipped together with Bonnie's—but this time wasn't—to form a double bag), he seemed reluctant to arise, to face reality again. Bonnie knew why.

She opened the nylon folds of the hood of his bag. By starlight he looked at her. Those bloodshot eyes seemed dim and small without their glasses. The nose had lost its luster. But he smiled.

She kissed him softly on the lips, nuzzled his nose, nibbled at the lobe of his ear. "Doc," she murmured. "I still love you, you fool. I always will, I guess. How can I help it?"

"Every sugar needs a daddy."

Their words turned to vapor in the frosty air. His arms came out of the sack and he hugged her.

Aware of Hayduke and Smith in the background, watching, she returned the embrace, kissed him some more. "Get up, Doc," she whispered in his ear. "Can't blow up any bridges without you."

He unzipped his bag, rolled slowly out, awkward, stiff, cradling a grand erection in his hand. "A shame to let this go to waste," he said. He stood upright now, swaying a little on his hind limbs, a great bulging bear of a man in thermal underwear.

"Later," she said.

"May never get another one."

"Oh come on. Put your pants on."

"Once more into your britches, friends." He found them, pulled them on, and shambled off to urinate, barefooted on the cold sand. Bonnie sipped her coffee by the picnic table, shivering despite the sweater she wore. Hayduke and Smith were busy reloading the vehicles, rearranging baggage and cargo. The plan of the moment, it seemed, was to take both Doc's station wagon and Hayduke's jeep to the site of the objective. Smith's camper truck would remain here, loaded and locked.

Captain Smith, old Seldom Seen, appeared not quite his usual jolly self. He looked thoughtful, an expression which made him hard to recognize. But Bonnie knew him; she knew the type. Like the doctor, Smith tended to suffer from scruples. Not a useful quality in this line of work. Bonnie wanted to go close to him, as she had to Doc, and whisper comfort in his ear.

As for George Hayduke, the very sight of that shaggy ape turned her stomach. She was glad, thirty minutes later, driving off in the dark with Doc and Smith at her side, to know that Hayduke, following in his jam-packed jeep, was choking on her dust.

She glanced up now and then from her steering wheel to look at one star, bright and alone, off in the velvet purple of the southeast. Words came out of nowhere: *It is a strange courage you give me, lonely star.*

"Turn right up yonder where it says Kaibito," Smith said. She turned. They glided over the new asphalt trail at a safe and sane eighty per, leaving Hayduke in his laboring jeep far behind. Only the distant yellow blur of his diminishing headlights, seen in the rearview mirror, reminded her of his presence. Soon that too was lost. They were alone at five in the morning on a long deserted highway, rushing galley west through the dark.

We don't *have* to do this, she thought. We *could* escape that lunatic back there, return to a decent law-abiding way of life with *some* sort of future.

The wind hissed softly swiftly by; the great motorcar plowed almost silently through the edge of night, wired to and guided by the quadruple beam of its powerful lamps. Behind them, over the rim of Black Mesa, the first virescent streaks of dawn appeared, announced by slash of meteor dying into flame and vapor down across the fatal sky.

They rushed ahead on a direct collision course with trouble. The lights of the instrument panel glowing under the hood of the dash illumined three solemn, sleepy faces: Doc's face grim, she thought, bearded, red-eyed and ruby-prowed; Seldom Seen Smith's face homely honest incorrigibly bucolic; and mine of course, that *très élégant* profile, that classic loveliness which drives men right out of their gourds. Yeah, sure.

"Right again, honey, about a mile ahead," Smith mutters. "Watch out for them horses."

Horses? What horses?

Brakes. Scream of rubber. Two tons of steel, flesh, dynamite fishtailing down the pike, weaving like a shadow through a band of ponies. Startled eyes big as cueballs gleamed in the dark: painted ponies in camouflage, inbred underfed Indian horses browsing on the weeds, tin cans and rabbit brush along the road. She missed them all.

Doc sighed. Smith grinned.

"Hope I didn't scare anyone," she said.

"Hell no," Smith said. "My asshole kind of puckered up, that's all."

"You can't see those animals till you're right on top of them," she explained.

"That's right," Smith said. "Maybe that's why they have them Watch Out for Animals Next Twenty Miles signs every two miles."

"It was pretty good driving," she said.

"Damned redskin savages," Doc said. "Too cheap to string up fences. What do we pay them welfare for? You can't rely on these aborigines to do anything right."

"That's right," Smith said. "Turn there on that dirt road where it says Shonto thirty-five miles."

They followed a dirt road with a surface like a washboard. Little blue lights stretched across the horizon: the BM & LP all-electric automated railway.

Darkness still surrounded them. They could see little but the road ahead, lined with sagebrush, and a few stars and the blue lights. Something like a tunnel appeared.

"Now," says Smith, "that's the railroad. Soon as you get through that underpass hang a hard left."

She did, leaving the Shonto road for a sandy wagon trail.

"Gun it hard," Smith says. "Deep sand."

The big car groaned, gearing down automatically as the tires sank into the sand, and wallowed on, pitching and yawning across sandy hummocks, undersides rasping over the cactus and weeds of the high center.

"Good going, honey," says Smith. "Keep it going far as you can. That's right. Now, there, see that fork? Stop there, turn it around. That's where we start walking."

She did. Lights off, motor silent (smell of overheated engine in the air), they got out and stretched and saw the dawn flowing toward them, violet clouds lighting up on the east.

"Where are we?"

"About a mile from the bridge. We picked this spot the other day. The car is out of sight of the railroad here and there ain't even a hogan within five miles. Nobody out here but us kangaroo rats and whiptail lizards."

Pause. In the silence of the desert, under a sky scattered with stars and tinted with the rush of the approaching sun, they stared—three small weak frightened mortals—at one another. Still time, she thought; still time, they were all thinking. The monster not even in sight yet. Still time for sober thought, order, decorum, sanity, all things good and safe and decent for *Christ's sake!*

They gazed at each other, smiles trembling on their cold lips. Each waited for another to speak the word of sense. But no one would be first.

Dr. Sarvis smiled broadly and opened his huge arms wide. "*Abrazo, compañeros.* Come to me." They came close and he embraced both—the exiled Jew, the outcast Mormon—in his vast Episcopalian anarcho-syndicalist libertarian tentacles. "Be of good cheer," he whispered to them. "We are going to face the Power Grid and clip its claws. We are going to be heroes and live in fame."

She leaned against his wide warm chest. "Yes," she said, shaking with cold and fear, "you're goddamn right."

And Captain Smith: "Why the hell not?"

To work. Smith and Sarvis hoisted each a case of Du Pont's finest up to shoulder and trudged westward through the sand. Bonnie followed with canteen, spade, pick; on her head the Garbo hat with floppy brim.

Somewhere back in the gloom, over the dunes, came the whine of jeep in four-wheel drive. The demon, following.

He caught up to them near the bridge.

"*Ya-ta-hay hosteen!*"

Grinning like a little boy at Hallowe'en, Hayduke swept upon them. He carried the balance of the necessary equipment: electrical blasting caps, reel of wire, crimpers, blasting machine (that reliable old workhorse the Du Pont No. 50, push-down type). Staggering over the sand in the twilight of morning, he stopped as they stopped and all four stared at the primary objective.

The bridge was the basic stringer type, forty feet long, supported by steel I beams abutted in concrete, grouted into the canyon walls; below the bridge was a chasm two hundred feet deep. Down in the cold and darkness of the bottom, among the slabs of rock and over the spongy quicksand, a trickle of water shone like tin, reflecting the last of the starlight. Willows grew down there, stunted cottonwoods and clumps of grass, horsetail reeds, watercress. Nothing moved below, no sign of animal life, though the stink of sheep was unmistakable.

Beyond the bridge the railway curved out of sight through a deep cut in the ridge. From where the gang stood they could see no more than half a mile of track in either direction.

"Okay, lookouts," Hayduke said. "Bonnie, you climb up on top of that cutbank"—pointing—"on the other side. Take these binocs. Doc—"

Bonnie said, "You said the train wouldn't get here till eight."

"Aha, right, but have you thought of this? The track crew puttputting down this way on their little car, the nosy motherfuckers, checking out the line ahead of the train. Hey? To your post, lookout. Don't fall asleep. Doc, why don't you go back the other way, find a comfortable spot up there under that cedar tree. Me and Captain Smith here will do the dirty work."

"You always get to do the dirty work," Bonnie grumbled.

Hayduke smiled like a cougar. "Don't you start whining already, Abbzug. I have a special treat for you, goddammit, right here in my arms." He set the blaster on the ground.

"Why are we doing this?" someone asked, one more time. Not Doc. Not Smith.

"Don't forget your spray paint either." He shoved the cans at her.

"Why?" she asked again.

"Because," Hayduke explained, one last time, patiently. "Because somebody has to do it. That's why."

Silence. The onward rush of the sun.

Doc scrambled up his hill, leaving tracks like a snowshoe trail in the loose sand. Bonnie climbed through the right-of-way fence and went to work on the beams of the bridge with her handy spray paint, on her way across to the other side.

Hayduke and Smith listened to the morning stillness. They watched the growing flush of light on the eastern horizon. One lizard rattled through the oak brush nearby, the only sound. When both lookouts were in position and gave them the all-clear signal, Smith and Hayduke took pliers, pick, spade and bar and went to work. Having inspected the target two days before, they had a clear idea of what they meant to do.

First, they cut the fence. Then they dug out the rock ballast from beneath the crosstie nearest the bridge, on the side of the train's scheduled approach. When a hole was cleared the size of an apple box, Hayduke consulted his demolition card (GTA 5-10-9), handy little item, pocket-size, sealed in plastic, which he had liberated from Special Forces during his previous career. He reviewed the formula: one kilogram equals 2.20 pounds; we want three charges 1.25 kilograms each, let's say three pounds each charge, to be on the safe side.

"Okay, Seldom," he says, "that excavation's big enough; you dig another five ties down. I'll place the charge."

Hayduke steps off the railway, back to the sealed boxes waiting on the dune. He rips open the first case—Du Pont Straight, 60 percent nitroglycerin, velocity 18,200 feet per pound, quick-shattering action. He removes six cartridges, tube-shaped sticks eight inches long, eight ounces heavy, wrapped in paraffined paper. He makes up a primer by punching a hole in one cartridge with the handle (nonsparking) of his crimping tool, inserting a blasting cap (electrical) into the hole, and knotting the cap's leg wires. Next he tapes the six sticks together in a bundle, the primed cartridge in the center. The charge is ready. He sets it respectfully in the hole under the first crosstie, attaches a connecting wire to the leg wires (all wires insulated) and replaces the ballast, covering concealing and tamping the charge. Only the wires are exposed, coiled in their red and yellow jackets, shining on the railway bed. He tucks them under the rail for the time being, where only an observer on foot would be likely to see them.

Checks the lookouts. Bonnie stands on the skyline west of the bridge, watching the curve of the railroad off to the west and north. He looks east. Doc leans against the cedar on the summit of the cutbank, smoking his cigar, and nods reassurance. The line is clear.

Hayduke prepares the second charge, same as the first, and places it in the second hole, which Seldom Seen has now completed. They work together on the third hole, ten crossties back from the bridge.

"Why don't we just blow the bridge?" Smith says.

"We will," says Hayduke. "But bridges are tricky, take a lot of time, a lot of H.E. I thought we ought to make sure we get the train first."

"The train is coming from this side?"

"Right. Downhill from Black Mesa, loaded with coal. Eighty cars with one hundred tons each. We blast the tracks right in front of the locomotive and the whole works goes ass over tincups into the canyon, bridge or no bridge."

"All of it?"

"It should. At least we're sure of getting the engine—that's the expensive item. They'll be pissed all right, old Pacific Gas and Electric, old Arizona Public Service, they'll be mighty pissed. Our name will be shit in public power circuits."

"That's a good name in them circuits."

The sun rises, a mighty asterisk of fire. Hayduke and Smith are sweating already. Third hole completed, Hayduke tapes and places the third charge, covers and tamps it. Resting for a moment, they grin at each other, white grins in sweaty faces.

"What the hell're you grinning about, Seldom?"

"I'm just scared shitless, that's all. What the hell *you* grinning about?"

"Same thing, *compadre*. Did you hear a hoot owl hoot?"

Bonnie Abbzug's face is turned their way, arms waving. Doc Sarvis too is sounding the alarm.

"Grab the tools. Everything out of sight."

Hayduke pushes the leg wires of the third charge out of view while Smith dashes toward the dunes dragging spade and pick. Hayduke scans his work, seeking some flaw in the arrangement, but all seems properly concealed.

They scuttle for cover, lugging their tools, leaving fat footprints all over the place. Can't be helped. They lie down and wait, listening, and hear the hum and rattle of one electric track car coming down the grade. Hayduke takes a peep, sees the square yellow cab on wheels, open windows, three men sitting inside, one at the throttle eyeballing the rails ahead.

Bonnie and Doc are down behind the bushes. Bonnie, on her belly in the sand, sees the track car coming her way, slowing at the bridge, stopping in the middle of it for a moment, starting again and passing through the deep cut beneath her (sound of laughter) and on around the curve, electric sparks flying from the trolley intersections, motor whining away into the stillness, out of sight and out of hearing. Gone.

The track crew had paused on the bridge, she realized suddenly, to look at her art-nouveau graffiti on the cement of the abutment, her red and black and decorative writing on the wall. CUSTER WEARS AN ARROW SHIRT—R E D P O W E R!

She unbuttoned her sweater as the sun began to bear down, put on her smoky shades, adjusted the brim of the huge and nonchalant hat. Garbo on guard duty. She watched Hayduke come tramping out of hiding, carrying what looked like a big metal spool. Squat and powerful, he resembled more than ever an anthropoid ape. Darwin was right. Seldom Seen Smith came out with him, lean and long. Mutation; the vastness of the gene pool; the infinite variables of combination and permutation. Who, she wondered vaguely, shall father my child? She saw no likely prospects in the vicinity.

Watching Hayduke kneeling by the tracks, she saw the knife blade flashing in his hand, watched him splice and tape a connection of unsheathed wire. When the fourth set of connections was completed, Hayduke joined the free ends of the blasting-cap wires to the shooting wires, making a single-series blasting circuit. He then unreeled the lead wires away from the bridge along the rim of the canyon to a point sheltered from the blast site, under an overhang. He set the reel down and followed the wires back to the railway; as he walked he pushed the wires over the edge of the canyon rim, letting them hang there hidden from view—from the view, that is, of any eyes coming from the east. At the tracks he took the exposed wires and taped them to the web of the rail, beneath the flange, concealing them there as well.

She watched him talking with Smith; saw Smith punch Hayduke lightly in the ribs, saw them place hands on each other's shoulders like a pair of Sumo wrestlers squaring off. There was something in the way they grinned at each other, something in the way they handled each other, that irked and offended her. All men at heart, she thought—at bottom should I say?—are really queer. The way ballplayers pat one another on the fannies, running onto the field or coming out of the huddle. The Greek quarterback and the nervous center. Queer as clams. Though of course none would have the decency or honesty or nerve to admit it. And of course they really are united against women. The swine. Who needs them? She stared fondly at the two oafs below, fondling one another. A pair of clowns. Queer as abalones. At least Doc, he has some dignity. Though not much. And where was he, by the way? She looked, looked hard, and finally made him out in the shade of a tree, head drooping, falling asleep on his feet. Jesus, she thought; this criminal anarchy is boring work.

Her name lofted through the sunlight. Faces facing her. That bisyllabic tremor rippled through the air, spreading past and beyond. *Bonnie!* . . .

Hayduke, Doc and Bonnie huddled at the spool of wire. Smith was working on the bridge. Hayduke cut the leads, while Doc and Bonnie watched, separated the wires and peeled two inches of insulating plastic from each shining strand of copper.

"These fuckers," he explains, "go here." He touches them to

the two terminals on the blaster. "This little fucker"—dropping the wires aside and lifting the handle of the blaster—"goes up like this." He lifts it all the way. "When the wires are connected to the terminals and you push down hard, hard as you can—don't be afraid to hurt the machine, you can't hurt her, just go ahead and try to knock the bottom out—when you do that you send a current through the circuit and the juice sets off the caps. The caps detonate the primers and the primers detonate the charges and—well, you'll see. But you have to push that handle down *hard*. Like cranking an old-fashioned country telephone; if you don't crank hard enough you don't send out any signal." Looking at Bonnie. "You listening to me, Abbzug?"

"Yes, I'm listening, Hayduke."

"What did I say?"

"Listen, Hayduke, I have a master's degree in French literature. I'm not a high school dropout like some people here I could mention though I won't name any names even though they're in spitting distance."

"Okay, try it then." He screwed the caps off the blasting machine terminals and placed his fingertips on them. "Go ahead. Slam that handle down. Give me a charge."

Bonnie grabbed the handle and pushed it down. It clunked against the top of the wooden casing.

"I felt a tingle," Hayduke said. "A tiny tingle. Try it again. *Slam* it down. Knock the bottom out."

She pulled the handle up, took a breath and drove it down. As it crashed into the box Hayduke's hand bounced up in sharp galvanic reflex.

"That's better. I felt it that time. Okay, Bonnie, you want to be the blaster on this operation?"

"Somebody has to do it."

"Doc can stand by, check the procedure, back you up. I'll be where I can see the train coming. When the train's in the right spot I'll give you a signal, like this." He raised an arm and paused. "When I raise my arm you pull up the blaster handle. Keep your eyes on me. When I lower my arm"—he slashed it downward—"you ram that handle down. Hard!"

"Then what?"

"Then we get the hell out of here. You and Doc take the station wagon; me and Seldom'll take the jeep. We should have at least an hour before they send up airplanes, so drive like hell for an hour, then stop somewhere under a tree, wait for evening. Take the old dirt road to Shonto. We'll meet back at Betatakin tonight to celebrate the victory. Don't look up at airplanes. Pale faces show up good from the air. Take it easy, keep cool, if anybody talks to you make like tourists. Put on your Bermuda shorts, Doc."

"Haven't got any, George, but I'll try."

"And you, keep those dark goggles on. Don't let the Indians see that crazy gleam in your eye."

"Sure," Bonnie says. "Where's the bathroom?" And she disappeared over the sand dunes.

Doc looked morose, staring after her.

"What's wrong?" says Hayduke.

"Nothing."

"You look sick, Doc."

Doc smiled, shrugged. "A little black magic is leaving my life."

"You mean her? You want to talk about it now?"

"Maybe later," Doc says. He returned to his lookout station.

Hayduke joined Smith at the bridge, laboring on the east abutment with pick and shove.

"This here's slave work, George."

"I know it," says Hayduke. "We need a jackhammer and a compressor like everybody else has. Let's study this project some more."

They leaned on their tools and contemplated the job. It appeared, at the present rate of progress, that two weeks of steady work would be required to hand-dig bore holes between abutment and canyon wall. Hayduke decided to attempt a simpler if less certain tactic.

"We'll try to cut the beams," he said. "Right there at the joints. Forget the abutment, we don't have time." He glanced at his watch. "We should have half an hour left. If that train ain't early." He looked up at Doc on his lookout; all clear. And who knows how much stray current—come to think of it—is flowing through these rails? The all-electric railway. Fifty thousand volts above our heads. Ionized air. Jesus Christ. Should have used the safety fuse. But we need precise timing. Stick with the plan.

He knew he had left the lead wires shorted out, away from the blasting machine. But a child, even Bonnie Abbzug, could hook them up. Where is that girl, goddamn her?

Nerves, nerves. He climbed to the tracks and disconnected the lead wire from the leg wire, breaking the circuit. Now he felt a little better. Three human lives hanging around. Four, counting his own, if you wanted to count his own. Should have done this job himself, or with Smith only. Doc and Bonnie, those innocents, bringing them along, there was his real mistake.

Better hurry. "How much?" Smith was saying.

How much? Yeah, the I beams. About two feet high at the web. Should have figured this all out before. An inch thick. He checked his demo card: 9.0 pounds. Flanges a foot wide and about—he crawled down under the bridge and measured them with the rule printed on the card—about exactly seven-eighths inch thick. He consulted the printed table: 9.0 for the web plus 8.0 for the two flanges adds up to 17.0 pounds of TNT. For each beam. We got three beams. That's one whole case and then some, or, about—let's see, unless I've miscalculated somewhere; let's see, old Smith standing there waiting, looking worried, Doc worried, that Abbzug wench fooling around somewhere, shit, should have used a pressure release—51.0 pounds. TNT. Add 10 percent for dynamite. Straight dynamite: 56.1.

"We better bring both cases," he said.

They got them, brought them back and set them down on the concrete ledge under the bridge. Hayduke cut the sealing tape, lifted the cover from the box and opened the polyethylene liner. The cartridges, sleek and fat in their waxy red wrappings, snugly packed, 102–106 per box, looked—well, looked definitely potent. Sensitive to shock and friction, highly inflammable—Hayduke's hands trembled slightly as he removed the cartridges, in bundles, from the box. Smith opened the other box.

"Don't like this stuff, George."

"You'll get used to it," Hayduke lied.

"Ain't sure I want to."

"I don't blame you. Dangerous to get used to it. Let me fix the charges. You get the sacks out of the jeep." He counted off the dynamite sticks, thirty-four to a bunch, added five more for good luck, and taped them together.

"What sacks?"

"There're a dozen burlap sacks in the front of the jeep, under the passenger seat. We'll fill them with sand to tamp the loads with. Where's that box of caps?"

"Right here, George." Smith rose, disappeared.

Hayduke primed the center cartridge in the first bundle, tied it with a half hitch, pushed the primer back into place and taped the assembly to the inside of the first I beam, letting the leg wires dangle to the ledge. He prepared and placed the second and third charges. He linked the leg wires to the shooting wires. The circuit was again complete, all but the final connections to the blasting machine. All loads in place. Smith returned with the sacks. They filled them and tamped the charges.

"We're ready to shoot," Hayduke says.

Bonnie was coming toward them. Smith lowered his voice and said, "You sure you want to let her handle the blaster?"

Hayduke hesitated, glancing at Bonnie, before looking back at Smith. Sweating, trembling with nervous fatigue, they stared at each other. The smell of hairy armpits in the air. The smell of fear. "Seldom," he says, "call it . . . democracy."

Smith frowned. "Who?"

"Democracy. You know . . . participation. We got to let Bonnie take part."

Smith looked uncertain. Sweat glistened like grease on the pale stubble of his upper lip. "Well," he says, "I don't know. . . ."

"Complicity," Hayduke adds. "Right? We can't afford to have any innocent parties with us anymore. Right?"

Smith studies Hayduke. "You don't trust nobody, do you, pardner?"

"Not right away. Not too quickly."

Abbzug comes breezing up, hat down on her back, a halo of sunshine backlighting her mahogany hair.

"So all right," she says breezily, "let's cut the crap. There's work to be done around here."

"Where's your hat?" snarls Hayduke.

"This?" She offers the bonnet.

"Your hard hat!"

"You don't have to fly off the handle, Hayduke. What are you anyway, some kind of manic paranoid? When's the last time you saw your shrink? Bet my shrink can lick your shrink."

"Where is it?"

"I don't know."

Smith knelt by the tracks, his hand and ear on a rail. Solemn vibrations in the iron.

"There's something for sure coming, George. Right now. Something big."

A lonesome hoot owl called. They looked up to the crown of the eastern cutbank, at Dr. Sarvis silhouetted against the morning sun. Both his arms were stretched high, hands fluttering like frantic birds. The binoculars dangled from his neck, swinging in alarm. "Train!" he shouts.

"How far?" Hayduke shouts back.

Doc raises binoculars, readjusting the focus, and studies the scene to eastward. He lowers the glasses, turns again.

"About five miles," he shouts.

"Okay, come on down. You—" Hayduke says to Bonnie, "put this on your goddamn head." Giving her his own hard hat; she puts it on, it drops around her ears. "Get back to that blasting machine. But don't raise the handle till I give you the signal. And don't come out from under the overhang till I say it's safe."

She stares at him, eyes bright with panic and delight, a twitch of the cynical smile touching her lips.

"Well," he says, "what are you gaping at me for? Take off."

"All right all right *all right*, don't get excited." She dashes away along the canyon rim.

Seldom Seen meanwhile is gathering up the tools and hoisting the leftover half case of dynamite to his shoulder. The box of caps, the crimpers, the bits and pieces of wiring, the roll of tape, still lie on the concrete ledge under the bridge, against the abutment where Bonnie has sprayed, in gorgeous red with charcoal black embroidery, the legend: HOKA HEY! HOSKINNINI RIDES AGAIN!

A grim vibration in the rails, coming closer.

"Let's go."

Dr. Sarvis is still up on the hill, watching them. "Train's coming," he hollers.

"Come on down, Doc," Smith yells. "We're gonna shoot."

Doc comes lumbering down the slope, taking giant strides through the sand, his morning shadow twenty feet long, stretching freely over Gambel oak and scrubby prickly pear and other vegetable organisms. A corona of blazing light shines behind his helmeted head. Accident. He pitches face first down a dune, boots and feet confused, betrayed by—they hear the quiet curse—an innocent shrub. He struggles to his feet again, comes on, upright, dignified, unruffled by mere mishap of gravity and chance.

"*Fallugia paradoxa*," he explains, wiping sand from his glasses. "Are we ready?"

Of course they hadn't picked the proper lookout point for Hayduke. He decides to climb up to where Doc has been—quickly. Doc and Smith will join Bonnie back at the blasting machine, Smith to hitch up the shooting wires and relay signals from Hayduke, Doc to supervise Bonnie at the controls.

Under the overhang below the canyon rim, Smith catches up the lead wires and tracing them straight to the box, finds them wound and screwed down fast to the terminals.

"Holy smoke, Bonnie, you already hooked them up!"

"Of course," she says.

"Well holy Moroni, we was all three out there not ten feet from a hundred pounds of straight dynamite."

"So?"

Hayduke at the same time is scrambling up the hill, slipping and sliding in the sand, clutching at the hairy prickly pear, the thorny oak. He claws his way to the top, panting like a dog, and looks eastward through the railway cut at the broad snout the blank eyes the rumbling muzzle of locomotive two hundred yards away, coming not fast but steadily, about to pass below him and over the first three charges and onto the bridge.

He looks back in the direction of the blasting crew, sees nobody in sight. Oh, *fuck!* Then Smith emerges from around a hump of sandstone and gives him the ready signal. Hayduke nods. The automatic train advances, blind, brutal, powerful, swaying on the tracks around the bend. Electric arcs flash and crackle as the bow-type trolley, rising and falling in its spring-action frame on the hood of the engine, jumps the synapses in the power line. Behind the engine comes the main mass, eighty loaded coal cars long, rolling into the Page of history at forty-five miles an hour down the grade. Slowing for the curve. Hayduke raises his arm.

Eyes fixed on the fifteenth crosstie back from the bridge, arm upright in guillotine position, he hears, smells and feels the train passing beneath him. The ongoing engine blocks the blasting site from his view. He swings his hand and arm down, a vigorous unmistakable gesture—

And sees, at the moment his hand slaps his hip, the face of a man at an open window in the cab of the locomotive, a man looking up at him, a young man with smooth, tanned and cheery countenance, good teeth, clear eyes, wearing a billed cap and tan twill workshirt open at the neck. True to all tradition, like a brave engineer, the young man returns Hayduke's wave.

Heart shocked to a stop, brain blanked dead, Hayduke dives into earth with hands locked over skull, waits for the earth to move, shock wave to come, projectiles to flutter past his plugged ears, the cordite odors creeping up his nose; waits for the screaming to begin. Anger more than horror numbs his mind.

They *lied*, he thinks, the sons of bitches *lied!*

"What are you waiting for?"

"I can't do it," she moans.

Smith, twenty yards away and helpless, stares at them, at Bonnie stooped over the infernal machine, at Dr. Sarvis stooped over her. She clutches the uplifted handle, her knuckles blanched with strain. Her eyes are shut tightly, squeezing forth at the corner of each eyelid one jewel of a tear.

"Bonnie: push it down."

"I can't do it."

"Why not?"

"I don't know. I just can't."

Doc catches a glimpse of the engine thundering over the bridge, passing out of sight into the cut beyond, followed, with only twinkles of daylight intervening, by the unplaced monotony of dark grimy overloaded coal cars. Black dust spreads through the otherwise clean air, accompanied by the grate and grind of steel, a smell of dingy iron, the roar of industry blundering across God's sweet desert country. Doctor Sarvis feels a surge of awful wrath rise to his craw.

"Are you going to shove that thing down, Bonnie?" His voice is tense with anger.

"I just can't do it," she moans, tears trailing down her cheeks. He stands directly behind her; she feels his groin and belly pressed against her back. He reaches around her, wraps his big white sensitive surgeon's hands over her hands, gripping them fast to the handle of the blasting machine, and forcing her to bend with and beneath him, he rams the plunger through radiant resistance coils hard and deep and true—all the way!—down to the cervix into the very womb of the cushioned box:

Wham! and—

B L A M !

—he keeps it there.

Oh no, she realizes, a bit late, while chunks and fragments and splinters of fossil fuel and inorganic matter trace parabolic hyperbolas, graceful and fiery, across the blue above her head; it always was his favorite position.

Thank you, ma'am.

Hayduke, meanwhile, had waited. When nothing happened he opened his eyes and raised his head in time to see the locomotive rumble over the mined bridge, clear the far side and enter the cut, pulling its train of cars. Sighing with relief, he started to get up.

At that moment the charges went off. The train rose up from the rails, great balls of fire mushrooming under its belly. Hayduke dropped again as pieces of steel, cement, rock, coal and wire hurtled past his ears and soared into the sky. At the same time loaded coal cars, completing their jump, came back down on the broken bridge. The girders gave, the bridge sank like molten plastic and one by one the coal cars—linked like sausages—trundled over the brink, disappearing into the roar the dust the chaos of the gorge.

And on the other side of the bridge?

Trouble. Nothing but trouble. Lines down, power grounded out, the electric locomotive had come to a halt, helpless. Now it was coming back, unwillingly, with locked brakes, sliding powerless toward a multi-million-dollar disaster. Still coupled to the train, the engine was being dragged backward by the weight of the cars falling into the canyon.

Hayduke watched as the young man, the engineer, observer, monitor, whatever he was, came out the side of the cab, climbed two rungs down the steel ladder and jumped. He landed easily, running a few steps down the embankment, and came to a stop in the ditch. Hands on hips he stood and witnessed, like Hayduke, the destruction of his train.

The locomotive slid with shrieking rigid wheels to the shattered bridge, toppled and fell. Out of sight. A moment elapsed: the boom of the crash rose to the sky.

The main body of the train continued rolling down the grade, off the warped tracks, through the wreckage of the bridge to crash, car after car, repetitive as mass production, down into the pain and confusion of the chasm. Nothing could be done and none were spared. Every single car, like dreaming sheep, bumbled over the edge and vanished.

Hayduke crawled through the brush on hands and knees, rolled off the side of the dune and stumbled down the sand to his companions. He found them still at the blaster, paralyzed, stunned by the roar of smashing coal cars and the grandeur of their deed. Hayduke roused them to flight. Lugging all equipment, the four hurried to the jeep, piled in and on and rode it back to Doc's car. They split, as planned.

All the way home to camp Doc and Bonnie sang old songs, including everybody's all-time favorite, "I Been Workin' on the Railroad."

George and Seldom did the same.

15

❧❦

Rest and Relaxation

The nice ranger had a few questions. "*You folks enjoying your visit to* Navajo National Monument?" Firelight glimmered on his honest, handsome, thoroughly shaven young face. He looked as a park ranger should look: tall, slim, able, not too bright.

"Excellent," said Dr. Sarvis. "Excellent."

"Where are you people from, if I may ask?"

Doc thought quickly. "California."

"We get a lot of people from California these days. What part of California?"

"Southern part," Bonnie said.

"How about a drink, Ranger?" Dr. Sarvis said.

"Thank you sir, but I can't drink on duty. Very kind of you to offer. Noticed your car has New Mexican plates, that's why I asked. I went to school in New Mexico."

"Is that so?" Bonnie said. "My husband and I live there now."

"Your husband's a doctor?"

"Why yes, as a matter of fact he is," Bonnie said.

"Saw the caduceus on the car. I was premed myself for a while but the biochemistry was too tough for me, so I switched to wildlife management and now I'm just a park ranger."

"That's all right," said Doc, "there is a place for everyone, however humble, in the general scheme of things."

"What part of New Mexico?"

"Southern part," Bonnie said.

"I thought you said southern California, pardon me."

"I said we're *from* California. My grandfather here"—Doc frowned—"is from California. My husband is a New Mexican."

"Mexican?"

"New Mexican. We don't like racist terms. You should call them Spanish-speaking Mexicans or Americans-with-Spanish-surnames. Mexican is an insult, in New Mexico."

"A proud, sensitive people," Dr. Sarvis explained, "with a grand tradition and glorious history behind them."

"Far behind," Bonnie said.

"Your husband must be the young fellow with the beard. Driving the blue jeep with the winch on front and the Idaho plates."

Another brief pause.

"He's my brother," Bonnie said.

"Haven't seen him around today."

"He's on his way down to Baja California. Should be in Caborca by now."

The ranger fiddled with his iron-brimmed Smokey-the-Bear-style ranger hat. "Caborca's generally found in the state of Sonora." He smiled sweetly; he had straight white teeth, pink and healthy gums. The flicker of firelight danced on his firmly knotted necktie, his brass insignia, his gold-plated ranger badge, the burnished nameplate over his right breast pocket: Edwin P. Abbott, Jr.

Dr. Sarvis began to sing, softly, to the tune of "Meet Me in St. Louis, Louis," "Meet me in Caborca, Lorca. . . ."

"What happened to your other friend?" the ranger said, addressing Bonnie.

"What other friend?"

"The owner of that vehicle there." Nodding toward Smith's big pickup off in the dark nearby, barely visible in the campfire's fitful gleam. Decals removed, of course. Old Seldom Seen—where was he?

Back of beyond? Out in the outback? Loning and longing for his wives?

"Really can't say," Doc said.

"Can't say?"

"He means we don't know exactly," Bonnie said. "He said he was going for a hike somewhere and would be back in five days."

"What's his name?"

Hesitation.

"Smith," Bonnie said. "Joe Smith."

The ranger smiled again. "Of course. Joe Smith. How do you like Page?"

"Page?"

"Black Mesa?"

"Black Mesa?"

"Did you hear the news this evening?"

"Sometimes."

"How do you feel about the energy crisis?"

"Tired," Doc said. "I think I'll go to bed."

"We're against it," Bonnie said.

"I'm for it," Doc said, after a moment's thought.

"Where were you people last night?"

"Can't say," Doc said.

"We were right here by this campfire," Bonnie said. "Where were you?"

"You left kind of early this morning."

"That's right," Bonnie said. "So what? My brother wanted to get an early start and we went along to see him off, that's all. Is there any law against that?"

"Now, now," Doc said.

"I'm sorry, miss," the ranger said. "I don't mean to pry into your affairs. Just curious, that's all. Mind if I take a look inside that car of yours?"

No reply.

"What did you think of the news?" the ranger asked.

Bonnie and Doc remained silent, staring at the fire. The young ranger, still standing, still turning his big hat in his hands, stared at them.

"I mean the train, of course," the ranger said.

Doc sighed and glumly shifted his Marsh-Wheeling to the other side of his mouth. "Well . . ." he said.

"We heard about it," Bonnie said, "and we think it's deplorable."

"I've said it before and I'll say it again," Doc said. "Anarchy is not the answer."

"Answer to what?" the ranger said.

"Sir?"

"Answer to what?"

"What was the question?"

"We heard it was an automated train," Bonnie said, "so at least nobody got hurt, I suppose."

"Automated, all right," the ranger said, "but there was an observer on board. He was lucky."

"What happened?"

"According to the news there was some kind of accident at Kaibito Canyon Bridge." The ranger watched them. No response. "But of course you heard the news."

"I used to eat in an automated restaurant," Dr. Sarvis said. "That was damn risky too. I remember one Automat on Amsterdam and 114th when I was a student at Columbia. Automatic cockroaches. Big, smart, aggressive *Blattella germanica*. Frightening creatures."

"What happened to this observer?" Bonnie asked.

"You didn't hear?"

"Not exactly."

"Well, it seems part of the train crossed the bridge before the bridge collapsed. The observer had time to get out of the engine before it rolled back into the canyon. The news said the whole train, engine and eighty coal cars, ended up in the bottom of Kaibito Canyon."

"Why didn't the observer or engineer or whatever he was just step on the brakes or step on the gas or whatever you do to a train engine?"

"There wasn't any power," the ranger said. "It's an electric railway. When the bridge collapsed the power line went down with it."

"Deplorable."

"Electrocuted some sheep before they got the power shut off. Now the Indians are mad."

"At who?"

"At who? At whoever cut the fence."

Pause. The juniper crackled nicely in the fire. The night chill sank deeper. The stars burned brighter. Bonnie turned up the hood of her parka. Doc chewed on the dead stub of his stogie.

The ranger waited. When there was no reply he went on, "Of course it might have been an Indian who cut the fence."

"They are a feckless people," Doc said.

"The railroad lost two million dollars in damage, according to the radio. The power plant will have to shut down for a few weeks."

"A few weeks?"

"That's what the radio said. Till they get the bridge replaced. Of course the plant has a big stockpile of coal on hand. Mind if I have a look inside your car?"

"Only a few weeks," Bonnie mused, staring at the flames.

"You go right ahead, young man," the doctor said.

"Thank you sir."

Bonnie woke from her reverie. "What? Wait a minute. Let's see your search warrant, buddy. We got rights."

"Of course," the ranger said. "I'm only making a request." Suavely he added, "If you'd rather I didn't see what you have in there . . . ?"

"You need a search warrant. Signed by a judge."

"You seem to be familiar with these legal technicalities, miss."

"Miz to you, pal."

"Miz, pardon me. Miz who?"

"Abbzug, that's who."

"Sorry. Thought you said you were married to a Mexican."

"New Mexican, I said."

"Pancho Abbzug," Doc explained.

"You better believe it," Bonnie said.

The ranger pulled a portable battery-powered radiotelephone from the case on his belt. Where he also carried his can of Mace and a five-celled flashlight. (Not too good for the kidneys, Doc noted.) "If you wish," he said, "I'll go ahead and see about getting a warrant. Of course I'll have to detain you while we're waiting." He extended the telescoping antenna.

"Where do you get a warrant?" Doc asked.

"Since this is U.S. Government property we fall under the jurisdiction of the nearest Federal district court, which happens to be in Phoenix."

"You're going to wake up the judge?"

"He's paid forty thousand a year."

"I thought you said this was a national park," Bonnie said.

"Strictly speaking, a national monument. Like Death Valley or Organ Pipe. There's a technical difference."

"But anyway it's the property of all Americans," Bonnie said.

The ranger hesitated. "Technically speaking, that is correct."

"So," Bonnie pursued, "this place is really a people's park. And you're going to search our car in a people's park."

"It's not a people's park, it's a national park."

"You ought to be ashamed of yourself."

The ranger blushed. Then he scowled. "Well I'm sorry but I have to do my duty. Since you refuse permission to search your car I'm going to get a search warrant." He raised the walkie-talkie to his lips.

"Wait a minute," Doc said. The ranger waited. Doc said, "How long is this going to take?"

"How long?" The ranger did some computations in his head. "If they bring the warrant up by car it will take about eight—ten hours, if the judge is home. Only an hour or two if they fly it up."

"And we have to wait all that time?"

"If they bring it up tonight. You might have to wait till tomorrow."

"May I ask," said Doc, "what is the purpose of this unwarranted search?"

"Just a routine investigation, sir. Won't take a minute."

Dr. Sarvis looked at Bonnie. She looked at him. "Well, Bonnie . . . ?"

She rolled her eyes and shrugged.

"All right," Doc said. He pulled the soggy cigar butt from his mouth and sighed heavily. "Go ahead. Search the car."

"Thank you."

The ranger sheathed his radio, unsheathed his flashlight and moved briskly to the car. Bonnie followed. Doc remained slumped on his folding canvas chair by the fire, sipping at his bourbon and branch, looking forlorn.

Bonnie opened the dust-covered back door of the station wagon. A dome light went on. Cascades of red sand and floury silt dripped on the ranger's shiny boots.

"Been out on the back roads, eh?" he said. Bonnie was silent. The ranger switched on his flashlight to take a close look at the stack of boxes in the cargo compartment. Heavy, waxy, fiberboard boxes of uniform size, closely packed. He read the labeling. Then he leaned closer and read it again. Hard to mistake that famous name in its familiar oval brand. Hard not to recall the famous slogan, "Better things for better living. . . ." Hard to ignore the pertinent descriptive data clearly printed on each box: 50 lbs. . . . 60% strength . . . $1\frac{1}{2} \times 8$, etc. etc. etc. . . .

It was the ranger's turn to sigh. Again he pulled out his handy little Motorola, while Bonnie looked sullenly on.

Dr. Sarvis set down his drink and rose from his fireside chair.

"Sir!" said the ranger sharply. Doc stepped toward the darkness of the woods. "You there!"

Doc stopped, looking at him. "Yes?"

"Just stay in your chair, please. Just stay right where you were." The ranger, as noted, was armed only with Mace, and the good doctor was fifty feet away, well out of range. But the firm authority in the young man's tone made even a middle-aged delinquent like Dr. Sarvis unwilling to risk direct confrontation. He sat down. Grumbling but obedient.

The ranger, keeping one eye on the girl at his side and the other on Dr. Sarvis—no easy feat, for the ranger was between the two—talked quietly but clearly into the mike of his radio telephone. "JB-3, this is JB-5."

He released the transmission button and from the built-in speaker came a quick response: "JB-3. Go ahead."

"Need assistance at Campsite Ten, Old Campground: 10-78, 10-78."

"Ten-four, Ed. We're on the way. JB-3."

"JB-5 clear."

The ranger turned to Bonnie. An entirely different quality appeared in his voice now. "Okay, miss—"

"Miz!"

"Okay, *miz—*"

His tone sank to a snarl. There was a nasty curl to the smooth-shaven upper lip. All that metal and leather and beaver fur getting in Ranger Abbott's eyes, in his heart. Park ranger: cactus fuzz: tree pig.

He pulled the nearest of the fiberboard cases onto the tailgate. "Open that box."

"You said you just wanted to take a look inside the car."

"Open that box!"

"I object."

"You . . . open . . . that . . . box."

Doc watched in sullen gloom from his chair, the firelight playing fitfully on his nose, on the bald dome of his oversize skull. He sipped at his drink and waited for the unmasking.

Bonnie pulled the tape from the cover. Again she hesitated.

"Open it!"

She shrugged, tightened her jaw (one stray chestnut curl lay like a caress along the curve of her glowing cheek; the long dark lashes lowered) and pulled off the cover of the box.

The ranger looked inside. He saw what appeared to be an assembly of jar lids and jars. Odd. He pulled out a jar and read the label:

Death Smith Brand old fashioned Peanut Butter. Very odd. He unscrewed the lid. Inside was an oily liquid. He sniffed, inserted a finger,
drew it out covered with a rich brown oleaginous substance. "Shit,"
he muttered in disbelief.

"No, peanut butter," Bonnie said.

He wiped his finger on the box.

"Taste it," Bonnie said. "You'll like it."

He clapped the jar shut and rammed it back. "Open the next
box," he snarled.

Bonnie opened the next, taking her time. And the next. Two
more rangers drove up. She opened them all, while Ranger Abbott
and his reinforcements stood by and watched, grim and silent. She
showed them her peanut butter, her baked beans, her Green Giant
Sweet Kernel Corn, her Aunt Jemima pancake mix, her tinned tuna,
her pinto beans, her baby clams, her Karo syrup, her tinned oysters
and kippered herring, her bags of sugar and flour, her cooking utensils
and her toiletries, her flower books and cookbooks and personally
autographed extremely valuable first-edition copy of *Desert Solipsism*,
her sweet bikini panties and Doc's foul socks, etc. etc., all neatly
packed and stowed in the handy, compact, strong and durable fiberboard dynamite boxes.

"Where'd you get these boxes?" the chief ranger demanded.

"You let her alone," said Doc from the fire, feebly.

"You shut up. Where'd you get them, girl?"

"We found them by your garbage can," Bonnie said, "right
there." And she pointed vaguely, with uncertain hand, toward several
badly littered but vacant campsites nearby.

The rangers looked at one another in wild surmise.

"It *was* them," the chief said and snapped his fingers. "Them
goddamn crazy Shoeshine Indians."

"You mean Shoshone—?"

"Shoshone, right, those long-haired bastards. Let's get going.
Ed, you call the SO, me and Jeff'll get ahold of DPS." The three men
hustled off into the night toward their patrol vehicles, talking fast and
low. Something about AIM, the Crazy Dogs, the Shoeshine Tribe and

the Reconstituted Native American Church of Latter-Day Shinola-
heads.

"Red Power!" Bonnie shouted after them, raising her clenched
fist above the peanut butter, but the rangers, roaring off in all directions, never heard.

A pause. . . .

Two rough fellows emerged from the shadows wearing dusty
clothes, adorned with sheepish grins, whiskers, holding beer cans.

"They gone now?" says old Seldom Seen.

"They're gone," Bonnie says.

"Took you long enough," says Hayduke.

16

✣

Saturday Night in America

Time for logistical maneuvering. All agreed (including Doc) that Doc should return to Albuquerque and tend his patients for a while, cash their checks (the patients' checks) and replenish the supply column.

Bonnie didn't want to go back to the office and who could blame her? She wanted to stay with Smith and Hayduke for the next adventure. Whatever it might be.

But Doc cannot drive a car, or pretends he cannot, or is at any rate unwilling to drive a car. It was necessary, therefore, to drive him to the nearest airport—Page, in this case—for the flight back to New Mexico. He left reluctantly, grumbling, drinking too much, eyes wet with sentiment, embracing his three comrades each in turn, Smith first.

"Smith," he says, "old Seldom Seen, I'm counting on you to look after these children. They're both crazy, you know, and innocent and absolutely helpless. You're the grown-up in this *ménage*. Take care of them."

Smith pats Doc on the back. "We'll do all right, Doc. Don't you worry none."

"Try to keep George from getting himself killed."

"I'll do that, pardner."

"Keep a sharp eye on Bonnie too. I think she's catching Hayduke's Disease."

"I'll keep *both* eyes on her, never you fear."

"Good man. Remember this: Though the way is hard, the hard is the way. Our cause is just (just one damn thing after another) and God's on our side. Or vice versa. We're up against a *mad machine*, Seldom, which mangles mountains and devours men. Somebody has to try and stop it. That's us. Especially you."

"You bet, Doc. You make some money now and hurry back." Smith grinned. "Don't forget the houseboats and the trained dolphins."

"My God," says Doc, "you're all crazy. Next!"

George Washington Hayduke, *muy hombre, muy macho pendejo*, steps forward. Dr. Sarvis draws him somewhat away from the others. "George," he says, "step aside here for a minute."

"It's all right, Doc, I know what you're going to say." Hayduke, burly as a beer barrel, reeking of sweat and dust and beer as always, looks almost . . . well, anxious. "Listen, Doc—"

"No, you listen to me."

"No, listen, this wasn't my idea. I never wanted her to come in the first place. She's nothing but trouble."

Doc smiled, his arm around Hayduke's brawny shoulders. Like hugging a linebacker. The bear and the buffalo, buffaloed. "George," he says, "listen carefully. I am forty-nine and a half years old. Over the hill. Bonnie knows it. You take her. It's your turn."

"I don't want her."

"Don't lie to me, George. Take her. If you can, that is. If you're man enough. Take her and my blessings on you both. Don't give me any argument."

Hayduke stared at the ground, silent for a moment, actually embarrassed. "Old Seldom, he's the one really wants her."

"Smith has a head on his shoulders. He's a man of taste and good sense. Not a fool like you. Let him take her then. Make a real ass of yourself."

Hayduke flushed. "I'm sure as hell not going to fight over her. I got more interesting things to do than that."

"There's nothing more interesting than a woman, George. Not in this world."

They marched around again in a second small circle while Doc's plane had its fuel tanks topped, turbochargers checked, tail stitched up and ailerons wired back on.

The Arizona summer sun blazed down on them all—airport, power plant, airplane, the citizens of Page, the passengers, parked cars, bystanders and loafers, and of them all the fairest that it shone upon by far was Ms. B. Abbzug.

Doc Sarvis, he knew; he knew the meaning of such a treasure. Why, any man of sane natural piety would get on his knees before that holy shrine, whimpering like a sick hound, and lick the tips of her ten pink toes with the abject slathering adoration of his tongue.

Smith knew; he was melting like a popsicle. Just like his daddy always said, you could eat that with a spoon. The Indians knew, lounging in the shade, watching her like hungry rabbits, laughing, telling their Pleistocene jokes (the best kind). Only Hayduke, stubborn and stupid, seemed oblivious to the Higher Knowledge.

"All right," Doc said. "Everything is settled. I'll say good-bye to Bonnie now."

She cried, a little.

"Now now, sweetheart, you're losing your mascara. Don't cry." He'd have been pained if she didn't, of course. He stroked her hair, the sweet curve of buttock and flank. The Indians giggled. To hell with *them*—Stone Age savages riding around in pickup trucks, eating Rainbo Bread and Hostess Twinkies, wearing bolo ties, their TVs tuned to *Mister Rogers' Neighborhood* every fucking afternoon.

"I'm not crying," she said, her tears soaking into Doc's smart new chamois vest.

"I'll be back in a couple of weeks," he said. "You look after those idiots, make sure they get their vitamin pellets and brush their teeth after every meal. Don't let George drink himself to death. See that Seldom Seen gets back to his wives now and then."

"Of course, Doc." She sobbed between his lapels, her bosom pressed against his stately paunch.

"Be careful. Never tell George you needed help with the blaster. He doesn't know. Make those maniacs exercise some restraint. Don't cry, darling. I love you. Are you listening to me?"

She nodded within his arms, still crying.

"Okay. Stay out of trouble until I get back. Do your work but make sure nobody gets hurt. And make sure you don't get caught."

She nodded. The pilot revved his engines. The shattering roar surged out in waves to Tower Butte, Vermilion Cliffs, Lone Rock and back, an insane clatter of lunatic pistons. Passengers were filing out the gate: cowboys with briefcases; rich hippies more beaded and banded than Ute or Paiute, on their way to the banks of the Ganges to find a new guru; U.S. Bureau of Wrecklamation officials with heads like turnips and eyes like pellets of rat poison, clutching snap-brims through the backwash of the props; sweet little old ladies in shawls bound for Phoenix to baby-sit the kids (Phoebe Sue's getting a divorce again)—half of Page, it seemed that day, was bound for elsewhere and who could blame them? Any town with more Baptists than Indians. With more beer drinkers than winos. With more motorboats than birchbark canoes. With more sunshine than sensibility. . . .

"Better go now."

He kissed her tear-streaked face, the fragrant mouth, the heavy lashes of her closed eyes.

"Doc . . . ?"

"Yes . . . ?"

"Still love you, Doc, you know. . . ."

"Sure, Bonnie. . . ."

"See you. . . ."

"Sure. . . ."

Dr. Sarvis, satchel, newspaper and topcoat in hand, hurries for the gangway, fumbling for his ticket as he goes. He pauses, theatrically, at the top of the steps, turning to wave—not farewell but so long for now—to his friends and comrades. Bonnie, leaning against

Seldom Seen's thin frame, dabs at her cheeks with a red bandanna and waves back.

They watched the plane go rumbling down the runway, engines howling like beasts in pain, saw airfoils work their magic one more time, the wheels rise from asphalt and fold into the nest of the wings as the awkward tin bird lurched over the power line beyond (barely clearing it) and rose and banked toward the blind stare of the sun.

Feeling vaguely amputated, they retired for consultation to the dim recesses of a familiar Page bar. Happy hour: the dive was full of thirsty men, including a table ringed with six leather-faced cowboys and their bouffant girl friends. Bonnie slipped a quarter into the jukebox, picked her favorites—first some *nouveau-riche* hard rock band from England. This was patiently endured. Then followed another rock group, surmounted by the hysteric stridulations of an imitation-Afro female vocalist, one Janis Joplin of martyred memory. Too much. The nearest cowboy rose to his feet—about six foot eight, he took some time to unlimber his full height—and walked on legs like calipers to the jukebox and kicked it, hard, and when this didn't work he kicked it again, harder. That worked. The needle slid crosswise against the groovy grain of the vinyl disc; a hideous squawk electronically amplified snaked like aural lightning through the ears, brains and central nervous systems of everybody present. Strong men cringed. The juke's reflexes, activated, moved swiftly into automatic servomechanism: the retrieval arm grasped the hated record and filed it back in the mute rack. As the cowboy slid another quarter in, there was a moment of that golden stuff, silence.

Only a moment.

"Hey!" yelled Bonnie Abbzug in her rawest Bronx snarl, "that was my record you kicked, you bowlegged sonofabitch."

Politely the cowboy ignored her. Calmly scanning the console, he pushed the Merle Haggard button, the Hank Snow button and (good God!) the Andy Williams button. He shoved another quarter in.

Bonnie jumped up. "You get my Janis back on there!" Ignoring her, the cowboy searched for three more selections. Bonnie leaned on him, tried to shoulder him aside. He gave her a shove.

Hayduke rose, three shooters of Beam and a quart of Coors gurgling in his gut. He felt the moment had come. Rising to his full five foot eight he reached up and tapped the cowboy on the shoulder. The cowboy turned.

"Hi," said Hayduke, grinning. "I'm a hippie." He swung for the stomach; the cowboy staggered back against the wall. Hayduke faced the five other cowboys (and their heifers) at the table. They were rising too, all smiles. He began his number.

"My name's Hayduke," he roared, "George Hayduke, and I'm happy to be here. I hear that sex revolution has finally come to Page Arizona, Shithead Capital of Coconino County. All I want to say is it's high fucking time. Why I hear even cowboys can get laid now. I hear—"

Well. Shit. Wrong cowboys this time.

Hayduke came back, gradually, painfully, through dreams and memories, a maze of nightmares and hallucinations in the middle of a roaring headache, to find himself in what appeared to be (good Christ!) a motel room. With gentle hands on his head and face, swabbing his wounds with a warm wet cloth. Her face, sweet and lovely as an angel's, gazed down at him through his pink mist of hurt and pain. . . .

"Idiot," she seemed to be saying, "you could have got yourself killed. There were six of them, only three of us."

Three who? Six of what?

"Poor old Seldom," Bonnie went on, "nearly got himself beaten up getting you out of there. They wanted to kill him too."

Who? He tried to rise. She leaned on him, pushed him back into the pillows.

"Relax, I'm not finished." She picked glass from the gash in his scalp. "We'll have to get this sewed up."

"Where's Seldom?" he croaked.

"In the bathroom soaking his bruises. He's all right, don't worry about him. You're the one got the worse of it. They mashed your head against the corner of the jukebox."

Jukebox? Jukebox. . . . Ahhhhh, now he began to remember. The Janis Jalopy record. A bit of a scuffle in a bar. Cowboys ten feet tall with eyes like falcons looming over him. Yeah. The wrong cowboys. About eighteen of them, maybe forty. All over the joint.

Seldom Seen Smith emerged from the bath, a towel wrapped around his lean torso, on what he called his face a crooked grin, one purple eyelid and an apparent deviated septum. Nostrils packed with blood-soaked cotton. Walking out on his extenuated legs he looked, more than ever, like some kind of bird—a talking buzzard, maybe, a blond vulture from the canyon rims.

"What's on the Monday Night Movie?" he says, turning on the television.

"The Saturday Night Movie," Bonnie says.

They spent the evening there in the stucco box of the Shady Rest Motel, an elderly economy lodge (no pool) but Page's pride. The air cooler rumbled, the TV maundered on and on. Smith stitched up Hayduke's scalp wound and taped on a bandage compress. He and Bonnie dressed the lesser wounds, then helped Hayduke into a warm bath. Smith went out for beer and food. Bonnie bathed Hayduke with tender hands and when his penis rose up in majesty, as it surely did, she caressed it with loving fingers, praised it with generous words. He was recovering rapidly. Hayduke knew, despite his battered stupor, that he had been chosen. Nothing he could do about it now. Beaten but grateful, he surrendered.

Smith returned. They ate. A tactful man, Smith withdrew when the movie was over, went out into the desert with his truck and bedroll, slept under the stars, on the sand with tarantulas and sidewinders for company, and dreamed no doubt of his neglected wives.

Abbzug and Hayduke, alone at last, crashed into one another like boxcars coupling in a railway yard. No one kept score that night but the rickety motel bed rocked on its legs and clattered against the wall more times than strictly seemly; the sound of Bonnie's cries and outcries rang out through the dark at unpredictable but frequent intervals, causing unfavorable comment in adjoining rooms.

Late next morning, at checkout time, after a grand finale, one replete the other depleted, they lay limp as kelp on a wet beach and listened for quite some time, before answering, to the gentle rapping of Smith's knuckles on the hollow-core plywood door. That door where the printed notice hung, tacked in a frame.

NOTICE

Check Out Time 10 A.M.
All Contents This Room
Were Itemized and Counted
Before Rental to You.
Your Name, Address &
License Number Will Be
Retained in Our Permanent
Files. Enjoy Your Stay
And—*COME AGAIN!*
    The Mgmt.
    Shady Rest Motel

17

❧❧

The American Logging Industry: Plans and Problems

He said he was going home for a while. He said he had thought about it a lot during the night and decided he really should visit wives and kids, sort his mail and other business and reschedule some boat trips down the Green before rejoining them. Besides, he was afraid that Bishop Love and the Search and Rescue Team would still be on the watch for him in San Juan and Garfield counties. He asked Abbzug and Hayduke to delay the next operation for at least a week.

The three had breakfast together in Mom's Café. An economy eatery (nothing fit to eat) and one of Page's finest. They drank the chlorinated orange "drink," ate the premixed frozen glue-and-cotton pancakes and the sodium-nitrate sodium-nitrite sausages and drank the carbolic coffee. Typical Page breakfast, they agreed, and "not half bad." It was all bad. They agreed as well on the contents of the near future.

Smith would make his four-hundred-mile all-Utah conjugal rounds, fulfilling his domestic obligations. Then they would reunite for the projected attack upon the Utah State Highway Department and its latest works.

And Bonnie and George? Well, George admitted he had plans for a premature premarital honeymoon in the cool high North Rim forests above Grand Canyon, a declivity of sorts which Bonnie wished to check out from above. Also, he wanted to investigate current activities of the U.S. Forest Service and the logging companies on the Kaibab Plateau.

The men locked wrists, à la Mallory and Irvine on Everest '24. Bonnie embraced Smith. They parted, Smith in his truck bound for Cedar City, Bountiful and Green River, George and Bonnie in the jeep driving from Page toward the Echo Cliffs, Marble Canyon and points beyond.

Bonnie remembered the last time she had been this way, headed for Lee's Ferry and the now historic river trip down through the Canyon. How could she forget the bearded bum on the beach? the rapids? the campfire conspiracy which had thickened from day to day, night after night, down there in the earth's Precambrian bowels, all the way from Lee's Ferry to Temple Bar? On the beach near Separation Wash the men swore to one another the pledge of eternal comradeship, sealing the oath with bourbon and with blood drawn by the nick of Hayduke's Buck knife from their outstretched palms. Bonnie, aloof in the empyrean of her weed, smiled at the ceremony but was tacitly included nonetheless. By campfire under midnight stars three thousand feet below the rim of the Shivwits Plateau the Monkey Wrench Gang was born. . . .

The lovers dropped through the notch, hung a hard right at Bitter Springs, sped north through the edge of Good-bye Come Again Navajoland to Marble Canyon Bridge ("this one, too, someday," Hayduke mused) and across into the Arizona Strip. Westward they raced in Hayduke's jeep, under the face of Paria Plateau and the Vermilion Cliffs, past Cliff Dwellers Lodge into Houserock Valley, through the red inferno of stone and heat waves, past the gateway to Buffalo Ranch and up the limestone bulk (like a beached whale on the desert plain) of the East Kaibab Monocline. Here the jeep climbed, laboring upward four thousand feet to the yellow pine and grassy meadows of Kaibab National Forest.

They paused like all good tourists at Jacob Lake for gasoline, for coffee and pie and take-out beer. The air was clean and sweet with the smell of sunshine, pine tars and grama grass, cool despite the awful desert heat waiting below. The translucent leaves of the aspen shimmered in the light, the slim white-barked trunks of this tree so ladylike against the dark background of conifers.

At Jacob Lake they turned south on the road which dead-ends at the North Rim of Grand Canyon. Bonnie had love and scenery and a cabin in the pines in mind; Hayduke, also a romantic and a dreamer, thought mostly of masochistic machinery, steel in pain, iron under unnatural duress, the multiple images of what he called "creative destruction." One way or another they were going to slow if not halt the advance of Technocracy, the growth of Growth, the spread of the ideology of the cancer cell. "I have sworn upon the altar of God," Hayduke bellows into the roaring wind (for the jeep's rag top is down), and he blinks, trying to remember Jefferson's words, "eternal hostility against *every fucking form of tyranny*"—getting it slightly wrong but absolutely right—"over the life of man."

"What about the life of woman?" screams Abbzug.

"Fuck woman," hollers Hayduke joyfully. And come to think of it—"And come to think of it," he adds, turning off the highway down a rare little lane into the woods, under the pines and tinkling aspens, out of sight of the road to the edge of a sunny meadow dappled with cow dung, "let's!"

He stopped the jeep, shut off the engine, grabbed her and dragged her down to the grass. She resisted manfully, clawing at his hair, tearing his shirt, trying to get her knee between his legs.

"You bitch," he snarls, "I'm going to fuck you."

"Yeah," she says, "you try it you degenerate bastard."

They rolled over and over on the cow-cropped meadow grass, over the fallen leaves, the pine needles, the neurotic and panicked ants.

She almost escaped. He tackled her, pulled her down again, crushed her in his big arms, buried his eyes his mouth his face in the fragrance of her hair, bit her on the nape of the neck, drawing blood, nibbled on the lobe of her ear. . . .

"Fucking fat Jewish bitch."

"You red-neck honky uncircumcised swine of a goy."

"Fucking bitch."

"High school dropout. Verbal paraplegic. Unemployed veteran."

"I want it."

"No good at Scrabble."

"Right now!"

"All right. So all right." But she was on top. "Your head's in a pile of cowshit, you know. You don't care. Of course not. All right. Okay. Where is it? Can't find it. This? You mean *this*? Hello, Mom, is that you? This is Sylvia. Yeah. Listen, Mom, I won't be able to make it for Chanukah. Yeah, that's what I said. Well, because my boyfriend—remember Ichabod Ignatz?—he blew up the airport. He's some kind of a—oooh!—a nut. . . ."

He plunged into her. She ingulfed him. The winds wailed through the yellow pines, the aspens shivered, leaves dancing with a sound like many minor waterfalls. The discreet chatter of little birds, the barking of a gray fox, the swish of tires on the distant paved road, all such normal, sane, moderate sounds were swept away over the edge of the world, lost in the rush.

Up and down, in and out of forest and meadow, past sinks and pits and bowls in the rolling terrain of the limestone plateau (riddled like a sponge with endless cavern systems), he piloted the jeep on, southward, toward the logging industry, its hopes and fears. She nestled against him, half upon him, long hair streaming like a banner in the wind.

They paused once again, near the north end of a meadow called Pleasant Valley, to edit and beautify an official U.S. Forest Service Smokey Bear sign. The sign was a life-size simulacrum of the notorious ursine bore, complete with ranger hat, blue jeans and shovel, and it said what these signs always say, to wit, "Only YOU can prevent forest fires."

Out with the paints again. They added a yellow mustache, which certainly improved Smokey's bland muzzle, and touched up his eyeballs with a hangover hue of red. He began to look like Robert Redford as the Sundance Kid. Bonnie unbuttoned Smokey's fly, pictorially speaking, and painted onto his crotch a limp pet-cock with hairy but shriveled balls. To Smokey's homily on fire prevention Hayduke attached an asterisk and footnote: "Smokey Bear is full of shit." (Most fires of course are caused by that vaporous hominoid in the sky, God; disguised, i.e., as lightning.)

Very funny. However, in 1968, the United States Congress made it a Federal offense to desecrate, mutilate or otherwise improve any official representation of Smokey the Bear. Aware of this legislation, Bonnie bullied Hayduke back into the jeep and out of there before he could carry out his urge to hang Smokey by the neck to any nearby tree, such as a *Pinus ponderosa,* and elevate likewise the bear's penis from flaccid pendency to full *in rigor extremis* erection.

"Enough," explained Abbzug, and she was right, as usual.

Four miles north of the entrance to the North Rim District of Grand Canyon National Park, they came to an intersection in the road. The sign said WATCH FOR TRUCKS. Hayduke turned left at this point, onto the unpaved but broad logging road which led eastward into the forest, and a new scene.

During the entire forty-mile drive from Jacob Lake they had seen nothing so far but green meadows decorated with herds of cattle and deer, and beyond the meadows the aspen, pine, spruce and fir of what appeared to be, uncut and intact, a people's national forest. Façade. Behind the false front of standing trees, a fringe of virgin growth a quarter mile deep, was the real business of the national forest: timber farms, lumber plantations, field factories for the joist, board, pulp and plywood industry.

Bonnie was astonished. She had never seen a clear-cut logging operation before.

"What happened to the trees?"

"What trees?" says Hayduke.

"That's what I mean."

He stopped the jeep. In silence they looked around at a scene of devastation. Within an area of half a square mile the forest had been stripped of every tree, big or small, healthy or diseased, seedling or ancient snag. Everything gone but the stumps. Where trees had been were now huge heaps of slash waiting to be burned when the winter snows arrived. A network of truck, skidder and bulldozer tracks wound among the total amputees.

"Explain this," she demanded. "What happened here?"

He attempted to explain. The Explainer's lot is not an easy one.

In clear-cutting, he said, you clear away the natural forest, or what the industrial forester calls "weed trees," and plant all one species of tree in neat straight functional rows like corn, sorghum, sugar beets or any other practical farm crop. You then dump on chemical fertilizers to replace the washed-away humus, inject the seedlings with growth-forcing hormones, surround your plot with deer repellants and raise a uniform crop of trees, all identical. When the trees reach a certain prespecified height (not maturity; that takes too long) you send in a fleet of tree-harvesting machines and cut the fuckers down. All of them. Then burn the slash, and harrow, seed, fertilize all over again, round and round and round again, faster and faster and tighter and tighter until, like the fabled Malaysian Concentric Bird which flies in ever-smaller circles, you disappear up your own asshole.

"You see?" he said.

"Well yes and no," she said, "except that, like if this . . ."—she waves her hand and bangled wrist at the surrounding wasteland—"I mean like if all that was a national forest—a *national* forest—then it belonged to us, right?"

"Wrong."

"But you said—"

"Can't you understand anything? Goddamned cocksucking New York Marxist liberal."

"I ain't no New York Marxist liberal."

Hayduke drove on past the clear-cut area. Although there was little natural forest remaining in the Kaibab it still looked, by and large, like a woods. The clear-cutting was only getting started. Though much was lost, much remained—though much was lost.

Still troubled, Bonnie asked, "They pay us for our trees, don't they?"

"The loggers bid for the right to log an area, sure. The top bidder writes a check to the U.S. Treasury. The Forest Service takes the money, our money, and spends it building new logging roads like this one, all banked and graded for the loggers to run their timber-hauling rigs on to see how many deer, tourists and chipmunks they can kill. A deer is ten points, chipmunk five, tourist one."

"Where are the loggers now?"

"Sunday. They're off."

"But America does need the lumber. People need some kind of shelter."

"All right," he said, "people need shelter." He said it grudgingly. "Let them build their houses out of rock, for chrissake, or out of mud and sticks like the Papagos do. Out of bricks or cinder blocks. Out of packing crates and Karo cans like my friends in Dak Tho. Let them build houses that will last a while, say for a hundred years, like my great-granpappy's cabin back in Pennsylvania. Then we won't have to strip the forests."

"All you're asking for is a counter-industrial revolution."

"Right. That's all."

"And how do you propose to bring it about?"

Hayduke thought about that question. He wished Doc were here. His own brain functioned like crankcase sludge on a winter day. Like grunge. Like Chairman Mao prose. Hayduke was a saboteur of much wrath but little brain. The jeep meanwhile sank deeper into Kaibab National Forest, into the late afternoon. Pine duff rose on dusty sunbeams, trees transpired, the hermit thrushes sang and over it all the sky (having no alternative) flourished its borrowed sundown colors—blue and gold.

Hayduke thought. Finally the idea arrived. He said, "My job is to save the fucking wilderness. I don't know anything else worth saving. That's simple, right?"

"Simpleminded," she said.

"Good enough for me."

They came to the work site Hayduke had been seeking. It was a clear-cut in progress with hulking machines standing around, nothing to do, in the evening twilight. Bulldozers, loaders, skidders, tankers, everything was waiting but the haulers, which had made their last run loaded down off the plateau to the sawmill in Fredonia the Friday before.

"Where's the watchman?"

"There won't be any," Hayduke said. "They're not on to us."

"Well if you don't mind I'd like to make sure."

"We'll do that."

Hayduke stopped his jeep, got out and locked the hubs, transferred into four-wheel drive. They drove up and down the skid trails, through mud and muck, around stacked logs and slash heaps, through the acreage of mutilated stumps. Massacre of the pines—not a standing tree within an area of two hundred acres.

They found the work-site office, a small house trailer locked and dark, nobody home. GEORGIA-PACIFIC CORP., SEATTLE, WASH., said the tin sign on the door. Them boys a long way from home, seems like, thought Hayduke.

He got out. He knocked on the padlocked door, rattled the hasp. Nobody answered; nothing answered. A squirrel chattered, a blue jay squawked off in the trees beyond the stumps, but nothing was stirring nearby. Even the wind had stopped, and the forest lay still as the death site it surrounded. Bonnie thought of the Traveler. Tell them he returned. Tell them he remembered, etc. Hayduke came back.

"Well?"

"I told you. There's nobody here. They all went to town for the weekend."

She turned her head, gazing over the battlefield at the inert but powerful machines close by, the defenseless trees beyond the clearcut. Then back to the machines.

"There must be a million dollars' worth of equipment here."

Hayduke surveyed the layout with appraising eyes. "About two and a half million," he said. One guess as good as another. They were both silent for a minute.

"What to do?" she said, feeling the chill of evening.

He grinned. The fangs came out, gleaming in the gloom. The big fists rose, thumbs up. "Time to do our chores."

18

❧❦

Dr. Sarvis at Home

A hard day at the shop. First, thoracic surgery, a tricky lobectomy on the left lung inferior lobe of a teenage boy who'd come to the Southwest ten years too late, after the old-fashioned nineteenth-century air had been replaced by modern scientific thinking, and had managed to contract pneumonitis compounded by the scars of bronchiectasis (rare in young mammals) compounded in turn, a few years later, by that most typical of Southwestern ailments, coccidioidomycosis or valley fever, a fungus infection associated with alkaline soils and carried far and wide by the winds wherever the desert surface is disturbed by agriculture, mining or construction. In the boy this expanding economy disease led in due course to severe hemorrhaging; there was no recourse but removal, suturing the bronchus, stitching up the lad's hide.

Second, for relaxation, Doc performed a hemorrhoidectomy, a simple operation—like coring an apple—that he always enjoyed, especially when his patient was the red-necked white-assed blue-nosed persecutor of topless dancers W. W. Dingledine (not *the* W. W. Dingledine? aye, the same!), District Attorney of Bernal County, New Mexico. Doc's fee for the ten-minute rectal reaming would be, in this case, a flat $500. Exorbitant? Of course; of course it was exorbitant; but, well, the D.A. had been warned: Prosecutors will be violated.

Finished, he dropped his blood-spattered gown, pinched the wrong nurse on the right buttock and shambled on shaky hind legs out the side door up the alleyway through the photochemical glare of the dimmed but unrelenting Albuquerque sun down a short flight of steps into the feel-your-way and padded darkness of the nearest bar.

The cocktail waitress came and went and came and went again, a disembodied smile gliding through the gloom. Doc sipped his martini and thought of the boy with the eight-inch cut now stitched and burning underneath the left shoulder blade. The Southwest had once been the place where Eastern physicians sent their more serious respiratory cases. No more; the developers—bankers, industrialists, subdividers, freeway builders and public utility chiefs—had succeeded with less than thirty years' effort in bringing the air of Southwestern cities "up to standard," that is, as foul as any other.

Doc thought he knew where the poison came from that had attacked the boy's lungs, the same poison eating into the mucous membranes of several million other citizens including himself. From poor visibility to eye irritation, from allergies to asthma to emphysema to general asthenia, the path lay straight ahead, pathogenic all the way. They were already having afternoons right here in Albuquerque when schoolchildren were forbidden to play outside in the "open" air, heavy breathing being more dangerous than child molesters.

He ordered a second martini, following with his gaze the movement of the girl's structurally perfect thighs as she withdrew in sinuous meander among the tables back to the chrome-plated rails of the service bar. He thought as she walked of those inner surfaces caressing one another in frictionless intimacy, how they led and where and why. He thought, with a pang as poignant as morning dreams, of Bonnie.

Enough. Enough of that.

Doc blundered forth into the fat sunshine, the traffic's rising involuntary roar, the unreal reality of the city. Found his bicycle, actually Bonnie's, where he had parked it (crookedly) in the rack near the entrance to the surgical ward. Wobbling badly at first, Dr. Sarvis piloted his ten-speed craft in first gear up the long grade of Iron Avenue. ("Wearing his legs out," the country boys would say, "to give his ass a ride.")

Mad motorists in arrogant chariots of iron brushed him by dangerously close. He struggled on, heroic and alone, holding up traffic all by himself. A contractor's menial at the controls of an oversize cement mixer honked his air horn immediately in the doctor's rear, nearly blasting him into the gutter. Doc refused to yield; pumping on he raised one hand, the big general-purpose finger rigidly extended—*Chinga!*—in direct retort. The truck driver pulled around him and passed, leaning recklessly far to the right in his cab to stick a beefy forearm, fist and finger out and up: *Chinga tu madre!* Doc replied with the well-known Neapolitan double thrust, little finger and forefinger extended like the prongs of a meat fork: *Chinga stugatz!* (Untranslatable and unnatural obscenity.) Oh-oh! Too much: went too far that time.

The truck driver swung his mixer to the curb with squealing brakes, opened the door on the driver's side and wallowed out. Doc bounced up on the sidewalk and pedaled smoothly by on the right, sitting up straight like a gentleman. He shifted into third. The truck driver ran a few steps after him, stopped and retreated to his cab as a chorus of horns began to sound, *tutti fortissima,* behind the truck.

Still on Iron, for him the most convenient route for another mile, Doc became unpleasantly aware that he was being pursued. A glance over the shoulder and he saw the cement truck gaining again, bearing down like Goliath. Heart beating fast, chewing desperately on his smoldering stogie, Doc made plans. The corner he had in mind, one block ahead, featured a vacant lot with a giant high-legged two-faced steel-beamed billboard already in view.

Doc slowed the bicycle a bit, pedaling as close to the curb as he could, and allowed a couple of cars to pass. The cement truck was now directly behind him. Doc glanced back once more and threw the driver another two-pronged unspeakable Calabrian insult. The air horn replied with a bray of rage. Doc stepped up the speed, shifting into sixth as the cement truck thundered at his rear. The corner came close; he focused on the narrow opening in the curb where a dirt driveway led to the billboards. (Doc and Bonnie had edited those signs before.) Giving the driver a sporting chance, Doc courteously signaled the oblique right turn he was about to make. Finger extended, of course.

The moment arrived. Doc banked gracefully into the turn, losing not a stroke at the pedals. Swift and sleek, sitting sedately upright on the tiny saddle of his bike, he passed between the steel posts and under the lower edge of the double billboard. The top of his hat cleared the steel crossbeam by six inches. The cement truck followed.

When he heard the crash, Doc slowed and circled, surveying the damage: spectacular but not serious. Both billboards were down, sprawled all over the cab and still-revolving mixer of the cement truck. Out of the midst of the tangled wreckage rose a spout of steam, hissing like a geyser from the ruptured radiator of Unit #17 Duke City Reddy-Mix Cement & Gravel Co.

Doc watched the driver crawl from his cab into the shade of the billboards. Except for a bleeding nose and minor contusions, lacerations and shock, the man appeared not seriously injured. The Dopplerian moan of sirens approached, arrived and died with the slamming of doors. The police took charge of the scene. Satisfied, Doc pedaled harmlessly away.

Supper was not quite so facile. Dr. Sarvis loved to eat but hated to cook. After banging about for a while up and down his kitchen with a package of pork chops, hard as quartzite from four weeks in the freezer, he settled—where in the *hell* is my *Bonnie*?—for a can of string beans, some old leftover Abbzug chicken salad, and a bottle of beer. He turned on the TV to watch the evening news with Walter Cronkite and his friends. He sat down at the table and studied once again the postcard he'd found in the mailbox.

Dear Daddy Doc having a great time up here in the woods picking flowres watching the deere and General Havick follows everywhere we go we miss you all of us and see you at Page? Fry

Canyon? In another week or two right? Will phone love Butch &
Bonnie & Seldom Seen Slim.

The card was postmarked Jacob Lake, Arizona, and showed on its picture side a view of mountain meadow, mule deer, and aspens in summer green.

He ate his lonesome bachelor supper, feeling as cold and glum as the chicken salad. He missed the gang. He missed the vivid air, the wastelands, the little yellow flowers, the smell of juniper smoke, the feel of sand and sandstone under his hands. He missed the pleasures, the action, the satisfaction of the good work. (Support Your Local Eco-Raiders.) But most he missed his Bonnie. The bonniest Abbzug who ever lived.

He watched the news. Same as yesterday's. The General Crisis coming along nicely. Nothing new except the commercials full of sly art and eco-porn. Scenes of the Louisiana bayous, strange birds in slow-motion flight, cypress trees bearded with Spanish moss. Above the primeval scene the voice of Power spoke, reeking with sincerity, in praise of itself, the Exxon Oil Company—its tidiness, its fastidious care for all things wild, its concern for human needs.

Coming back from the refrigerator, second beer in hand, Doc paused for a moment in front of the television screen. Long shot of an offshore drilling rig. Music rising on concluding phrase. The words "We thought you'd like to know" passing across the screen. Too much for Doc. All of a sudden it was all too much. He drew back his big booted right foot and kicked the picture tube square in the eye. It imploded-exploded with a sound like the popping of a grandiose light bulb. A blue glare filled the kitchen and then died in the instant of its birth; shards and flakes of fluorescent glass slid down the walls.

Doc paused to contemplate the awful thing he had done. "Thus I refute McLuhan," he muttered.

He sat down again at the table. The smell of zinc sulfide floated on the air. He finished his supper and dumped the dishes onto the pile of dirty dishes already overflowing the dishwashing machine. He crammed them down, leaning heavily on the lid. A crunch of splintering glass. He fed Bonnie's cat and threw it out, left the kitchen, sat down in the living room and lit a cigar, gazing out through the big west window at the sullen magnificence, like a bed of embers, of the city. Above the city and beyond the Rio Grande, the crescent moon hung pale as platinum in the evening sky, shining down on city, river and desert plain.

Doc thought of his friends out there somewhere, far away to the north and west, among the rocks, under that simple light, doing their necessary work while he idled away his middle age. The devil finds work for idle hands. Dr. Sarvis reached for the newspaper. Saw the full-page ad on the back. Boat Show, Duke City Ice Arena. He thought he might go have a look at the new houseboats. Tomorrow, or the next day. Soon.

19

❦

Strangers in the Night

Hayduke parked his jeep out of sight among the pines near the entrance to the logging area and stationed Bonnie on the hood with instructions to keep her eyes open and ears clean. She nodded impatiently.

He put on hard hat, coveralls, gun and gun belt, work gloves, took a small flashlight and his other tools and disappeared from Bonnie's ken into the deep twilight of the cut-over site, fading like a shadow among the giant machines. She wanted to read but it was already too dark. She sang songs for a while, softly, and listened to the cries of birds, unknown and unseen birds, off in the forest, retreating to their nests for the night, heads nestled under fold of wing, retiring into the simple harmless dreams of avian sleep. (A bird has no cerebrum.)

The forest seemed eternal. The winds had stopped some time ago and the stillness, as the birds settled down, became finer and deeper. Bonnie was aware of tall presences around her, the brooding yellow pines, the somber shaggy personalities of the Engelmann spruce and white fir, their high crowns pointing like cathedral spires, at variant angles (for everything which rises must diverge), toward that luxurious fireball array of first-magnitude stars which ornament, as they illuminate, doing the best they can, the vast interior of our expanding universe. Bonnie though had seen it before: she rolled and lit a joint.

Meanwhile under the belly of a bulldozer George W. Hayduke was tugging at an oversize spanner, trying to open the drain plug in the crankcase of an Allis-Chalmers HD-41. Merely the biggest tractor Allis-Chalmers makes. His wrench was three feet long—he'd taken it from the tractor's toolbox—but he couldn't turn that square nut. He reached for his cheater, a three-foot length of steel pipe, fitted it like a sleeve over the end of the wrench handle and tugged again. This time the nut gave, a fraction of a millimeter. All he needed; Hayduke yanked again and the nut began to turn.

So far he'd done nothing dramatic, merely following routine procedures. Where possible, as in the case of this HD-41, he decided to drain the crankcase oil, planning to start up the engine just before leaving. (Noise factor.) He had no keys but assumed he would find what was needed by breaking into the office trailer.

Another turn on the plug and the oil would begin to drain. Hayduke eased his body out of the way, regripped his pipe-handled wrench. And froze.

"How you doin', pard?" said a man's voice, deep and low, not more than twenty feet away.

Hayduke reached for his sidearm.

"Naw, don't do that." The man flicked a switch, training the beam of a powerful electric torch directly into Hayduke's eyes. "I got this," he explained, pushing the muzzle of what certainly looked to be a twelve-gauge shotgun into the light, where Hayduke could see it. "Yeah, it's loaded," he said. "And it's cocked and it's touchy as a rattlesnake."

He paused. Hayduke waited.

"Okay," the man said, "now you go ahead and finish what you're a-doin' under there."

"Finish?"

"Go ahead."

"I was looking for something," Hayduke said.

The man laughed, an easy, pleasant laugh, but not without menace. "Is that right?" he said. "Now what the hell you a-lookin' for under the crankcase guard of a goldang bulldozer after dark?"

Hayduke thought carefully. It *was* a good question. "Well," he said, and hesitated.

"You think it over now. Take your time."

"Well . . ."

"This oughta be pretty good."

"Yeah. Well, I was looking for—well, I'm writing a book about bulldozers and I thought I ought to see what they look like. Underneath."

"That ain't very good. How do they look?"

"Greasy."

"I coulda told you that, pard, saved you all the trouble. What's that three-foot end wrench for you got in your hands? That what you write your book with?"

Hayduke said nothing.

"Okay," the man said, "go ahead and finish your job." Hayduke hesitated. "I mean it. Turn that plug. Let the oil out."

Hayduke did as he was told. The shotgun, after all, like the flashlight was aimed straight at his face. A shotgun at close range is a powerful argument. He worked, loosened the plug; the oil streamed out, sleek, rich and liberated, onto and into the churned-up soil.

"Now," the man said, "drop the wrench, put your hands behind your head and kinda sidewind outa there on your back."

Hayduke obeyed. Wasn't easy, wriggling out from under a tractor without using the hands. But he did it.

"Now roll over on your face." Again Hayduke obeyed. The man rose from his squatting position, came close, unholstered Hayduke's gun, stepped back and hunkered down again. "Okay," he said, "you can turn over now and sit up." He examined Hayduke's piece. "Ruger, .357 mag. That's power all right."

Hayduke faced him. "You don't have to shine that light right in my eyes."

"You're right, pard." The stranger switched off the light. "Sorry about that."

They faced each other in the sudden darkness, each wondering, perhaps, who had the quicker and better night vision. But the stranger had his forefinger on the trigger of the shotgun. They could see each other well enough in the high-plateau starlight. Neither made a move for some time.

The stranger cleared his throat. "You sure work slow," he complained. "I been watchin' you for seems like an hour."

Hayduke said nothing.

"But I can see you do a good job. Thorough. I like that." The man spat on the ground. "Not like some of them half-assed dudes I seen up on the Powder River. Or them kids down around Tucson. Or them nuts that derailed— What's your name?"

Hayduke opened his mouth. Henry Lightcap? he thought. Joe Smith? How about—

"Forget it," the man said, "I don't want to know."

Hayduke stared harder at the face before him, ten feet away in the starlight, gradually becoming clear. He saw that the stranger was wearing a mask. Not a black mask over the eyes but simply a big bandanna draped outlaw-style over the nose, mouth and chin. Above the mask one dark right eye, vaguely shining, peered at him from under the droopy brim of a black hat. The other eye stayed closed in what appeared to be a permanent wink. Hayduke finally realized that the man's left eyeball was gone, long gone, lost and forgotten no doubt in some ancient barroom quarrel, some legendary war.

"Who are you?" Hayduke said.

The masked man spoke in a tone both surprised and hurt. "You don't want to know that. That's not a nice question."

Silence. They stared at each other.

The stranger chuckled. "Bet you thought I was the night watchman, didn't you? Made you sweat a little, huh?"

"Where is the watchman?"

"In there." The stranger jerked a thumb toward the nearby office trailer, where a pickup truck stood parked, company decals on the doors.

"What's he doing?"

"Nothin'. I got him hogtied and gagged. He's all right. He'll keep till Monday morning. The loggers'll be back then and turn him loose."

"Monday morning is tomorrow morning."

"Yeah, I reckon I oughta mosey on outa here."

"How'd you get here?"

"I like to use a horse for this kind of work. Not so fast, maybe, but quieter."

Another pause.

"What do you mean?" Hayduke said, "by 'this kind of work'?"

"Same thing you're doin'. You sure ask a lot of questions. You wanta see my horse?"

"No. I want my gun back."

"Okay." The stranger handed it back. "Next time you better keep your lookout a little closer."

"Where is she?" Hayduke reholstered his weapon.

"Right on that jeep where you left her, puffin' on one of them little Mary Jane cigarettes. Or she was." The stranger paused to look at the surrounding night, then turned back to Hayduke. "Here's somethin' else you want too," he said, fishing in his pocket and handing over a bunch of keys. "Now you can start them engines and burn 'em up real good."

Hayduke jingled the keys; he looked toward the office trailer. "You certain that watchman is secure?"

"I got him handcuffed, hogtied, gagged, dead drunk and locked up."

"Dead drunk?"

"He was half drunk when I got here. After I got the drop on him I made him finish up a pint of bourbon he was suckin' on. He passed out scared and happy."

So that's why nobody squeaked when I knocked on the door.

Hayduke looked at the masked stranger, who was shuffling his feet, apparently ready to leave.

A high voice, strained and frightened, came out of the dark. "George, are you all right?"

"I'm all right," he shouted back. "You stay out there, Natalie. Keep watch. Also, my name is Leopold."

"Okay, Leopold."

Hayduke jingled the keys, looking at the dark hulk of the tractor at his side. "Not sure I know how to start this thing," he said.

The masked man said, "I'll give you a hand. I ain't in that big of a hurry." Off in the woods somewhere a horse stomped, shuffled, nickered. The man listened, turned his head that way. "You be quiet, Rosie. I'll come and git you in a minute." He turned back to Hayduke. "Come on."

They climbed to the driver's seat of the big tractor. Taking back the keys, the stranger chose one and unlocked the access plate behind the braking pedals on the floor of the operator's compartment. He showed Hayduke the master switch and turned it on. Unlike the old-fashioned Cat at Hite Marina, this machine was started entirely by the power of a series of batteries.

"Okay," said the one-eyed man, "now you push that little button there by the speed shift."

Hayduke pushed the button. The starter solenoid engaged starter pinion with flywheel ring gear: the twelve-cylinder four-cycle turbo-charged Cummins diesel coughed into life—1710 cubic inches of packed piston power. Hayduke was delighted. He pulled back on the throttle lever and the engine revved up smoothly, ready to work. (But heating rapidly.)

"I'm gonna do something with this machine," he announced to the stranger.

"Yes you are."

"I mean move things around."

"You better move quick then. It ain't goin' to last but a few minutes." The stranger eyed the instrument panel: oil pressure zero, engine temperature rising. An odd unhealthy noise, like the whine of a sick dog, could be heard already.

Hayduke unlocked the lock lever and pulled the speed shift lever into gear. The tractor bucked forward against the lowered dozer blade, shoving a ton of mud and two yellow pine stumps into the side of the Georgia-Pacific office.

"Not that way," the stranger shouted. "There's a man in there."

"Right." Hayduke stopped the machine, leaving his load piled high against the buckled trailer wall. He shifted into reverse and the tractor backed over the Georgia-Pacific pickup truck; the truck collapsed like a beer can. He rotated the bulldozer over it, grinding the wreckage into the muck.

Next? Hayduke looked around through the starlight for another target.

"See what you can do with that new Clark skidder over there," the masked man suggested.

"Check." Hayduke raised the dozer blade, turned the tractor and charged at full throttle—five miles per hour—into the skidder. It crumpled with a rich and satisfying *crunch* of steel flesh, iron bones. He pivoted the tractor 200 degrees and aimed it at a tanker truck full of diesel fuel.

Somebody was screaming at him. Something was screaming at him.

Full throttle forward. The tractor lurched ahead one turn of the sprocket wheels and stopped. The engine block cracked; a jet of steam shot forth, whistling urgently. The engine fought for life. Something exploded inside the manifold and a gush of blue flame belched from the exhaust stack, launching hot sparks at the stars. Seized-up tight within their chambers, the twelve pistons became one—wedded and welded—with cylinders and block, one unified immovable entropic white-hot molecular mass. All Is One. The screaming went on. Fifty-one tons of tractor, screaming in the night.

"She's foundered," the masked man said. "There ain't nothin' we can do." He clambered off over the rear, under the eight-ton rippers. "Let's go," he shouted. "There's somebody comin'!" And he melted into the darkness.

Hayduke pulled himself together, got off the tractor. He still heard somebody screaming at him. Bonnie.

She yanked at his sleeve, pointing away into the woods. "Can't you see?" she screamed. "Lights, lights! What's the matter with you?"

Hayduke stared, then grabbed her arm. "This way."

They ran across the clearing, among the stumps, toward the shelter of the forest as a truck came rumbling into the open area. Headlights flared, a spotlight swept across the open and *almost* caught them.

Not quite. They were in the woods, among the friendly trees. Feeling the way through the dark in what he thought was the direction of his jeep, Hayduke heard a thunder of hoofs. Somebody on a horse galloped past at a full run. The truck, which had come to a stop beside the whistling bulldozer, discharged some men: one, two, three—impossible to count them in the dark. Hayduke and Abbzug watched a spotlight probe the clearing, the trees, seeking the horse.

Again too late: one glimpse of the horseman and he was gone, into the forest and down the road, riding off to the end of the night. A gun barked once, twice, in futile remonstration and subsided. The hoofbeats faded away. The men at the truck moved to the assistance of somebody inside the office trailer, who was kicking at the walls. They'd have a tough time getting him out with that load of rubble banked against the jammed door.

Bonnie and George got into the jeep.

"Who's in God's name was that?" Bonnie demanded.

"The watchman, I guess."

"No, I mean the man on the horse."

"I don't know."

"You were with him."

"I don't know anything about him. Shut your door and let's get out of here." Hayduke started the motor.

"They'll hear us," she said.

"Not with that bulldozer howling they won't." He drove without any light but starlight out of the trees, slowly, and onto the main forest road, heading back toward the highway and North Rim. When he felt he had gone a safe distance he turned on the headlights and stepped on the gas. The well-tuned jeep purred smoothly forward.

"You really don't know who that man was?"

"I don't know, sweetheart. All I know is what I told you. Call him Kemosabe."

"What kind of name is that?"

"It's a Paiute word."

"Meaning what?"

"Shithead."

"That figures. That fits. I'm hungry. Feed me."

"Wait'll we get a few more miles from that logging outfit."

"Who was in that truck?"

"I don't know and I didn't want to stick around to find out, did you?" He decided to stick it to her. "Did *you*, my hotshot lookout?"

"Listen," she said, "don't give me any hard time about that. You wanted me to stay with the jeep and that's what I did. I was watching the road like you wanted me to."

"Okay," he said.

"So shut up."

"Okay."

"And amuse me, I'm bored."

"Okay. Here's one for you. A real conundrum. What is the difference between the Lone Ranger and God?"

Bonnie thought about it as they rattled through the woods. She rolled a little cigarette and thought and thought. At last she said, "What a stupid conundrum. I give up."

Hayduke said, "There really is a Lone Ranger."

"I don't understand."

He reached over, grabbed her, pulled her snug against his side. "Forget it."

20

Return to the Scene of the Crime

Hayduke and Abbzug camped illegally (not even a fire permit) against all regulations far from the blacktop down a closed-off fire road under the aspen trees.

They woke up late and had breakfast in bed.

Birds singing, sunshine, et cetera. Afterwards she said, "Now I want something to eat."

He took her to North Rim Lodge for brunch. They had orange juice, pecan waffles, fried eggs sunny side up, hash-brown potatoes, ham, toast, milk, coffee and Irish coffee and a sprig of parsley each. All marvelous. He led her out on the terrace of the lodge and showed her the high rim view of the Grand Canyon of the Colorado.

"Neat," she said.

"See one Grand Canyon you've seen 'em all," he agreed. He took her to Cape Royal, Point Imperial and finally to Point Sublime, where they camped illegally the second night. As the sun sank legally (in the west) they gazed down six thousand vertical feet, into the yawning abyss.

"That abyss is yawning at me," Hayduke observed.

"I'm sleepy," she said.

"Christ, it's only sundown. What's the matter with you?"

"I don't know. Let's take a nap before we go to bed."

It had been an active weekend. They lay down again to rest some more.

From down down far down below, carried on the wind, came the applause of Boucher Rapids. The dried stalk and empty seed husks of the yucca rattled in the breeze, on the rimrock, under the stars. Bats dipped and zigzagged, chittering, chasing insects taking evasive action flying for their lives. Off in the dark of the woods one vulgar nightbird honked. Nighthawks rose against the gaudy sunset, soared and circled and plunged suddenly for bugs, wings making a sound like the roar of a remote bull as they pulled abruptly out of headlong dives. Bullbats. Back in the forest deep in the gloom of the pines a hermit thrush called—called who?—in flutelike silver tones. The pining poet. Answered promptly by the other bird, the clown, the raven, the Kaibab crake, with a noise like a farmhand blowing his nose.

They passed her placebo back and forth in exceeding slow slow-motion. Reefer madness. I love you, Mary Jane.

"Listen," murmured George W. Hayduke, his heart corrupted and his brain damaged by too much beauty, love, tenderness, dope, cunt, sunset, canyon scenery and fluty woodland notes. "You know something, Bonnie?"

"What?"

"You know we don't *have* to go on like we been. You know?"

She opened her heavy eyes. "Don't have to what?"

"Don't *have* to keep on risking our necks. They're gonna catch us you know. They'll kill me. They'll have to."

"What? Who? Who is?"

"If we keep on. We could go to Oregon. I heard there's human beings there. We could go to New Zealand, raise lambs."

She rose on her elbows. "Are you talking to me? Are you out of your *mind*? Are you *sick* or something, George? How many—gimme that joint—who *are* you anyway?"

His drugged eyes stared at her from forty miles away, the dark-brown pupils big as checkers. Poker chips. Mushrooms. Magic morels.

Slowly the wide evil gleaming grin appeared, wicked as a wolf's in the smokeblue twilight.

"Men call me . . ." he said, tongue thick and numb as a turnip's tuber, "men—"

"*Men* call you?" she said.

He tried again. "They call me . . . persons call me . . ." He put a finger on his numb lips. "Shhhhhhhh. . . . Kemo . . . sabe. . . ."

"Shithead?"

"Right," he said, nodding his stone-heavy head and grinning happily. He laughed and sank again, beside her. They sank together, laughing, sprawled on the lofty fluff of their goosedown zip-together.

In the morning he had recovered, was his normal bale and fulsome self again, despite a wracking marijuana headache. "Back to work," he growled, rousing her. "We got three bridges, a railroad, a strip mine, a power plant, two dams, a nuclear reactor, one computer data center, six highway projects and a BLM scenic overlook to take care of this week. Up, up, up. Make me some coffee, godfuckingdammit, or I'll ship you back to the Bronx."

"You and who else, buster?"

They headed north, out of the national park into the national forest. Property of all Americans administered for *you* by your friendly (Amer. Forestry Assoc.) forest rangers. Their Smokey Bear sign had been removed. At Jacob Lake they stopped for fuel, replenished the beer chest (back to normalcy, says Hayduke) and mailed a few incriminatory picture postcards. Onward. Hayduke took the right fork out of the woods, eastward down the monocline toward the Martian-red desert, floating in heat waves, of Houserock Valley. Pleased with themselves and the world, they drove on down and away across the desert and up the Kaibito Plateau and southeast beyond Page to see how the Black Mesa & Lake Powell Railroad was doing. Concealing the jeep off the road near the crossing of Kaibito Canyon, they hiked north for a couple of miles through the psychedelic Navajo sunshine. They saw the railway in the distance. Properly oriented, they made their way to a high point on the slickrock from which, through field glasses, they could study the progress of repair work at Kaibito Canyon Bridge.

"Power's restored," he said.

"Let me see."

She looked through the glasses at the tracks, the repair train, a big green Bucyrus-Erie crane lifting I beams from a flatcar, revolving on its bed and lowering the beams onto the rebuilt bridge abutments. Engineers, technicians and laborers swarmed like ants over the work site. The power line, spliced and re-erected, hung across the gap of the canyon bringing high-voltage energy to those in need. Coal cars down in the shadows, piled upon one another like junkyard wreckage, waited for possible recovery.

"Determined organization," Bonnie said. Now we know, she thought, how the pyramids were built, how the Great Wall of China came to be, and why.

"The power plant wants that coal," said George, "and wants it bad. P. G. and E needs their Krunchies. We're going to have to stop them again, Abbzug."

Back to the highway across the sandstone reefs, slogging through shoals of sand. Back to the camouflaged jeep among the desert trees, where a flock of pinyon jays swirled away like confetti at their approach.

"Tools, gloves, hard hats," Hayduke barked.

"What tools?"

"Fence pliers. Power saw."

Armed and equipped, munching on beef jerky, fig newtons and apples, they marched toward the railway but this time on a different tangent. Lying on their bellies on a dune, they watched a work train rattle past, headed back to Page for more supplies. The train vanished around a curve. Bonnie stood guard, field glasses in hand, beneath a shady juniper, as Hayduke went to work.

He shuffled through the sand to the railway, cut the stock fence, pushed aside an embankment of tumbleweeds and stepped to the nearest power-line pole. Like the others, it was guyed to the ground. He looked up at Bonnie. She gave him the go-ahead sign. He started the chain saw and noisily but quickly cut a deep notch in the base of the pole. He shut off the saw, looked at Bonnie and listened. She gave him the all-clear sign.

Hayduke trotted to the next pole, made the same kind of cut. Finished, he stopped the engine and checked with his lookout. Okay. He notched three more. Only the guy wires kept the poles standing. He was about to start on a sixth pole when he noticed from the corner of his eye that Bonnie—too far away to be heard above the whine of the saw—was making frantic arm signals. At the same moment he felt, even before he heard, the hated and dreaded *whock! whock! whock! whock!* of a helicopter. He stopped the saw and dove with it down the bank of the roadbed into the waist-high mass of tumbleweeds piled in the ditch. Curling and shriveling beneath them, willing himself invisible, he drew his revolver and waited for fiery death.

The helicopter came over the ridge and the sound was suddenly much louder, terrible, insane. The air shuddered as the machine passed overhead by a hundred feet, clattering like a pteranodon. The turbulence pressed Hayduke to the ground. He thought he was dead but the thing flew on. He squinted through the weeds and saw the helicopter receding down the right-of-way, following the convergence of the rails toward the east. The notched poles swayed slightly in its wake but did not fall.

The helicopter was gone. He waited. No sign of Bonnie; she too must have buried herself somehow. He waited until the last imperceptible vibration of the air machine was gone. As his terror drained away its place was filled by the old and futile and unappeasable outrage.

I hate them, George Hayduke said, under the sun of Arizona, I hate them all. The moment he'd heard that bubble-nosed dragon approach one memory before all others flashed on the screen of his mind: by a dusty road in Cambodia, the bodies of a woman and child fused together in a black burning mass of napalm.

He stood up. The helicopter was gone. He waved at Bonnie, now appearing from under her tree. Go back, he signaled. She didn't seem to understand.

"Go back," he shouted. "Back to the jeep." She was shaking her head.

Hayduke gave up on her. He stumbled out of the thicket of tumbleweed, up the roadbed and on to the next power-line pole. He jerked the starter cord of the chain saw; the motor growled. Hayduke set the guide bar against the pole, thumbed the oiler button, squeezed the power trigger. The saw snarled like a cat; the chrome-plated cutting teeth slashed into the tender wood. First a slanting cut at 45 degrees; then a horizontal cut intersecting the first halfway into the heart of the pole. Eight seconds. He shut off the engine, pulled free the saw. A wedge of pinewood tumbled out.

On to the next. And the next. He paused to look and listen. Nothing. Nobody in sight but Bonnie, high on the ridge above the railway, five hundred yards away now, almost out of earshot. Hayduke notched three more poles. Stopped again to look and listen. No sound but that of his own breathing, his trickling sweat, the singing of the blood in his ears. Once again he signaled Bonnie to go. Again she ignored the command. Okay, he thought. Now. Down with it.

He had notched eleven poles. Should be enough. Time to uncouple the guy lines. He hid the saw under the nearest juniper and got out the fencing pliers. Using the pliers like a capstan handle, he unscrewed the turnbuckles which kept each guy anchored to the ground. As he moved down the line he undid each one. On number nine the whole array of notched poles began to lean. With number ten they fell.

They fell inward, upon the tracks, pulled by the weight of the cantilevered power line. An instant before the crash Hayduke saw a blue spark 50,000 volts strong leap the gap from cable to rail. He thought of God. And then the *clang!* of the collision, like eighty-eight grand pianos committing simultaneous suicide. The smell of ozone.

All Power, down and out. He scrambled up the cutbank and through the fence and jogged south over the slickrock among the admiring junipers. Clutched in his right hand was the chain saw, in his left the pliers. He paused now and then under the concealment of the trees to look and listen. Somewhere along the line somebody must already be in radio contact with the helicopter, giving the word. General alarm.

And where was Bonnie? He looked but could not see her. If she was half as scared as he was she'd be halfway back to the jeep.

Scared, yes, and happy too. Scared but happy, thinks Hayduke, panting like a dog, tongue lolling. He ran on, bolting across exposed places, pausing under trees to rest and gasp for air and listen to the sounds of the listening sky. Proud as pie, he stopped again for breath. A big black bird with a great big mouth began to sing:

> They gonna get you, Jawge Hayduke.
> They gonna hang youah ass, man.
> You cain't hide. You cain't git away. You cain't do nothin they
> don't know about.
> They on the roads, lookin for you.
> They comin down the railroad, lookin for you.
> They back in them data banks, trackin you down.
> They up in the sky, lookin for you.
> You a gone goose, Jawge Hayduke. You a broken-down bum.
> You a fucked duck, man. Yeah!

He pitched a stone at the big-mouthed bird. It flapped off, yakking like a clown. The wings flapped heavy on the thin air, going *whock whock whock,* making a heavy, heavy, heavy sound. . . .

> *Whock whock whock*
> *Whock whock whock*
> WHOCK WHOCK WHOCK WHOCK WHOCK WHOCK WHOCK
> They up in the sky.
> They lookin for you.

21

Seldom Seen at Home

Green River, Utah. Susan's house. The watermelon ranch. An easy day's drive from Sheila's place at Bountiful, which was in turn an easy day's drive from Kathy's house near Cedar City. He'd planned it all that way, of course from the beginning. Seldom Seen Smith hearkened to the prophet Brigham: he was polygamous as a rabbit.

Three o'clock in the morning and the bedroom was full of dreams. Oh pearl of great price! Through the open windows floated the smell of ripening watermelons, the sweet odor of cut alfalfla. (Second cutting of the summer.) Also the smells, poignant and irrevocable, of apple trees, horseshit, and wild asparagus along the irrigation ditches. From the embankment only one field away came the sound of whispering willow, the flat *whack!* of a beaver's tail slapping the river water.

That river. That river, that golden Green, flowing down from the snows of the Wind River Range, through Flaming Gorge and Echo Park, Split Mountain and The Gates of Lodore, down from the hills of Ow-Wi-Yu-Kuts, from the Yampa, Bitter Creek and Sweetwater, down the canyon called Desolation through the Tavaputs Plateau to emerge from the portal of the Book Cliffs—which John Wesley Powell thought "one of the most wonderful facades in the world"—and there to roll across the Green River Desert into a second world of canyons, where the river gives itself to Labyrinth and Stillwater and the Confluence with the Grand, under the rim of The Maze and into the roaring depths of Cataract. . . .

Smith lay in his bed beside his third wife and dreamed his troublesome dream. They were after him again. His truck had been identified. His rocks had rolled too far. The Search and Rescue Team was howling mad. A warrant for his arrest had been issued in San Juan County. The Bishop of Blanding raged like a strictured bull over half of Utah. Smith fled down endless corridors of sweating concrete. Under the Dam. Trapped again in a recurring nightmare of That Dam.

Down in the dank bowels of Reclamation. Engineers on skateboards glided past, clipboards in hand. Pneumatic panels opened before him, closed behind him, drawing Smith deeper and deeper into the dynamo heart of the Enemy. Magnetic webs pulled him toward the Inner Office. Where the Director waited, waiting for him. Like Doc and Bonnie and George, also locked up somewhere in here, Smith knew he was going to be punished.

The final door opened. Smith was dragged inside. The door slid shut and sealed itself. He stood again before the ultimate eye. *In the presence.*

The Director peered at Smith from the center of an array of metric dials, scintilometers, temblor screens, Visographs and sensorscopes. Tape reels spun, their circuits humming, before the quiet buzz of electronic thought at work.

The Director was monocular. The red beam of its unlidded Cyclops eye played on the face of Seldom Seen, scanning his brain, his nerves, his soul. Paralyzed by that hypnotic ray, Smith waited helpless as a babe.

The Director spoke. Its voice resembled the whine of an electronic violin, pitched in highest register to C-sharp, that same internal note which drove the deaf Smetana insane. "Smith," the voice began, "we know why you are here."

Smith gulped. "Where's George?" he croaked. "What you done to Bonnie?"

"Never mind that." The red beam glanced aside for a moment, shifty-gimbaled in its hooded carapace. The tape reels stopped, reversed, stopped, rolled forward again, recording all. Coded messages flickered in sleek electric flow, transistor-relayed through ten thousand miles of printed circuitry. Beneath the superstructure the dynamo purred on, murmuring the basic message: Power . . . profit . . . prestige . . . pleasure . . . profit . . . prestige . . . pleasure . . . power . . .

"Seldom Seen Smith," the Director said, its voice now tuned to a human intonation (modeled it would seem on the voice of an aging teenybopper balladeer whose scraggly-bearded unisex face has appeared on the cover of *Rolling Stone* seventeen times since 1964), "where are your pants?"

Pants? Smith looked down. Good Gawd Almighty!

The scanning beam returned to Smith's face. "Come closer, fellow," the voice commanded.

Smith hesitated.

"Come closer, Joseph Fielding Smith, known informally as 'Seldom Seen,' born Salt Lake City, Utah, Shithead Capital of the Inter-Mountain West, for behold art thou not he who was foretold in 1 Nephi 2:1–4, *The Book of Mormon,* wherein it is written, 'The Lord commanded him, even in a dream, that he should take his family and depart into the wilderness'? With ample provision, such as organic peanut butter, and with his family known as one Doc Sarvis, one George W. Hayduke, and one Miz B. Abbzug?"

Some tongue from a higher world answered for Smith, in words he knew not: "Datsa me, Boss."

"Good. But unfortunately for you, fellow, the prophecy cannot be fulfilled. We cannot allow it. We have decreed, Smith, that you shalt become as one of us."

What?

Four green bulbs winked in the Director's frontal lobes. The voice changed again, becoming clipped and cryptic, clearly Oxfordian. "Seize him."

Smith found himself pinioned instantly by rigid, though invisible, bonds. "Hey—?" He struggled feebly.

"Good. Affix the electrodes. Insert the anode into his penis. Quite so. The cathode goes up the rectum. Half a meter. Yes, all the way. Don't be squeamish." The Director issued his orders to invisible assistants, who bustled about Smith's paralyzed body. "Good. Imprint the flip-flop circuits on his semi-circular canal. Below the ear drum. Right. Five thousand volts should be sufficient. Attach sensor wires by strontium suction cup to his coccyx. Firmly. Plug the high-voltage adapter into the frontal sockets of his receptor node. The head, idiots, the head! Yes—right up the nostrils. Be firm. Push hard. Quite so. Very good. Now close circuit breakers. Quickly. Thank you."

Horrified, Smith tried to speak, to protest. But his tongue, like his limbs, seemed gripped in an absolute and infantile paralysis. He gaped in terror at the cables now joining his head and body to the computer bank before him.

"Well now, Smith," the Director said, "—or should we call you (heh heh) Seldom Scanned?—are you ready for your program? What's that? Now now, buck up. That's a good lad. You have nothing to fear if you can pass this simple test we have prepared for you. Call the taper, please. Good. Insert the magnetic tape. No tape slot? Then make one. Between the anode and cathode attachments, of course. Right up through the old perineum. Precisely. Never mind the blood, we'll have George clean that up later. Ready? Insert the tape. All the way. Hold his other foot down. What? Then nail it down! Good. Quite so."

The Director's single eye beamed into Smith's pineal gland. "Now Smith, your instructions. We want you to expand the simple exponential function $y = e^x$ into an infinite series. Proceed as follows: Bn: transfer contents of storage location n to working register; Tn: transfer contents of working register to location n; $+ n$: add contents of location n to contents of working register; xn: multiply contents of working register by contents of location n; $\div n$: divide contents of working register by contents of location n; V: make sign of contents of working register positive; Pn: transfer address n to accumulator if contents of working register are positive; Rn: transfer address in location n to accumulator; Z: stop program. Is that clear, Smith?"

Numb as novocaine, Seldom could not speak.

"Good. Get ready. You have 0.000012 milliseconds in which to perform this basic operation. If you fail we will have no choice but to transplant your vital organs into more adaptable specimens and to recycle your residue through the thermite crucibles. Are you ready? Good lad. Have fun now. Set the timer, please. On your toes, Smith. Count down from five. Here we go. Five! Four! Three! Two! One! Zero! THROW THE GODDAMNED SWITCH!"

"Aaaaaaaaaaaaah. . . ." Smith rose in his bed, filmed with cold sweat, turned and clutched at his wife like a drowning man. "Sheila," he groaned, struggling toward the surface of consciousness, "great almighty Gawd—!"

"Seldom!" She was awake at once. "Wake up, Seldom!"

"Sheila, Sheila. . . ."

"There's nobody here named Sheila. Wake up."

"Oh Lord . . ." He fumbled at her in the dark, feeling a warm hip, a soft belly. "Kathy?"

"You were at Kathy's last night. You have one more guess and it better be right."

He groped higher and fondled her breasts. The right one. The left one. Two of them. "Susan?"

"That's better."

Vision adapting to the starlit darkness, he found her smiling at him, reaching down for him with both arms from the warmth of their lawful conjugal bed. Her smile, like her sweet eyes, like her bountiful bosom, was rich with love. He sighed in relief. "Susan . . ."

"Seldom, you are a caution. You are something else. I never."

And she consoled, caressed and loved him, her trembling, stricken man.

While outside in the fields of desert summer the melons ripened at their leisure in the nest of their vines, and a restless rooster, perched on the roof of the hencoop, fired his premature ejaculation at the waning moon, and in the pasture the horses lifted noble Roman heads to stare in the night at something humans cannot see.

Far away in Utah on the farm, by the side of a golden river called the Green.

22

✤

George and Bonnie Carry On

He spotted the helicopter at once. It was not, however, pursuing him. Not yet. Half a mile to the east, circling over something of interest on the ground below, it had its antennae fixed on Bonnie Abbzug.

He crawled to the crest of a sand dune and watched. Bonnie was running toward a cleft or gulch in the slickrock which led like a roofless tunnel to a deeper gulch beyond, and from there into Kaibito Canyon. He understood her plan of escape.

The helicopter landed within fifty yards of the gulch, in the nearest open area available. The motor expired. Two men jumped from the Plexiglas cockpit, bending under the free-wheeling arms of the rotor, and ran toward Bonnie. One carried a carbine.

But Bonnie—good girl! She was gone, out of sight down the eroded gulch and running, no doubt, toward the canyon. One of the two men climbed down into the gulch. The other, with the carbine, ran along its rim, trying to head her off. Hayduke saw him stumble, fall on his face and lie there for a moment, stunned. Slowly he got up, picked up his weapon and started off again, running. In a few minutes he was out of sight.

The empty helicopter waited behind them, the big rotor turning slower and slower.

Hayduke drew his revolver, opened the loading gate and pushed a sixth cartridge into the one chamber which, for safety's sake, he usually left empty in the breech. Leaving the chain saw and pliers under a juniper, he climbed the dune, descended the slip face in three giant leaps and ran toward the helicopter.

He could hear the crewmen shouting in the distance, out of sight. He ran straight for the objective. When he reached it, five minutes later, the first thing he did was tip the muzzle of his gun into the face of the helicopter's radio transmitter. About to squeeze the trigger, he reconsidered and chose a less noisy implement, a fire extinguisher, wrenching it from its bracket and smashing the radio. A futile gesture perhaps; another helicopter might even now be on the way.

What choice did he have? Had to get Bonnie out of this. Hayduke looked around for a place of concealment. There was nothing much at hand. Certainly not within or behind the helicopter itself, a skeletal machine with transparent three-passenger cabin and no true fuselage at all, sitting high off the ground on its steel skids. There was the usual assortment of junipers nearby, but a juniper, while it can conceal a man from aerial observation, is no good from ground level at close range. The trunk is too small, the foliage too sparse, the branches too thin for hiding. Can't set up an ambush without a proper bush. Having no alternative, he descended into the same gulch Bonnie had taken, crawled beneath a ledge, pulled in some tumbleweed for camouflage and waited.

Dust. Spider webs. The allergenic Russian thistle in front of his face. A layer of juniper twigs and cactus joints sprinkled with tiny turds covered the floor under his belly—some provident pack rat, years before, had left this behind. Waiting, not patiently, palms sweaty and stomach sick with fear, Hayduke watched a pair of ants climb up the barrel of his revolver. Where'd they come from? The ants clung to the front sight. Before he could flick them off they crawled down the sight and disappeared into the bore. Now there's the place to hide. What would they make of the groovy rifling and the hollow-pointed bulge of lead blocking the end of the tunnel?

Hayduke wiped his damp hands on his shirt, one at a time, keeping the revolver out of the dirt. He cleared his throat, as if about to speak, and steadied his grip on the weapon—that comforting, solid and hefty magnum presence in his hand.

Male voices approaching. He reversed the greasy bandanna around his neck and pulled it up to his eyes. What was it Doc always liked to say? To the question: Wilderness, who needs it? Doc would say: Because we like the taste of freedom, comrades. Because we like the smell of danger. But, thought Hayduke, what about the smell of fear, Dad? Masked like a frontier outlaw, filled with dread, he waited for his next big moment.

Here they come.

The three approached in single file, for the gulch was narrow. From fifty feet away Hayduke could smell their sweat, feel their weariness. In the lead was the helicopter pilot, a red-faced young man with a big mustache, wearing army-style green fatigues, a long-billed cap, Wellington boots; like a combat pilot he wore a pistol in a shoulder holster under his left arm.

In the rear walked the man with the carbine, which he now carried slung over one shoulder. He was dressed in the uniform of a Burns Agency security guard: tight shirt with tin pawnshop badge and shoulder patch, straw cowboy hat, tight pants, cowboy-style boots with high heels and pointy toes, not good for desert exercises. This man looked older, bigger and brawnier than the pilot and just as tired. He limped. Both were sweating hard. Bonnie had given them a good run.

In the middle walked the captive, not too proudly, looking sullen, frightened and beautiful. Her hat was missing, the long mane of hair hung half across her heat-flushed face. She held her hands clasped together in front of her stomach, the wrists bound with handcuffs.

Hayduke had only a vague notion of what ought to happen next. Should we begin shooting? Shoot to kill or shoot to maim? With that cannon he held in both hands now it would be hard to merely maim; any hit would remove something substantial. Doc and Smith and Bonnie would not approve. So what? He had them covered now, he had the drop. Should he stop them at once? Or wait until they began the climb up over the slippery sandstone to the rim above?

The trio approached. The pilot was frowning. "That's right, kid," he said, looking for a way up out of the gulch, "you don't have to tell him anything. Name, rank and measurements, that's all."

The guard said, "I don't care what the hell her name is but she got to show me her sex identification. I guess I know my Constitutional rights. Right, girlie?" He poked her in the butt with two large stiff fingers.

Bonnie jerked aside. "Keep your hands off me." The guard, stumbling, did something painful to his game leg.

"Oh, shit," he moaned.

The pilot stopped, looking back. "Leave her alone, leave her alone."

The guard sat down on the ground, massaging his ankle. "Christ, that hurts. You got an Ace bandage in that kit of yours?"

"Maybe I do and maybe I don't. Leave the girl alone." The pilot looked around—toward the black shadow of the ledge where Hayduke lay crouched twenty feet away, toward the dry watercourse beyond, and up at the rounded hump of sandstone over his head.

"Isn't this where you came down?" The slickrock, easy enough to descend, not so easy to climb, rose twelve feet at this point above the bottom of the gully. "How about it?" he said to Bonnie.

"I don't know." She stared at the ground.

"Well it looks right to me. I don't see anyplace else unless we go clear back to where the great lover"—jerking a thumb at the guard—"where he came in." A false smile from the Burns man.

The pilot gave it a try. The rock curved upward at an average angle of 30 degrees. There were some niches big enough for fingers and toes. His leather-soled boots gave him little traction but he was agile. Using all fours, he had climbed halfway up the face of the rock when he heard, everybody heard, loud and clear, the sound of someone cocking a revolver. First click: half cock. Second click: full cock.

Perched uneasily on fingertips and toes, the pilot stopped and looked down. The security guard, surprised but reacting, raised a hand to unsling the carbine. Hayduke fired a shot over his head, closer than intended; the slug nicked the crown of the guard's hat. Two ants were launched on ballistic flight into the wild blue yonder.

The discharge made a shocking blast which startled everyone, not least of all Hayduke, and he was familiar with the roar of a .357 magnum. There were no echoes. In the one percent humidity of desert air the sound vanished almost as quickly as the bullet. A clang of hammer on anvil—and the stillness rushed back.

No one moved though all looked toward the dark shadow under the ledge.

Hayduke tried to think of what to do next. The pilot, finely balanced on his rock, was immobilized for the moment. That left the man with the carbine.

"Bonnie," he whispered. It sounded like the rustling of a dead leaf. He cleared his throat. "Bonnie," he croaked, "get that carbine."

Bonnie stared toward the hidden voice. "Carbine?" she said. "Carbine?"

The guard was alert. His furtive hand began to move again. Hayduke recocked the revolver, firm and businesslike. The hand stopped.

"Get the guy's gun," Hayduke said. He glanced up at the perched helicopter pilot. Two keen blue eyes burned back at him through the concealing weed, into his shadow.

Bonnie stepped close to the guard's shoulder, extending her handcuffed hands toward the forestock of the carbine. His hands, resting on the ground, were doing a nervous finger dance.

"Don't get between me and him."

Bonnie gulped. "Right." Moving behind the guard she stepped, not necessarily meaning to, on the man's hand with her lug-soled boot.

"Jesus!"

"Sorry." She took the weapon from his shoulder and backed off. The guard scowled, looking at the waffle-iron imprint on the back of his hand.

Hayduke slid out from under the ledge, rose to his knees and aimed his revolver up at the pilot's crotch. "All right. Now you. Unbuckle that holster."

"I can't let go," the pilot said. "I'll slip."

"Then slip."

"Okay, okay, wait a minute." The pilot raised one hand and fumbled with the buckle. "Man," he sighed, muscles quivering, calves beginning to tremble from the strain.

Holster, strap and weapon came sliding down the rock. Hayduke stood up a bit shakily, unholstered the pistol and stuck it in his belt. "Bon—Gertrude, you stand over here beside me." He waited. She came. "All right, now you come on down." He waved the big revolver at the pilot. The pilot eased himself down. The two men faced Hayduke. What to do now? "I think I'll kill you both," he said.

"Wait a minute, friend," the pilot began.

"He's kidding," Bonnie said. She looked more frightened than the men.

"Well goddammit, I don't know why I shouldn't," Hayduke said. The intoxication of absolute power, the power of life and death, was getting to him all right. Despite twelve months in the Central Highlands with the Montagnards, despite his Green Beret and Special Forces rating as demolitions specialist, George Hayduke had never killed a man. Not even a Vietnamese man. Not even a Vietnamese woman. Not even a Vietnamese child. At least, not to the best of his knowledge.

The fury and frustration of those years bubbled up like swamp gas, like an evil methane, to the surface of his consciousness. And here was a helicopter pilot, most despised of all, a real live helicopter pilot, probably from Vietnam, at his mercy. The right age: he looked like a vet. Why not kill the evil bastard? Hayduke like many men had a not-so-secret longing to cut at least one notch on his gun butt. He too wanted a tragic past. At another man's expense.

Providing, of course, that he could get away with it. Providing of course it was "justifiable homicide."

"Why shouldn't I kill the bastard?" he said aloud.

"Well you're not going to," his love said, hanging on to his right arm.

He shrugged off her restraining hands. Shifting the revolver to his left hand but keeping it trained on the pilot—"You sit down beside your buddy. Yeah, that's right. Just sit down there on the rocks"—he took the carbine from Bonnie and checked the action. One in the chamber and a full clip. Both hands full, he reholstered his revolver and leveled the carbine, hip high, point blank, at the two human beings sitting there, twenty feet away, alive and breathing in the fresh air, the cheerful sunlight, of the great American Southwest. A bird sang (rufous-sided towhee) down the gulch somewhere, and life generally looked good. A good day for dying too, no doubt, but all present were willing to put off till tomorrow what they didn't have to do today.

"How about—" Bonnie began.

"Why the hell shouldn't I?" Hayduke was dripping sweat, the little carbine shaking in his hairy, white-knuckled hands.

"Don't be crazy," she said. "They didn't hurt me. Now get this thing off me."

He blinked at the handcuffs. Two bracelets of black plastic, joined by a twelve-inch band of the same. "Where's the key?" He turned his masked face, red eyes glaring in the shade of the hard hat's beak, toward the security guard. "Where's the key?" he roared.

"Ain't no key," the man mumbled. "You got to cut it."

"You dirty liar."

"No, no, he's right." Bonnie's hands were on his arm again. "They're plastic throwaways. Get your knife out."

"Can't you see I'm busy?"

"Please, get your knife."

The men watched him closely. The pilot, big mustache drooping, grinned a nervous grin, his blue eyes bright and alert. A nice-looking kid, by recruiting-poster standards. He probably had a mother and a little sister back in Homer City, Pennsylvania. Never mind that he was also, in Hayduke's inflamed imagination, a mass murderer, a burner of huts, a roaster of children.

"Okay, Leopold," Hayduke said, slightly confused, "you too, fella; both of you lie down. Face down. Yeah. Hands on the back of your head. That's right. Stay that way. Don't move." Hayduke tucked the carbine between his thighs, pulled his knife and sliced apart Abbzug's bonds. "Let's get out of here," he whispered. "Quick. Before I kill somebody."

"Give me the gun."

"No."

"Give it to me."

"No. You climb up there. I'll hand it up to you."

Bonnie picked off her manacles. "All right." She put her lips close to Hayduke's filthy ear, bit the lobe, whispered, "I love you you crazy bastard."

"Get up there."

She scrambled up the slope of stone easily, her Vibram soles gripping the surface like lizard pads.

Hayduke handed up the carbine. "Keep them covered." He drew his revolver, cocked it. "Okay, you guys, roll over. Right. Now pull off your boots. That's right. Now throw them up to . . . to Thelma there." They obeyed. "That's right. Now."

The two men waited, watching him intently, eagerly, with complete undivided attention. As any sane man would, facing the dark hole, bottomless as oblivion, of a .357 magnum held in the shaky hand of an obvious lunatic.

Kill them now? Or later?

"Take off your pants."

This command drew protest. The guard, with a feeble laugh, perhaps an attempt at levity, said, "There's a lady present."

Hayduke raised his gun and squeezed off a shot two feet above the guard's head, knocking a chunk of stone out of the wall. The dart of flame, the crash of shock waves splitting the air. The invisible bullet, a mangled asteroid of lead, ricocheted off the rock and zigzagged down the gulch. A cascade of pulverized sandstone pattered on the brim of the guard's hat and into the neck of his shirt.

Hayduke recocked.

Skinner was right; persuasive reinforcement works. Both men pulled off their pants, quickly if not gracefully. The pilot wore, underneath, chic trim purple briefs which he may have been pleased to reveal to Bonnie, watching from above. The guard, older and more conservative, probably a Republican, wore conventional middle-American pee-stained shorts. He had a right to object.

"Okay," said Hayduke, "now take out your billfolds or whatever—keep that—and throw your pants up on top." They obeyed, though the guard had to throw his pants up twice before they reached the rim and stayed. "Now lie down again, on your stomach, like before, hands on your necks. Right. Stay that way, please, or I'll blast both you cocksuckers into eternity." Hayduke liked that majestic phrase so much he repeated it. "Blast you cocksuckers—into eternity!" he hollered, holstering his gun and creeping up the slope of stone.

On the rim they held a hurried consultation, then Hayduke hustled off to the helicopter with an armload of pants and boots. Bonnie stayed where she was, carbine cradled in her slender arms, watching the prisoners. The sun, plying westward, had only an inch to go to reach the horizon.

Hayduke, at the helicopter, tossed the clothes into the cockpit. He glanced at the smashed-up radio and regretted his haste. Would be nice to know what communications were flying back and forth right now, on the short waves of the air. He considered for a moment the controls of the machine. I wonder. . . . No, no, there was no time for that. Though he could go back and get the pilot, make him. . . . No! Not enough time; have to get out of here. Fast.

He drew the pilot's automatic from his belt and fired a shot into the instrument panel. Messy. He turned to the rotor head and shot up the swash-plate, the lag hinges, the rotor blades, the fucking ball bearings. Only three or four rounds left and he didn't want to waste any of his own ammunition. He fired the last two rounds into the fuel tanks, mounted on cross plates above the engine, close behind the cockpit. High-octane aviation gasoline streamed down into the works.

He found some flight maps in the cockpit, crumpled them together, lit them with a match and tossed the flaming ball onto the sand beneath the engine. He backed away. The ball of paper burned, then soared upward in a rich yellow spurt of flame as the first dribbles of fuel got to it.

Hayduke threw the pilot's gun into the flames and turned and moved off farther, quickly, as the fire spread over the engine and reached toward the fuel tanks. A mushrooming explosion shook the air—*whoomp!*—and the fire leaped upward, casting a violent glare across the sundown scene, paused at apogee and sank back upon the helicopter, draping the entire machine from cockpit to tail rotor in a film of sticky, busy, energetic flames.

Well, surmised Hayduke, feeling satisfied at last, I reckon this one's had it. Cooked. This fuckin' fucker's fucked. Full of goodwill, he turned to Bonnie. "Come on."

"What about these men?"

"Shoot them, kiss them, what do I care?" he yelled gaily. "Come on, come on."

Bonnie looked at Hayduke, then down at her two prisoners. She hesitated. "Here's your gun," she said, lobbing it down into the twilight of the gulch. The handy little firearm (U.S. Army .30 caliber semiautomatic) clattered brutally on the rocks, breaking. "Sorry. We have to go now. You can—"

"Come on!" barked Hayduke, waving his arm.

"You can get warm at the fire after we leave." She took off after her lover.

Side by side they ran past the melting helicopter into the shadows of the junipers.

"Where's the carbine?"

"I gave it back to them."

"You what!"

"It was their gun."

"For Christ's sake." Hayduke paused to look back. Nobody had yet begun to emerge from the dark cleft in the slickrock. Bonnie stopped too. "You keep going, I'll catch up." He drew his revolver and fired a snap shot over the rim of the gulch, just to keep things quiet and respectful down in there. Nobody replied. They ran on. The sun went down.

"What about your . . . fingerprints?" he panted.

"What finger . . . prints?"

"On the carbine."

"Won't do them . . . any good."

"Oh no? They can . . . trace anybody . . . for chrissake."

"Not me." Bonnie ran, proud hair streaming, breathing hard but steady. "I have never . . . been fingerprinted . . . in . . . my . . . life."

Hayduke was impressed. Well I'll be fucked, he thought. "Never even once?"

"Not even once."

All went well. Sun down, the hasty desert twilight darkened swiftly into night. The sky like a purple colander admitted points of starry light from the burning sphere beyond. No aircraft appeared. Hayduke recovered the fencing pliers and chain saw (property of Dr. Sarvis). They walked through the night back to the jeep which they also found, after a number of false ventures, under its Vietnam camouflage net, undisturbed.

As they were removing the net, folding it up and packing it away, they heard the unnecessary sirens, saw the superfluous whirling red lights of a Navajo Tribal Police van charging down the highway toward the bonfire of the helicopter. Standing on the hood of the jeep while Hayduke packed, Bonnie watched the police van stop, turn and charge through a barbed-wire fence and across the dunes toward the fire. The truck advanced a hundred yards before bogging down in the sand. She could see, even by the poor light of the stars, that the van's rear end was sinking deeper and deeper as the man at the wheel (Officer Nokai Begay) kept on stubbornly gunning his engine while his assistant (Officer Alvin T. Peshlakai) stood outside waving a flashlight in his eyes and shouting instructions. Their wheels were still spinning, their motor howling, their voices still yelling when Hayduke slipped his own vehicle, lights out, quietly back to the highway.

The highway should be swarming with *les flics*? Quite so. Hayduke kept his lights off and when the first headlights appeared coming his way he turned the keep onto the wagon road which paralleled the highway. Stopped and waited. An unmarked car rushed past, followed immediately by another.

He turned back on the highway and followed it for another ten miles, driving without lights. Dangerous? Perhaps. But not impossible. Hayduke had not too much difficulty staying on the road. Bonnie Abbzug chewed her anxious knuckles and offered plenty of unwanted advice like, "For God's sake turn the lights on. You want to get us both killed?" His only immediate worry was horses: hard enough to see horses at night even with the lights.

They arrived at the dirt road leading northeast to Shonto and Betatakin. Hayduke turned and once well away from the state road switched on the lights. They made good time, stopping only at a lonely spot out in the desert, between two wind-stripped, dead and silvery junipers to recover the goods, packed in heavy canvas duffel bags, which the Gang had cached there after the railway bridge operation. That had been Hayduke's idea—he wanted the dynamite in the bags for what he called "sanitary" reasons and for easier backpacking later. Abbzug had salvaged the empty boxes; that was her idea.

As Hayduke loaded the two bulging bags into the rear she again complained, "I'm not going to ride in the same car with *that* stuff!" but again—"Walk then!"—she was overruled. They trundled on. Getting low on fuel. Hayduke stopped near the familiar Park Service campground at Betatakin. He groped under the seats until he found his Oklahoma credit card, a length of neoprene tubing—*My leetle robber hose, señor,* as he called it fondly—and disappeared into the darkness with siphon and two gasoline cans.

Bonnie waited, rehearsing once again all the tedious questions about her own sanity. No question at all about that of her companion, or that polygamous jack-Mormon river guide, or poor mad Doc. But what am *I* doing here? Me, a nice Jewish girl, with an M.A. in Classical (*yech!*) French Lit. With a mother who worries about me and a father who makes 40,000 a year. Forty thousand what? Forty thousand ladies' foundation garments, what else. Me, Abbzug. A solid, sensible *gril* with a *keppela* on her shoulders. Running around with these crazy *goyim* in the middle of Arabia. We'll never get away with it. They got laws."

Hayduke came back, two full cans pulling his arms down straight. Groping again under the front seats—copping as he did a free feel between Bonnie's thighs—he found his spout and poured ten gallons into the tank. Started to walk away again with the empties.

"Where're you going now?"

"Got to fill the auxiliary tank."

God! Gone. She waited, cursing herself, wanting to sleep and quite unable, dozing in fits and waking up in terror.

Sound and smell of pouring gasoline. They were off again, into the night, running as Hayduke liked it best, full and cool. With trans-figured license plates both fore and aft. "We're from South Dakota tonight," he explained.

Bonnie groaned.

"Relax," he said, "we're crossing the river soon. We're getting out of this overdeveloped hypercivilized goddamn fucking Indian country. Going back to the canyons where people like us belong. They won't find us in a million years."

"Ought to call Doc," she mumbled.

"We will. Soon as we get to Kayenta. We'll stop at the Holiday Inn, have some coffee and pie."

That thought cheered her for a moment. The image of bright lights. Formica-topped tables, central heating, actual regular dues-paying American citizens with shaves! and haircuts! eating New-York-cut steaks with two vegetables on the side, salad, warm rolls wrapped in a cloth, a split of wine—no! yes!—recalled home, and decency, and hope.

The road passed through a galvanized tunnel underneath the Black Mesa & Lake Powell Railroad. Hayduke stopped.

"Now what?"

"This'll only take a minute."

"No," she cried, "no. I'm tired and I'm hungry and the police are all over the reservation and I'm scared."

"Only take a minute." He was gone.

She put her face in her hands and cried a little, then dozed off. In her dreams she heard the click of snapping fence cutters, the vicious whine of something like a tiger in the jungle of the night, sinking its teeth into helpless flesh. She was awakened by the sound of a crash, authoritative, and a cacophonic jangle of falling wire.

Hayduke rushed back, breathing hard, scowling with ill-suppressed delight. He jumped in, jumped the clutch and burned away, turned left at the highway and drove north toward Kayenta, Monument Valley, Mexican Hat, the trackless canyons of Utah—*escape*.

Passing through Black Mesa Junction in a light traffic of summer tourists, Navajo pickups and state police, they saw the lights of the loading depot burning brightly. Separate power source. The coal conveyor, bridging the highway forty feet above their heads, was also moving. Slowing his jeep, Hayduke stared at this critical node of the power complex.

"Keep going," she said.

"All right," he said. "Sure."

But one mile farther and he had to stop. He pulled off on a side road, shut off lights and cut the motor. He looked at Bonnie's pale face in the dark.

"Now what's the matter?" she said, coming fully awake.

"Got to," he muttered.

"Got to what?"

"Take a piss."

"What else?"

"Finish the job."

"I thought so. I knew it. Well listen to me, George Hayduke, you're not going to do it."

"Got to finish the job."

"Well I'm not going with you. I'm tired. I need some rest. I've had enough explosions and fires and wrecks and guns. I'm sick of it all. Sick of it. Sick of it. Just *sick* of it."

"I know." And as he took out his backpack and stuffed it with the food and water and tools he would need, he gave his girl her

working orders. She would drive on and wait for him at the Holiday
Inn at Kayenta; who could think of a safer place? How much money
did she have? About forty dollars. She could use her father's Gulf Oil
card, good at Holiday Inns. Establish credit and credibility. Never
mind the risk. Too late now. Take a hot bath. Call Doc and Smith,
arrange a meeting at the abandoned Hidden Splendor Mine, on Deer
Flat near Woodenshoe Butte. If he, Hayduke, didn't make it to Kayenta by night after tomorrow, she should leave the jeep there and go
on to Hidden Splendor with Doc and Seldom. Tell Doc not to forget
the magnesium. Very important. What else? He removed one of the
duffel bags from the jeep, and the chain saw, sharpener and fuel can.

"I wish you wouldn't do this," she said. "You need rest too."

"Don't worry, I'll be under a tree somewhere tomorrow and I'll
sleep all day."

"You haven't had a decent meal since noon."

"I got enough gorp and jerky in the pack to last me a week. Also
we got a cache near here. Take off."

"Tell me what you're going to do."

"You don't want to know. You'll read about it in the papers."

She sighed. "Give me a kiss." He gave her an impatient kiss.

"Do you love me?" she asked. He said he did.

"How much?" she wanted to know.

"Will you get the fuck out of here!" he roared.

"All right all right, you don't have to yell." Sitting now behind
the wheel of the jeep, she started the motor. Her eyes shone with
moisture in the dim glow from the dashboard. He didn't care. She
raised a knuckled forefinger to her cheeks and rubbed away the preliminary leakage. Exchanging his hard hat for the salt-rimed leather
sombrero, he didn't even notice. She raced the engine. "Can I have
your attention for a moment?"

"Yeah?" Pulling on gloves, he stared at the bright lights of the
loading towers.

"Just one thing I want to say to you, Hayduke, before I go. Just
in case I never see you again."

He looked everywhere but at her. "Try to make it short."

"Bastard. You sonofabitch. What I wanted to say is I love you, you ugly sonofabitch."

"Fine."

"Did you hear me?"

"Yes."

"What did I say?"

"You love me and I'm glad. Now get the hell out of here."

"Good-bye."

"Good-bye!"

Eyes blurred, she drove away. Alone, buzzing down the asphalt trail to Kayenta, heart beating, her pistons leaping madly up and down, Bonnie Abbzug relapsed into the sweet luxury of tears. Hard to see the road. She turned on the windshield wipers but that didn't help much.

Alone at last (Jesus *Christ* what a relief) Hayduke unbuttoned the fly of his jeans and fumbled it out and staled proudly, like a stallion, upon the hard ground, the beer cans and pop bottles, the squashed aluminum and broken glass, the plastic six-pack carriers and forgotten wine jugs of Navajoland USA. (Jesus Christ what a *relief*.) As he pissed he saw particulated images of stars a hundred thousand light years beyond our solar system glittering briefly, but bravely, on the trembling mirrors of his golden dew. He pondered for a moment the oceanic unity of things. Like the witch doctors say, we are truly all one. One what? What difference does that make?

The grandeur of his reflections gave him solace as he bent to his lonely and ill-rewarded labors. Reconstituted, the chain saw in one hand, the loaded duffel bag in the other hand and an eighty-pound pack on his broad mortal back, George W. Hayduke tramped forward—a staunch and unplacated force—toward the clanking apparatus the tough red eyes the armored jaws the tall floodlit and brazen towers of . . . the Enemy. His enemy? Whose enemy? The Enemy.

23

At the Hidden Splendor

Bonnie raised her stick from the juniper coals and checked the cremated marshmallow impaled on the tip. She pulled it off with her teeth and swallowed it down in one gulp, like a burnt oyster.

"I always thought only little childern ate them things," Smith said.

"Well, I like them," Bonnie said, "and I'm an old crone of twenty-eight. Doc, hand me some more."

He tossed her the bag; she put another on the stick. Sun going down behind the Henry Mountains. Cool shadows sweeping down from Elk Ridge. Below, a thousand feet down and five miles south by line of sight, the nude rock of Natural Bridges National Monument shone dull gold in the waning evening light.

Waiting.

She sighed. "Let me see those newspapers." Munching on her crisp black marshmallow, she read for the fourth time—or was it the tenth?—the account, on page eleven, of recent depredations in the Black Mesa area. Authorities Reveal Widespread Sabotage. Coal Train Derailed Second Time. Steel wedges found near tracks. Mysterious explosion blows top off loading and storage towers. Name scrawled in sand: "Rudolf the Red, Native Avenger." Investigations continue.

Police suspect large-scale organized band known as "Crazy Dogs." Renegade clan from Shoshone tribe. Coal conveyor destroyed by explosives in four different places. Gem of Arizona, world's largest dragline excavator, partly destroyed by fire in engine room. Damage estimated at one and a half million dollars. Only clue: "Rudolf Knows." Power line leading to strip mine cut for second consecutive night. Message scrawled in sand: "Rudolf the Red Knows." Cooling fins riddled with bullet holes, 80,000-volt transformer ruined. Pipe fitters strike in third week. Railway and power lines patrolled by aircraft. Coal company officials mystified and angered by wave of vandalism, "Work of idiots," says Arizona Public Service Company Environmental Coordinator. Secret monitoring device installed on coal conveyor. Pipe fitters' union denies allegation of industrial sabotage. "Remember Fort Sumner—Rudolf." Tribal Council promises inquiry into secret Navajo dissident group known as Ch'indy Begays (Sons of the Devil). "Remember Wounded Knee—Rudolf the Red." American Indian Movement denies any knowledge of Black Mesa incidents. Arizona Department of Public Safety, Navajo Tribal Police and Coconino County Sheriff's Office request assistance from FBI.

Bonnie folded the paper in disgust. "I don't see why they have to bury us in the back pages. We worked hard." She extended a hand to Doc. "Let me see that other paper. No, the old one. Last week's."

She opened last week's paper (the *Arizona Republic*, Phoenix) to page seventeen and looked at her picture again, an "artist's conception" based on verbal descriptions by the helicopter pilot and the Burns security guard. A poor likeness, she thought. Her hair too dark, her chest much too prominent. "Why do they have to make me look like Liz Taylor?" she complained.

"What's wrong with that?" Doc said.

"It's not just, that's what's wrong with it. Liz Taylor is an overweight, double-chinned, middle-aged matron. I am a petite and strikingly beautiful young woman."

"I'd call the drawing an idealization."

"You would." She looked at Hayduke's picture. The drawing showed simply the head and bulky shoulders of a man wearing a construction worker's helmet and a bandanna which covered all of his face but the eyes.

HELICOPTER DESTROYED IN FIRE. Pilot and guard assaulted and robbed by saboteur and female companion. ("Female companion" indeed.) Discovered near site of power-line sabotage, girl fled when approached for questioning. Caught by pilot and security guard, abducted at gunpoint by construction worker wearing handkerchief as mask, both wanted for questioning by authorities. ("Abducted!") Armed and dangerous. Pipe fitters deny any involvement. Rudolf the Red is not an Indian, asserts Navajo Tribal Chairman. Rudolf the Red *is* an Indian, insists Jack Broken-Nose Watahomagie, self-styled "war chief" of the Shoeshine Crazy Dogs. Speculations rife. Indian or non-Indian, these depredations are the work not of one man but of a well-organized and large-scale conspiracy, informed sources disclosed privately. Coal company has long history of labor troubles.

Bonnie refolded the paper. "What rubbish." She made as if to toss it in the fire. "Do we need this anymore?"

"Save it for George," Doc said. "He'll get a big kick out of it."

"Don't put anything more on the fire," Smith said. "Gettin' too dark. Gotta let that fire die out. Don't want ol' J. Dudley Love to spot us from down below there, do we now."

"He's looking for all of us, eh?" says Doc.

"Well, we're what they call wanted for questioning."

"How did he get my name?"

"I figure he must of got it from that pilot picked you up at Fry Canyon that time."

"That pilot is a friend of mine."

"No comment."

Bonnie studied her watch in the coagulating dusk. "That George," she said, "is now exactly four days and five hours late."

Nobody said anything. They watched the dying fire and thought each his own and her own thought. And that thought which each thought secretly was: Maybe we've gone far enough. Maybe George has gone too far. Maybe it's time to stop. But only Doc would confess it.

"You know what I've been thinking," he said. The others waited. He took a puff on his stogie, savored the smoke, expelled it in a flat blue stream. Poorwills called from the oak brush. Bats gathered and dispersed, out hunting under the blue-gold sky. "I've been thinking that after we finish this bridge job . . ."—if George ever gets here, that is, but he did not speak the thought—"that perhaps we should, well, give ourselves a bit of vacation. Say for a few months, at least. Only a few months," he added quickly, as he noticed Bonnie appear to stiffen. "Then, when things are quiet again and this area is not so hot, we can, so to speak, resume."

They considered the proposition in silence, a long pause following Dr. Sarvis's remarks. The coals of the fire shone on. Waves of darkness moved westward over the plateaus. Nighthawks patrolled for supper.

"We're not deciding anything until George gets here," Bonnie said. Chin set, lips compressed, she stared darkly into the remains of the fire.

"Of course," Doc said. "But the rest of us have to make contingency plans all the same."

"Doc, you know what I found yesterday down there at the mine works?" Smith said. "You see that big tank sets up above the road, on that wooden frame? That thing is half full of diesel fuel. Yessir. Five hundred gallons of diesel fuel in that thing if there's a drop."

Doc failed to reply.

"You just think what we can do with that, Doc."

Doc thought. "I see. But let me tell you something, Seldom Seen Smith. The kind of houseboat you want would cost me at least forty-five thousand dollars. I went to the boat show last week."

"We need four. Four sixty-footers," Smith said.

"That's only a hundred and eighty thousand," Bonnie said. "Doc can afford that, can't you, Doc?"

Doc smiled, a thin smile, around his cigar.

"Well, Doc," Smith said, "I'm gonna save you about a hundred and seventy-nine thousand and six hundred dollars, right here and now." He waited. No response. "We don't have to buy any houseboats. We rent them at Wahweap Marina for a hundred a day. We take them up Wahweap Bay past Lone Rock, clear out all the cabin space and load 'em up with ammonium nitrate. That's powerful fertilizer, Doc. I got all we need at the watermelon ranch. Then we pour on the diesel and seal the windows tight and our boy here . . . there . . . wherever he is, old George he fixes them up with a detonator charge and late at night we go down the bay and through the channel and cut that cable boom acrost the water and then we get that dam."

"I see," Doc said. "I'm supposed to walk into the marina office and I'm supposed to say to the clerk, 'Look here, lad, I want to hire four houseboats for the day; I'll take those big ones over there, four of them please, that one, that one, that one and that one.' That's what I'm supposed to do?"

Seldom smiled. "We'll all go in with you, Doc, the four of us together, and you can say, 'I need a houseboat for my friends here, one for the gal too, that'll be sixty-footers, please.' The man at the desk he'll be kind of surprised but he'll oblige. Them people'll do anything for money. You'd be surprised. They ain't like us, Doc. They're Christians."

"You're both insane," Bonnie said.

"Well," Smith said, "we could go to four different marinas, Wahweap, Bullfrog, Rainbow Bridge and Hall's Crossing. That'll take a few days longer, but we could do it that way. Then we turn 'em around and head down the lake."

"Renting a forty-five-thousand-dollar houseboat is not quite as simple as renting a car," Doc said.

"And then," Smith concluded, "we can take that vacation. We'll go to Florida, see the alligators. My Susan always wanted to see what them scaly bastards look like. Stop in Atlanta on the way." Seldom grinned. "We'll plant some watermelon seeds on old Martin Luther King's grave."

"Oh, mother," Bonnie groaned, raising her head to the velvet sky, the lavender night, the first faint pinpoints of the stars. "What am I *doing* here?" She looked at her watch.

"Try to relax," said Doc. "Drink your Ovaltine and stop whining."

A pause.

Bonnie stood up. "I'm taking a walk."

"Take a long walk," Doc said.

"I think I'll do just that." She left.

Smith said, "The poor little gal's in love, Doc. Worryin' herself sick, that's why she's so touchy."

"Seldom, you are a penetrating observer of human nature. And why am *I* so touchy?"

"You're the doctor, Doc."

They stared at the fading fire. One small bed of dying coals, like the lights of a lonely desert town, after dark, lost in the wastes of the great Southwest. Doc thought of New Mexico, of his empty house. Smith thought of Green River, Utah.

Change the subject, doctor.

"First the bridgework," he said, "then maybe the dam. Then we quit for a while. No matter what George says."

"You think we can get them houseboats lined up all right?"

"All we need is to make one little crack in it, Doc. One crack in that dam and nature she'll take care of the rest. Nature and God."

"Whose side is God on?"

"That's something I wanta find out."

Far away and below, down in the purple gloom, a pair of headlights made one convergent light in the dark, thin as a pencil flashlight's beam—some late-arriving tourist, no doubt, searching for the campground. They watched the light move slowly on its curving track, vanish under the trees, reappear, vanish again, go out for good.

Northeast and above, high on the slopes of North Woodenshoe Butte, a coyote barked at the fading sunset. The last bark, finely modulated, *andante sostenuto,* became a prolonged archaic and anarchic howl. The desert wolf, his serenade, his nocturne.

Waiting.

Doc removed the chewed-up stub of the stogie from his teeth. He looked at it. The Conestoga cigar, hand-rolled in the wagon seat, westward bound. He flipped it into the coals. "You think he'll make it?"

Smith mulled over the question before answering. After due consideration he said, "He'll make it. Nothing can stop that boy but hisself."

"Precisely the difficulty," Doc agreed.

That's the trouble, she thought. Something lacking in his instinct for self-preservation. Without me around to advise him he's like a child. A hotheaded brain-damaged overemotional child. Hyperactive type. Subconsciously wants to obliterate himself and so forth, that old bit. I don't believe in that *Psychology Today* schlock. Encounter groupies and Esalen oilers. Yes you do. No I don't.

She walked among the wind-ripped sun-bleached shacks. Uranium miners two decades before had lived here, somehow, on this waterless bench below the ridge, above the arboreal branchings of the canyons. Rusted oil drums stood against the canted walls. Mattresses the color of carnotite, urine, yellowcake, unstuffed by pack rats, raddled by rock squirrels and field mice, lay on the rotted floors. Sunken privies expired in the backyards. An old car tire hung by wire rope from the branch of a pinyon pine: children once played here. Garbage dumps like tailing heaps sprawled over the rimrock in a welter of metal, plastic, plywood, plasterboard, chicken wire, ketchup bottles, mundane shoes and eternal Clorox jugs, treadless and threadbare auto tires.

Down the gullied surface of a truck road she walked, under the loading chutes, past storage bins, water tanks, fuel tanks. Smells of sulfur, diesel fuel, decaying wood, bat dung, oiled timbers, oxidizing iron. From the black mouths of the mineshaft adits issued cloudy wraiths of unknown gases—radon? carbon dioxide?—drooling forth like smoke but odorless, heavier than air, creeping with languid sloth over the ground. The Hidden Splendor. Lovely place you picked for a rendezvous, George Hayduke. Pig that you are. Reptile. Toad. Horned toad. (I may be horny, George replied, but I ain't no toad.) She stepped cautiously around the foggy tongues, the slithering fingers of gas, and followed the rails that led, narrow-gauged, askew and rusty, out from the mine's foul maw across the road to the tailings dump.

She sat on the iron flange of an overturned mine car and gazed far out toward the south, through the veils of evening, for a hundred miles as thought can sail, over Owachomo Natural Bridge, over Grand Gulch, Muley Point and the gooseneck meanders of the San Juan River, past Organ Rock, Monument Valley, the volcanic hulk of Agáthalan, over the Monument Upwarp and beyond the rim of the visible world to Kayenta, the Holiday Inn, and the battered blue jeep still waiting there.

24

Escape of the Depredator

Hayduke ate one can of Brazilian corned beef, sodium nitrite and all (those fascist bastards make good corned beef) and drank two whole cans of diced pineapple, including the dice, for dessert. He rested awhile, then packed the canned goods back into the storage locker and reburied the locker in the cache hole. He disassembled the chain saw, oiled all parts and packed them into the canvas duffel bag and stored the bag with the food. He covered the cache with dirt, rocks and sticks; by starlight at least it appeared well concealed. What remained went into his backpack, which he reshouldered.

He put on his hat and looked at the stars. The Big Dipper lay upside down, from his point of view: about one o'clock in the morning. Hayduke moved down the talus slope below the rim and headed north straight across the country, toward the lights of Kayenta.

He felt good. His load seemed very easy after the burdens of the last few days, his feet were in good shape, his heart and head replenished by the sweet pleasure of success.

He made good time, despite the dogs that barked from every hogan clearing, and the anticipated police roadblock on the highway south of the Kayenta junction, forcing him to circle wide. In the pregnant hour between false and true dawn he reached the complex of motels, gas stations and curio shops at the junction itself. Stashing his pack in the bushes—for nothing looks more suspicious in the eyes of townsfolk, whether red-skinned or white, than a bearded man on foot with a pack on his back—he scouted the perimeter of the Holiday Inn parking lot.

The jeep was still there, complete with hidden key and note.

> *Sam, I waited for you three whole days. The Latter-Day Saint came and we went to pick up His Lordship at the Mexican Hat International Airport. Will meet you at the Plaza, as agreed. Please hurry as I don't like to be kept waiting. No more monkey business. And help beautify America—take a bath. Your friend and legal counselor,*
>
> *Thelma*

Nobody around but a few aborigines passed out against a cinder-block wall, empty bottles nearby. Hayduke started his jeep, retrieved his pack and drove north through Kayenta to the San Juan River and the village of Mexican Hat. The sun was rising as he rattled over the bridge. Back in Utah, back in the crazy canyon country, he felt safer, better and very much at home. Good to be back in good old San Juan County.

He noticed that the café was open and against his better judgment, knowing he had to get away from all towns and paved roads as soon as possible, he stopped. He suffered from a craving, irresistible, for a mug of coffee and a ham-and-eggs breakfast. Five days of nothing but raisins, nuts, sunflower seeds and chocolate chips, nothing but Granola and powdered milk, peanut butter and corned beef out of a can, did that to him.

He parked his jeep two blocks from the café, behind the Frigid Queen Drive-In (closed till noon), walked back and took a stool at the feeding counter. A Ute Indian girl with acne but a facial structure like that of a Mongolian movie-star princess took his order. He went into the men's room to splash some water on his face and attempt to wet down and smooth out his shaggy mane.

Relieving, he read, as always, the writing on the wall, the voice of the people: *Free love,* they said, *is priced right. There is no gravity; Earth sucks. Help Fem-Lib: Liberate A Woman Tonight. White man we gave you corn you give us clap.* He followed one message up the wall and onto the ceiling, where it said: *What're you looking up here for stupid? You're pissing on your shoes.*

Hayduke returned to the dining room and found two broad backs in tight cowboy shirts sitting adjacent to his ham and eggs, hash browns and coffee. Two silver-gray cowboy hats and two wide important rumps in gabardine. He spotted them instantly as the kind of men who wear bolo ties and shoot doves and eat Vienna sausages out of a can on fishing jaunts. The kind of folks that made America what it is today.

"Morning," Hayduke said, sitting down and facing his food. The wide tired brim of his sombrero would shield, he figured, the upper part of his face, the dangerous part. (Those red-rimmed eyeballs glaring at him wearily, like a lemur in a cave, from the cracked glass of the men's room mirror.) The moment he sat down however he knew he had made a serious mistake. From one corner of his left eye he saw the bright yellow Blazer parked hard-nosed against the log outside, the big official decal on the driver's door. He was tireder than he thought. The synapses in his brain, such as they were, had misfired or maybe never fired at all. His reflexes were not flexing. He knew he was tired but didn't know—hadn't known—he was too tired to see.

What the fuck. Let's eat anyhow and do something about it later.

The muscular brown jaws next to his paused for a moment in their work. The leather-skinned face turned his way and the eyes, pale blue as juniper berries, radiating wrinkles from a lifetime of squinting into the desert glare, fixed on Hayduke's hairy hostile face.

"How's my boy ol' Seldom Seen?" the bishop said, staring hard.

Dismayed but too worn out to care, Hayduke stared back, thinking, *George, you ever look a horse's ass in the face? Well here's your chance.* "Don't know him," he mumbled through a mouthful of breakfast.

"Is that right?" The bishop's huge red hands, bigger than Doc's and not half so kind, resumed their feeding motions. "Well, he knows you, boy."

The man on the bishop's right, who looked like Love's younger brother, stopped eating for the moment, looking at his eggs, and waited for Hayduke's response.

Hayduke hesitated only slightly. "Don't know anybody by that name." Adding a lot more sugar to his coffee: quick energy.

"You sure?"

"Never heard of him."

All three resumed eating, steadily: Hayduke his ham and eggs, the Bishop of Blanding also ham and eggs, the younger Love, sausage (four links) and scrambled eggs. The munch and chomp of manly mastication. The Ute princess shuffled from kitchen to counter in her bobby-soxer saddle shoes. The screen door slammed again. Two Navajos with retreaded heads, looking like school administrators or tribal bureaucrats, sat down at a table near the door, setting their attaché cases on the floor. They too wore bolo ties. Hayduke began to get that crowded, confined sensation.

Out of here!

The bishop continued: "Well, boy, I seen you with him that day at Bridges. And I never forget a face. Specially a face like yours. There was you and him and that young gal with the voice that carries so good and that big bald-headed man with the salty-black beard. And we stopped to ask you about some depredations on the road project. Somebody leavin' tracks with lug boots, size ten or eleven, all the way from Comb Wash to Hall's Crossing Junction. If that wasn't you that must of been your twin brother." The bishop's brother leaned back on his stool for a glance at Hayduke's footgear.

Hayduke's toes curled inside his lug-soled mountain boots. "Must've been my twin brother," he said, swabbing up the last of the yolk with the final slice of toast. Good, by God. He held up his mug toward the princess. "Coffee?"

She filled it, giving him a shy smile that under ordinary circumstances would have haunted Hayduke's memory for the next two months. Hope springs eternal in the male gonad.

"You don't remember nothin' about that?"

Hayduke poured more sugar in his coffee. "Nope," he explained.

"You are a liar, boy."

Hayduke took a sip, then another. He felt the sweat begin to trickle from the old pits and slide, drop by oily drop, down the ladderway of his ribs. The shirt he'd been wearing for five days was stinking bad enough as was without this extra bouquet. Ah, what to do, what to do? The old question. Of course he had the .357 stuck in his belt, concealed by his jacket, but he could hardly get it out and throw down on these Love brothers—two of them, big fellas—in front of so many witnesses. Should he throw the hot coffee in the bishop's face? Run for the door? Trouble like roses always seems to come in bunches.

"You hear me, boy?"

There's an idea. Play deaf and dumb. "Sir?" he said, and to the waitress, with a smile, "Check, miss?"

The girl took out her little green order pad. "Is this all on one?" she said, looking at Hayduke and the other two gentlemen. Their conversation had misled her.

Hayduke thought of Our Lord's words to the waiter at the Last Supper: "Separate checks, please." God but she was lovely. Confused but lovely. Those cheekbones. Those Aztec eyes. But he had more important things to think about. "Separate," he said. "I got to go."

"You ain't goin' nowhere," the bishop said quietly. "Not yet you ain't. We got some things to talk about."

"Sir?" Fumbling for his money. He fished it out.

"Yessir. Like a bulldozer jumpin' into Lake Powell all by itself. Like somebody rollin' rocks down onto my other Blazer. Like the whereabouts of one Seldom Seen Smith. Few little things like that, boy."

The bishop and his brother continued to scarf up their scoffings but kept their feet set back under their butts, ready to move, quickly. Their bleak and only faintly amused eyes did not leave Hayduke's face, not for a moment.

Still sitting at the counter, he paid his bill and a generous tip and was ready to depart. But how? He still hoped, somehow, to leave with dignity, with cool and grace. "Well, Dad," he said, "you got me mixed up with somebody else, that's all I can say." He started to rise.

The bishop reached out a heavy hand and yanked him back. "Sit down."

The bishop's younger brother grinned at him. "We'll all leave together," he explained.

A blue funk enveloped Hayduke's head. He hated jails. They gave him claustrophobia. That trapped feeling. Sighing, he said, "Well in that case I guess I'll need another cup of coffee." He held out the big mug; the girl refilled it, steadying Hayduke's wobbling hand with a touch of her own. "Thanks."

The steam spiraled up from the coffee in the shape, transient but clear, of a question mark. The question was not the practical one—Are they armed?—for if they carried weapons they kept them, like Hayduke's, concealed. In Hayduke's case, illegal; but the brothers doubtless held deputy sheriff commissions. The question was: Will the sphincter hold till I get out of here and free and clear? The riddle of the sphincter. That was the question.

"What's your name?" the bishop asked.

"Herman Smith."

"You don't look very American to me. Sure it ain't Rudolf?"

"Who?"

"Rudolf the Red?"

Hayduke threw his mugful of coffee into the bishop's face and dashed for the doorway. Two Navajo attaché cases big as satchel charges obstructed his passage. He leaped over them, crashed through the screen door.

"Have a nice day," the waitress screamed after him, obeying her standing orders from the management; "come back again soon."

Hayduke bolted past the bishop's new V-8 Blazer, regretting he lacked time to snatch the keys or shoot up the tires. He had only a glimpse of Love's loaded gun racks inside, the pennant on the aerial, before he pivoted around the corner and galloped up the road toward the Frigid Queen. Energy he never knew he had coursed through his veins, arced the spark gaps of his nerves, electrified his muscles. Feet don't fail me now. Roars of rage followed not far behind, the slamming and reslamming of the door, outcries, shouts, the thump of running feet. Look back? Not yet.

The drive-in. He swung around the corner and slid behind the wheel of the jeep. As he started the engine he allowed himself a glance back. The younger Love, running full tilt toward him, had covered half the distance. A big man but not fast. Bishop Love, swabbing his face with a towel, staggered out the door of the café, howling for his brother, and groped toward the door of his Blazer.

Drive wheels spinning, flinging gravel, Hayduke fishtailed his jeep toward the highway. The younger Love sagged against the wall of the Frigid Queen, gasping, then wheeled around and lumbered back toward his bellowing brother.

Hayduke's Plan: get the hell out of there. He coaxed his groaning jeep toward its maximum speed. Not near fast enough. He'd have a lead of maybe a mile before the Love brothers stopped fighting over who's to drive and got their powerful vehicle cranked up, turned around and started on his trail. Not nearly enough. Hayduke's only chance was to get off the pavement and out into the bush. What bush? He was down in the San Juan River desert, a wasteland of red rock and purple conglomerate where nothing grew but snakeweed, matchweed, povertyweed and tumbleweed. The high plateau where shelter lay was ten miles to the north. All uphill. He'd never make it. Think of something else, man.

Mexican Hat's one and only auto graveyard came into view, a decorative sprawl of old, wrecked, abandoned and cannibalized motorcars. Hayduke looked in his rearview mirror: the yellow Blazer not yet in sight. He whipped the jeep off the highway, through a gap in the fence and into the middle of the derelicts. Stopped and waited. Half a minute later the Love brothers came over the hill and rushed past not fifty yards from Hayduke's nose. By the sound of their engine they were still in second gear, winding it up. The bishop drove; his brother held a shotgun upright between his knees.

Hayduke gave them a mile lead, then followed. No choice. He

couldn't go the other way, south, back to Arizona. No friends down there anymore. He had to get up on that plateau and through the woods to his mates at the Hidden Splendor. So he followed his pursuers.

Three miles out of Mexican Hat the highway forked, the main branch leading east to Bluff and Blanding, the left branch—only partially paved—leading north to the high country, the canyons, liberty, sex and free beer.

The bishop, pursuing an out-of-sight fugitive, had to make the first decision. Would he be dumb enough to choose the east branch, leaving Hayduke a wide-open avenue of escape? Or would he take the road to the left, meanwhile radioing ahead to Bluff and Blanding, alerting the Utah Highway Patrol, the Sheriff's Office, the rest of the San Juan County Search and Rescue Team? Bishop Love, though full of rage and no intellectual, took the left fork.

Hayduke, lagging far behind, saw the bishop's choice and took the right fork. Directly into the waiting arms of the "authorities"? Maybe, and then again, maybe not. Though not intimately familiar with this area, as Seldom Seen was and as the bishop surely was, Hayduke had studied the maps often enough to remember that several miles ahead there was a dirt road leading off the highway to the left into something which the county Chamber of Commerce had named Valley of the Gods. Did the road dead-end? Climb to the plateau? Loop back to the highway? Hayduke didn't know and he didn't have time to make local inquiries. In a few minutes the bishop was going to realize that his quarry had somehow doubled back and was behind not ahead of him.

Grinding up the highway on the shoulder of an utterly treeless monocline, Hayduke watched for the dirt road, found it and veered left, gearing down. He bounced through a rocky gully and splashed across a sheet of water spread six inches thin on a slab of bedrock. He followed the road up the other side, which was bad but not bad enough. Sometime in the recent past someone had worked the road with a grader, trying to make it accessible to tourist traffic. Hayduke kept going, raising a cloud of dust across the wide-open desert plain. If the bishop didn't see that he was indeed blind with rage.

The road proceeded generally northward, following the contours of the landscape. Ahead a group of monoliths loomed against the sky, eroded remnants of naked rock with the profiles of Egyptian deities. Beyond stood the red wall of the plateau, rising fifteen hundred feet above the desert in straight, unscaled, perhaps unscalable cliffs. Hayduke had to find his way to the top of that plateau if he was to join his friends at the assembly point.

The jeep was stirring up too much dust. Hayduke stopped to look around, relax for a few minutes. He was beginning to think he might already have escaped. He hung his field glasses around his neck and climbed to the high point on a nearby stub of a hill.

All around, nothing but the wilds. Mexican Hat, the only humanly inhabited place within a radius of twenty miles, lay out of view below the swell of the monocline. In all directions he saw only the rolling desert, red rock dotted by scrubby vegetation, with a few cottonwoods down in the washes. Mountains and plateaus, floating on heat waves, walled the far horizon.

Dust clouds approached from the south and west. He raised the glasses to his eyes. On the road to the west, beyond the buttes and pinnacles in the foreground, he saw a shiny object made of metal coming fast—right: one yellow Chevy Blazer jouncing over ruts and rocks, scarlet pennon flying from the tip of the whiptail radio antenna. Rolling up from the south on the road Hayduke himself was taking came another Blazer, and another, both advancing at a fast clip, aerials gleaming, hardware sparkling under the glance of the sun. Hayduke followed the two roads with the glasses and found where they connected a few miles farther, westward among the Chamber of Commerce gods. The Searchers and Rescuers had him cut off and they were closing in. No more than ten, maybe fifteen minutes away.

"But I ain't lost," Hayduke said, "I don't wanta be rescued." For a moment panic struck him: Throw down your pack and run. Crawl in a hole and weep. Lay down, shut your eyes, give up.

But he suppressed the panic—the sphincter held—and turning

away from his pursuers he studied the lay of the land to the north and northeast. North he found nothing but the wall of the plateau; northeast, however, a trace of a trail road wound among the gods, dipped into a ravine and disappeared, reappearing on a narrow juniper-studded ridge toward a drop-off point. A dead end? From here he could not tell.

Hayduke sprang down the knoll and into his jeep. He started the engine, then jumped out again to lock the front wheel hubs and remove some brush caught in the winch. Seated once more, he shifted into first and drove off. Immediately the rooster tail of dust began to rise, revealing his position. Couldn't be helped.

Rumbling on at maximum feasible speed plus ten, he scanned the terrain ahead for the trail road he'd spotted from the knoll. Though not hard to see from up there, it was now invisible. Slabs of sunburnt sandstone in stratified terraces blocked his view. A lone juniper moved past on his left. He remembered it; the trail road diverged in this vicinity. Though the seconds were suddenly vital again, he had to stop and climb onto the hood of the jeep. Surveying the rocky jumble beyond his radiator he saw the parallel tracks peeling off through sand across a wash and up the hill eastward.

Back at the wheel, Hayduke geared down to first, transferred into low range and plowed through the sand and up over the rocks. At the top he paused to glance back. Three dust clouds were coming closer from two directions, closing a ten-mile triangle of which he was the vertex.

He hurried on. The road twisted among clumps of rabbit brush and scrub thorn, detoured around the pedestals of five-hundred-foot-high monuments. Despite local variations the trail kept rising; the needle on his altimeter gained another hundred feet, a few more scrubby junipers appeared. Hayduke realized that he was proceeding up the escarpment which he had seen from the lookout point at his first stop—junipers getting bigger, more numerous as the road wound toward the eastern skyline. Riding mostly on rock now, his vehicle no longer stirred up a funnel of dust. But that was not much help.

Though three miles behind and not gaining, the bishop and his Team could see Hayduke's jeep plain enough by line of sight.

What did Hayduke hope to find at the end of this rising wave of slickrock and juniper? He didn't know; he no longer had a plan. He merely hoped, and kept going.

One tall and healthy-looking juniper, well anchored in the stone, as its wind-sculpted branches testified, stood in photogenic silhouette against the sky. Beyond it, apparently, lay a void. With that tree as his goal, for want of any better, Hayduke drove on and upward. He was no longer following anything that resembled a road. The road had faded out on the slickrock a half mile behind.

He drove as far as the tree and there he had to halt. Land's end. Fifteen feet beyond the tree was the edge, the rimrock, the verge of a big drop-off. Hayduke got out and looked, and found himself on the brink of a cliff. Not merely a vertical cliff but an overhanging cliff, the rim of a projecting scarp. Hayduke was unable, because of the overhang, to see down to the juncture of the cliff face and bench of stone below. How far below? He estimated the fall at one hundred feet.

The lower bench or ledge sloped gently into a sandy wash which led in turn, through badland domes, knobs and turrets of eroded stone, to the broad avenue of sand, gray-green with sage and shaded by groves of cottonwoods, called Comb Wash. Comb Wash ran north and south for fifty miles below the wall of Comb Ridge. Some forty miles north of this point ran the highway project. Beyond that was the old road to Natural Bridges, Fry Canyon, Hite—and off on a northerly spur (abandoned), the remains of the Hidden Splendor uranium mine, sixty-five miles away.

A long hike and Hayduke was already four days late for the get-together. He might escape on foot, even from here—somewhere along this bluff there might be a place where he could rappel down by rope from the rim—but that meant surrendering his prize jeep with its roll bars, winch, auxiliary fuel tank, beer-can holder tilt meters, Guru Maharaji decal, "Think Hopi" sticker, wide wheels, special weapons, tools, camping and climbing gear, topo maps, Gideon's Bible and *The Book of Mormon* (stolen from the Page motel) and other treasures to that bunch of vigilantes behind him. *No way.* Not if he could help it. But could he? He looked over the edge of the cliff again. It really was an overhanging drop-off. It really was at least a hundred feet down. He recalled Dr. Sarvis's favorite apothegm: "When the situation is hopeless, there's nothing to worry about."

He turned to weigh the pursuit. The bishop and his Team were two miles back, coming slowly but steadily up the scarp. In the stillness he could hear, despite the distance, the throaty roar of those big V-8 engines. Gas hogs but powerful. Hayduke estimated he had about ten minutes.

Bishop Love was a patient man. Patient, methodical and painstaking. Though his face and neck still burned from the scalding coffee, he would not allow hatred to interfere with his judgment, his caution, his concern for his men. With the hairy gentile still distant but plainly trapped, he called by radio for consultation and stopped. Waiting for the others, he got out and studied the subject through binoculars. Focusing, he looked at bulging stone, the scattered trees and yucca plants in organic pockets of soil and, farthest out, way on the end of a geological limb, the patch of sun-bleached blue which gave away the location of the jeep, pitifully ill-concealed behind that large but final juniper.

Love knew what lay beyond that edge of rock. He himself had pioneered this very road, decades before, when staking out his claims during the first big uranium rush in '52. You heathen sonofabitch, the bishop thought, grinning in his entrails, we got you now. Glassing the criminal youth's position, he detected furtive movements behind the tree. Take care, he reminded himself. Consider armed and dangerous.

His men came up and joined him. They conferred. Bishop Love advised a vehicular advance of one more mile, stopping just beyond rifle range. From there they would proceed on foot, armed of course, in a broad skirmish line, with one man out wide on either flank to prevent the fugitive's possible escape along the rimrock. Agreed? Bishop Love's request for consensus was a courtesy only; in fact his suggestions, in the firm hierarchy of the Church, carried the authority

of commands. His companions, all of them full-grown men with busi-
nesses of their own, nodded like good soldiers. All but the bishop's
younger brother, who was, sad to say, somewhat of a jack Mormon.

"And be careful," the bishop concluded. "That unwashed bastard might have a gun. He just might be crazy enough to shoot."

"Well then," said the brother, "maybe we *should* radio the sheriff. Might be a good idea to have a little air support here. In case that
rascal manages to creep away over the rocks, maybe?"

The bishop, fifty-five, looked with humorous squint of eye and a
hint of sarcastic grin at his kid brother, forty-eight. "Think we need
help, Sam? There's one of him and six of us and you think we need
help?"

"He'd be a lot easier to spot from the air."

"How's he gonna get down off that rim out there?"

"I don't know."

"Maybe we ought to call in the state police too? Maybe the Air
National Guard? Helicopters, maybe? Puff the Magic Dragon? Maybe
a tank?"

The other men chuckled, shuffling their feet in embarrassment.
Big men, strong, competent, shrewd; two of them ran gas stations
and auto repair shops in Blanding; one owned and operated a motel
in the village of Bluff; one managed a feedlot and a six-hundred-acre
pinto-bean ranch on the dry upland near Monticello; the bishop's
brother worked as chief engineer for the El Paso Natural Gas Company's pumping station at Aneth, southeast of Blanding. (A very responsible position.)

As for Bishop Love himself, Search and Rescue was only a hobby;
he was not only a bishop of the church but also served as chairman of
the county commission, planned to run soon for the Utah State Assembly and higher office after that, owned the Chevrolet agency in
Blanding, several uranium mines active and inactive (including that
old one on Deer Flat above Natural Bridges), and a half interest in
the marina complex at Hall's Crossing. And eight children. A busy
man; too busy, perhaps. His physician, frowning over Love's cardio-

grams, advised him twice a year to slow down a bit; the bishop said he would when he got the time.

"Okay, Dudley," the younger brother said, "make a joke out of it. All the same, we ought to call the Sheriff's Office."

"I don't need any help," the bishop said. "I got a deputy's commission and I aim to use it. I'm gonna take care of that hairy little hoodlum up there and I'll do it all by myself if I have to. You fellas can go home if that's what you want to do."

"Hold it, Bishop," the motel operator said, "don't get your back up. We're all goin' with you."

"That's right," the bean-ranch manager said.

"Just what do you have in mind when we get him, Dudley?" his brother said.

The bishop grinned and tenderly, gingerly, touched his inflamed face. "Well first I'll take my needle-nose pliers and remove a couple of his toenails. Then his back teeth. Then I'm gonna ask him where Seldom Seen is, and that Dr. Sarvis and that little whore of a girl they transport around with 'em. We might get them all on the Mann Act, come to think of it—crossing the state line for immoral purposes. Then we'll bring in the whole bunch ourselves and we won't need no sheriff's department or state police to help neither. I don't have anything else I have to do today. You fellas with me?"

They all nodded, except the brother.

"How about you?" the bishop said.

"I'm coming," he said. "Somebody has to keep a rein on you, J. Dudley, or next thing we know you'll be running for Governor."

The men smiled, including the bishop himself.

"I'll get around to that later. Right now let's go jump that rabbit out of his bush."

They climbed back in their machines and advanced as planned. Within a mile of the objective Love stopped and got out. The others joined him. All were well armed—pistols, carbines, shotguns. Love issued his orders and the Team spread out laterally toward the sides of the ridge. He raised his field glasses to check on the quarry but the rise of the land prevented direct observation. He looked to either side;

his men were ready, watching him. He made a forward motion with his right arm, the squad leader's signal to advance. All began to walk forward, crouching, keeping in the cover of junipers and pinyon pines, holding their weapons at port. The bishop's brother Sam stayed close by the bishop: where each wanted the other.

A fierce hot high noon in San Juan County—thunder on the air, some more than decorative clouds in the southeast quarter of the sky, dazzling sunlight on the stone, the trees, the bayonetlike leaves of the yucca. No one noticed the desert marigolds, purple asters, mule-ear sunflowers in bloom here and there, in the sandy basins in the rock. The Team had better game.

"Did you take your digitalis today, Dudley?"

"Yes, I took my digitalis today, Sam."

"Just asking."

"Okay. Then shut up."

Bishop Love jacked a cartridge into the firing chamber of his carbine and lowered the hammer. He was enjoying himself; hadn't felt so good since mopping-up days on Okinawa. He was Lieutenant Love then, platoon leader, Bronze Star, building a good war record for later use. Heart expanding, the bishop even felt for a moment a trace of sympathy for the trapped Jap, the loser out there on land's end, cowering behind his jeep, pants stinking with fear.

The Search and Rescue Team advanced tactically, two dodging forward while the others stood ready to provide covering fire if needed. But there was no shooting from the fugitive's position. The Team advanced, crouching low, for the rim was less than four hundred yards away and the trees were scattered. The six men crept forward in plain view of one another, halted, waited, listened.

"I heard a motor," the brother said.

"That ain't possible, Sam," the bishop replied. He wanted to use his field glasses but so close to the enemy hesitated to put down his weapon. "I don't hear nothin'."

They listened intently. There was no sound, no sound whatsoever but the faintest sighing of the breeze in the juniper boughs and the occasional irrelevant twittering of birds.

"I thought I did," the brother said. "You say he's behind that last tree?"

"That's right."

"I can't see the jeep."

"It's there, don't worry about that." The bishop looked left then right at his men. They waited, watching him. All were sweating, all looked red-faced but resolute. The bishop turned toward the point of the ridge, the last juniper tree, which was obscured by other trees and barely visible from where he stood. He cupped his hands around his mouth and shouted, "You up there! Rudolf, whatever your name is! You hear me?"

No answer but the passing air, the distant jabbering of pinyon jays, the soft hoot of one great horned owl from beyond and below the rim.

The bishop yelled again. "You better come down outa there, Rudolf. There's six of us. You answer or we're gonna shoot." He waited.

No response except a second useless taunt from the owl.

The bishop cocked his weapon, nodded to his men. They took aim and fired, all but the brother, in the general area of the tall juniper, which shook visibly from the blast of buckshot and bullets.

The bishop raised his hand. "Hold your fire!" The echoes of the gunnery rolled away, down the monocline and off across the Valley of the Gods, dying out against the walls and promontories of the plateau, five, ten, twenty miles away.

"Rudolf?" the bishop shouted. "You comin' down?" He waited. No reply but the birds. "Keep me covered," he said to his brother. "I'm gonna root that devil outa there."

"I'm going with you."

"Stay here." Whispering: "That's an order."

"Don't give me that bullshit, Dudley. I'm going with you."

Bishop Love spat on the ground. "All right, Sam, get yourself killed." He yelled at the other four men, "Keep us covered." To his brother: "Let's go."

They dodged from tree to tree up the last rise of land and hit the dirt—but there was no dirt—hit the rock within plain view of the ultimate tree, the rim of the drop-off.

Nobody there.

No question about it now, he was gone. Rudolf had disappeared. His jeep had disappeared too. Nothing remained but the lone juniper, a cracked plate of sandstone lying near its base and a few spots of grease, a few slivers of steel scattered about on the ground.

"He's not here," the brother said.

"It ain't possible."

"Even the jeep's not here."

"I can see that. I ain't blind, goddammit." Bishop Love rose to his knees, staring at the positive, definite, almost tangible, almost palpable presence of nothing. Sweat dripped from his nose. "But it ain't possible."

They walked to the edge and looked over. All they saw was what was there: the bench of bare stone a hundred feet or so below, the corroded badlands, the gulches, draws and arroyos draining their arid beds of sand and rubble toward Comb Wash, the high sheer façade of Comb Ridge beyond the wash, the mountains beyond the ridge.

Sam smiled at his brother. "Well, Governor . . . ?"

"Shut up. I'm trying to think."

"First time for everything."

"Shut up. Hunker down in the shade here and let's figure this out."

"Maybe now you'll radio the sheriff."

Bishop Love plucked a stem of grass and stuck it in his teeth. Squatting on his broad hams he scratched at the ground with a stick. "I'll call the sheriff when I catch this bastard," he said. "Him and his evil crew. That's when I call the sheriff. Not before."

"Okay. Fine. Let's catch them. How?"

The bishop squinted at the sun and frowned at his brother and looked again at the tree and back at the stony ground between his boots. He chewed and he scratched and he thought. "I'm workin' on it."

25

Rest Stop

"Gee, then what happened?" She stared at him with awestruck eyes, mouth agape in mock astonishment.

"There you were," Doc said, "trapped on the edge of a hundred-foot cliff . . ."

"There I was."

"With the bishop and his fanatic henchmen coming toward you, armed to the teeth and black vengeance in their hearts . . ."

"That's about it." George popped the top from his fourth can of Schlitz within the last thirty minutes.

"No way down and no way out . . ."

"That's right."

"Six of them against one of you . . ."

"Six of them against only one of me. Yeah. Shit." He tilted the can to his grimy muzzle. They heard these awful schlurping sounds, watched his hairy Adam's apple bobbing. Smith, turning the spit on which their supper was impaled, smiled thoughtfully, gazing at the flames. Dr. Sarvis sipped at his Wild Turkey and pothole water, while Bonnie Abbzug smoked her "Ovaltine."

Back in the evening shadows, under the dappled light and shade cast by the camouflage net draped from the pinyon pines, Smith's truck stood parked; snug against it the blanched, blue and wrinkled jeep, its hood, top, seat and tarp-covered load all coated with an inch of auburn dust. There was a jagged, star-shaped hole big as a football in the windshield.

"Well?"

"Well, shit."

"Well, what did you do?"

"When?"

"Come on, George."

George lowered the can of beer. Smith was looking at him; he winked at Smith. He looked at Bonnie and Doc. "Oh, Christ, it's a complicated story. You don't want to hear it all. Let's just say I got down off of there and drove up Comb Wash and hit the road and what the fuck here I am. Give me a hit on that."

They stared at him in silence. Bonnie passed the weed. Doc lit up a fresh Marsh-Wheeling. Seldom Seen turned the spit.

"Okay," Bonnie said, "forget it. Let's talk about something else. What shall we talk about?"

"But if you insist—"

"No, that's all right."

"If you insist—"

Smith said, "You winched her down."

"Of course. How else." George grinned proudly at them all and in the short pause which followed elbowed the beer once more up to his face. He looked gaunt, filthy, starving, his eyes bloodshot from sun glare and strain, ringed like a raccoon's with dark circles of exhaustion. Nevertheless he wasn't ready to crash. Too tired to sleep, he had explained.

"What's this about a wench?" Bonnie wanted to know.

"The winch," Hayduke said. "That thing on the front. Got a hundred and fifty foot of cable there. Nothing to it."

"Now wait a minute," Doc said. "Are you trying to tell us you winched that jeep down over the cliff?"

"Yeah."

"An overhanging cliff?"

"Wasn't easy."

"That's what us rock climbers call a free rappel," Smith explained.

"Free repel?" says Doc. "What you mean, free repel?"

"Rappel, rappel. *Rappel de corde,*" Bonnie explains. "*C'est un moyen de déscendre une roche verticale avec une corde double, récupérable ensuite.*"

"Exactly," says Hayduke.

"We do it all the time," Smith said. "Only not with a jeep very often. In fact nobody never done it with a jeep before, far as I know, and if I didn't know George here was an honest man I'd be inclined to suspect he was maybe stretching the truth a *little* bit. Not exactly lying, mind you, I'd never suspect George of anything like that, but maybe just, well—"

"Simplifying the truth," Bonnie suggested.

"That's right, or maybe even oversimplifying it some."

"Yeah," Hayduke said. "Well, shit, don't believe me if you don't want to. But there's the jeep, right before your goddamned eyes." He passed Bonnie's little custom-made back to her.

"It looks like the same jeep," Smith admitted. "But it don't have to be. It could be one of them what they call reasonable fact-similes. But I ain't saying it ain't possible. I've winched my truck up and down some pretty steep pitches. But I got to admit I hain't never done a free rappel with a truck."

"Very well," Doc said, "let's assume, if only for the novelty of it, that George is not lying. But I have some technical questions. I didn't know, for one thing, that a winch can be operated in reverse."

"Wouldn't be much use if it couldn't," Hayduke said.

"And you anchored the cable to that juniper tree?"

"That's right."

Bonnie started to interrupt. "But—"

Hayduke set down his beer can, already empty, and reached for another. "Listen," he said, "do you want to hear the whole story or not? Okay, then shut up and I'll tell you exactly what I did. When I saw the bishop and his men were going to give me enough time, the first thing I did was get out my rock rope and measure the descent. My rope is a hundred and twenty feet long. The drop was about one hundred and ten feet. That meant problems. If the descent was seventy-five feet or less I could've done a true rappel with the jeep. There's one hundred and fifty feet of cable on the winch, remember. I could've doubled the cable around the tree trunk and hooked the running end to the frame and drove the jeep down to the bottom—"

"And sawed off the tree," said Smith.

"Right. Maybe. And when I got to the bottom I could've unhooked the running end and retrieved the cable without any trouble. But it was too far down. That meant I had to leave the running end of the cable on top, hooked around the tree. That meant I had to figure some other way to get it down after the jeep was down."

"Why couldn't you detach the cable from the winch," says Doc, "after you reached bottom?"

"I didn't think I'd have time. Besides it's against climber's ethics to leave aids in place after you finish a descent. Also I didn't want Bishop Love to know where I was, or how I got down, or *if* I got down. I wanted to give him something to think about for the next few years. So I *had* to get the cable off the tree and retrieve it. The only question was how. While I was thinking about that I secured everything tight inside and jockeyed the jeep between the tree and the cliff, back end at the edge. All this time the bishop and the Team were coming up the ridge but it looked to me like I still had at least five minutes. They were taking their time. And then they stopped about a mile below and got out and palavered awhile and started to walk up the ridge, deployed for combat but not too good; I could've killed every one of them if I wanted to. But—pass me that joint again—you know . . . bad PR."

"Finish the goddamn story," Bonnie said, "and let's eat."

"So I had the time. I hooked the winch cable around the bottom of the juniper. I tied one end of my rope to the cable hook—that's a big open slip hook, if you want to look at it. Since you don't believe me."

"No digressions." Smiling at him, eyes shining with ill-concealed love, Bonnie field-stripped the roach and packed the remains into her Tampax tube. "Go on."

"Okay, I put the jeep in neutral, started the motor and pushed the jeep back over the edge far enough to take up the slack in the cable—about four feet. Winch is locked now, you see, and the jeep hangs there, just the front wheels still on solid rock, motor idling. Then I put the winch in reverse and rode her down."

"You rode her down?" Doc says.

"That's right."

"You rode the jeep down? Down through the air?"

"Yeah."

"What were you going to do if the winch failed?"

"It didn't."

"But suppose it did?"

"I'd rappel down the rope."

Silence. "I see," Doc said. "Or I think I do. How much does your jeep weigh, Hayduke?"

"About thirty-five hundred pounds with all that gear in it. And the gasoline."

"And the winch held it?"

"It's a good winch. A Warn winch. Of course we twisted a lot going down and that worried me more than anything else. I was afraid the cable would twist itself in two. But it didn't."

Smith rotated the shish kebab (sirloin tips, sliced tomatoes, bell peppers, cherry tomatoes, onions—nothing is too good for the wooden-shoe people) and looked away and below at the canyon rims, the forested plateau, the distant road coming from the east. "George," he says, "you're something else."

Hayduke opened another beer. *La penultima.* The next to last. Every beer is *la penultima.* He said, "I was sweating some, I don't mind telling you. We hit bottom pretty hard but nothing got busted. I braked the jeep and let the winch unwind far enough to get slack in the cable, gave a good yank on my rope, pulled the hook free, and let go of the rope. The cable came down like a ton of bricks, and the rope after it. The hook went through the windshield and mashed up some gear but I didn't feel like complaining about it. Maybe I should have put the jeep under the overhang first, but you can't think of every-thing. I was feeling pretty fucking good anyhow. After the cable dropped I drove the jeep under the overhang, out of sight, and pulled in the cable. Then we waited. We had a long wait."

Bonnie said, "Who's we?"

"Why, me and my jeep."

Smith began removing dinner from the spit. "Grab your plates, pardners."

Doc said, "They couldn't see you down there?"

"It was an alcove in the cliff. Like a cave. There was no way they could see me or the jeep from the rim. But they hung around all afternoon. I could hear them arguing up above, with J. Dudley doing almost all the talking, of course. My main problem then was how to keep from laughing. Along about evening they left. I could hear them driving away. I waited until midnight to make sure they were gone. Then I wound up the cable on the winch and picked out a route down to Comb Wash. That took me all the rest of the night. In the morning I hid out under the cottonwoods. When nothing showed up by after-noon I came on up here. Let's eat."

"George," said Doc.

"Yeah?"

"*George . . .*"

"Yeah?"

"George, do you really expect anybody to believe that story?"

Hayduke grinned. "Fuck no. Let's eat. But next time you see the bishop, ask him what happened to Rudolf the Red."

"*Deus ex machina,*" Bonnie said.

They ate and drank and watched the sunset flare and fade. Dr. Sarvis gave his celebrated lecture on the megamachine. The fire flick-ered low. Smug Hayduke, victorious, gazed inwardly toward the smoldering coals of juniper and thought of the look on the bishop's face. Had he risked his life for a laugh? Yes and it was worth it. While Seldom Seen, quietly alert, relaxed but attentive, looked west at the mellow sunset, south into twilit canyons, east toward encroaching night, and north at the butte, Elk Ridge, the Abajo Mountains. Not worried, not anxious—but aware.

Don't like it here too good, he thought.

Hayduke yawned, beginning to unwind at last. Bonnie opened one more beer for him. "Time for you to get some rest, beast."

Dr. Sarvis dried his hands on a rag and contemplated the rich red-golden half-clouded sky. "Well done, Yahweh."

"Weather's comin'," Smith said, following the doctor's gaze. He wet his finger and held it in the air. "Wind's right. We might have a sprinkle or two tonight. On the other hand we might not. You can't never depend on the weather in these parts, like my daddy used to say. When he couldn't think of anything else to say, which was kind of often."

"I'm taking to the sack," says Hayduke.

"And like I *meant* to say," Smith went on, "reckon we might as well keep a lookout from now on. I'll stand the first watch myself."

"Wake me up at midnight," Hayduke said, "and I'll spell you."

"George, you better sleep. I'll get Doc here."

"How about a friendly little game?" says Doc. "A little nickel ante? Table stakes? Pot limit?" No response.

"Doc's drunk," Bonnie said. "Wake me."

"You and George can stand watch tomorrow night."

Bonnie led Hayduke to the love nest she had prepared: their sleeping bags zipped together on a pair of sheepskins on the rim of the mesa under the sweet air of pinyon pines.

"I don't know," said Hayduke.

"Don't know what?"

"If we should do this. Tonight."

Bonnie's voice became chill. "And why not?"

Hayduke hesitated. "Well . . . Doc's here."

"So?"

"Well, won't he . . . I mean, Doc's still in love with you, isn't he? I mean—Jesus Christ."

Bonnie stared scornfully at Hayduke, her eyes twelve inches away, six inches below. He could smell the smell of her wilderness cologne—what did she call it?—L'Air du Temps. That fragrance meaning: North Rim. Cape Royal. Point Sublime.

"Such delicacy," she said. She grabbed him by the shirtfront, firmly. "Listen Hayduke, you flake, you yo-yo, Doc's not like you. Doc's a grown-up. He accepts the fact that you and I are lovers. We don't have to be sneaky about anything."

"He doesn't care?"

"Care? He cares about me and he cares about you. He's a decent man. What are you afraid of?"

"I don't know. He's not jealous?"

"No, he's not jealous. Now are you going to go to bed with me or are you going to stand here arguing all evening while *I* go to bed? Make up your mind quick because I am not a patient woman and I detest wishy-washy men."

Hayduke considered the matter carefully for two and a half seconds. The broad and bristly face softened to a sheepish grin. "Well, shit . . . I am sort of tired."

Late that night, with Doc on guard by the coffeepot, where it simmered on the hot ashes of the fire, Hayduke was awakened, gently, by a few raindrops falling on his face. He came out of a troubled sleep—dreams of falling—to find himself staring straight up at a black and inky sky. No stars. For a moment, terror gripped him. Then he felt Bonnie's warm smooth body stirring at his side, and comfort came back, peace and reassurance; and a sense of laughter.

"What's the matter, Rudolf?" she said.

"It's raining."

"You're nuts. It's not raining. Go to sleep."

"It is. I felt it."

She poked her head out of the hood of the bag. "Dark all right . . . but it's not raining."

"Well it was a minute ago. I know it was."

"You were dreaming."

"Am I Rudolf the Red or ain't I?"

"So?"

"Well goddammit, Rudolf the Red knows rain, dear."

"Say that again?"

Early in the morning, up in the cloudy sunrise sky, they heard an airplane.

"Don't move," Smith said. They were all except Hayduke eating breakfast under the trees, under one corner of the camouflage net. "And don't look up. Where's George?"

"Still sleeping."

"Is he under cover?"

"Yes."

Smith glanced at the ashes of yesterday's fire. Cold and dead. Breakfast they'd cooked on the Coleman stove. The airplane droned past, slowly, not far overhead, bearing west. As it went on toward Hite Marina on Lake Powell, Smith scanned it with binoculars.

"Anybody you know?" says Doc. He thought of heat sensors, infrared spectrography. No place to hide from the techno-tyrant.

"Can't read the markings. But it ain't the state police or the SO. Probably one of them Search and Rescue boys. Eldon flies a plane. So does Love himself, come to think of it."

"So what do we do?" Bonnie says.

"We stay under the trees all day and keep a lookout on the road below. And listen for planes."

"I'd say we'll need a little amusement to pass the time," says Doc. "How about a friendly game of five-card stud?" No response from his victims. "Two-bit limit? Just happen to have this deck here. . . ."

Smith sighed. "Three things my daddy tried to learn me. 'Son,' he always said, 'remember these three percepts and you can't go wrong: One. Never eat a place called Mom's. Two. Never play cards with a man named Doc.' " He halted. "Deal me in."

"That's only two," Bonnie said.

"I never can recollect the third, and that's what worries me."

"Seldom, put your money where your mouth is and shut up."

Doc riffled the cards; they sounded like autumn leaves, beaded curtains in a Spanish bordello, the fall of Venetian blinds, Friday night

in Tonopah, a babbling brook, all things good and sweet and innocent.

"We need another hand."

"Let the boy sleep. We'll play stud till he wakes up."

Ten minutes later the airplane came back, cruising slowly past
two miles to the north. It disappeared over Elk Ridge, headed toward
Blanding or Monticello. A morning of silence followed. The game
went on, through the heat of a humid day, in the shade of the trees,
under a solumn sky, far out on the wooded flat beyond the end of the
stub road to Hidden Splendor. Hayduke joined them at noon.

"Where's the magnesium?"

"Buried."

"Whose deal?"

"Doc's."

"Deal me in anyway."

The plane, or a plane, made another pass and return, two and
four miles south.

"How many time's that fucking plane been over?"

"Check the bet. Four times."

"Make it a dime."

"Raise you a dime, pardner."

"Called. What do you have?"

"Aces over, pardner."

"Flush here. Who's watchin' the road?"

"I can see it. Deal 'em."

"Cards?"

"Three."

"Three."

"One."

"Dealer takes two."

"Watch that bastard. Your bet, Abbzug."

"Don't rush me, I get nervous."

The play: Abbzug lost her last chip.

"This is a crooked, dumb, boring game," she said, "and if I had
my Scrabble set here I'd show you dudes some real action."

Hayduke was the next to fold. Siesta time.

All but Smith crept into sleep. He climbed to a high point east of camp, above the mine, sat on a slab in the piney shade, binoculars in hand, and watched.

He could see for a hundred miles. Though the sky was lidded with heavy clouds there was no wind. The air was clear. The stillness was impressive. Filtered sunlight lay on the strange land, and waves of heat, shimmering like water, floated above the canyons. Must be a hundred ten in the shade down there. He could see Shiprock, Ute Mountain, Monument Valley, Navajo Mountain, Kaiparowits, the red walls of Narrow Canyon, the dark gorge of the Dirty Devil River. He could see the five peaks of the Henrys—Ellsworth, Holmes, Hillers, Pennell and Ellen—rising behind the maze of the canyons, beyond the sandstone domes and pinnacles of Glen Canyon.

Hell of a place to lose a cow. Hell of a place to lose your heart. Hell of a place, thought Seldom Seen, to lose. Period.

26

Bridgework: Prolegomena to the Final Chase

"Okay okay okay, let's get this motherfucking show on the road. Come on, Doc. Off your ass and on your feet. Out of the shade and into the heat. Come on, Abbzug, fix us some supper. Where's Smith?"

"Cook it yourself you're in such a big hurry."

"Goddammit, where's Smith?"

"Up on the hill. He's coming."

"Bloat and sloth, sloth and bloat; the sun is going down."

"What do you want me to do about it? Jump off the rim or something?"

"Both." Hayduke, now feverishly coming back to life after twenty-four hours of recuperation, pumps up the Coleman, lights the burners. He peers inside their big blue battered community coffeepot, dumps out grounds and leftover coffee and one sleek soaked drowned mouse. "How'd he get in there? Don't tell Bonnie," he adds to the figure at his left rear.

"I'm Bonnie."

"Don't tell her." He shovels in eight tablespoonfuls of coffee, fills with water, sets back on stove. "Chemicals, chemicals, I need chemicals."

"Aren't you even going to rinse the pot out?"

"Why?"

"There was a dead mouse in there."

"I threw the fucker out. You saw me. What're you worried about? He was dead. Start slicing potatoes. Open four cans of chili. We're going to *eat* for chrissake." Pulling his warlike Buck knife from its sheath, Hayduke slices a two-pound slab of bacon into thick strips, lays them overlapping in the camp-size cast-iron skillet. At once they commence to sizzle.

"Who's going to eat all that?"

"I am. You are. We are. We got a hard night's work ahead." He starts opening four cans of beans. "Will you open that chili or do I have to do every fucking thing around here? And boil some eggs. You're a woman, you understand about eggs."

"What are you in such a bitchy mood for?"

"I'm nervous. I'm always like this when I'm nervous."

"You're making me nervous. Not to mention mad."

"Sorry."

"Sorry? I think that's the first time I ever heard you use that word. Is that all you can say?"

"I take it back."

Dr. Sarvis and Seldom Seen Smith now join them; late-afternoon supper begins. The four discuss the Plan. The Plan is for Hayduke and Smith to work on the bridge, or bridges, depending on amount of time, materials and "local conditions," and for Abbzug and Sarvis to act as sentries, one at either end of the project. Which bridge of the three is to be restructured first? They agree on the smallest—the White Canyon bridge. The second, time permitting, shall be the Dirty Devil bridge. With the two access bridges knocked out, the central bridge over Narrow Canyon, Lake Powell, the inundated Colorado River, will be rendered useless. A bridge without approaches. With or without it, the road—Utah State Highway 95 joining Hanksville to Blanding, the east and west rims of Lake Powell, the western canyonlands to the eastern canyonlands—will be effectively cut. Sundered. Broken. For months at least. Maybe for years. Maybe for good.

"But if the people want this road?" asks Bonnie.

"The only folks want this road," says Smith, "are the mining companies and the oil companies and people like Bishop Love. And the Highway Department, which their religion is building roads. Nobody else ever heard of it."

"Just thought I'd ask," says Bonnie.

"Are we through with this fucking philosophizing?" says Hayduke. "Okay. Now let's get to work. Doc and Bonnie, you two see if you can't find something we can make signs with. We're gonna need four large ROAD CLOSED: BRIDGE OUT signs. Don't want any tourists in Winnebagos taking nosedives into the Dirty Devil River. Wouldn't want the Search and Rescue Team flying ass over tincups down into White Canyon Gorge, would we? Or would we? Do you have enough paint?"

"Why do I always get the dull uninteresting jobs?" whines Bonnie.

"We got a full case of Day-Glo spray paint," Smith says.

"Good. Me and Seldom we'll get to work on the thermite crucibles. We're going to need, let's see, about—"

"Why?" she whines.

"Because you're a woman. About four cardboard drums. Maybe six. Where's the stuff?"

"In the cache."

"That's what I thought," she says.

"Look," says Hayduke patiently, "Jesus Christ, would you really rather crawl around under the bridges? Down there with the rats and rattlers and scorpions."

"I'll paint signs."

"Then shut up and get to work."

"But I won't shut up."

"Okay. Who's going to wash the dishes?"

"It always comes down to that in the end," says Doc. "I'll wash the dishes. A surgeon should always keep his hands clean . . . somehow."

"We're going to hide this camp," says Hayduke, "so no one will ever know we were here."

"Which vehicle?" says Smith.

Hayduke thinks. "Better take both. Then we can split up if we get chased. Or have a backup if one breaks down. Gonna have a lot of stuff to haul."

Out of chaos, order. All hands falling to, they packed their gear into the camper of Smith's truck, leaving the giant camouflage net till last. They burned and flattened their tin cans and dropped them in a pit beside the remains of the campfire. (Good for the soil.) They buried the ashes of the fire in the same pit, filled it in, swept burial site and fire site with juniper boughs. The blackened stones which had formed their fire circle they threw over the rim.

Bonnie and Doc went off to the old mining camp, claw hammer and spray paint in hand. There they found sheets of plywood and fiberboard and made their signs, big ones, six feet by ten, lettered so:

DANGER
ROAD CLOSED
BRIDGE OUT!
THANK YOU

They salvaged some two-by-fours, knocked together props to hold the signs erect and lashed the signs to the roll bars of Hayduke's jeep.

Hayduke and Smith dug out the thermite materials from the cache under the trees: 45 pounds of iron oxide flakes, 30 pounds of aluminum powder, 10 pounds of powdered barium peroxide and 2½ pounds of powdered magnesium, all of it packed in round cardboard containers with metal ends.

"This all there is?" says Hayduke.

"Ain't that enough?"

"Hope so."

"Whaddaya mean you hope so?"

"I mean I don't really know how much it'll take to burn through those bridge members."

"Why don't we blow them?"

"We'd need ten times the dynamite we've got." Hayduke picks

up two cartons. "Let's get this stuff into the jeep. We'll need some kind of big can with a lid to mix the stuff in."

"Them cache tins will be okay, won't they?"

"They'll do."

"Why don't we mix the stuff here?"

"Be safer to mix it on the job," Hayduke says.

They loaded as much as would fit into Hayduke's jeep—the powders, the fuses, the last of the leftover dynamite—and the rest into the back of Smith's truck. The sun was gone, the sunset fading behind a dull gray overcast. They took down the camouflage net. Hayduke took his juniper broom and swept away the last footprints.

"Let's go," he says.

Smith and Doc leading in the pickup, they drove very slowly without lights down the ten miles of trail road to the highway. Hayduke and Bonnie followed in the overloaded jeep. Communications had been prearranged. If either party ran into trouble the other would be warned by light signals.

Bonnie felt the heavy fatalism coming on again, that flu-like feeling in her heart, her stomach. She was glad, exceeding glad, that tonight's raid would be the last for a long time to come. I fear nothing but danger, she quoted to herself. She glanced aside at Hayduke, caught in the reflex act of tossing a beer can out the window. She heard the tinkle of aluminum on the pavement. You slob, she thought, you filthy, foul-mouthed slob. She remembered the night and the morning in their zipped-together sack: other sensations. Did I take my pill today? Good God! Brief moment of panic. One thing we don't need now, a little bungle from heaven. She fumbled through her beaded medicine pouch, found the dispenser, popped a tiny tab in her mouth and reached for the fresh can of beer Hayduke had already opened. His hand—the sensitive plant—yielded the can reluctantly.

"What're you popping?" he asked, suspicious.

"Just a little Sunshine," she said, washing it down with Schlitz.

"You better be kidding."

"Worry."

"I got more important things to worry about."

Evil fanatic. Nobody had yet told George about the Larger Plan. The plan to suspend operations after tonight's assault on the Power Complex. Not terminate—but suspend. No one had dared. And now, certainly, was not the time.

There was also the question of interpersonal relations. Bonnie couldn't help it, pill or no pill: she thought about the days and weeks, even the months and years to come. Something inside, deep within her, longed for a sense of what lay ahead. For the gestation of something like a home, if only in her mind. With whom? With whom indeed? Abbzug liked living alone, part of the time, but never imagined for a moment that she might spend the rest of her life in such unthinkable exile.

We are lonely. I am lonely, she thought. Only her need and love kept loneliness at bay—the darkness surrounding a forest campfire, that bitter misery of loss. George . . . if only the bastard would talk to me.

"Say something," she said.

"Gimme back my beer."

Vast walls of sandstone rose on their left, south of the road. The pavement ended; they drove into the dust of Smith's pickup, following him westward over the forty miles of dirt road that led to the three bridges. No traffic on this lonesome byway tonight, though ore haulers from the uranium mines had left the surface beaten and corrugated like a washboard. The noise of the jeep and its rattling cargo made conversation uncomfortable, but since there was no conversation anyway she knew he wouldn't mind, the moody brooding sonofabitch.

They passed Fry Canyon gas station and food store, bathed in the ghastly blue glow of its mercury vapor "security lights." Nobody there. And drove onward down the winding bench of desert scrub and sand toward Glen Canyon, Narrow Canyon, the slickrock wilderness.

Stars appeared, a few of them, dim beyond the cloudy veil. She could barely see the road.

"Shouldn't you turn on the lights?"

He ignored her or didn't hear her. Hayduke was staring at something ahead, away from the road. Bulky black silhouettes of steel against the green glow of sunset lingering in the sky. He switched his headlights on and off four times. Halt signal. He pulled the jeep off the road and parked it behind a clump of trees. When he shut off the engine she heard at once, off in the distance, the dreary chanting of a poorwill.

"Now what?" she said.

"Bulldozers." Alive again, animated, his moroseness gone. "Two of them. Big mothers."

"Well?"

"Better check them out."

"Oh no. Not now, George. What about the bridges?"

"They'll keep. This won't take long."

"You always say that. And then you disappear for seven days. Shit."

"Bulldozers," he muttered hoarsely, eyes glittering, leaning toward her, stinking of Schlitz. "It's our duty." He pulled the boxes of rotor arms from beneath the seat, kissed her square and fair on the mouth, then scrambled out.

"George!"

"Be right back."

She sat and waited in furious despair, watching his blue-lensed light dancing about in the operator's compartment of a bulldozer that looked to be about forty hands high. The iron tyrannosaurs.

Smith approached. "What's wrong?"

She nodded toward the bulldozers.

"Thought so," Smith says. "I hoped—"

He was interrupted by the roar of a twelve-cylinder Cummins turbo-charged diesel, starting up.

"Excuse me." Smith disappears. She hears a consultation: two men shouting at one another under the raving of the mighty engine. Smith climbs down from Hayduke's tractor, makes his way to the second; she sees his flashlight wink on briefly near the control panel and hears the second motor revving up.

After a minute's delay both tractors rumble off on parallel course, into the gloom. They are about fifty feet apart. Between them is a tanker truck, a BLM public-relations billboard on posts and a sort of metal shed mounted on a sledge. These objects come suddenly alive, wrenched into movement by an unseen force, and move away between the two tractors, as if pulled by invisible bonds. The billboard topples, the shed sways, the truck rolls on its side, as all diminish steadily toward the rim (as she will later learn) of Armstrong Canyon nearby.

Twilight silhouettes, blurred by dust, Hayduke and Smith stand at the controls of their tractors, peering forward. Then very quickly they climb off. The tractors go on without human hands, clanking like tanks toward the canyon, and drop abruptly from sight. The tanker, the shed, the billboard follow.

Pause for gravitational acceleration.

A bright explosion flares beyond the rimrock, a second and a third. Bonnie hears the thunderous barrage of avalanching iron, uprooted trees, slabs of rock embraced in gravity, falling toward the canyon floor. Dust clouds rise above the edge, lit up in lurid hues of red and yellow by a crescendo of flames from somewhere below.

Hayduke comes back to the jeep, his smoky eyes alight with happiness. On his head he wears a billed cap of yellow twill with a harmless legend stitched on the forepeak:

"I want it!" She grabs the cap and tries it on. It slumps over her eyes.

He opens another beer. "Adjust the band in back." He starts the engine, pulls back to the road and drives into the cool darkness.

"Okay," she says, "so what was going on out there? Where's Seldom?"

Hayduke explained. They had stumbled onto a tree-chaining project. The two bulldozers had been joined to each other by a fifty-foot length of navy anchor chain, strong enough to uproot trees. By this simple means the Government was clearing hundreds of thousands of acres of juniper forest in the West. With the same chain, by the same method, Hayduke and Smith had simply cleared away into the canyon the support equipment which had been assembled for protection and convenience between the two bulldozers. As for Seldom, he was up ahead in his truck.

"Okay," Bonnie says, "but I'm not sure that stunt was so smart." She looks back. A flower of fire burns under the canyon rim, growing brighter as the night descends. "Anybody can see that fire for fifty miles. You'll bring the Team down on us for sure now."

"Naw," says Hayduke. "They'll be too busy investigating the fire. And while they're busy at that we're thirty miles beyond, down by the black lagoon, melting their bridges in front of them."

They came to the first bridge. Finally. Smith and Doc waited for them in the darkness. Below the bridge was the apparently bottomless gorge of White Canyon. Leaning over the steel parapet Bonnie heard water gurgling below but could see nothing. She picked up a rock and lugged it, two handed, to the rail, let it teeter over and fall. She listened and heard only the water churning down below. She was about to turn away when the sound of colliding rock, exploding sandstone and small assorted splashes came up from the gorge. Prone to acrophobia, Bonnie shivered.

"Abbzug!"

A blue light danced before her, painting phosphorescent figure-eights on the velvet dark. She turned her head aside, blinking away the retinal afterimage, which lingered like a fading stain of color.

"Yeah?"

"Give us a hand, kid."

She found Hayduke and Smith mixing their powders, rolling them back and forth in a big closed canister: three parts iron oxide to two parts pulverized aluminum equals thermite. Then the igniting mixture: four parts barium peroxide to one part magnesium powder. A potent dish. Doc Sarvis stood nearby, cigar smoldering in his teeth.

Bonnie was appalled by this display of reckless nonchalance. Her boys seemed unaware of danger, stoned on their delusions of power.

"Who's standing watch?" she demanded.

"Waiting for you, my sweet," says Doc. "You are the catalytic agent in this unprecipitated *mélange*. This retort malign of dissident chemicals."

"Then let's get cracking," she says. "Who's putting up the road signs?"

"We are," says Doc. "You and I. But one moment, please. I'm watching Dr. Faustus at work."

"All finished with this batch," Hayduke says. "Now I need sentries out. I'm going to blast a couple of holes in the roadway above the main arch of the bridge, one on each side. The idea is, we expose the arches, set up the thermite crucibles over the holes, ignite the thermite and let it flow down onto the steel. Should burn right through it—if we got enough mix. Gonna be some trial and error involved, so watch out."

"You're not sure it'll work?"

"I'm not sure what'll happen. But there is gonna be noise and there is gonna be some white heat."

"Just how hot does this stuff burn?"

"Three thousand degrees centigrade. About six thousand degrees Fahrenheit, right, Doc?"

"Negative," says Doc. "The equivalence formula goes like this: degrees Fahrenheit equals nine-fifths degrees centigrade plus thirty-two. Three thousand degrees centigrade therefore is about, let's see, five thousand four hundred and thirty-two degrees Fahrenheit."

"All right," says Hayduke. "I want security on all perimeters. Lookouts, set up your road signs."

The crew begins to function. Doc and Bonnie take two of the road signs from Hayduke's jeep and load them into Smith's truck. Hayduke takes what he needs—dynamite, blasting caps, safety fuse—from the jeep, before Smith drives it off to the west. Doc and Bonnie drive a mile east of the bridge in the truck and set up the first sign, then a quarter mile farther, where they set up the second. They wait.

Sound of three sharp whistles: alert. After a moment they hear the shot, the massive muffled *thump*—well tamped—of high explosive doing its thing.

"Now what?" says Doc. "Does that mean the bridge is already out? How do we get back?"

Again Bonnie explains the procedure. She and Doc are to stand guard at this point, from which they can see ten miles up the desert valley. They will wait for Hayduke's come-in signal, which means he has the thermite "crucible" set up and ready to ignite. Smith meanwhile is doing the same on the west of the bridge. After that—

Sound of the second blast.

"After that," Bonnie goes on, "we pick up the warning signs west of the bridge and take them across the middle bridge and across the Dirty Devil bridge and set them up again west of the Dirty Devil. Then George takes out the Dirty Devil bridge."

"Simple," Doc says.

"Simple."

"What's the middle bridge?"

"That's the one across the Colorado River."

"I believe George said the Colorado River has been temporarily removed." Doc's fiery eye, the burning stogie, flares and then dims as a sprawl of smoke lofts toward the stars.

"The river is still there but now it flows under the reservoir."

"What do you mean?"

Silence.

"Bonnie, my child, what are we doing here?"

Silence. Together they stare up the road, a pale and winding dirt track in the starlight, toward the black outline of mesa, butte, plateau and mountain. Old moon later than ever. Nowhere a single human light. Nowhere a sign. Or sound. Even the poorwills are taking a break. Nothing but the whisper of night breezes rising off the super-heated rock. And the far-off murmur of jet engines, 29,000 feet in the sky on the air lane to the north. No escape, anywhere, from *that* sound. Bonnie looks for the source of the noise and discovers tiny moving lights tracing a course westward through the arms of Cassiopeia. Bound for San Francisco, maybe, or L.A. *Civilization!* She feels a pang of longing.

Sound of a whistle. One long, one short, one long. Time to return.

Leaving their signs erect and in place, Bonnie and Doc climb into the pickup and drive back to the White Canyon bridge, Bonnie at the wheel. They find a rubble of concrete scattered the length of the roadway, through and over which Bonnie is forced to pick a way, driving the truck in low.

In the middle of the bridge she stops to look at two witch's nests of reinforcing rods splayed upward like electrified hair—black, crooked, smoking and hot, stinking of nitrates and vaporized wood pulp. Within these craters the bridge's support members are exposed, the great beams of structural steel plate designed to last for centuries.

Here Hayduke has set up his "crucibles," the five-gallon cartons resting on two-by-fours above the holes. Each carton is two thirds full of thermite; on top of the thermite is a two-inch layer of igniter mix. Buried in the center of the igniter is the business end of a fuse cord, taped to the rim of the carton so that it cannot be accidentally dislodged. The fuses lie draped over the sides of the cartons, running separately over the rubble toward the west end of the bridge, where George is waving his flashlight up and down, the brakeman's come-ahead signal, at those two idiots parked in the center of his bridge. A fuse lighter burns in his left hand, coruscating like a Fourth of July sparkler.

"Where's George?" says Doc, peering about through his spectacles.

"Maybe that's him waving the light at us."

"What's he want?"

"Come on," Hayduke roars. "Get the fuck outa there!"

"That's George," Bonnie says, nervously. She shoves the transmission into low and engages the clutch, too fast. The truck lurches forward, stalls.

"Come on," roars Hayduke again, the fulminating human

bomb. Somewhere beyond him, out in the darkness, Seldom Seen Smith is waiting, watching, listening.

"Dear Bonnie," Doc says in sympathy.

She gets the truck going and rumbles forward over the debris. They stop a few feet past Hayduke to watch the lighting of the fuses.

"Go on," he says.

"We want to watch."

"Go on!"

"No."

"All right, good Christ!"

Hayduke applies his lighter to the first fuse, then to the second. A coil of greasy smoke rises from each tip; the powder inside the lacquered casing burns speedily toward its goal.

"What happens next?" Bonnie says. "Will it explode?"

Hayduke shrugs.

"You haven't used thermite before?"

Hayduke frowns, making no answer. Doc puffs on his cigar. Bonnie twists her fingers. The three of them stand and stare at the two pale tubs of thermite out on the roadway in the center of the bridge. The fuses cannot be seen, and only a faint trace of burning wax on the air reveals the progress of the initiators.

Hayduke's lips move. He is counting the seconds. "Now," he says.

A glow appears in first one then the other of the containers. A hissing sound. The glow brightens, becomes an intense white light fierce as a welder's arc, painful to the eyes. The entire length of the bridge is brilliantly illuminated. They hear a soft thud, followed by a second, as the tin bottoms drop out of the cartons. A flow of molten metal pure and bright as sunlight streams down into the craters of the roadway, pouring onto the steel beams. The interior of the gorge far below is lit up, each detail of rock and crag and fissure now revealed, down to the pools of water on the canyon floor. Gobs and gouts of burning slag fall through space, flaring hotter as their descent accelerates, and splash with a steaming sizzle into the water. Fragments of red-hot welded steel and broiled concrete follow.

The molten masses clustered like horrible tumors on the bridge beams start to cool, a cooling apparent to the eye, a clearly diminishing incandescence. Darkness creeps back on all sides. The stars can be seen again.

The bridge still stands, apparently essentially intact, arched above the flood, above the trench of the darkening canyon.

A red glow remains, like the coal of Doc's cigar, under the span of the bridge, glaring like two red eyes through the sockets in the roadway. There is some sputtering and fizzling, some creaking and cracking sounds, as molecular adjustments take place, accompanied by the splash and kiss of fiery shards dropping into the water below.

Quietude. The bridge remains. The three watch the failing light show. "Well," says Doc, drawing on his smoke—the twin pinpoints of fire glint for a moment on the lenses of his glasses—"what do you think, George? Have we or have we not?"

Hayduke scowls. "Have a feeling we been fucked. Let's take a look."

"Don't go out there," Bonnie says.

"Why not?"

"How do you know it's not right on the point of collapsing? The whole thing?"

"That's what I want to find out." Hayduke steps forth onto the bridge, springs up and down, walks out to the smoldering center and looks into one of his glowing handmade volcanoes, his face lit up pink as a rose.

Bonnie follows. Doc comes slowly after.

"Well?"

Far off in the east, a green light rises in an arc, descends and fades.

"Falling star," Bonnie says. *How I wish*, she thinks.

They stare like kids. "More like a flare," says Hayduke. "I wonder— What the fuck, let's see what we got here. . . ."

They look down through a hole at the dull red blob of heat and steel, seeing what resembles a glowing jumbo-size wad of chewing gum mashed to the arch of the bridge.

"Didn't cut," mumbles Hayduke. "Didn't cut through." Checking the other hole. "What we got is just two big motherfucking spot welds on the beams. I think maybe I made the sombitch stronger than it was before." He kicks at a smoking rod.

"Now now," says Doc, "don't be too hasty. The temper of that steel will never be the same again. Suppose someone tried to bring a tractor-trailer across here? Or a bulldozer?"

Hayduke considers. "Don't think so. Doubt it. Need plastique, goddammit, plastique. About two hundred pounds of plastique."

"How about more of the thermite? How much is left?"

"I used exactly half of it. Was saving the other half for the other bridge."

Bonnie, looking westward toward the river, the reservoir, the black bulk of the Dirty Devil Plateau, sees a pair of headlights creeping down the road, five miles or more away. "Here comes Seldom."

"Well," Doc continues, "why don't we give one of these beams a second application? The full and intensive thermite treatment? Better to get one bridge than none. Run a big truck across it. A road grader, perhaps. Whatever we can find over toward Hite."

"We'll try it," Hayduke says, looking at the approaching lights. "That ain't my jeep."

Three long hoot-owl hoots from Smith's lookout post float on the air, accompanied by warning signals from his blue flashlight, a frantic X-ing in the dark.

The first pair of lights is followed by a second, and a third.

"Let's go," says Hayduke.

"Which way?" says Bonnie. "There's somebody coming the other way too."

They turn and look. Two pairs of headlights are swinging down into the red-rock country from the east.

"I thought you said there was never any traffic on this road at night," Doc says to Hayduke, who is staring at the lights.

"I think we better get out of here," Hayduke says. He fingers the butt of the revolver in his belt. "It's my opinion we better go." He starts toward the truck at a run.

"Which way?" Bonnie yells, looking over her shoulder as she runs, stumbling over a chunk of bristling concrete.

Doc jogs along in the rear, clutching at his hat and his cigar and his spectacles, big feet slapping on the pavement. "No cause for panic now, no cause for panic."

Hayduke and Bonnie pile into the truck. Hayduke guns the motor, waiting. Doc climbs in and slams his door.

"Which way?"

"We'll ask Seldom," Hayduke says, driving ahead into the dark without lights, toward the blue of Smith's circling flashlight.

They find him standing on the road beside the idling jeep, an anxious smile on the buzzard-beaked face. "How's the bridge?"

"Still there."

"But weakened," Doc insists. "Structurally impaired and on the verge of collapse."

"Maybe," says Hayduke, "but I doubt it."

"Those people are coming," Bonnie points out. "Let's discuss the bridge later."

"What's the escape plan?" Hayduke asks Smith.

Smith smiles. "Escape plan?" he says. "I thought Bonnie she was in charge of escape plans."

"Let's not be funny," Abbzug snaps. "Which way out of here, Smith?"

"Now don't get your bowels in an uproar." He looks up the road to the west. The lights, flickering behind an intervening rise of land, are making slow progress. "We still got a couple of minutes, so we'll take this abandoned loop yonder and wait for that bunch to go on past. Then we cut back to the road and head on up to the Maze and that Robbers' Roost country. We can hide for ten years in there if we have to, unless you'd rather hide somewheres else. Or maybe we oughta split up beyond the middle bridge and half of us borrow a boat at Hite and go down the sewage lagoon." He stares at more lights approaching from the east. "Damn if it don't look like the whole returned-missionary brigade is out tonight. That Bishop Love, he's bound to make Governor yet, the cottonmouthed sonofabitch. What'd you say, Bonnie?"

"I said let's get going. And I don't want us to split up."

"Might be smarter," Hayduke says.

"What do you say, Doc?" Smith asks.

Dr. Sarvis withdraws the cigar for a moment. "Let's stay together, friends."

Smith smiles happily. "That suits me fine. Now, follow me. And no lights." He gets into the jeep and drives it down the cut-off loop of the original road. Hayduke follows. Five hundred yards farther, down in a deep arroyo, Smith stops. Hayduke stops. All wait in the dark, eyes wide, hearts beating, motors idling.

"Better snuff out the cigar, Doc."

"Of course."

The lights come over the hill and around the bend—the first, the second. East of the bridge the other group also approaches, but slowly, having passed the first of the DANGER signs. In the middle of the bridge a rosy glow can still be seen. Barely there, cooling, dying out: 5432° C. of molten thermite all for naught, a splash of magma in the night and nothing more.

Headlights and taillights go by on the road beyond. Dim-lit interiors where men sit, shotguns and rifles clutched between their knees, eyes peering ahead. Sound of thrashing pistons, popping valves, fat stagger-block wide-treaded steel-belted radials gritting on sand and stone. Spotlights play toward the bridge, up the hillsides, over their heads.

The third vehicle does not follow the others. It diverges to the driver's left, off the main road down some alternate route. Advancing slowly but steadily *this way*. Disappears.

"Well, shoot," mutters Smith, who has left the jeep and is leaning against the front fender of his truck.

Hayduke pulls out his short piece. Loaded, naturally. "What's wrong?"

"That third party thinks he's playing it pretty smart. Put that iron back where you got it. He's a-comin' right down this road."

"Well," Hayduke says, "I guess we'll just have to ram the fucker head on. Crush him like a grape."

Smith stares into the darkness, his wise and wrinkled coyote eyes scanning the immediate terrain. "Here's what we'll do. He has to come over that hump in front there so he won't see us till he's on top of us. But he won't see us for certain then neither 'cause just about that time we turn on our lights and we charge right past him on the left there, through the blackbrush, before he figures out who we are."

"What blackbrush?"

"That blackbrush. You just follow me, George old horse. Lock your hubs and put her in all four and turn that spotlight on him and keep it right in his eyes till we both get past. Then we cut out for the canyons hell bent for election. Just follow me." Smith goes back to the jeep.

Hayduke gets out and locks the front wheel hubs, gets back in, shifts into four-wheel drive, revs the engine.

"What spotlight?" Bonnie says. "This it?"

"That's the control handle." He shows her how to train it forward. "Beam it on the man beside the driver. He's the one that'll be doing the shooting."

"What shall *I* do?" Doc says.

"Take this." Hayduke hands him the .357 magnum.

"No."

"Take it, Doc. You're gonna be on the hot side."

"We agreed a long time ago," Doc says, "that we'd have no bodily violence."

"I'll do it," Bonnie says.

"No you won't," Doc says.

"Hang on," Hayduke says, "we're ready to go."

"Caltrops!" Doc cries.

"What?"

"They're in the back of the camper. That's what I can do—sow the caltrops." The truck is already moving. "Let me out of here."

"Use the crawl hole, Doc."

"The what?"

"Never mind."

Smith in front has switched on the jeep headlights and is climbing the far bank of the arroyo. Hayduke follows through the swirl of dust, switching on his own lights.

"Turn on the spotlight, Bonnie."

She flips the switch; the powerful beam lies hard on Smith's neck.

"Get it off him. Just a hair to the right."

Bonnie swivels the light so that it pours beyond the jeep directly between the pair of lights coming up the other side.

They top the rise. Lights glare in their faces. Hayduke swings the truck to the left, out of the path of the oncoming vehicle. The spotlight blinds the driver—Hayduke has a glimpse of Bishop Love's scowling face—and then the man beside him, hat brim down over his eyes. Crackle of smashing brush, clatter of stones against the skid plate. Love has stopped his Blazer, unable to see.

"Dim your goddamn lights!" the bishop howls as they storm past him. Glint of gunmetal, sound of unholy curses, clash and click of gunlock meshing. Even above the whine of the engines, the snap of breaking branches, Hayduke hears and recognizes that slight but unmistakable noise.

"Everybody down!" he yells.

Something hot, heavy and vicious, magnum and hollow-pointed, whips through the space of the truck cab, leaving in its quick wake a pair of matched stars in the camper's rear window and the windshield, a ragged tear in the crawl-hole canvas. Tailed one microsecond later by the crash of muzzle blast—the gun's report.

"Keep your heads down." Hayduke reaches for the spotlight control, turns the beam 180 degrees into the eyes of the men behind. A second star appears like a miracle in the shatterproof glass of the windshield, this one six inches nearer Hayduke's right ear. The cobweb pattern of fractures overlaps the pattern of the first shot. Hayduke shifts into second, double-clutching, gas pedal jammed to the floor, almost overrunning Smith in the tired jeep.

He glances in the rearview mirror and sees, through the dense billow of dust floating in the spotlight's column, the lights of the bishop's vehicle backing, attempting a turn, jockeying back and forth in the narrow roadway.

Well, thinks Hayduke, they're coming after us. Naturally. Radios busy back there. That herd down by the bridge, coming across, getting the word, coming this way. Certainly. What else? So: the chase begins. Begins again. What else did you expect, flowers, ribbons, medals? Doc said something about caltrops. Caltrops?

27

On Your Feet: The Chase Begins

Yes, caltrops, medieval weapons from the Age of Faith. Dr. Sarvis tries to explain to George Hayduke what he is talking about, then gives it up and crawls into the back. His head disappears; his shoulders, trunk, wide bottom; his legs; his boots. They hear him rummaging around in the camper as the truck rocks, sways, rumbles and rattles down the dirt road hard on the tail of Smith in the jeep.

A glance in the mirror. Hayduke sees the entire Search and Rescue Team now on the trail: eight pairs of blazing headlights not half a mile behind. He steps harder on the gas but has to ease up almost immediately to avoid running into the jeep. Maybe I should give him a boost anyhow; and he pulls closer, eases the front of the truck into the rear of the jeep, accelerates against the drag. Smith in the jeep feels that buoyant lift in the hinder end, as if the jeep were launching into overdrive, spreading wings, taking off.

Doc's burnished head reappears through the drapery of the crawl hole. "Need a light."

They give him a flashlight; he disappears.

"Whatever they are he better find 'em quick," says Hayduke, watching those dazzling high-beam lights in the mirror.

"He can't hear you," Bonnie says.

"Keep that spotlight trained on the lead car back there," George says. "Blind the bastards."

"I am but they're gaining anyhow."

Hayduke hands the girl his revolver. "If they get too close use that."

She takes it. "I don't want to kill anybody, though. I don't think I do." She turns the weapon over in her hands, looking into the muzzle. "Is it loaded?"

"Of course it's loaded. What the fuck good is a gun if it's not loaded? What are you doing? Don't do that! Jesus Christ. Aim at their lights. Shoot out their tires."

Jeep and tailgating truck bound over the curves, in and out of ruts and chuckholes, over rocks, across washouts, through a drift of blow sand. Bumpers clang, clash, engage and lock. Hayduke realizes suddenly, in deep disgust, that the two vehicles are now coupled. One flesh. That settles the question of splitting up at the Dirty Devil.

Their pursuers are coming closer, closer, through the fog of dust, up the long rise before the descent to the gorge of the Colorado.

Bonnie points the gun out the window at her side, aiming perhaps at the mountains, and tries to pull the trigger. Nothing happens. She can't pull it. "What's the matter with this gun?" she hollers. "It won't work." She pulls it back in, letting the heavy barrel sag toward Hayduke's groin.

"Nothing's wrong with it and for chrissakes keep it pointed away."

"I can't pull the trigger. See?"

"Single action, single action, good God! You have to thumb the hammer back first."

"Hammer? What hammer?"

"Give me that thing." Hayduke snatches it back. "Here, get over here, slide over me. You drive."

At that moment the dirt road ends, succeeded by pavement. They are nearing the Colorado bridge. The rattle, bang and clatter of jostled equipment abruptly stops. No more dust, no more mechanical clamor—and no chance of escape.

"Hurry up!" Hayduke commands.

"All right!"

"Wait!"

Hayduke notices that the back door of the camper is open and that Doc, a black tuberous bulk against the lights of the Team, is tossing out handfuls of something like oversize jackstones. He looks like a man feeding pigeons in the park. He shuts the door, crawls toward the cab over a chaotic jumble of hardware and canoe paddles, peanut butter and blasting caps, and pokes his head into the cab. From Hayduke's point of view the doctor appears as a disembodied head—bald, sweating, bearded, teeth and spectacles gleaming, an apparition made tolerable only by familiarity.

"I think I've stopped them," he says.

They look. The lights are still back there and still coming closer.

"Doesn't look like it," Bonnie says.

"In a moment. Be patient." Doc turns his head to see through the bullet-shattered window in the rear door.

Presently, within a few more seconds, it becomes clear that the Team is indeed falling back. Their light beams wobble, turning erratically aside to the shoulder of the road. There is a confused cluster of lights—white, red, amber—merged in the middle of the road. Plainly the pursuers have halted, apparently regrouping for conference.

Hayduke and Smith, in pickup and jeep, bumpers locked, rumble together like Siamese twins over the asphalt between the great arches of the central bridge. They do not pause but continue on for another mile to the turnoff leading north, the jeep road to the Maze and whatever lies beyond. Off the pavement a short distance Hayduke stops the truck, forcing Smith to stop as well. They shut off their lights and get out for relief and study, staring back at the collection of headlights beyond the middle bridge, where the whole Team for some reason has come to a halt.

"They couldn't all of run outa gas at the same time," says Smith. He turns suspiciously to Hayduke. "Was you shootin' at them boys, George?"

"No."

"Flats," says the doctor. "They've all got flats."

"What?"

"Flat tires." Doc unwraps a fresh Marsh-Wheeling, gazing with satisfaction at the havoc he has wrought.

"You mean they all got flat tires at the same time?"

"Precisely." He rolls the stogie in his mouth, bites off the tip, spits, lights up. "Perhaps not all."

"How'd that happen?"

"Caltrops." Doc reaches in his pocket and removes an object the size of a golf ball with four projecting spikes. Crown-of-thorns starfish. He gives it to Smith. "An ancient device, old as warfare. Anticavalry weapon. Drop it on the ground. Right. You will notice that, however it comes to rest, one spike points up. These will puncture any tire up to ten ply, steel-belted or whatnot."

"Where'd you get these things?"

Doc smiles. "Made to order by a fiendish friend."

"Pongee stakes," says Hayduke. "Let's get these fucking bumpers unhooked, men, and get the hell out of here."

Bonnie and the doctor bounce on the jeep bumper while Smith and Hayduke lift on the other. The vehicles are freed from their unnatural conjugation. A transfer of drivers; Hayduke resumes control of his jeep, Smith goes back in the truck, to the great relief of Dr. Sarvis, who will ride with him. Bonnie gets in with Hayduke.

"That boy makes me nervous sometimes," Doc admits to Smith.

"George he's kind of crazy," Smith agrees, "ain't no question about that, which makes me mighty glad he's on our side and not the bishop's, all things considered. Though if you wanted to look at this business from a strickly practical kind of way you might think maybe it'd be better to stay as far away from both of them as a man could get. Better fasten that seat belt, Doc; mighty rough road ahead."

"An excess of a rather desperate . . . *panache*."

"Exackly, Doc. What's he waitin' for?" Smith looks back toward the bridge. Two pairs of lights have detached themselves from the immobilized group and are coming on. "Head out, George," Smith says softly, revving his engine up to an important roar.

Hayduke gets the jeep going. Without lights, following the pale path of the trail road by starlight, the two vehicles proceed northward, slow and cautious in the dark, over a road which makes the former dirt road seem like a ribbon of silk.

"Will this work?" Doc asks. "Why not turn on the lights and go as fast as we can?"

"Maybe it will and prob'ly it won't," says Seldom. "Old Love, he'll stop and find our tracks back there at the turnoff and be right on our tails again in five minutes. But you can't drive much faster than this on this road anyhow."

"What road? I don't see any road."

"Well I don't neither, Doc, but I know it's there."

"You've been here before?"

"A few times. It was only three weeks ago, you'll recollect, me and George led our friend Love up here. When George rolled the rock on him and smashed the bishop's Blazer flat as a flapjack. From what I hear Love is still sore as a boil about that. No sense of humor, that bishop. Mean as a junkyard dog when you cross him. *Watch* out!"

Billows of dust rise in the starlight as Hayduke and jeep drop into a deep pothole in the road. Smith is forced to step on his brake pedal for a moment, sending a bright red signal through the dark. Hayduke stops, wanting to talk.

"Break anything?" Smith asks.

"Don't think so. See any lights behind us yet?"

"Not yet. Love prob'ly went on down to the marina for some hot patches for his boys' tires. But he knows we're up this way. He's stupid, but he ain't near as stupid as we are."

"Should we try that old mine road we took last time?"

"Not unless you want to spend half the night moving your rocks off it. Besides, you want to hide in the Maze."

"Right. Okay. But how do we know the bishop hasn't got a squad of state troopers and sheriff's deputies coming down the Flint Trail to meet us? Or a couple of eager-beaver park rangers from up at Land's End?"

"We don't know, George, but it's the chance we got to take. If it's anybody but the Park Service they'll have to come all the way from Green River or Hanksville, so we'll beat 'em to the Maze junction easy, unless the sons of bitches are riding in them goldamn helicopters. Besides, old Love is too stiff-necked to call for help; he wants to catch us all by hisself, if I know that burr-headed bastard like I think I do. What're we standin' here for?"

"Where's the icebox?"

"Why?"

"I need a beer. I need two beers. How far to the Maze anyhow?"

"About thirty miles by air and about forty-five by road."

"I see lights," Bonnie says.

"So do I, honey, and I'd say that's kind of a hint we ought to head on up the trail."

Hayduke is already moving. Switching the headlights on, Smith follows the taillights of the jeep, which wink back, two bloodshot eyes, as Hayduke steps lightly, now and then, on his brake.

The road becomes steadily worse. Sand. Rock. Brush. Chuckhole, rut, washout, high center, gully, gulch and ravine. Forty-five miles of *this?* thinks Doc. After the easy victory of the caltrops, he now feels fatigue reaching for his eyelids, brain cells, spinal column. Smith talking. . . .

"What's that?" Doc says.

"I said," says Seldom Seen, "it's a damn good thing we all had an easy day back in the shade up on Deer Flat. What time you reckon it is, Doc?"

Doc checked the chronometer on his wrist. The instrument reported 1635 hours, Rocky Mountain Standard Time. That can't be right. He held it to his ear. Of course, he'd again forgotten to wind the thing. Bonnie's birthday gift, The kid must have saved a month's pay for this trinket. He winds it.

"Don't know," he tells Smith.

Smith stuck his head out the open window at his side and saw the glow of moonrise. "About midnight," he says. He looks back. "Them fellers are hangin' on. You got any more of them calitropes?"

"No."

"Sure could use some more," Smith says and starts humming a tune.

This is madness, thinks the doctor. A delirium, an insane dream. Pinch yourself, Doc. Okay. This is me, Sarvis, M.D., Fellow, American College of Surgeons. Well-known if not generally liked member of the medical fraternity. Tolerated though distrusted resident of Twenty-second Precinct, Duke City, New Mexico. A mourning widower with two fool-grown sons launched in full career. Rakes and no-goods, both of them. Like their father, *el viejo verde*. When I am old and bald and fat and impotent, will you still love me then, my moxie-doxie? But that's been clearly settled, has it not?

Doc stares at the dust-covered rear of Hayduke's jeep laboring ahead, the boy and the girl concealed by the pile of baggage under a lashed-down tarpaulin. He looks to the side, out his window, and sees furtive clumps of blackbrush and rabbit brush passing slowly amid a dim expanse of rock and dust and sand. He looks back and sees two pairs of headlights, one well in front of the other, glowing faint as fireflies through the floating dust, far behind but creeping onward, neither gaining nor losing distance.

What of it? says Doc to himself. What is it I fear? If death is truly the worst that can happen to a man there is nothing to fear. But death is not the worst.

He dozes off, wakes, dozes and wakes again.

They rattle ahead, mile after mile, over the stones and ruts. The adversary follows at a discreet distance, far back but seldom out of sight. Smith, studying the stubborn lights in the rearview mirror, says, "You know something, Doc, I don't think them fellas are trying to catch us right now. I think they're just trying to keep us in sight. Maybe they do have somebody coming down from Flint Trail to meet us. Which means I wouldn't be too surprised to find somebody laying for us up ahead about dawn."

"You said we could beat them to the Maze turnoff."

"That's right, but them fellas don't think we're headin' for the Maze."

"Why not?"

"Because the Maze is a dead end, Doc. The end of the road. The big jump-off. Nobody ever goes to the Maze."

"And that's why we're going?"

"Doc, you figured it out."

"And why does nobody ever go to the Maze?"

"Well, because there's no gasoline there, no roads, no people, no food, most of the time no water and no way out, that's why. Like I told you, it's a dead end."

Lovely, thought the doctor. And that is where we are going to hide for the next ten years.

"But *we* got some food there," Smith went on. "We cached some at Lizard Rock and some over at Frenchy's Spring. We'll be all right if we can get to it before the Team gets to us. We might have a little trouble finding water right away, though if we get rain tonight or tomorrow, and it sure smells like rain, then we'll be all right for a few days. If the Team don't press us too hard."

Not bad, thought Doc. Not half bad. We are four jokers on a dead limb. I'm afraid this night will never end. I'm afraid it will. He looks east at the rising waning sick oblate and gibbous moon. Not much hope there. He sees a jackrabbit scuttle across the roadway through the dusty columns of the light beams. Smith swerves to avoid it. Doc realizes that he has not seen cattle or horses now for many miles. Why so? he asks.

"No water," Smith replies.

"No water? But the whole Colorado River is over there on our right somewhere. Can't be more than a couple of miles to the east."

"Doc, the river is down in there all right but unless you was a butterfly or a buzzard you couldn't get down to it. Unless you feel like doing a two-thousand-foot swan dive off the rimrock."

"I see. There's no way down."

"Hardly any, Doc. I know one old trail down from Lizard Rock to Spanish Bottom but I never found any others." Smith checks the rearview mirror again. "Still doggin' our tail. Them fellas don't give up easy. Think maybe we ought to hide these here vehicles and take off afoot."

Doc turns in his seat, peering back through the crawl hole and the bullet-shattered window in the rear door of the camper. A mile, perhaps five miles, in their rear—impossible to gauge the distance in the night—comes a pair of headlights, rising and falling on the rocky road. He is about to face forward again when he sees a streak of green fire glide upward, higher and higher, reach apogee and turn back to earth, trailing a wake of phosphorescent, slowly fading coals.

"Did you see that?"

"I seen it, Doc. They're signaling somebody again. We better have a look around."

Smith blinks his headlights. Hayduke stops, shutting off headlights but not motor. Smith does the same. All four get out.

"What's up?" says Abbzug.

"They're shooting flares again."

"Where the fuck are we anyhow?" Hayduke says. He looks tired and depressed, his eyes bloodshot, hands shaky. "I need a beer."

"Kind of parched myself," says Smith, gazing ahead toward the dark walls of the plateau, then back at their pursuers. The lights have stopped for the moment. "Get me one too, George." He looks into the sky, hooding his eyes with his hands, toward the north, northeast, east. "There it is. Forget the beer, George, we ain't got time."

"Whaddaya see?"

"A plane, I guess."

They follow the line of his pointing arm and finger. One tiny red light blinks up there in the violet night, passing through the handle of the Big Dipper. Still too far away to be heard, it quarters across the northeastern sky.

"It's a helicopter," Hayduke says. "I can feel the vibrations. It'll be coming this way in a minute. You'll hear it."

"So what do we do?"

"I'm having a beer," says Hayduke, opening the rear of the camper.

He takes a warm six-pack from the icebox. No ice for days now. "Anybody else?"

A second Very light soars skyward from their enemy in the rear, at some indeterminate range, and rises to its zenith, hesitates and sinks, an elegant parabola of green flame. All watch, momentarily paralyzed.

"Why flares? Why don't they use their radios?"

"Don't know, honey. Different frequencies maybe."

Pop! goes the top. A fountain of warm Schlitz rises over the truck, mimicking the flare, and showers down on Doc, Bonnie and Smith in a fine, diffuse spray. Hayduke cuts off the throbbing jet of beer by clamping his mouth over the bunghole. Sound of earnest suckling.

"Well," Bonnie says, "let's do something." Silence. "Anything."

"It appears to me—" the doctor commences.

Whock whock whock whock: rotating blades chop at the air. Coming this way, comrades.

"We better head out on foot," Smith says. He gropes with both arms into the tumbled baggage in the rear of his camper and pulls out packs, day packs, six-packs, backpacks, all loaded with food and gear. Somebody thought of that (Abbzug); at least one thing has been done right this time. He throws out canteens, a half dozen of them, mostly full. He finds one small hiking boot and tosses it at Bonnie. "There's your boot, honey."

"I have two feet."

"Here's the other."

Hayduke gapes stupidly at Bonnie sitting down to put on her boots, at Doc struggling into his sixty-pound pack, at Smith closing the back of the camper. Hayduke holds his foaming can of beer in one hand, the other five cans—bound together in a plastic collar—in the other hand. What to do? In order to function he must put down the beer. But in order to function he has to drink the beer. A cruel bind. He tilts the open beer to his mouth, chugalugs it all down, tries to jam the remaining five into the top of his backpack. Can't be done. No room. He ties them on the outside.

"We got to hide these vehicles," he says to Smith.

"I know, but where?"

Hayduke waves vaguely toward the black gulf of Cataract Canyon. "Down that way."

Smith glances up at the helicopter, now cutting a big circle in the sky a few minutes to the north. Hunting for somebody.

"Don't know as we have the time, George."

"But we got to. All our shit in there—guns, dynamite, chemicals, peanut butter. We'll need that stuff."

Smith looks again at the circling helicopter, sinking toward the road a few miles to the north, and at the lights approaching from the opposite direction, now less than two or three miles away. Ambush in preparation: the closing jaws.

"Well, let's get them as far off the road as we can. Down that way, over the slickrock so we don't leave tracks. Maybe we can find a deep gulch we can drive into."

"Okay, let's go." Hayduke squeezes the beer can in his hand. "You and Bonnie wait here," he says to Doc.

"We're staying together," Bonnie says.

Hayduke tosses his crumpled beer can onto the road where Bishop Love can pick it up conveniently. "Then back in the truck, quick."

"No need for panic," Doc says, sweating already, "no need for panic."

All aboard once again. Smith leads the way with his truck, pulling around Hayduke and the jeep, off the road and over the rocks between clumps of desert shrubbery to the open surface of the sandstone. Hayduke follows. Without lights, edging forward, they drive downslope toward the dark gulfs of space beyond the canyon rim. In the faint light from the moon, distances and depths become ambiguous, deceptive, offering shadows and obscurity but little cover, little safety.

No cover, thinks Hayduke, looking for the helicopter; we're caught in the open again. Now comes the napalm. Smith eases to a stop in front of him. Unwilling to step on the brake pedal and flash a red signal to the enemy, Hayduke pulls his hand brake and lets the jeep bump gently into the rear of Smith's truck.

Smith gets out to examine the lay of the land. Looks, comes back, drives on. Hayduke follows close, grinding ahead in low gear. They creep toward someplace to hide. The helicopter, apparently set down on the road with lights switched off, can no longer be seen.

Good, thinks Hayduke. They're waiting for us up there. Good. Let the fuckers wait. He pops the top one-handed from another Schlitz. When you're out of Schlitz you're out of Schlitz. Long dry march ahead, got to keep that old kidney stone built up, can't have it dissolving on us in a lather of sweat and pothole water.

What else? He does a rapid inventory in his mind. What to carry: packs; the .357 and twenty rounds in his gun belt; the .30-.06 with variable sniper scope slung on his back, under the Kelty—"for deer, of course" (anticipating Bonnie's question and Doc's objections)—the Buck Special on his belt; carabiners, rope, chock nuts . . . what else? what else? Now, above all, must not forget something essential. Survival is the question coming up now. Survival with fucking honor, of course. With fucking honor at all costs. What else?

Smith stops again. Again Hayduke brakes by hand, bumping bumpers. Letting his engine idle, he gets out, walks to the lean arm hanging from the driver's side of the pickup cab. Six eyes and a red cigar confront him from the dark interior of Smith's truck.

"Yeah?"

Smith points. "Right down in there, old horse."

Hayduke looks where Seldom indicates. Another ravine divides the slickrock, this one maybe ten or maybe thirty feet deep, hard to tell in the moonlight. Sandy floor. Much brush—scrub oak, juniper, sage. Overhanging wall on the outside of the curve, a rounded incline on this side. It might go, Hayduke thinks. It might.

"You think we can hide them down in there?"

"Yep."

Pause. In the silence they hear only . . . more silence. No lights visible anywhere. All jeeps, Blazers, trucks, helicopters have been stopped and shut off. The Team will not so easily be outflanked this time. Over there in the dark, in those shadows under the plateau wall, the Searchers and Rescuers are waiting. Or not waiting; perhaps a scouting party has already been sent out, up the road, down the road, looking, listening.

"Too quiet," Bonnie says.

"They're still a mile away, at least," Hayduke says.

"You hope."

"I hope."

"We hope," says Doc, red eye glowing.

"Okay," Hayduke says, "let's drop 'em down in the gulch. Want me to winch you down?"

"No," says Smith, "can't have no motors running now, they might hear us. I'll ride the brake down."

"Use your hand brake."

"Too steep. Can't trust it."

"Your brake lights will show," Hayduke says.

"Smash 'em."

Done. Smith eases his truck down the bulge of rock, twenty feet to the sandy bottom, and noses it into the shadows under the oak brush and juniper. Hayduke follows in the jeep. Dim moonlight falls on the wall above, that flowing curvature of stone stained with oxides of manganese and iron, but down in the bottom under the overhang all is dark. They unfold the camouflage net, stretch it over the trees and tie it down; concealing truck and jeep from aerial observation. Hayduke cases his extra firearms and hides them in a grotto in the wall, above the high-water line.

Floods? The sand is powder dry, the bedrock of the gulch as arid as iron. Nevertheless, it is a drainage channel.

"We'll be shit out of luck if this place gets flooded," Hayduke says.

"We'll take some losses," says Smith, "and I wish we had time to find a better hiding place. Sure as shootin' it's gonna rain."

"Pretty clear now."

"It's building. See that ring around the moon? Tomorrow night you'll see a solid overcast. Next day it'll rain."

"Is that a weather forecast?" Bonnie asks.

"Well," hedges Smith, "like you might of noticed by now there's two things a person can't depend on. One of them is the weather and I ain't sayin' what the other one is."

Three low hoot-owl hoots from Doc on lookout.

"Reckon we better go, George," says Smith, hoisting his pack on his back, buckling the hip band.

Hayduke slings the rifle across his back and the pack on top of it. The rifle is light, a chopped-down sporting model, but it makes an awkward package wedged between his clavicles and the pack frame. He could sling it over one shoulder, and will later, but right now needs both hands free to scramble up the sandstone. He thinks: Ready anyhow, I guess, if a man is ever ready for anything.

Reinforcements coming for the Team. Three more pairs of head-lights are moving up from the south, amber-colored in the dust. Got their flats fixed. The other vehicles remain shut down, invisible, their crews unseen. Same goes for the helicopter.

"They'll be spreading out, I'd say," Smith says. "We better head this gulch here and then turn north, single file if you'll kindly foller me. Keep your feet on stone and leave no tracks and we'll be all right, least as long as this slickrock holds out which it won't all the way, naturally. Huh?"

"I said," Bonnie says, "how far to the Maze?"

"Ain't far. Watch out for this prickly pear, honey."

"How far is that?"

"Well, Bonnie, I'd say we're only about two miles—three miles at the most—from the turnoff."

"You mean the turnoff to the Maze?"

"That's right."

"Good. So how far from the turnoff to the Maze itself? In miles."

"Well it's a pretty good walk but it's a nice night."

"How far?"

"The Maze, that's a mighty big piece of country, Bonnie, and if you mean the near end of it or the far end of it that makes considerable difference. And that's not counting the up and down."

"The up and down what?"

"Canyon walls. The fins."

"What exactly are you talking about?"

"I mean this country, it's mostly stood on edge, honey. Some of it you can stand on but most of it goes straight up or straight down. You can get boxed in or rimmed up pretty easy. Which means that usually the long way around is the shortest way. Usually the only way."

"How far, please?"

"Walk ten miles to get one mile, if you see what I mean."

"How far?"

"Thirty-five miles to Lizard Rock. Where we cached some water. We could take shortcuts if there was any but there ain't. None that I know about. But it's complicated country and you never know what you're gonna find."

"So we won't get there tonight?"

"We won't even try."

Hayduke, bringing up the rear of the file, stops to remove his pack and re-sling the rifle. In the pack he carries food, six quarts of water, ammunition and too much else. Plus the rifle on his shoulder, the loaded gun belt and holstered revolver, the knife sheathed on his hip. A walking arsenal and it hurts; but he is too stubborn to leave any more behind.

They pad ahead through the vague moonlight, staying on solid stone, skirting the lip of the shadowy ravine on their right. Smith pauses frequently to look and listen, then leads on. No sign anywhere of their enemy; nevertheless the enemy waits out there somewhere, in those shadows under the fifteen-hundred-foot cliffs, among the quietly breathing junipers.

Bonnie's head is full of questions. Who brought in the helicopter—state police, Sheriff's Office, Park Service, or other members of the Search and Rescue Team? If we can't get to the Maze tonight, what do we do when the sun comes up? Also I'm hungry and my feet are going to hurt pretty soon and who put the pig iron in my pack?

"I'm hungry," she says.

Smith halts, hushing her. He whispers, "Them other folks is out there, Bonnie. We're gettin' close. Wait here a minute."

He puts down his pack and glides off like a phantom, a shadow, a Paiute, across the rolling sea of petrified dunes toward the road. Bonnie watches his lanky figure recede into the moonlight, fading into moonshade, phasing itself out. Now you see him, now you don't. Seldom becoming Never Seen. Bonnie and the others remove their packs. She unzips the side pocket and pulls out a Baggie full of her personal mixture of raisins, nuts, M & Ms, sunflower seeds. Doc chews on a stick of jerky. Hayduke stands and waits, staring after Smith. He unslings the rifle, resting the rubber butt plate on his boot.

"Why the gun?" Bonnie whispers.

"This?" Hayduke stares at her. "This is a rifle." He grins. "*This* is my gun."

"Don't be vulgar."

"Then don't ask dumb questions."

"Why did you bring that gun?"

Doc intervenes, the moderator. "Now now, let's keep it down."

For a minute or so they remain silent, listening.

Off in the desert, at an indefinable distance, an owl calls. One call. The great horned owl. They hear a second call.

"Two hoots?" Bonnie says. "What's that mean, I forget."

"Wait. . . ."

From farther away again, or not so far, but from an opposite direction, comes the sound of another great horned owl, hooting gently into the moonshine and the night. The second owl calls three times. Meaning danger, on guard; meaning distress, trouble, I need help. Or meaning in owl language: You there, little bunny rabbit hiding under that bush, I know you're there, you know I'm here and we both know your ass is mine. Come.

Which call is true? Which owl is false? Neither? Both? They hadn't planned on real owls.

A whisper of light feet on rock. Seldom Seen emerges from the moonlight. Eyes shining, all tooth and ear and leather and hair, breathing slightly harder than normal, he says, very quietly, "Let's go."

Groaning and creaking, they struggle back into their packs. "What'd you see?" asks Hayduke.

"Them Search and Rescue people are all over the place and they're not waiting till sunup to come find us. I saw six of 'em along the road and I don't know how many more come in that goddanged infernal helicopter up ahead. Every man I saw has a shotgun or a carbine and they're all carrying them little walkie-talkie radios and spreading out in a skirmish line. Like beating the brush for rabbits."

"We're the rabbits."

"We're the rabbits. We can't get back to the road so let's find a way across this gulch here. Follow me."

Smith leads back for a short distance along the route they had come, finds a descent into the gulch and disappears. The others, Hayduke on rearguard duty, scramble down after him and find Smith ahead in the sandy wash, making tracks. Can't be helped. On either side the walls are nearly perpendicular, twenty to forty feet high. They stumble through the shadows, blindly following their guide.

After a while Smith finds an opening in the wall, a tributary wash. They go upwash over the dry sand and within a hundred yards reach an exit, a sloping dome of stone on the inside of a curve. Up they scramble like monkeys, on fingers and toes, Doc puffing a bit, and regain the moonlight and open terrain. Smith strikes off northeasterly toward a sharply defined skyline of buttes and pinnacles. He walks like an old-time prewar pre-pickup-truck Indian, with a steady loping stride, the feet pointed straight ahead, perfectly parallel. The others hurry to keep up.

"How many more . . . little canyons . . . like that?" Bonnie gasps. "Between here and . . . I mean . . . where we're going?".

"Seventy-five, maybe two hundred. Save your wind, honey."

The long march is under way. At every hundred paces or so Smith pauses to look, listen, test the air currents, feel the vibrations. Hayduke at the end of the file, catching his rhythm, alternates Smith's vigils with his own, stopping while the others march for an extra look around. He is thinking of that helicopter: what a nice coup it would make. If he could only slip away for a half hour. . . .

. Hayduke lingers behind, pausing to tap a kidney. Absorbed, self-satisfied, he contemplates with pleasure the steady drumming on the stone. Purified Schlitz, shining by the moon. Thank God I am a man. Flat rock. Splashing his boots. He is shaking it, trying to free that last drop which will inevitably drip down his leg anyhow, about to tuck it away and rezip, when he hears a sound. A foreign noise, alien to the desert peace. A metallic click and clash.

A powerful ray of light sweeps across the slickrock—from a spotlight attached to the helicopter?—impaling Smith and Abbzug on its beam. They stand frozen for a moment, pinned by the white lance, then start running among the junipers. The light beam follows, catching them, losing them, catching Doc Sarvis lagging behind.

Hayduke draws his revolver. He kneels, steadies his gun hand with his left and aims at the turning light. Fires. The shattering muzzle blast stuns him for a second, as always. Missed the target too, of course. The disembodied light, like a great glaring eye, comes searching Hayduke's way. He fires and misses again. Should unsling the rifle but there isn't time. He is about to fire his third shot when the light goes out. Whoever was guiding it has suddenly realized that he is too close to the target. That he is the target.

Hayduke runs awkwardly after the others, the enormous pack riding on his back. From behind comes the sound of running feet, shouts, a spasm of symbolic gunfire. Hayduke stops long enough to snap off three shots, aiming at nothing in particular—for in the vague and treacherous moonlight there is nothing in particular to shoot at that he can see, and even if there were he couldn't hit it with this jolting cannon in his hand. But the noise slows the pursuers, makes them cautious. The shouting dies away; the Team is busy with its radios. Scrambled transmissions jam the airwaves, excited voices canceling one another out.

Running, the awkward burden on his back, Hayduke catches up to Doc, huffing along like a steam engine far behind Smith and Abbzug—dim figures jogging over the rise ahead. Hayduke can see that they have shed their big backpacks. In his rear the shouts resume, orders, instructions, the thump of running boots. Spotlight on the move again. Two spotlights.

"We got to . . . dump these packs," he says to Doc.

"God yes!"

"Not right here—wait. . . ."

They reach the rim of another incipient canyon, a typical slick-rock-country gash in the stone, with overhanging walls and inaccessible floor—a cleft too wide to leap, too deep and too precipitous to descend.

"Here," says Hayduke, stopping. Doc stops beside him, blowing like a horse. "We'll drop them here," Hayduke says, "under the wall here. Come back and get them later." He takes off his pack, pulls out a coiled rope, then gropes deep in the big pocket for his box of rifle ammunition. Can't immediately find it, jammed as it is beneath sixty pounds of other gear. Sound of pursuit coming closer, the heavy boots running. Too close. Hayduke lowers his pack and pack frame over the edge, lets go: they drop fifteen feet onto something rough. *Crump!* That beautiful new Kelty. Attachment to possessions. Yes! He slings the coil of rope across his back, carries the rifle in his hand.

"Hurry up, Doc."

Dr. Sarvis is wrestling with something in his pack, trying to draw a black leather bag up and out from its tight fit in the center of the load.

"Come on *come on!* What're you doing?"

"Just a moment, George. Have to get my . . . bag out of here."

"Drop it!"

"Can't go on without my bag, George."

"What the hell is that?"

"My medical bag."

"For chrissake, we don't need that. Let's go."

"Just a moment." Doc finally gets his satchel out, shoves the rest of the backpack over the edge. "I'm ready."

Hayduke glances back. Shadows scamper over the rock, flitting among the junipers, approaching rapidly. How far? One hundred, two hundred, five hundred yards? In the crazy moonlight he can hardly guess. A hand-carried spotlight flicks on, the bright beam seeking prey.

"Run for it, Doc."

They pound over the stony terrace where they'd last glimpsed Bonnie and Smith. And find them waiting on the other side. They carry only a couple of canteens.

"Right behind us," Hayduke gasps, running past them. "Keep going."

Without a word all follow, Smith moving up to run at Hayduke's side. "George," he says, "let's use that rope . . . before we get . . . rimmed up. . . ."

"Right."

Doc lags again, blowing hard, the satchel bumping against his knee at every pace. Bonnie grabs it, carries it on.

They run along the edge of the small canyon, Hayduke looking for a tree, a shrub, a boulder, a stony knob, some sort of projection to double the rope around. Rappel time again. But there is nothing usable in sight. How far down? Ten feet? Thirty? A hundred?

Hayduke stops at a point where the wall below is neither overhanging nor vertical but bulges outward, sloping a bit, not much, toward the bottom. Good rappel pitch. He peers down. Can't see the bottom. Darkness and silence below, the faintly perceived forms of shrub and juniper.

"Here." He uncoils his rope, shakes it out and, as Doc and Bonnie come close, panting desperately, faces flushed and glistening with sweat, he takes them both without a word in a big embrace, loops one end of the rope around them and ties it snug with a nonslipping bowline knot.

"Now what?" Bonnie says.

"We're going down into the canyon. You and Doc first."

Bonnie looks over the edge. "You're crazy."

"Don't worry, we'll belay you. You'll be all right. Seldom, gimme a hand here. Okay, down you go. Back off the edge."

"We'll get killed."

"No you won't. We've got you. Back over the edge there. Lean back. Lean way back, goddammit. Both of you. Keep your feet flat against the rock. Okay, that's better. Now, walk down, backward. Don't try to crawl down, there's no way. And don't grab the rope so hard, that won't help. Lean back. *Lean back* for chrissake or I'll kill you! Feet flat on the rock. Just use the rope for balance. Walk on down. Easy, see? That's better. Keep going. Keep going. Holy sweet motherfuck. Okay. Fine. Where are you? You down?"

Muted grumbles from the shadows below. Sounds of crackling brush, the scuffle of tangled feet.

Hayduke peers down into the gloom. "Untie the knot, Bonnie. Free the rope. Hurry up!" The rope comes slack. He hauls it up. "Okay, Seldom, your turn."

"How're you gonna get down, George? Who's to belay you?"

"I'll get down, don't worry."

"How?" Smith runs the doubled rope between his legs, around one side and over the opposite shoulder, preparing to rappel.

"You'll see." Hayduke unslings the rifle. "Take this down for me. Wait a minute." He stares back the way they've come, trying to spot their pursuers. The pallid moonlight lies weak on stone and sand, on juniper and yucca and blackbrush, and on the cliffs beyond, a shifty and deceptive illumination. You can hear men's voices and the slap of big feet on sandstone. "You see them, Seldom?"

Smith is squinting in the same direction, shading his eyes from the moon. "See two of them, George. Three more way behind."

"Ought to crack off one little shot, slow 'em down again."

"Don't do it, George."

"Make Christians out of them Saints. Put the fear of Rudolf Hayduke into them. A rifle shot would make them stop and think."

"Gimme the rifle, George."

"I'll shoot over the fuckers' heads."

"They might be safer if you aimed at 'em."

"Those fuckers were shooting at us. Shooting to kill and maim."

Smith extricates the rifle gently from Hayduke's hands and slings it over his free shoulder. "Belay me, George." He backs to the edge. "Testing belay, George."

Hayduke takes up the slack, plants his feet, the rope around his hips. "Okay. Belay on."

Smith backs over the rim and disappears. Hayduke holds the rope lightly in his hands as Smith goes quickly down the pitch. Smith's weight, transmitted by the rope, is supported by Hayduke's pelvis and legs. In a moment he feels the rope go slack; the voice of Smith rises from the darkness below. "Okay, George, off belay."

Hayduke looks back. The enemy is moving closer. And now that hand-carried spotlight is switched on and the dazzling beam turns directly toward him, at once, blind bad luck, no escape.

Nowhere to go. Nothing but air to rappel from.

"How far down there?" Hayduke croaks.

"About thirty feet I'd say," replies Smith.

Hayduke lets the rope, now useless to him, fall into the canyon. The light beam sweeps over him, goes past. A double take by the glaring Cyclops eye. The beam is jerked back and stops, fixed on Hayduke's crouching figure, burning into his eyes, blinding him.

"You there," someone bellows—a vaguely familiar voice, amplified majestically by bullhorn. "You stand *right* there. Don't you make a move, son."

Hayduke drops to his belly on the verge of the rock. The light remains on him. Something cruel, silent, swift as thought, sharp as a needle, keen as a snake, whips at the sleeve of his shirt, stinging the flesh beneath. He draws his gun; the light goes out. He hears at the same instant the crack of a second rifle shot. (In the east a crack of dawn.)

He calls down to the others, "That a juniper below me?" The light comes on again, pinning him down.

"Yeah"—Smith's warm and homely voice—"but I wouldn't try that if . . ." His words fade off in doubt.

Hayduke holsters his revolver and slides on his stomach over the edge, facing the wall, feeling the cool unyielding bulge of the stone against his chest and thighs. He hangs for a moment to the last possible handhold. Friction descent, he thinks, what they call a friction fucking descent. He looks below, sees only shadows, no bottom at all.

"I change my mind," he says desperately, inaudibly (losing his grip), speaking to nobody in particular—and who is listening?—"I'm not going to do this, this is insane." But his sweaty hands know better. They release him.

Coming down, he yells. Thinks he yells. The words never get past his teeth.

28

❧ ❧

Into the Heat: The Chase Continues

This vulture soars above the Fins, the Land of Standing Rocks. Soaring is the vulture's life, death his dinner. Evil foul black scavenger of the dead and dying, his bald red head and red neck featherless—the better to slip his greedy beak deep into the entrails of his prey—he feeds on corruption. *Cathartes aura,* his Latin title, derived from the Greek *katharsis,* meaning purification, and *aura* from the Greek for air, emanation or vapor. The airy purifier.

Bird of the sun. The contemplator. The only known philosophizing bird, thus his serene and insufferable placidity. Rocking gently on his coal-black wings, he watches a metallic dragonfly tracking methodically back and forth above the Fins, above the Standing Rocks, making a violent unfitting noise.

The vulture circles higher and tilts his wrinkled head to observe with keener interest, three thousand feet below, the movement of four tiny wingless bipeds who scurry, like mice in a roofless maze, down a winding corridor between towering red walls of stone. They dash furtively from shadow to shade, as if the sand were too hot for their feet, as if hiding from the blaze of the sun or the other searching eyes in the sky.

Something limp and halting in the gait of two of those creatures suggests to the vulture the thought of lunch, arousing his memory of meat. Although all four appear to be still alive and active, it is nevertheless a well-known truth, the vulture reasons, that where there is life there is also death—that is, hope. He circles round again for a better look.

But they are gone.

"Didn't know they could fly them goldanged things right down into a little canyon like this'n here," he says, "and what's more I say there oughta be a law agin it; it's bad for the nervous system. Makes my whole system nervous."

"I'm hungry," she says. "And my feet hurt."

"They try that again I'll drop them," Hayduke says. He holds his rifle cradled in his arms. Proud sweet weapon. The walnut stock polished with his sweat, hand-rubbed, the sniper scope sooty blue, the bolt, breech and barrel glowing with a silky sheen. Trigger, trigger guard, the checkered pistol grip, the rigorous precision of the action as he opens the bolt and inspects the firing chamber, slams it closed and springs the trigger. *Click.* Chamber empty; seven rounds in magazine.

"Thirsty and hungry and my feet hurt and I'm bored. Somehow it just isn't much fun anymore."

"Well I just hope they didn't spot our tracks. Can they set that thing down in here?" Smith, his hat off, hair plastered down with perspiration, looks out from under the overhang, out of the shade into the heat, the glare, toward the sunbaked stone, the leaning red walls of the gorge. " 'Cause if they can I'd reckon we got to find another hole mighty quick. Maybe quicker." He wipes his shining and unshaven face with a red bandanna that is already dark and greasy from sweat. "How about it, George?"

"Not right here. But maybe up the canyon, around the bend. Or down the canyon. Fuckers might be creeping up on us right now. Shotguns loaded with buckshot."

"If they seen us."

"They saw us. If they didn't they will next time."

"How many men can they get into that thing?"

"Three in that model."

"There's four of us."

Hayduke grins bitterly. "Yeah, four. With one handgun and one rifle." He turns to the dozing Dr. Sarvis. "Unless Doc has a pistol in that bag of his." Doc grunts, a vague but negative reply. "Maybe," Hayduke adds, "we could shoot 'em with one of Doc's needles. Give 'em each a shot of Demerol in the ass." He rubs his bruised limbs and abraded hide, the lacerated palms.

"You're due for another shot yourself," Bonnie says.

"Not now," Hayduke says. "The stuff makes me too groggy. Got to keep awake now." Pause. "Anyway, you can bet your bottom dollar if they did see us they've radioed the Team. That whole crew will be marching down here in an hour." Another pause. "We have to get out of here." Shifts the rifle from crook of arm to right hand. "Can't wait for sundown."

"I'll tote that rifle for a while," Smith says.

"I'll keep it."

"How do you feel?" Bonnie asks Hayduke. She gets a mumble for an answer. Bonnie appears on the verge of heat exhaustion herself. Her face is flushed, damp with sweat, eyes a bit dreamy. But she looks better than the battered Hayduke, with his clothes in shreds and his elbows and knees stiff with bandages, so that he walks when he walks like a prefabricated man, Dr. Sarvis's hand-made monster. "George," she says, "let me give you another shot."

"No." He modifies the growl. "Not right now. Wait till we find a better hole." He looks at Doc. "Doc?" No response; the doctor lies sprawled on his back in the deepest coolest corner of the alcove under the cliff, eyes closed.

"Let him rest," she says.

"We ought to get going."

"Give him ten more minutes."

Hayduke looks at Smith. Smith nods. They both look up at the narrow strip of blue between the canyon walls. The sun has drifted high into noon. Wisps and horsetails of vapor hang on the planes of heat. One of these days it's going to rain. One of these days it's got to rain.

"I'm not asleep," Doc says, his eyes shut. "Be up in a minute. . . ." He sighs. "Tell us about the war, George."

"What war?"

"Yours."

"That war?" Hayduke smiles. "You don't want to hear all that. Seldom, where the shit are we anyhow?"

"Well, I ain't sure, but if we're in the canyon I think we're in, then we're in the middle of what they call the Fins."

"I thought we were in the Maze," Bonnie says.

"Not yet. The Maze is different."

"How so?"

"Worse."

"That war," says George Hayduke to nobody in particular and also to nobody in general, "they want to forget it. But I won't let them. I won't ever let the bastards forget that war." Talking like a dreamer, a sleepwalker, talking not to himself but to the stony silence of the desert. "Never," he says. Silence. "Never."

The others wait. When Hayduke fails to go on, Bonnie says to Smith, "Do you think we'll find some water? Pretty soon?"

"Bonnie honey, it ain't too far now. We'll find water somewheres up in here, and if we don't it's there waitin' for us on the shady side of Lizard Rock. Water and food."

"How far?"

"Where?"

"How far to Lizard Rock?"

"Well now, if you mean in miles I'd be kind of hard up to say on account of the way these canyons meander around so. Also I ain't absolutely sure we can get out of this canyon at the other end because maybe it boxes up. We might have to backtrack some, try to find a way out along the sides."

"Can we get there tonight?"

"No," says Hayduke, gazing at the sand between his thick white knees, bound in layers of filthy gauze. "Never." He scratches his crotch. "Never."

Smith is silent. Bonnie stares at him, waiting for the answer. He squints, frowns, grimaces, scratches his sunburnt neck, tilts his green eyes up at the canyon wall. "Well . . ." he says. Sound of a canyon wren.

"Well?"

"Well I wouldn't want to lie to you, Bonnie."

"Don't."

"We ain't gonna get there tonight."

"I see."

"Maybe tomorrow night."

"But we will find water? I mean soon. In this canyon."

Smith relaxes a bit. "Very likely." He offers her his canteen. "Have a few good swallers outa there. Plenty left."

"No thanks."

"Go ahead."

He unscrews the cap and shoves it in her hands. Bonnie drinks, hands it back. "We should've kept our packs."

"Maybe," Smith says. "And if we done that we'd be in Bishop Love's Fry Canyon icebox now too, waitin' for the sheriff's van. And Love, that crazy sonofabitch, he'd be one more step up on his way to the Governor's mansion, as if the sonofabitch we have squattin' in there now selling out the state as fast as he can ain't bad enough."

"What do you mean?"

"I mean those people like Love and the Governor got no conscience. They'd sell their own mothers to Exxon and Peabody Coal if they thought there was money in it; have the old ladies rendered down for the oil. Them's the kind of folks we got runnin' this state, honey: Christians; my kind of folks."

"Just won't let 'em," Hayduke mumbles. "No, I won't."

Smith stirs, reaching for his hat. "We oughta get ourselves on our feet, friends, make some tracks north."

"I was a POW," mutters Hayduke.

Doc opens his eyes for a moment, sighing.

"I was a VC prisoner," Hayduke goes on. "Fourteen months in the jungle, always on the move. They'd chain me to a tree at night except when the planes were coming. I was more trouble to those little gooks than a French newspaper correspondent. Fed me moldy rice, snakes, rats, cats, dogs, liana vines, bamboo shoots, whatever we could find. Even worse than what they ate themselves. Fourteen months. I was their unit medic, the little brown bastards. We used to hug each other down in the bunkers, curled up in a heap like fucking kittens, when the B-52s came over. It seemed to help absorb the shocks. We always got word when they were coming but you never heard them, they flew so high. Only the bombs. We were ten feet sometimes twenty feet under the ground but afterwards there'd be these little guys running around with blood coming out of their ears from the concussions. Some of them went crazy. Kids, most of them. Teenagers. They wanted me to help plan their raids. Satchel charges and that kind of thing. I wanted to but I couldn't quite do it. Not that. So they made me their medic. Some medic. I was sick half the time. Once I watched them shoot down a helicopter with one of those twenty-foot steel crossbows they had. Made out of shot-down helicopters. They all cheered when the sonofabitch crashed. I wanted to cheer myself. Couldn't quite do that either though. We had a party that night, C rations and Budweiser for all the Charlies and me. The ham and beans made them sick. After fourteen months they threw me out—said I was a burden on them. The ungrateful little Communist robots. Said I ate too much. Said I was homesick. And I was. I sat in that rotting jungle every night, playing with my chain, and all I could think about was home. And I don't mean Tucson. I had to think about something clean and decent or go crazy, so I thought about the canyons. I thought about the desert down along the Gulf coast. I thought about the mountains, from Flagstaff up to the Wind Rivers. So they turned me loose. Then came six months in Army psycho wards—Manila, Honolulu, Seattle. My parents needed two lawyers and a U.S. Senator to get me out. The Army thought I wasn't adjusted right for civilian life. Am I crazy, Doc?"

"Absolutely," Doc says. "A certifiable psychopath if I ever saw one."

"I get a pension too. Twenty-five percent disability. Head case. One quarter lunatic. I must have a dozen checks waiting for me back at the old man's place. The Army sure didn't want to let me go. Said I had to be 'processed and rehabilitated.' Said I couldn't wear the VC flag pin on my Green Beret. Finally I caught on and said what you're supposed to say and the Senator turned a screw on the Pentagon, and about the time we were ready for court action they let me go. Medical discharge. They really wanted to court-martial me but Mom wouldn't stand for it. Anyhow, when I finally got free of those jail-hospitals and found out they were trying to do the same thing to the West that they did to that little country over there, I got mad all over again." Hayduke grins like a lion. "So here I am."

Silence. A perfect silence. Too clear, too calm, too perfect. Seldom Seen slips from his customary squatting position, kneels and puts one large ear to the ground. Bonnie opens her mouth; he lifts a warning hand. The others wait.

"What'd you hear?"

"Nothing. . . ." Gazing up the canyon, up at that sky. "But I sure felt something."

"Like what?"

"I don't know. Just something. Let's saddle up and move on out of here."

Doc, still sprawled in the coolest corner of the shade, sighs once more and says, "I hear a koto. One koto, one bamboo flute and a drum. Way out yonder in the heart of the wilderness. Under a grandfather juniper tree. The Izum-kai are playing the Haru-No-Kyoku. Not well." Wipes his broad and sweating physiognomy with handkerchief. "But with absolute insouciance. Which is to say, as befits the place and the occasion."

"Doc's cracking up," Bonnie explains.

"It's the heat," says Doc.

Smith staring down the canyon. "We better march along, folks."

Slings his canteen over one shoulder, Hayduke's coiled rope over the other.

They all rise, Doc last with his precious black bag, and shamble forth into the dazzling sunlight, the blaze of noon, under the endless roar of the sun. Smith leads the way up-canyon, walking where possible on stone. Although the canyon walls are hundreds of feet high and often overhanging, there is little shade. Too dry for cottonwood. The only plant growth in sight is a clump of datura with wilted blooms, a dead pinyon pine, some snakeweed, and lichens on the rock.

The canyon curves left, curves right, ascending by gradual degrees toward—they hope—a hidden spring, an unknown seep where water oozes cool though alkaline from the pores of the sandstone, to trickle down through hanging gardens of ivy, columbine, club moss and monkeyflower to an accessible outlet. To a tin-cup spout, a canteen-mouth drip. They long for the tinkle of waterdrops, sweetest of all possible sounds in this superheated red-walled giants' passageway of stone.

Smith points to an alcove in the canyon wall, fifty feet above their heads. They stop and stare.

"I don't see anything," Bonnie says.

"Don't you see that little wall, honey, with the rafters stickin' out of it and the little square hole in the middle?"

"Is that a window?"

"More likely a door. The kind of door you have to get down on hands and knees to crawl through."

They are staring at the remains of an Anasazi cliff dwelling, abandoned seven hundred years ago but well preserved in the desert's aridity. Dust and potsherds wait up there, burnt corncobs and a smoke-blackened ceiling in the cave and old old bones.

The four tramp on over the sloping beds of sandstone, over the rocks and gravel of the waterless stream bed, through the endless sand, through the heat.

"Maybe back there's where I should live," muses Hayduke aloud. "Up in that cave with the ghosts."

"Not my kinda life," Smith says.

Nobody responds. All trudge wearily ahead.

"Never did have much use for farmers," Smith goes on. (Trudge trudge.) "And that includes melon growers. Before farming was invented we was all hunters or stockmen. We lived in the open, and every man had at least ten square miles all his own. Then they went and invented agriculture and the human race took a big step backwards. From hunters and ranchers down to farmers, that was one hell of a Fall. And even worse to come. No wonder Cain murdered that tomato picker Abel. The sonofabitch had it coming for what he done."

"Nonsense," grumbles Doc, but he is too thirsty, too tired, too resigned to deliver his famous lecture on civilization and the birth of reason (O rarest and sweetest of history's flowers).

No sound but the shuffle of eight leaden feet.

"Wet sand here," says Smith. "Water up ahead somewheres." He leads his column in detour around the telltale sand, over a tumble of rocks and past the mouth of a side canyon.

Hayduke, at the rear, pauses to stare up into the lateral branch. Narrow and winding, with a flat sandy floor devoid of any vegetation, and perpendicular walls standing five hundred feet toward the sky, it looks like a hallway into the Minotaur's labyrinth. The sky above is reduced to a narrow strip of clouded blue, pinching out at the turn of the walls.

"Where's this one go?" he says.

Smith stops, looks back. "Up into the Fins somewhere. That's all I can tell you."

"Isn't that where we want to go?"

"Yeah but this canyon is a lot bigger and it ought to lead up there too and ain't so likely to box up. That little gulch is a box if I ever seen one and I seen a few. A dead-end no-way-out surefire trap. You walk two hundred yards up that one and I'll bet *my* bottom dollar you come to a hundred-foot overhang."

Hayduke hesitates, looking up the side canyon, then into the stifling heat and meandering turns of the larger canyon. "Maybe this one does too."

"Maybe it does," Smith says, "but this one's bigger and besides it leads to water."

"What makes you so sure?"

Seldom Seen lifts his long anxious beak into the air currents. "I can smell it." He points again to the smooth expanse of dampish sand near the junction of the two canyons. "Most of that seepage is a-comin' from up this way."

"We could dig for water right here," Hayduke says.

"You could get a little out of that. Enough maybe to wet your whistle. But you'll spend half an hour diggin'. There's surface water up this way. I can smell it and I can feel it."

"Come on, George," Bonnie says. "If we don't get to water soon I think Doc is going to drop. And me with him."

Water. All they can seriously think about is water. Yet it's all around them. Mountainous cumuli-nimbi hang above their heads filled with the stuff, in vaporous form. Carloads of water. High over the plateau rims, three thousand feet above at Land's End and all across the canyonlands float huge, massive clouds trailing streamers of rain, all of which evaporates, it is true, before reaching the earth. Two thousand feet below and only a few miles away, as a bird flies, deep in the trench of Cataract Canyon, the Green and the Colorado pour their united waters through the rapids in roaring tons per second, enough to assuage any thirst, drown any sorrow. If you could reach it.

Hayduke yields to Smith and reason. The gang marches onward, over rock and pebble, sand and gravel and terraces of slick unbroken sandstone. They go around another deep bend in the canyon. Smith stops to stare. The others bunch up close behind him.

Three hundred yards ahead, where the canyon makes its next turn, they see a jumble of boulders big as bungalows tumbled in casual, haphazard disarray across the canyon bottom. On the far side of that pile of rocks, at a higher level, rising softly green and vividly alive into the twilight of the shadows—for here the walls tower so high that two hours past noon the direct rays of the sun are cut off—stands a prime cottonwood tree. In this red labyrinth it is the tree of life. Seedling cottonwoods, and willow, and tamarisk with lavender plumes, line an unseen watercourse beyond. A shy fragrance floats on the air. The light in the canyon, though indirect, is golden and warm, reflected and refracted from the monolithic walls above, where swallows dart beneath the rimrock.

"The Greeks," Dr. Sarvis says hoarsely, hopelessly, with parched throat and heavy tongue, "were the first to make fully conscious—" He tries to clear his throat.

Smith holds up his hand. "Doc," he says, so softly the others strain to hear him. "You hear what I hear?"

They listen. The canyon seems filled with an absolute stillness. An immaculate, crystalline and timeless perfection. Except for one faint flaw, which exaggerates the silence, underscoring without contradicting it. The sound of someone or something plucking at the G string of a bass viol, poorly strung. A rhythmic croak.

"What is it?" Bonnie asks.

Smith smiles at last. "That there's the sound of water, honey. Up in them rocks, beyond the cottonwood."

"Sounds more like a frog."

"Where there's frog there's water."

All stare at the marvelous green of the tree.

"Well let's go," Bonnie says. "What're we standing here for?" She takes a step forward. Doc leans ahead.

Hayduke whispers, "Wait."

"What?"

"Don't go up there."

Something in his voice, his stance, makes them all freeze. Again they listen. Now the silence is complete. The frog, the bass viol, has ceased, and even the delicate leaves of the big tree have stopped their quaking.

"What do you hear?"

"Nothing."

"You see something?"

"No."

"Then why—?"

"I don't like it," Hayduke whispers. "It's not right. Something moved up in there. I think they're around that next bend, watching the spring."

"They?"

"The men in the helicopter. Somebody. We better back out of here."

Bonnie stares at the waiting cottonwood tree, the water-loving tamarisk and willow, the firm-tensioned repose of the rocks, waiting unhurried for the deliberations of time and geology, the next catastrophe. She glances aside at Smith, who is now looking back the way they've come. "What do you say, Seldom?"

"Something scared that frog. George is right."

On Bonnie's lovely face appears a look of anguish. "But we're *thirsty*," she moans, and the first tears appear.

"Just a little sort of strategic withdrawal," Smith says quietly, leading them back again, over the burnt bleached stones of the stream bed, which looks as if it hasn't seen water for seventeen years. "We'll find water; don't you worry, honey. Stay off the sand now. Can't afford to leave no tracks here. Real sorry about this, folks, but I got the same feeling George had when that frog shut his mouth. And it ain't just the frog. There's something wrong back there, and as far as I know there ain't no reason why they couldn't of landed some men beyond that next bend."

Bonnie looks back. "Why aren't they chasing us?"

"Maybe they know they don't have to."

"I don't get it."

"Maybe we're already in the trap."

"Oh. Oh no."

Smith leads at a brisk pace, half loping half striding along, his big feet (size 12-E) aligned in perfect parallel, flopping along in synchronous counterstroke, wasting not a centimeter of precious distance. Bonnie and Doc shuffle blindly after him, Bonnie sniffling, Doc still maundering in a mad monotone about Pythagoras, ratio, the golden mean, Greek quarterbacks, nervous centers, Coney Island hotdog stands, his mind somewhere—anywhere!—leagues beyond his feet. Hayduke guards the rear, rifle at port arms, stopping at every other step to glance back, listen. His yellow CAT cap is dark with sweat.

We turned our backs on water, Bonnie thinks. Real liquid H_2O not half a block away. I saw the tree. A living tree. First one we've seen all day. A tree with little green leaves on it like in the picture books. With a green frog in a green pond. My God, my mind is going. Is that what happens first? My tongue feels like a—well, say it, like a frog in my throat. Named Pierre. Good God, I am going around the bend. Wonder if your tongue really turns black, like they say? Or purple? Your teeth fall out, eyes fall in, worms crawl over your purple skin and so forth and I'm tired of this shit and if I don't get a big frosted glass of iced tea *right now* with cracked ice and slice of lemon I am going to scream.

But she doesn't. Only the sun screams, ninety-three million miles away, that insane ceaseless cry of the hydrogen inferno which we will never never never hear because, dreams Doc, because we are born with that horror ringing in our ears. And when it stops at last we shall not hear the solar stillness either. We will be . . . elsewhere, then. We will never know. What *do* we know? What do we really know? He licks his dried cracked lips. We know this apodictic rock beneath our feet. That dogmatic sun above our heads. The world of dreams, the agony of love and the foreknowledge of death. That is all we know. And all we need to know? Challenge that statement. I challenge that statement. With what? I don't know.

I don't care, thinks Hayduke. Let them try it. Just let them try something, the fucking swine. Whatever they try I'm taking seven into hell with me. Seven of them for every one of me, sorry about that, men, but that's regulations. He caresses the polished walnut of the pistol-grip stock, which fits so fitting to his hand. Who needs their bloody stinking law? Who needs their filthy polluted water? I'll drink blood if I need it. Let them try something, the fuckers, I'll never let them forget. I'll never let them do it here. This is my country. Mine and Seldom's and Doc's—yeah, hers too—and just let them try and fuck up any of this and they're in real trouble. Real deep trouble, the fuckers. Got to draw that line somewhere and we might as well draw it right along Comb Ridge, the Monument Upwarp and the Book Cliffs.

While Smith, concentrating on the task at hand, thinks mainly about the three innocents following his lead, depending on him to find a way through the maze of the Fins, to find water, to find a route to Lizard Rock and food and fresh supplies, and from there to find a way down into the maze of the Maze, and safety, and freedom, and a happy ending.

He stops. Suddenly. Doc and Bonnie, heads down, and Hayduke, looking backward, stumble into his rear like the Three Stooges, three clowns in a silent movie. All stop once again. No one speaks.

Past the mouth of the side canyon opening on their right, Smith peers down the main canyon toward the first bend in that direction, five hundred years away. He listens with the concentrated intensity of a buck in hunting season. The silence, except for the derisive call of one canyon wren, high on the wall and perched on a point, seems perfect as before, an unmarred stasis sealed in the paralyzing, stagnant heat.

But Smith hears that sound again. Or rather, he feels it again. Feet. Many feet. Many big feet, marching over rock and shuffling through the sand. An echo perhaps? Delayed by some peculiar acoustic property of this grotesque place, a replay of the sound of their own feet? Not likely.

"They're still a-comin'," he mutters.

"Who?"

"Them other fellers."

"What?"

"The Team."

Whispering, Smith points to the patch of firm and seepage-darkened sand before them. "You watch what I do," he says, "and then each one of you do the same thing I do." He looks at Bonnie, at her flushed face and anxious eyes, and gives her a squeeze on the shoulder. He looks at Doc, who is trying to focus his eyes on something not of a visual nature, and at Hayduke, glaring about, tense as a cougar. "You understand?"

Bonnie nods. Doc is nodding. Hayduke growls, "Hurry up," before looking back over his shoulder again.

"Okay now, here I go." Smith turns himself around and walks backward, facing them, over the stretch of damp sand. At each step he makes a little extra effort with the heel of his boot, sinking it deeper, so that the footprint will resemble that of a man walking normally. He walks backward in a curve around the sand and into the mouth of the side canyon and up into it until he comes to stone again. There he halts, waiting for the others.

The others follow, walking backward.

"Hurry it up," Hayduke whispers.

Doc comes, shambling heavily, backward, watching his big feet. Bonnie walks beside him, reversing her steps with grace and care. Then, finally, Hayduke. He joins his friends. All four stand on rock and admire for a moment the trail they have invented. Clearly, four people have walked *out* of this side canyon.

"You think a trick like that will fool a bunch of grown men?" Bonnie asks.

Seldom allows himself a cautious smile. "Well now, honey, if Love was by himself I'd say no, you wouldn't fool him so easy. But with his Team it's different. One man alone can be pretty dumb sometimes, but for real bona fide stupidity there ain't nothing can beat teamwork." He pauses, listening again. "Hear them?" he whispers.

Now even Doc can hear the tramp of boots around the corner down-canyon, the hollow sound of unintelligible but human voices approaching through a stony echo chamber.

"That's them," Smith says. "Let's move out, pardners."

Half in shade and half in sun they hustle up the bare slickrock, shuffle through more of the dragging nightmarish sand, clamber over spalled-off slabs and struggle on, straggle upward, into the barren tributary canyon. Which rises at a steep gradient, narrowing rapidly toward the almost-certain cul-de-sac. The trap within the trap. The walls lean smooth and vertical on either side, offering fewer finger-holds and toe grips than the façade of an office building. At each turn of the canyon Smith searches the walls ahead for an exit, for some way up and out. He hopes he may have ten minutes to find an escape route, ten minutes before Love and Team decide to make a second study of those human shoe tracks coming inexplicably out of where they should be explicably going in. Even a man who wants to be Governor can't be that dumb.

The canyon turns and turns again, looping back and forth in close meanders. On the outside of the curves the walls arch over the canyon floor, forming hollow half domes deeper and higher than the Hollywood Bowl. On the inside of the curves the walls flow in corresponding but opposite fashion, smooth, rounded, rising so sharply from the canyon bottom that Smith can see no way for a human to get started up those slick and tricky surfaces. Perhaps a human fly. Perhaps a human Hayduke. . . .

Quite suddenly, without preliminary, they reach the end of the corridor. The predictable overhang bars their advance—a battlement of eroded sandstone sixty feet high, curving outward above their heads, with a spout or pour-off at the notch where the next flash flood, already in preparation on the high plateau, will come crashing down in turgid splendor, rich with powdered clays, muds, shales, uprooted trees, rolling rocks and crumbling sheets of cliff face. To climb this obstacle a man would have to go first upward at 90 degrees, then out under the overhang, hanging like a spider upside down, fingertips and toenails glued to open-angled facets of the stone, his body defying not only gravity but reality as well. It has been done.

Hayduke appraises the pitch. "I can get up there," he says, "but it'll take some time. It's hairy. I'll need jumars, stirrup ladders, hex nuts, pitons, cliff hangers, hammer, star drill and expansion bolts, all which we ain't got."

"Is this water?" Bonnie says, canteen in hand, kneeling on the lip of a basin-shaped plunge pool below the drop-off. The wet sand on which she kneels is quicksand, slowly shifting beneath her, but she doesn't notice, yet. In the center of the basin is a pool eighteen inches wide, consisting of what looks like a cloudy broth and smells like decay. A few flies and fleas hover above the soup; a few horsehair worms and mosquito larvae wriggle about within it; on the bottom of the tiny bowl, scarcely visible, is the inevitable blanched cadaver of drowned centipede, eight inches long.

"Can we drink this stuff?" she asks.

"*I* sure can," Smith says, "and what's more I sure as hell aim to drink it. Go ahead, you fill your canteen, honey, and we'll strain it into mine."

"Good God, there's a dead centipede in here. Also I'm sinking in this muck. Seldom . . . ?" The quicksand quivers like gelatin, oozing and burbling. "What *is* this?"

"You're all right," he says. "We'll help you out. Fill the canteen."

While Bonnie fills her canteen, Hayduke takes the rope from Smith's shoulder and retreats a short distance back the way they've come. He has noticed a cleavage in the wall, a crack extending upward far enough to give possible access to the gently curving dome beyond, where boot-sole friction may be sufficient for further ascent. A hundred feet above his head the wall slopes off beyond his line of sight; what lies above they'll have to find out when and if they get there.

Draping the coiled Perlon across his shoulders, dropping his gun belt and revolver and stacking the rifle, he essays the rock. The wall is vertical at its base but the crack wide enough to admit his hands, one above the other, and the toe of his boot turned sideways. He places opposing pressure on the rock with his fingers, for there is nothing to pull downward on, and inserts the toe of his left boot, gently, into the crevice at knee height. Pulling laterally, with fingertips, he gets enough traction to rise. His right foot dangles uselessly; no place to put it. He slides his fingers up, inside the lip of the crack, exerts lateral force again, unwedges the left foot, lifts it higher and reinserts. This enables him to ascend another two feet. Again he slides his fingers up, first one, then the other, feeling for a fresh grip.

Should have uncoiled and tied on the rope; the thick coil interferes with his movements, endangers his balance. Too late now. He lifts the left boot as far as he can, places it higher and wedges it. Just barely enough pressure there to support most of his weight. He repeats the finger technique and straightens up. Again. And again.

He is now fifteen feet above the foot of the wall, and the sandstone starts to round a hair, one degree at a time, off the vertical plane. He climbs. Twenty feet. Thirty. The cleavage pinches out above him, fading into its matrix, the monolithic wall, but the degree of favorable curvature increases. Hayduke finds he can get some support for his right foot. He ventures two more hand slides up the crack before it narrows too much for even a fingertip.

Time to try the open face of the wall, which here curves inward like the dome of a capitol, the angle approaching 50 degrees. No alternative. Hayduke gropes outward, his fingers walking over the stone, feeling for a hold, a knob, an eyebrow, a crevice, an angle, the tiniest of holes. Nothing. Nothing out there but the abrasive, finely textured, totally indifferent wall. Well then, it's got to be friction and nothing else. If only I had my chock nuts, a bong, a rurp, a plumber's helper, a pair of big tits on my elbows. But you don't. Have faith in friction. Time to withdraw that left foot from the top of the crack.

Hayduke hesitates. Naturally. He looks down. A natural mistake. Three pale faces shaded by hats, three small human figures, are staring up at him. They seem to be far below, very very far below. They hold canteens, now full of murky water. No one speaks. They are waiting for him to come sliding, sprawling, tumbling down, to smash and crumple on the broken slabs below. No one speaks; a breath might knock him loose. *Exposure* is the word.

For a few moments Hayduke feels that sick panic of the unbelayed and unaided climber. The nausea and the terror. Impossible to go on, impossible to descend, impossible to stay where he is. The muscles of his left calf are beginning to tremble and the sweat percolates, drop by drop, through his eyebrows into his eyes. With cheek and ear pressed against the canyonland bedrock he feels, hears, shares the beating of some massive heart, a heavy murmur buried under mountains, old as Mesozoic time. His own heart. A heavy thick remote and subterranean thumping sound. The fear.

Dr. Sarvis, someone calls, years away, a phantom voice, like the bellowing of the Minotaur off around the many turns of many sunken canyons in this labyrinth of red stone. *Doctor. . . .*

Raising his head, Hayduke leans out away from the dome, placing the weight of his body on his right foot in its lug-soled boot, the boot supported by the curving rock—nothing more. He gently unwedges his left foot, draws it out and sets it down beside its mate, two big strong feet planted on the surface of a curvilinear plane. He stands erect. Friction functions. He's going nowhere now but up. Sound of helicopter rising—*whock whock whock whock*—off beyond the walls and domes and fins and pinnacles. No matter. That can wait. Walking upward, one firm step at a time, Hayduke thinks: We're going to live forever. Or know the reason why not.

So much for that. Safety. Now we need a belay point. He finds it immediately, a narrow but solid ledge dipping into the fall line of the wall (the right way) where a century or two before a slab had yielded to impulse and slipped, shattering into that pile of rubble on which Hayduke's friends stand now. He looks up. Waiting above is a long slope of stone littered with hamburger-shaped rocks on pedestals, some reposing beds of gravel, a few shrubs—cliff rose, yucca, gnarled twisted half-dead but also half-alive junipers. The way leads upward into the petrified mysteries of the Fins, toward (he hopes) Lizard Rock and finally the Maze.

"Next!" Hayduke shouts, taking one end of the rope around his waist and tossing the coil out into space. The running end sails out and down to the others, ninety feet below. Thirty feet to spare.

There is some resistance down there among the neophytes but finally Smith and Bonnie succeed in browbeating Doc into making the ascent. Smith lashes the rope snug below Doc's big chest, above the belly, hangs his medical kit to his belt, and boosts him up the first few steps. Doc is terrified, of course, but also feeling better as a result of at last getting some water, however warm and foul, into his spongy cell tissue. He tries at first to crawl up the rock amoeba-style, one sweaty pod at a time, but gets nowhere. They convince him that he has to lean out, lean back, in direct violation of all common sense and instinct, and walk up the wall, letting Hayduke pull him up with full tension on the line. He does it, somehow, and sinks near Hayduke's feet, wiping his face.

Next comes Bonnie loaded with gurgling canteens. "This is ridiculous," she says, "absolutely ridiculous, and if you let me drop, George Hayduke you pig, I'll never speak to you again." Pale and a bit shaky, she sits beside Doc.

Sound of a helicopter cruising somewhere near, off among the spires and turrets and domes, searching for something, anything, if only a place to put down, and finding nothing but an unearthly landscape of standing rock, rows of parallel three-hundred-foot-high tapering stone plates set on edge—the Fins. But at least it's not the Maze, the pilot thinks, thinks Hayduke, who is also unfamiliar with the region but at least he, Hayduke, has both feet on the ground: solid stone. Plus a strong flexible umbilical cord belayed around his hips connecting him to Seldom Seen Smith, who waits out of view below the hemisphere of sandstone.

"Don't forget my guns," Hayduke calls down.

Dr. Sarvis, calls somebody else, in a bull-like megaphonic voice grotesquely amplified, booming up the canyon from a hidden source, much closer than before, and coming closer. *Doctor, we need you. . . .*

Doc sits beside Hayduke, wiping his brow, still pale from the exposure and fear, trembling like a foundered horse. With shaky fingers he tries to relight his cigar, can't connect. Burns his fingers instead. "Goodness gracious."

Dr. Sarvis, sir, where are you?

Nobody pays much attention to the disembodied voice. Why should they? Who can believe it? Each thinks he alone is going crazy.

Bonnie strikes a match for him, lights the doctor's cigar. "Poor Doc." The acrophobes lean on one another.

"Thanks, nurse," he mumbles, regaining a measure of steadiness. "My goodness but this is a strange place." Looking around. "Naked rock, nothing but naked rock, everywhere you look. A surrealist dream world, eh, nurse? Dali. Tanguy. Yes, Yves Tanguy, his landscape. What's George doing there with that rope? If he's not careful someone will yank him off his perch."

"He's waiting for Seldom, love. Have another drink of water."

"Smith," yells Hayduke, "what the fuck are you waiting for?"

"I'm a-comin', I'm a-comin'. Belay ready?"

"Belay is fucking ready." Hayduke braced and waiting.

"Testing belay." Sharp tug on the rope. Hayduke stands firm.

"Give me tension."

"You got it."

Smith comes walking up the wall, hand over hand up the rope, feet flat against the stone, joins the crew and drops the rope. Breathing hard but looking relieved.

"What were you doing down there?" Hayduke says.

"Had to take a leak."

DR. SARVIS PLEASE. DR. SARVIS.

"What the hell *is* that?" Hayduke says.

"Sounds like God," Bonnie says. "With a country-western accent. Just what I was always afraid of."

"Gimme the rifle," Hayduke says. "And the cannon." Reluctantly, Smith hands them over. "Rest of you start up the slope." George buckles on his gun belt.

"Now George—"

"Go on!"

DOCTOR SARVIS!

Nobody moves. They stare down the canyon, from which direction the mighty appeal comes. Sound of heavy boots slogging over sand and gravel, busting through brush.

HEY, DOC SARVIS!

"Somebody with a bullhorn," Hayduke mutters. "Some kind of trick that bishop's up to."

"Only it don't sound quite like the bishop."

"Watch behind us. They're pulling something here. Everybody out of sight." Hayduke holds the rifle aimed down-canyon; nervously he works the bolt, slides a round into the firing chamber, closes the bolt.

Waiting. They stare at the bend of the canyon wall as the tramping feet come near. A man appears, large, heavy, a two-hundred-pound six-footer, sweating like a hog, unshaven, red-faced, anxious. A big canteen dangles from his shoulder. He stops, holding the battery-powered bullhorn in one hand, a dirty white T-shirt drooping from a stick in the other, and stares at the empty box of the canyon, unaware of the gang ninety feet above, looking down at him. The man looks something like Bishop Love. But not quite. He carries no weapons.

"What's the bastard want?" Hayduke whispers.

"That ain't the bishop," Smith says. "It's his little brother, Sam."

Their whispers carry. The man looks up, first to the left, the wrong side, hearing not the original sounds but their echoes. On that side he sees only the shadowy ceiling of the royal alcove arching above his head, two hundred feet high.

"We're up here, Sam," Smith says. "What you doin' anyway? You lost?"

Sam spots them and raises the dirty undershirt in a weary gesture of either surrender or parlay. Parlay: he raises the bullhorn to his mouth.

Smith lifts a hand. "We can hear you without that goddamn thing. What's on your mind, Sam?"

"We need the doc," the brother says.

"I knew it," Hayduke mutters savagely.

"What for?" Smith says.

"I knew it was a trick all along. Watch behind us, Bonnie."

Bonnie ignores him.

"The bishop's having a heart attack. Or some kind of stroke. I don't know just what it is but I think it's a heart attack."

Doc lifts his head with interest.

"Call in your helicopter," Smith says. "Get him to the hospital."

"The helicopter's coming but it can't set down closer'n a mile and we need the doctor right away."

"Describe the symptoms," Doc mumbles, reaching for his black bag.

Bonnie puts a hand on his shoulder. "No you don't."

The man below addresses himself directly to Dr. Sarvis. "Doctor," he shouts, "can you come down off of there? We need you real bad."

"Of course," Doc mumbles, blinking, groping around for the bag. Tied to his rear, he can't get it free. "Be right there."

"No!" Bonnie cries. "Tell them you don't make house calls. Office visits only," she shouts at Sam.

"Be right back," Doc mumbles, scrabbling to his feet. He pulls the bag to his side. Eyes clearing a bit now. "George," he says, "the rope . . . ?"

"It's a trick," Hayduke growls, stupefied.

"The rope, George?" Doc takes the running end and starts tying a large granny knot around his belly. Hands still too shaky. Puffing on the cigar. "Be right down," he mumbles to the man below, unheard.

"Doc!"

"Dr. Sarvis," the man hollers.

"Be right down. Somebody tell him. George, give me a hand here. We need a nonslip suture, right? Can't remember how you did that one of yours."

"Christ." George moves in close, undoes the granny, whips on a bowline. "Listen carefully, Doc," he begins. "They can't prove you were in on this."

"Of course not."

"No, you listen to me," Bonnie cuts in. "This is no good. They'll put you in jail. I'm not going to let you do this. All we have to do"—Bonnies gestures wildly toward the silent rock above, the blasé brooding monuments of stone; that dead city, that Jurassic morgue—"is get up there. Somehow. Then over into the Maze. Seldom says they'll never find us once we get in there."

"Now now, Bonnie," he says, embracing her, "I've got a good lawyer. Expensive but very good. We'll get together later. Can't go on much more like this anyway. Then there's the— Be down in a minute!" he shouts to the waiting man. "—You know, my oath and all that rubbish. Can't hardly be a Hippocratic hypocrite now, can we? I'm ready, George. Lower away."

"All right," Hayduke says, getting ready to belay, "but don't tell them fuckers anything, Doc. Don't admit to a goddamn thing. Make them prove it."

"Yes, yes, of course. Sorry we haven't time for—well, you know, proper—" Doc nods to Smith. "Good man. Keep these imbeciles out of trouble. Take care, George. Bonnie. . . ."

"You're not going!"

Doc smiles, shuts his eyes, leans outward and backs off over the brink. Struggling down the wall, bag hanging to his belt, both hands clutching desperately, knuckles white, at the rope, he keeps his eyes shut while Hayduke repeats the routine instructions.

"Lean back. Seldom, you better back me up. Lean back, Doc. Lean back. Feet flat on the stone. *Don't* squeeze the fucking rope to death. Relax. Enjoy it. That's right. Keep going. Keep going, Doc. That's the way."

Bonnie stares in amazement. "Doc . . ." she moans.

Doc reaches or, more precisely, is lowered to the bottom of the wall. Sam Love unties the medical bag, unties the climbing rope and assists the doctor over the rubble toward the canyon floor. Doc waves good-bye to his comrades, then weaves down the canyon side by side with Sam, who carries the bag.

"We'll see you soon, Doc," Smith calls. "You be careful and take care of that sonofabitch the bishop and make sure he pays you in cash. Don't take any checks."

Doc waves again, not looking back.

"Let's get out of here." Hayduke starts to coil his rope, pulling it up.

"Wait a minute," Bonnie says. "I'm going down too."

"What?"

"You heard me."

"Well, shit. Well, holy sweet motherfuck."

"No obscenities, please. Just give me a good belay."

"Well, shit, wait'll I get the rope up."

"You don't have to lower me down like a baby. I'll rappel down." Bonnie stuffs something—a wadded bandanna for padding—into the seat of her jeans and steps astride the rope. (That lucky rope, thinks Smith.) "Just give me a good belay and shut up." She passes the rope between her legs, across her back, over the shoulder. "Belay me, goddammit."

"You can't do it that way. You don't have the rope right. Where the fuck you think you're going anyhow?"

"Where does it look like I'm going?"

"You're my woman now." Hayduke's voice slips a notch, sounding almost like a lover's bleat. "Shit," he snarls, recovering quickly. "What the fuck's the matter with you?"

Bonnie turns to Smith. "Seldom," she commands, "give me a belay."

Smith hesitates while Hayduke tugs at the rope, now wound around Abbzug's fragile frame.

"Hell, Bonnie . . ." Smith says, and clears his throat.

"Good God," Bonnie says, "what a pair of wishy-washy mealy-mouthed juveniles you two really are anyhow, I mean *really*." Rope in corrected rappel position, one end still around Hayduke's waist, she backs toward the drop-off. "If you don't give me a good belay you're coming down with me."

"Jesus Christ!" Hayduke snorts, stepping back to the solid ledge, planting his boots. "Just a second! Don't *do* that." He glowers at her.

"Really I don't know how you two are going to survive without me. Or how I am going to survive without George's *brilliant* and *elegant* and oh so *refined* and *tender* conversation." Pause. "Lout! I'm going with Doc!"

"The hell you are." Pulling in the rope.

"The hell I'm not." Backing off.

"George." Smith speaks. "Let her go."

"You stay out of this."

"Let her go."

"You stay out of this, Seldom," Bonnie says. "I can handle this punk myself." Yanking at the line: "Testing belay!"

"Belay ready!" Hayduke replies, automatically bracing himself. Half the rope lies coiled at his feet.

Bonnie starts down over the dome of sandstone, the taut rope rasping across her jeans and shirt, the pressure of it bending her nearly double. Ninety feet down. Eighty. Seventy. From Hayduke's position he can see only her hat and head and shoulders. Then only the hat. Then nothing. Out of sight.

"More rope!" comes a terrified small voice from below.

Hayduke pays out the rope. "Should let her hang there. Stubborn little bitch. Nothing but trouble ever since I met her. Goddammit, Seldom, didn't I say in the very beginning we didn't need any goddamn *girls* in this goddamn fucking organization? Didn't I? You're damn right I did. Nothing but trouble and misery." The rope vibrates like a bowstring in his hand, a straight Euclidean line from his hipbone to the eyebrow of the canyon wall. "Where are you now?" he bellows. No answer. "Seldom, can you see what that crazy ginch is doing down there?"

A weak and piteous cry from far below: ". . . end of the rope. Gimme more rope, you bastard. . . ."

Smith peering over the edge. "She's near all the way, George. Let her down another twenty feet."

"Christ," Hayduke goes on, tears leaking down his hog-bristled cheeks, gliding like melted pearls along the flanges of his nose and into the hairy underbrush of jaw and jowl, "when you think of all we did for her too, goddamn her, and just when we're almost there she has to sneak off like this, just because she feels sorry for Doc. Well to hell with her, that's all I can say. To hell with her, Seldom, we'll just go on without her, that's all. To hell with her."

The rope goes slack in his hands but he seems unaware of it.

"She's down now, George," Smith says. "Pull up your line, she's cast off. So long, honey," he yells as Bonnie walks out to the center of the canyon floor, hastening after the departed Doc.

Bonnie stops and blows Seldom a kiss, a big triumphant smile on her lovely face. She looks radiant. Eyes sparkling, sunlight glowing in her hair, she waves at Hayduke. "Good-bye."

He coils his rope, looking sullen. Makes no reply. Manic-depressive psychopaths are hard to please. He won't even look at her.

"You too, schmuck," she calls gaily, blowing Hayduke a rosy

kiss. He shrugs, coiling his precious rope. Bonnie Abbzug laughs and turns and hurries away.

Silence. More silence.

"Now I remember that third precept," Smith says, smiling at grim, glum, grimy Hayduke: "Never get in bed with a gal that's got more problems than you have."

Hayduke's face relaxes into a grudging but widening grin.

Or almost as many, Seldom adds, speaking to himself only.

Whock whock whock whock. . . .

Sunlight flashes on whirling rotor, glances off the Plexiglas bubble, as the recon helicopter passes swiftly, like an afterthought, briefly glimpsed, across the slot of cloudy sky between two towering canyon walls, a mile away. The vibrations sweep toward them, the circles reaching out and closing, a glassy lasso looping down from heaven.

Smith picks up the canteen, Hayduke slings his rifle. They scramble up the stony slope, minute figures on a huge eyeless face of sculptured sandstone, two small human beings lost in an outsize kingdom of towers, walls, empty streets, and abandoned metropolis of rock and more rock and nothing but rock, silent and uninhabited for thirty million years. You can hear their voices in that barren waste from a league away, as they shrink and dwindle far off and far below, buglike micro-busybodies from the vulture's point of view.

George, says one tiny voice, incredibly remote but clear, *goldangit George you know I didn't think you could do it, when it come right down to the nubbin of it. I thought sure you'd wrinkle up like a mountain oyster and just sort of fold in and pizzle down and leak out and piss away like a sick snake.*

Why Seldom Seen you buzzard-beaked Mormon motherfucker I can do anything I want to if I want to do it and what's more I will and what's more they're never I mean never I mean never absolutely NEVER gonna catch me. No. Never. Nor you either if I can help it.

The micro-voices fade but not completely: the gibberish and laughter go on and on and on, for miles. . . .

The vulture smiles his crooked smile.

* * *

"You're under arrest, Dr. Sarvis. I suppose I ought to tell you that before you look at Dudley."

Doc shrugs, returning Sam his canteen. "Of course. Where's the patient?"

"We got him laid out under that cottonwood where those other men are. You too, sister."

Sister? Bonnie reflects, but only for a moment. "Don't call me sister, brother, unless you mean it. Also I'm still thirsty and *very* hungry and I demand my rights as a common legal criminal and if I don't get them there's going to be nothing but trouble around here."

"Take it easy."

"You'll get no rest whatsoever."

"All right, all right."

"Nothing but heartache."

"All right. Here he is, Doc."

The patient is sitting up against the bole of the tree, one large and heavy man with square handsome Anglo-Saxon cattleman's face. J. Dudley Love, Bishop of Blanding. His eyes glitter, his skin has a parboiled tinge, he looks overenthusiastic, agitated, not quite entirely present. "Hello, Doc, where the hell you been? Sam," he says to his brother, "what'd I tell you? I told you he'd come. Am I gonna be Governor of the great beehive state of Utah or ain't I? 'Industry,' Doctor, that's our state motto, 'industry,' and our state symbol is the golden beehive, solid gold forty-karat goddamn beehive, and by God we *are* busy little bees, ain't we, Sam? Who's this girl? Am I gonna be Governor or ain't I?"

"You're gonna be Governor."

"Am I gonna be Governor this goddamn state or ain't I?"

"Sure thing, Dud."

"Okay, now where's them other boys? I want them all, specially that turncoat renegade jackrabbit Smith. You got him?"

"Not yet, Dudley. But we're getting help. We contacted the DPS and the SO and the FBI and just about everybody else with jurisdiction here except the Park Service."

"No, Sam, I don't want any help. I can catch them boys all by myself. How many times do I have to tell you that?" The next Governor of Utah watches abstractedly as Bonnie, stethoscope hanging from her neck, rolls up his sleeve and wraps the pleats of the blood-pressure cuff snugly around his upper arm. Blood trickles from the bishop's nostrils. Doc holds a shining hypodermic syringe against the light, a vial impaled on the needle. "You're a fine-looking young woman. You a doctor too? What's your name? It hurts right down my left arm. Right down to the fingers. And least of all we don't want the park rangers bumbling around in here. They don't even belong here. We're gonna transfer this whole goddamned so-called national park to state ownership soon as I'm in, mark my words, Sam. What're you fellas gaping at? Get out of here. Find Smith; tell him he better show up for the next ward Mutual Improvement Society meeting or we're gonna revise his genealogy. The only thing worse than a gentile is a goddamned jack Mormon. Are you a gentile, young lady?"

"I'm Jewish," she murmurs, placing the horns of the stethoscope in her ears and reading the pressure gauge. Systole, diastole, mercury and millimeter. "One-sixty over eight-five," she says to Doc. He nods. She unwraps the cuff.

"You don't look Jewish even if you are a gentile. You look like Liz Taylor. I mean when she was young like you."

"You're so sweet, Bishop. Just relax now."

Doc moves in with the needle, laying a large, steady, calming hand on the bishop's damp brow. "This will hurt a bit, Governor."

"I ain't Governor yet. I'm only another bishop now. But I soon will be. Are you the—oof!—you the doctor? You look like a doctor. Sam, goddamn, didn't I tell you the doctor would come? You don't get many like this anymore. Sam, I like this little girl. What's your name, cutie pie? *Abb*zug? What the hell kind of a name is that? It don't sound American somehow. Who stole my tricycle? Sam, get on the radio. All-points alarm. Description: dark-complected, greasy, pimple on the ass, scar on left testicle. Baggy pants. Believed armed and dangerous. Alias Rudolf the Red. Alias Herman Smith. Smith? Where's that Seldom Seen? Wanted for burglary, armed robbery, kidnapping, destruction of private property, industrial sabotage, felonious assault, unlawful use of explosives, conspiracy to disrupt interstate commerce, flight across state lines to avoid prosecution for immoral purposes, horse stealing and rolling rocks. Sam? You there, Sam? Sam, where in the name of Moroni, Nephi, Mormon, Mosiah and Omni are you? What? What'd you say, Doctor?"

"Count backward from twenty."

"From what?"

"From twenty."

"Twenty? Twenty. Right. Count backward from twenty. Yes sir. Why not. Twenty. Nineteen. Eighteen . . . seventeen . . . sixteen. . . ."

29

✿✿

Land's End: One Man Left

Obscure and ambivalent gloom of dawn. Sky an unbroken mass of violet clouds, immanent with storm. What they saw, staring from the rimrock above the Fins toward Lizard Rock, looked neither right nor good. A fresh and bigger helicopter by a smoky fire, four trucks, two big wall tents, bedrolls or men scattered about over the sand and stone, either dead or asleep or both. But that wasn't the whole of the difficulty.

"Why'd they have to camp there?" Hayduke says. "All that empty beautiful clean desert and they had to camp there. Why right *there?*"

Oughta get back to my alfalfa and my melons, Smith is thinking. Both of them. Green River they need you. Rains a-comin'. Children miss their daddy. Get started on the Big Houseboat. Seldom's Ark.

The morning star shines in the east through one window in the overcast. Jupiter Pluvius, planet of rain, beaming like chromium in a sky of ivory, lavender dusk, the twilight of liberty.

"Why right there for chrissakes? Right on top of our goddamn fucking food cache?"

"Don't know, George," he says. "Dumb luck, I reckon. We got another up near Frenchy's Spring."

"We ain't going that way. We're going into the Maze."

"Don't know about that Maze, George. It's mighty hard to find a way down into that Maze. And harder to find a way out. There ain't no permanent water. No slow elk *a*-tall. Hardly no game. I've been thinkin', maybe we ought to climb up to the rim, hike north to Green River."

"You're crazy. That must be eighty miles. They'll have your house staked out night and day. You try to go home you'll find yourself in jail."

Smith chews on a stem of grass. "Maybe. Maybe not. My old lady there's pretty damn smart. She can find a way around Bishop Love."

"Bishop Love? It's not gonna be just him and the Team anymore, Seldom. It'll be the state police. Maybe the FBI. Maybe the CIA, for all I know. We've got to hide out for a while. At least through the winter."

Smith is quiet as they watch the camp below, half a mile away. No sign of movement down there yet. Beyond the camp and Lizard Rock are the many shadowy canyons of the Maze. "Well, George, I don't know. You might make it down in there. If you could get to the river, you'd have a good chance. There's plenty of catfish in the Green, I mean channel cat, that's good eatin', and generally easy to catch, and there is some deer in the side canyons. Not much but some. And some wild horses and a few bighorns, and now and then of course there'll be a dead cow floatin' down the river. Maybe I could send one down to you now and then myself. Along with a fleet of watermelons in late August."

"You didn't answer what I said," Hayduke says.

Smith makes no reply to this. Hayduke continues on the other track.

"If I can get one deer a month I'll survive. I can jerk the meat. If I can get one every two weeks I'll be fat and happy as a beaver. I'll build a smoker for the fish. Besides what's in the food caches—enough beans there for a month. I won't need any dead cows. A watermelon would be nice, I guess, if you want to float some down to me. But you better stay."

Smith smiles, sadly. "George," he says, "I already done that kind of thing. Several times. It ain't the food that's the problem."

"Well, fuck, I'm not worried about the winter either. I'll fix up one of those old Anasazi ruins or a good snug cave in the rock and keep enough juniper and pinyon pine on hand and I'll be ready for any blizzard you got. When these vigilantes leave the area I'll hike back and get my pack and bedroll. Not a thing to worry about."

"It ain't the winter either."

Silence. They lie on the rock, watching the enemy. Sleep by day, advance by night. But hunger gnaws at their bellies. Both canteens are empty again. Hayduke, stiff from his wounds and bandages, his clothes in rags, retains only his knife, revolver, rifle and rope, a few matches in his pocket. Smith is gaunt and weary, dirty, starved and homesick, beginning to feel his beginning middle age.

"You think I'll get lonesome," Hayduke says.

"That's right."

"You think I can't take the lonesomeness."

"It can get bad, George."

A pause. "You could be right, maybe. We'll see." Hayduke rubs the gnat bites on his hairy neck. "But I'm going to give it a try. You know, this is something I've wanted to do all my life. I mean live on my own, out in the wilderness." He pats the stock of his rifle. He touches the grip of the Buck Special. "I think we'll be all right. I just think maybe we'll be fucking all right, Seldom. And sometime next spring I'll come up the river and pay you a visit. Or pay your wife a visit. You'll be in jail, naturally."

Another wan smile by Smith. "You're always welcome, George. If I ain't there you can help with the kids and the housework while Susan drives the tractor. Keep the old place going."

"I thought you had no use for farming?"

"I'm a river guide," Smith says. "I'm a boatman. That ranch is only what they call social security. Susan's the farmer, she's good at it; me I've got a black thumb. Anyhow I want to get back there for a few days."

"They'll be waiting for you."

"Only a few days. Then maybe I'll load up one of the boats and come down the river a-lookin' for you. Let's say about a couple weeks from now. I'll bring you some watermelons and the newspapers so you can read all about yourself."

"What about your other wife?"

"I got *three* wives," Smith says proudly.

"What about them?"

Smith considers. "Susan's the one I want to see." He glances toward the dawning east. "Reckon we oughta hole up now, George, get some sleep. Our friends out there are gonna be lookin' for us pretty soon."

"I am so goddamned fucking hungry. . . ."

"You and me both, George. But we got to hole up now."

"If there was some way we could divert those guys away from their camp down there. Distract them just for a few minutes, sneak in and dig up our cache. . . ."

"Let's get some rest first, George, and then we'll think about it. Let's wait till the rain starts."

They retreat five hundred yards into the darkness of the Fins, walking on rock, leaving no tracks, and bed down under a deep ledge, hidden by fallen slabs of sandstone from anything but the closest inspection. Mumbling and grumbling, stomachs aching, limbs weak and flabby from lack of protein, throats dry from thirst, they try to sleep, and pass after a while into a twilight consciousness, half awake half asleep, shaking with little nightmares, groaning.

Far off over the plateau, three thousand feet above, lightning whips the pinyon pines, followed by rumbles of thunder rolling across the canyons, through the clouds, into the heavy silence of a sunless dawn. A few drops fall on the slickrock beyond the shelter of their ledge, making damp spots that fade quickly, evaporating into the thirsty air. Finally Smith, curled on his side, falls into deep sleep.

Hayduke schemes and dreams and cannot sleep. Too tired to

sleep. Too hungry, angry, excited and fearful to sleep. It appears to him that only one obstacle remains between himself and a wilderness autumn and winter down in the Maze, down there where he can lose himself at last, forget himself for good, become pure predator dedicated to nothing but survival, nothing but the clean hard bright pursuit of game. That ultimate world, he thinks, or rather dreams, the final world of meat, blood, fire, water, rock, wood, sun, wind, sky, night, cold, dawn, warmth, life. Those short, blunt and irreducible words which stand for almost everything he thinks he has lost. Or never really had. And loneliness? *Loneliness?* Is that all he has to fear?

But there remains the one obstacle: the enemy camp beside his supply cache at Lizard Rock.

A dazzle of sudden light penetrates his closed eyes. Suspense. Then comes the savage crash of thunder, a roar like the splitting of the belly of the sky. Cannonballs bombard the stone. Another flash of blue-white light, scorching the canyon wall. Jolted fully awake, Hayduke waits for the boom, counting the seconds. One . . . two . . .

C R A C K ! K A - P O W !

That was close. Two seconds. About twenty-two hundred feet away. A steady fall of rain comes down, shining like a bead curtain beyond the overhang of the ledge. He turns to look at Smith, meaning to speak to him, but checks himself.

Old Seldom Seen lies on his side, fast asleep despite the thunder (for him a familiar and maybe soothing sound), head cradled on his arm, a smile on the homely face. The sonofabitch is smiling. Good dream for a change. He looks so vulnerable at the moment, so helpless and happy and almost human, Hayduke cannot disturb him. He thinks: Why wake him at all? We got to split up anyhow. And Hayduke hates farewells.

He takes off his boots and turns his greasy, worn socks inside out, caressing the hot spots on his feet. No change of socks, no foot powder, no warm bath, those feet will just have to hold up for a few more hours till we get that cache opened. He puts the socks and boots back on. More lightning, another drum roll of thunder cascading off the cliffs. Hayduke finds the effect temporarily stimulating. Invigorating. The rain comes down, heavily now, like a waterfall, visibility less than a hundred feet. Good, excellent, exactly what they were hoping for.

Hayduke buckles on his gun belt and the holstered .357, slings rifle and rope across his shoulders, takes one of the two remaining (and empty) canteens and slips away. Outside, the rain beats down on his head and shoulders, drips from beak of cap to tip of nose as he forces himself into an uphill trot. In the thick gray light, flaring from moment to moment with blinding swords of lightning, the Fins gleam like old pewter, four-hundred-foot walls of wet silver, hulking in the mist, streaming with water.

He emerges in a few minutes from the defile and pauses to look out at a world much smaller than before, with eerie forms of stone rising through a sheet of rain, plateau walls lost beyond the obscurity, Lizard Rock itself no longer in sight. But he knows the way. Pulling tighter on the cap, he jogs into the storm.

Smith is not surprised to wake and find his buddy gone. Not surprised but a little hurt. Would have liked at least a chance to say good-bye (God be with you) or fare (thee) well or at least so long (for now), old buddy, till we meet once more. Along the river, maybe. Or down in Arizona for the glorious finale to the campaign, the rupturing, re-moval and obliteration of, of course, that Glen Canyon National Sew-age Lagoon Dam. We never did get all together on that one.

Smith wakes slowly, taking his time. No rush at all, now that Hayduke's gone. The rain pours down in steady monotone beyond the ledge, streams of water trickling into the cave, seeping under his shoulder. It was the water, not the rain or lightning, which finally woke him up. Crawling about for dryer ground he had noticed Hay-duke absent, together with Hayduke's last belongings, and realized without surprise but with some sense of deprivation that he, Smith, was the last one left, from his point of view.

Well, like Hayduke, he'd make the most of the rain. Should be able to slip around the Search and Rescuers now, hike the jeep trail to the Golden Stairs, climb to Flint Trail and up to Land's End, Flint

Cove, Flint Flat, Flint Spring, from there an easy ten-mile walk on level ground through the woods to Frenchy's Spring and another food cache. All he needs now is food. Some beef and bacon and beans, some biscuits and cheese, and he'd be ready for the sixty-mile walk home to Green River.

Mumbling to himself, Smith crawls out of the hole in the rock and lifts his face to the rain. Lovely. Sweet cool rain. Thank you very much, You up yonder. He cups his hands beneath the spout of water at the point of the ledge and drinks. Good, by God, good, but also mighty stimulating to the appetite. Refreshed but hungry he fills the canteen and moves off, up the eroded joint of stone between the towering Fins, as Hayduke has done. But at the exit, where Hayduke went straight ahead toward Lizard Rock, Smith cuts left, westerly and southerly, following a long contour of bench rock around the head of the nearest side canyon. He has only a notion of the time of day, for no trace of the sun is visible, but he *feels like* afternoon; his nerves and muscles tell him he has slept for hours.

The heavy rain continues. Visibility, two hundred yards. Smith strides across a desert of red rock, red sand, scrubby shrubs of cliff rose, juniper, yucca, sage, blackbrush and chamisa, all well scattered, each plant separated from its nearest neighbor by ten feet or more of uncontested rock and sand. No human concealment possible here, but the ledges, gulches, fins and stony depths lie nearby on his left. Nor does he attempt to conceal his tracks; where the most direct route lies across sand, Smith takes it. He knows that he'll soon be up on solid rock again, on the Stairs trail, and through the gap toward Flint Trail.

His loping pace soon brings him to the jeep track, which he cuts across and parallels for a while until the road is confined between the head of another box canyon and the plateau wall. No choice here; Smith strides down the road, leaving in the wet sand and clay the clear imprint of his big feet. Can't be helped. The road follows its only possible route, the path pioneered by deer and bighorn sheep twenty thousand years before, along the curving terrace to broader ground, where he leaves the road with relief, hoping the rain will wash out his tracks before the next patrol comes by.

And if it don't, he thinks, then it won't. Smith moves across the contours of the land to higher ground, angling toward the gap in the ridge known as the Golden Stairs, the only trail that leads from the benchlands where he climbs to the plateau above.

Crazy country, half of it perpendicular to the rest, much of it inaccessible even to a man on foot simply because so much consists of nothing but vertical walls. Seldom Seen Smith's country and the only country in which he feels comfortable, secure, at home.

A true autochthonic patriot, Smith swears allegiance only to the land he knows, not to that swollen bulge of real estate, industry and swarming populations of displaced British Islanders and Europeans and misplaced Africans known collectively as the United States; his loyalties phase out toward the borders of the Colorado Plateau.

He sees headlights passing below, through the rain, one—two—three vehicles like a military convoy creeping over the wet rock, grinding through a muddy wash, passing out of sight around the next turn of the bench. He hears the rumble of a rock fall. Some of them machines ain't gonna get out of here alive, he thinks, leaving the shelter of his juniper and moving on. God rolls rocks too. Should roll more.

He finds the trail and slogs upward, climbing four hundred feet in close switchbacks to the next bench. Here the trail makes a long traverse to the northeast, following the contour, until another break in the wall is reached. Three hundred feet higher and a mile farther brings Smith into the pass. Below is the upper end of a drainage known as Elaterite Basin; he's already halfway to the foot of Flint Trail. Beyond, barely visible through the rain, is Bagpipe Butte; above and beyond that the Orange Cliffs, the rim of the high plateau a thousand feet above and still five miles away. The sun is blazing through a hole in the clouds.

Smith rests for a while. Dozes off. He hears gunfire, far away, remote, hardly within the realm of his consciousness. He looks back, toward Lizard Rock, the Maze. Maybe he was dreaming the sound—hearing things.

The rain has stopped. More gunfire, a rolling barrage.

You're hearing things, he tells himself. The boy can't be that dumb. Not even George, not even him, could be dumb enough to get in a gun battle with all them, whoever they are in there now, state police, prob'ly, whole goddamned sheriff's departments of Wayne and Emery and Grand and San Juan counties, not to mention whatever's left of the bishop and his team of bean farmers and used-car dealers. No, he can't be; he's got to be down in the Maze now skinning a deer, that's his shots I heard. Sounds like a medium-size war, though, to tell the truth.

Too late to turn back. Hayduke wanted to be on his own. Now he is. Two helicopters clatter by, headed for the Maze. Smith gets up and marches on into the late afternoon. The storm clouds are breaking up, drifting eastward. Spokes of sunlight radiate like enormous golden searchlights across the renovated sky. He drags himself the last few feet to the top of Flint Trail.

Starved, soaked, exhausted, blister-footed, cold, Seldom shambles past the tourists huddled on the Park Service viewpoint platform at the rim. The Maze Overlook. Four women, elderly, passing binoculars back and forth, stare at Smith with fear and suspicion, then return to their study of something fascinating taking place off toward the Maze. They watch a panoramic ten-ring circus miles deep and wide. Circling aircraft down there. Red fire, writhing mists of smoke and fog floating out of canyons, a bronze waterfall of liquid mud thundering from the brink of a thousand-foot cliff while moving shafts of heavenly spotlights pick out this point, that point, all the remainder in the shadow of the clouds.

Smith ignores the tourists, seeking only to get beyond this public place into the piney woods as quickly as possible. Ten more miles to Frenchy's Spring and food. His shortcut takes him past the ladies' parked car and a picnic table on which they've left a big Coleman ice chest containing—denture cream? Preparation H? Food, perhaps?

Smith's faint knees almost collapse. He senses meat. He hesitates at the table, opens the ice chest, can't help it, reaches for the topmost package, checks himself. Looks back. Two of the women are gaping at him, astonished, their eyeglasses catching sunbeams for a moment, blazing in his eyes. He feels in his pocket. One greasy two-bit piece in there—hardly enough. But all he's got. He drops the quarter on the table and takes two cool packages wrapped in white butcher paper, touched with blood.

One woman shrieks, "You put that back, you filthy thief!"

"Sorry, ladies," Smith mumbles. He cuddles the packages to his chest and runs off into the woods, drops one, goes on, clomping through muck, pine needles and puddles to a sunny spot near a boulder. Listens. No sign of pursuit.

Good Gawd but I'm tired. He sinks to the ground, opens the package. Two pounds of lean red hamburger reeking with protein. He chomps into it like a starving dog, eating it raw. Eating it all. Gobbling, he hears a car rush down the road. No other sound but the chatter of a squirrel, a choral jabber of bluejays off among the pinyon pines. Evening summer sunshine. Peace. Exhaustion.

Belly fulfilled, Smith leans back against the sun-warmed rock and closes his weary eyes. A chorus of evening birds celebrates the end of the storm; bluebird, pinyon jay, thrush, mockingbird and thrasher sing among the trees, in the high-country air, seven thousand feet above sea level. The sun sinks into archipelagos of clouds, the broken ranges of the sky.

Smith falls asleep. His dreams are strange, troubled—dreams, those shabby and evasive imitations of reality. Poor Smith sleeps. . . .

Or thinks he sleeps. Some sonofabitch keeps kicking at his foot.

"Wake up, mister."

Whack whack whack.

"Wake up!"

Smith opens an eye. Forest green pants and shiny shoes. Opens the other eye. A clean fresh pink-cheeked young man in a Smokey Bear hat is glaring down at him, holding in one hand what appears to be a plucked chicken. Another young man nearby, armed with Mace and pistol, raps a billy club against a tree, watching Smith gravely. Both are wearing the uniform and badge of National Park Service rangers.

"Get up."

Smith groans and pulls himself half erect, sitting up against the boulder. He feels awful, and a dawning sense of disaster does not help. He rubs his eyes, picks at his ears with his little fingers and looks again. Sure enough, a plucked chicken. The young man dangling it before him looks familiar.

"Get up!"

Smith gropes around for his old mashed slouch hat and clamps it on his head. But then irritation sets in. He does not rise. "You fellas go away," he says. "I'm trying to sleep."

"We've got a complaint against you, mister."

"What's the complaint?"

"The ladies said you stole their hamburger and their chicken."

"What chicken?"

"This chicken."

Smith swivels his head a bit and studies the naked bird. "Never saw him before."

"We found it on your trail. You dropped it running away."

Raising his eyes from the chicken, Smith reads the ranger's name tag: Edwin P. Abbott, Jr. Now he remembers. "Say," he says, "weren't you down there at Navajo National Park in Arizona just a couple months ago?"

"I was transferred. They also say you stole two pounds of hamburger."

"That's true."

"You admit it."

"Yep."

"You don't deny it?"

"Nope."

The two rangers glance at one another, nod, then return their grave and serious eyes to Smith. Ranger Abbott says, "So you confess?"

"I was starvin' to death," Smith explains, "and I think I left them ladies some money. Meant to anyhow. Now you fellas got important work to do and I don't want to take up your time; go away and lemme get some sleep."

"You are under arrest, mister. You're coming with us."

"What for?"

"For theft and for camping in a nondesignated camping area."

"This here's *my* country."

"This is a national park."

"I mean I *live* here. I'm a Utahn."

"You can explain it to the magistrate."

Smith sighs and turns away, closing his eyes. "All right, but just lemme get a little more sleep. I am really tired, boys. Just a little more . . ." he mumbles, fading off.

"Get up."

"Go to hell," he whispers dreamily.

"Get up!"

"Zzzzzzzz. . . ." Smith slumps sideways, relaxing into the warm and friendly corner of the rock.

The rangers look at the sleeping Smith, then at each other.

"Why don't I just Mace the bastard?" the second ranger says. "That'll wake him up."

"No, wait a minute." Ranger Abbott pulls a set of the new disposable plastic handcuffs from his belt. "We'll handcuff him first. We won't need the Mace." Quickly, deftly—for this was one thing he'd been well trained in at the Park Service's Horace P. Albright Ranger Training Academy at South Rim, Grand Canyon—he loops the bands around Smith's wrists and draws them tight. Smith stirs feebly, growling in his sleep, but does not resist. Does not even wake up. Does not even care anymore.

Ranger Abbott and his assistant hoist their prisoner to his feet and haul him, his relaxed legs dragging in the duff, back through the woods to the road and their patrol truck. Where to put him now? They prop him up between them in the middle of the pickup's single seat. Smiling in his dreams, snoring softly, Smith sags against the man on his right.

"Heavy bastard," the assistant ranger says.

"Don't worry."

"What'd we do with that chicken?"

"Left it back in the woods."

"Don't we need it? For evidence?"

Ranger Abbott grins at his companion. "Forget the chicken. We have the real chicken right here. Can't you figure out who this man is?"

The other, shifting uncomfortably under Smith's dead weight, says after a moment, "Well, I *was* wondering about it. I was thinking he could be. That's why I thought we should just go ahead and Mace the bastard first. You mean we got Rudolf the Red?"

"We got Rudolf the Red."

Ranger Abbott starts the engine, picks up the mike and radios news of the capture to his chief.

"Congratulations, Abbott," the chief ranger replies, through heavy static, "but you didn't get Rudolf the Red. They shot Rudolf the Red an hour ago. You got somebody else. Bring him in anyhow. And don't forget your time-and-activity report."

"Yessir."

"Shee-it," says the assistant.

They are about to turn around and drive off when a tourist car pulls alongside. The couple inside look anxious. "Oh, ranger," the wife calls.

"Yes ma'am?" says Abbott.

"Would you tell us, please"—the woman smiles in faint embarrassment—"where the nearest comfort stations are?"

"Yes ma'am. The comfort stations are beside the parking lot at Maze Overlook and also at Land's End Viewpoint. You can't miss them."

"Thank you very much."

"You're welcome."

The visitors drive away, carefully (wet surface conditions). Ranger Abbott guns his engine and performs a screaming U-turn, rear end sashaying all over the road. Gobbets of mud splatter the roadside pinyon pines.

"I like this work," he says, roaring off to district headquarters.

"Yeah, me too," the assistant ranger says.

"You get so many opportunities to be *helpful* to people."

Ten thousand square miles of wilderness, dreams Seldom in his dream, and not a pot to piss in. Comfort stations! George Hayduke ol' buddy, we sure need you now. Rudolf the Red is dead.

30

Edge of the Maze: The Chase Concluded

Well, it all depends on your point of view, thought Hayduke as he paced through the rain toward the last-observed location of Lizard Rock. If you look at it from the buzzard's point of view the rain is a drag. No visibility, no lunch. But from my point of view, from the guerrilla's point of view—

He had only a mile and a half to go, rounding the heads of a branchwork of ravines in the slickrock, dark little canyons deeper than wide, all of them starting to run with water now, red-brown silt-laden stuff, a foamy spongy bubbling liquid too thick to drink, too thin to walk on.

He halted behind a wet bedraggled bush (cliff-rose) to let a pair of jeeps go by, their amber headlights burning through the downpour. Regained his breath and strength, getting the second wind, and jogged on, across the muddy jeep trail and far around the helicopter encampment, approaching the side of the secret supply cache. When the tent and vehicles and helicopter became visible through the rain, he got down on knees and elbows and crawled another fifty yards and stopped.

Squinting through the rain from behind a pile of rubble fallen from the crags of Lizard Rock, he scans the scene. Two armed men in ponchos stand beside a fire, guarding a coffeepot. Another sticks his head out of the nearer olive-drab military wall tent. The big gray helicopter—Department of Public Safety, State of Utah—rests on its skids, useless in the rain. Department of Public Safety, that's the new and sweeter name for State Police, which has too much of a—well, regimental sound.

"Coffee ready?"

"She's almost."

"Well, bring it in when it's ready."

The head retires within the tent. Hayduke looks to the right; two men with shotguns sit smoking in one of the DPS four-wheel-drive vans. The other vehicles are empty. He looks along the talus of Lizard Rock toward a certain jumble of debris—near that snaggle-toothed juniper, right?—where they cached the supplies. Food and water. First-aid kit. Clean socks. And ammo, two full boxes; he'd packed that himself, taking no chances.

What to do what to do; the same old question. That cache so near and precious remained beyond his reach, hidden only a hundred yards from the tents and campfire. What to do? We need a diversion here. The rain drummed down on his patient head, pouring like a cascade off the bill of his cap. He could wait, of course, wait for *them* to do something, go away, leave him in peace. But obviously they wouldn't move with that helicopter until the rain slowed down. Or leave it behind unguarded. Lose too many helicopters that way. He could crawl back, move off to another side, snap off a couple of shots, attract attention, circle around back here and move in on whoever stays behind.

He backs off, crawling on his belly, over the wet sand until out of sight of the camp, then moves up the talus under the cliff and takes shelter under an overhanging alcove. Sits there in the dust and bones and old coyote turds and tries to think of what to do. Should have made Smith come along. How? Should have kept his backpack on his back, where it belongs. Should never have thrown that backpack away. But he had to. But shouldn't have done it. But he had to do it. At the time it seemed like the right thing to do. But they never had a chance to go back. He can't quite convince himself. Of this, that or much of anything. The hunger in his hollow arms and legs, the echoing cavern of his belly, makes all else seem unreal, speculative, relatively unimportant. Academic.

Got to eat. He gnaws on his knuckle, tentatively. God, he thinks, a man really could get a little nourishment, some, just nibbling on his fingers. You can always get along with one hand, if you have to. Maybe. With help. Not out here, though. Not down in there. He stares toward the Maze and sees, through the silver screen of the rain, a bewildering jungle of rock: domes, elephant backs, potholes and basins, cut and carved and divided by canyons, side canyons, side canyons to the side canyons, all of them winding like worms, all sheer-walled and apparently bottomless. What a mess, he thinks. A man could get lost in there.

Safe for the moment, though starving and without a plan, hungry Hayduke unslings his rifle, takes the coil of rope from his shoulder and lies down to rest for a few minutes, again. He dozes off at once into dreams. The dreams are quick, erratic and uncomfortable, waking him. God, I must be getting weak, he thinks. Can't stay awake. He drifts back into slumber.

He wakes up to the sound of racing motors. The rain has slackened off. Maybe that's what woke him. Quiet followed by action. Groggy and uncertain, Hayduke picks up the rifle and stumbles to his feet. The police camp is hidden by the wall of Lizard Rock. He stumbles down the loose talus, nearly falling once, and reaches a vantage point.

He can see them now, the men, the tents, the smoldering fire, the vehicles and the revolving rotors of the helicopter. They're warming it up. Two men sit in the open side door of the machine, checking their weapons, smoking. They wear brown-green camouflage suits, like bow hunters or combat soldiers. One has binoculars dangling by a strap from his neck. Both wear crash helmets and also, judging from the stiff bulge of their suits, bulletproof vests.

Hayduke studies them through the telescope sights of his rifle, the cross hairs aimed first on one man, then the other. On their faces:

one needs a shave, looks a bit red-eyed and tired; the other wears a bushy mustache, has the moist nose, thin lips, heavy brows, sharp restless roving eyes of a hunter. At any moment he'll be leveling those 5-by-50 eyes up this way, the sombitch. And when he does he gets it, right in the neck.

Hayduke lowers the cross hairs a touch to read the name tag on the chest. They all wear name tags these days. And every man has a number. The name is Jim Crumbo and his hand, holding what looks like—Hayduke sharpens the focus—a Browning 3-inch magnum 12-gauge semiautomatic shotgun (the bastard!), is steady as a vise. His number he probably wears on that ID bracelet on his wrist, and that leather-holstered badge in his zippered left breast pocket. He looks like a fucking *officer*.

Oh it's 'Nam again all right all over again. Nothing missing here but the weed and Westmoreland, the whores and the Confederate flags. With me as the last VC in the jungle. Or am I the first? In the jungle of silence and stone. Take off, you swine; what're you waiting for? Hayduke, impatient, roves round the camp with his telescopic eye, the anarchist voyeur, looking for something to shoot, something to eat.

Less rain. Visibility up to five miles. The pilot appears in the cockpit. Crumbo and his mate swing inside the helicopter, close the doors, and the machine, bellowing, rises into the gray-green drizzle of the air. Hayduke crouches deep among his rocks, watching the copter's pilot through the telescope. Pale face behind Plexiglas. Metallic, helmeted, mike at mouth, grimly goggled in Polaroid glareproofs. Looks semihuman in that rig. Not a friend.

The helicopter merges with the mist, south toward the Fins, and disappears for the time being. Hayduke returns his full attention to the camp.

Two men are driving off in a four-wheel-drive pickup, heading down the slimy trail toward Candlestick Spire and the Standing Rocks. All gone? He examines the scene with care. Two vehicles remain, and the wall tents, the smoky fire. No humans apparent. The others, perhaps, have gone off on a foot patrol.

He waits, nevertheless, though the hunger lust is whistling in his ear. (Gawd! that peanut butter! that jerky! them beans!) Waits for half an hour, or so it seems to him. Nobody in sight. He can wait no more.

Carrying the rifle, Hayduke moves down and across the talus slope, toward the hidden cache. He takes concealment where he can, behind balanced boulders and under junipers, but there is not much cover.

He gets to within a few yards of his objective, a hundred yards from the camp, when—Jesus Christ!—a dog comes bounding out through the flaps of the near tent, barking like a maniac. It looks like an Airedale puppy, black and tan, half grown. Spotting Hayduke at once, the puppy runs toward him, then stops halfway, uncertain, barking and wagging its stub of a tail at the same time, doing its duty. Hayduke curses—goddamn dog!—as two men come out of the tent holding coffee cups, looking around. They see him. Caught in the open, Hayduke acts reflexively, snapping off a shot from the hip that shatters a window in the nearest truck. The men dive back into the vain shelter of the tent. Where their weapons are. And the radio.

Hayduke retreats. The puppy pursues him for another hundred feet and stops, still barking, wagging its foolish tail.

Hayduke runs toward the rim of the Maze, the first and only shelter he can see or think of. Never been there before. He doesn't care. Goddamn pet dogs. Ought to feed them all to the coyotes, he thinks, pounding along. Avoiding the wide-open rimrock, he runs through a growth of junipers down a peninsula of stone that thrusts like a pointing finger into the heart of the Maze. The finger is long, two miles long, and the cover meager. Halfway to the end of the rock, he hears that sound again, the air-shattering rotors of a helicopter. Glances back, can't see it yet; he keeps on running, though his ribs are cracking from the pain, his throat burning for more air, more space, more energy, more love, more anything but this.

But this is it, he thinks in wonder, sprinting down the shining rock, while one stray sunbeam, falling through a break in the rolling clouds, follows him like God's own spotlight (*There he goes!*) across the esplanade of stone, beyond the last of the trees, stage left, down below the galleries of the cliffs, into the open-air theater of the desert. Hayduke at last is sole star of the show, top banana, alone and exposed.

He runs across open slickrock toward the nose, the point, the tip of the peninsula. Sheer canyons close in on either side a hundred feet away, four hundred, five hundred feet deep, with walls as clean and straight and sheer as the flanks of what Bonnie calls the Vampire State Building.

Hopeless? Then there's nothing to worry about, he remembers, gasping like a marathon runner down the final lap. This is it, I've done it now, they'll shoot me down like a dog, there's no way off of here, no way, I don't even have my rope anymore—*forget the rope!*—and the situation is absolutely hopeless and there's not a fucking thing to worry about and furthermore I got six shots left in the rifle and five and twenty for the .357.

Thus Hayduke, his ruminations, as gunfire breaks out like a high-decibel heat rash in his rear, as the helicopter returns, as a dozen men on foot and a dozen more in radio-equipped patrol vehicles stop and turn and head this way, converging all of them on one exhausted, unfed, lone and lonesome, trapped and cornered psychopath.

Late afternoon. The sun breaks brighter than the ragged mass of storm clouds, more natural golden searchlights play over the canyon country, as Hayduke, spotted by the helicopter, stumbles unprepared to the final point of rock and teeters on the edge, arms flailing for balance.

He looks down over the brink and sees, five hundred vertical feet below, a semiliquid red frothy mass of mud hurling itself in a torrent down the canyon floor, a wall-to-wall flash flood hurtling around the bend, thundering over the jump-off, roaring toward the hidden Green River some five or twenty-five (he has no notion of the distance) miles away. Rolling boulders clash and clack beneath the surge, logs float past, uprooted trees pitching on the waves—he'd be not much worse off jumping into a river of lava.

The helicopter approaches in a wide circle. Hayduke slips into a crack in the rimrock, a jagged, curving crevice barely wide enough to admit his body, so deep and warped he cannot see to the bottom. A cliff-rose on one side, an infant juniper on the other. There is nothing to support his feet; he wedges himself in the crack, back against one wall, knees against the other, chimney-style. Jammed between the mass of the peninsula and the split-off block, only his eyes and arms and rifle above the surface of the ground, he waits for the first assault.

Is he afraid? Hell, no, he's not afraid. Hayduke has gone beyond terror. Scared finally shitless, purged and purified, he is now at last too tired for fear, too exhausted to think of surrender. The foul stench rising from the seat of his jeans, the warm loose structurally imperfect mass drooling down his right pant leg, hardly seems a product of himself. He, Hayduke, has found a simpler realm, centered on the eyepiece of his scope, resolving itself simply to the coordinate precision of forefinger and trigger, eye and cross hairs, muzzle point, windage and lead time. His mind, now clean as his bowels and clarified by fast, is sharp and eager.

The helicopter rattles in for the kill. Without thinking, as trained, Hayduke places his first shot through the pilot's window, accidentally missing the pilot's face. The helicopter veers off suddenly, wildly, and the multiple shotgun blasts from the side-door gunner flail the sandstone a comfortable ten to twenty yards from Hayduke's position. The bird's tail toward him, he places his second shot into the gearbox of the rear rotor. The helicopter, more insulted than injured, limps back to camp for minor repairs and a coffee break for the crew.

Hayduke waits. The men on the ground keep a cautious distance, six hundred yards away across the open slickrock peninsula, and wait for reinforcements and field command. Seeing that there is going to be a slight technical delay in the proceedings, Hayduke finds a more secure niche in the rimrock crevasse and pulls off his stinking pants. He believes he is willing to die today but he is not willing to die sitting in his own shit. After getting them off (the rifle at rest on the rock in front of his chin) his first thought is to drop the pants and the mess down the chute below him. But then he has a better idea. Nothing else to do at the moment anyway. He breaks a small branch from the cliff-rose, its lovely orangelike perfumed blossoms now going to seed.

He scrapes the shit out of his pants. Why? Under the circumstances, why bother? Well, thinks George Hayduke, it's a question of dignity.

Leaving the pants off to dry out a bit, he waits for the next assault. Four rounds left in the rifle: two for the next helicopter charge, two for whatever's next, and the loaded .357 for whatever's last.

It shouldn't be long.

Sam Love arrived late for the first of the action but not too late for the fun part. It would have made no difference in any case. He was no longer in charge of anything, including his own baffled curiosity. The time was twenty-four hours past when he'd launched his raving brother off in the helicopter, attended by Doc and Bonnie, to a bed in the Intensive Care Unit of the Moab hospital.

Sam was merely an onlooker now, a bystander and a spectator, and glad of it. He and a newspaper reporter from Salt Lake City sat on a block of stone and watched the scene of the battle. Lit by the falling sun, the wide and rosy proscenium of the Maze faced them like a great stage, with red pinnacles, purple buttes and blue mountains serving as backdrop. In the foreground, downstage, a light but steady crackle of rifle fire proved that where there's life there's hope. Two helicopters and a spotter plane buzzed about uselessly off toward the wings, wasting gas.

"Which one did he shoot down?" Sam asked.

"That big one from Public Safety. What they call a civilian Huey, I think. Only he didn't really shoot it down. Just nicked the tail rotor and put a hole through a window. Nobody got hurt but they had to set it down for a while."

"Where exactly is he anyway?"

"Out there on that point." The journalist raised his field glasses to his eyes; Sam did the same. "He's bunkered down in a joint in the rock, between those two bushes out there. About five or six hundred yards, I'd guess."

Sam focused his glasses. He could see the two shrubs, both of them almost leafless, and half branchless too, stripped apparently by rifle fire, but he saw no sign of the fugitive. "How do you know he's still there?"

"He fired two shots an hour ago, when they tried to drop grenades on him. Damn near got the pilot of the other helicopter."

They watched; from either side, a little below and in front, occasional rifle shots snapped out, cracking like whips.

"What are those men shooting at?"

"The bushes, I guess. Maybe they figure a lucky ricochet will get him. It's a way of killing time."

Without hurting anybody, Sam thought. "How long's he been there now?"

The reporter looked at his watch. "Six and a half goddamned fucking hours."

"He's probably out of shells. Might be a good idea to rush him before it gets dark."

The reporter smiled. "You want to lead the charge?"

"No."

"Nobody else does either. They have a respectable sharpshooter out there in that crack. He might be saving up for some last shots. They'll just wait him out."

"They better watch close," Sam said. "That Rudolf has a funny way of disappearing over canyon rims. Are they certain he's not already down inside the Maze?"

"They put two men down on that butte out there, on the other side of the canyon. It's a five-hundred-foot drop-off where Rudolf is, nearly straight down. Sheer sandstone, no way to climb down it. Even if he tries they'll see him. And if he falls he'd bounce into the biggest flood they've had go down Horse Canyon in forty years, according to the sheriff. I'd say your Rudolf is screwed."

"He's not mine, thanks. But he's got a long rope."

"Not anymore. They found his rope too."

The rifle fire continued, all one-sided.

"I'll bet he's out of ammunition," Sam said. "Maybe he'll surrender."

"Maybe. If he was a regular criminal that's what you'd expect. He must be plenty thirst by now. But the Public Safety boys say they have a real weirdo on their hands today."

"That I can believe."

Sam lowered his glasses. As he played with them, wondering what he was doing here, he heard a shout from nearby. A fusillade of gunfire burst out from the entire length of the firing line: a dozen or more automatic rifles in rapid fire. Streams of bullets converged on one target.

"My God," Sam muttered. He raised the glasses again, searching for the object of this concentrated interest. He looked and quickly found the target out on the point, within a few feet of the extreme edge of the cliff, a stiff awkward semihuman figure rising to the waist out of what appeared to be, from Love's angle of vision, a solid mass of stone. He saw the yellow billed cap, a bristly shaggy sort of head, the shoulders, chest and torso of something clothed in faded blue denim, exactly as he remembered Rudolf's garb from their hasty encounters before. The man's arms seemed to be holding, or to be wrapped around, a rifle. At so great a range, however, even though he was looking through field glasses, Sam could not be certain, could not be absolutely certain of identification—yet it surely must be the same person. Had to be. But with one obvious and significant difference: this man was being torn apart before his eyes.

Sam Love had led a sheltered life, minding mostly his own business; he had never personally witnessed the physical destruction of a human being. Horrified, sickened and fascinated, he watched Rudolf's figure seeming to crawl or slide sideways, half in and half out (for the love of God, why?) of the crevice, saw him swept with a storm of bullets, the body ripped and fragmented, chips, rags, splinters, slivers flying off, the arms flopping as if broken, the rifle dropped, the head itself shattered into bits and pieces—the collapsing wreckage of what *could* have been, seconds earlier, a living, laughing, loving, red-blooded *American boy.*

Sam stared. The riddled body hung on the rimrock for a final moment before the impact of the hail of steel, like hammer blows, literally pushed it over the edge. The remains of Rudolf the Red fell like a sack of garbage into the foaming gulf of the canyon, vanishing forever from men's eyes. And women's too. (For indeed, the body was never found.)

Sam felt ill. For a few minutes, as the reporter and all the others ran forward, shouting, he thought (as his daughter would say) he was going to toss his cookies. But he did not; the visceral revulsion passed, though the memory of this horror would taint his dreams for months and years to come. He drank water from his canteen, ate some soda crackers from his lunch bucket, and after another minute felt well enough to join the police, the sheriffs of three counties and their deputies, the assistant superintendent of a national park, two rangers, three journalists and the residue (four members) of the San Juan County Search and Rescue Team, out on the far end of the point of rock.

They found no trace of flesh or bone. But there was a generous trail of blood across the stone, leading to the rim. They found Rudolf's rifle, the splintered remnants of a once-beautiful scope-mounted Remington .30-.06—with one cartridge, unfired, still in the chamber. Some wondered at that, while others inspected the bullet-shredded vestiges of the cliff-rose and the juniper, which had given the outlaw, through the long afternoon, what little concealment they could when he lifted his head to fire.

Others examined the bullet-pocked sandstone, the smudged patches of fire and powder where the grenades had exploded some distance away, and idly kicked a few stones into the crevasse which divided the main body of the point from its ultimate tip. The stones clattered down into the shadows, disappearing, and clunked and thumped onto the accumulated debris of centuries at the bottom.

The captain of the state police company radioed his men on the opposite rim and confirmed that Rudolf had clearly and beyond dispute fallen into the canyon. Two men had observed the whole length of the body's descent, had seen it carom from a crag and vanish beneath the roiling waters of the flood. Furthermore they had observed the dismembered limbs of the body, still clad in denim, rise to the surface downstream and bob away out of sight around the first bend.

The pilot of one helicopter attempted but failed to follow the course of the remains down over the falls to the river.

The captain gathered up the broken rifle and the spent shells. All the men walked slowly and thoughtfully, not talking much, back to the camp at Lizard Rock.

All but Sam Love. Last to arrive at the death scene, he was the last to leave. He lingered and lingered, not knowing why, staring down into the roaring canyon. Bemused by the sound and a little frightened—for he felt the eerie pull of the depths—he backed a few steps, raised his eyes and looked out over the walls and canyons and tablets of the Maze, that grotesque labyrinth of stone gilded by the glow of the setting sun. Longing for distance and a sense of detachment, he gazed northward at the remote Book Cliffs, fifty miles away by line of sight, and east to the snow-dappled thirteen-thousand-foot peaks beyond Moab. Finally Sam turned and looked back the long way that he (and Rudolf) had come, past Candlestick Spire, past Lizard Rock, toward the unexplored Fins, the little-known depths of the Standing Rock country, all of it darkened now by the vast blue shadow of Land's End.

Sun going down. Time to get out of here. Sam knelt to peer one last time into the deep dim slot of the crack in the rock. He tried to see to the bottom. Too dark, too dark.

"Rudolf," he said, "are you down in there?" He waited. No reply. "You can't fool everybody, son. Not all the time." Pause. "You hear me?" No answer but the silence.

Sam waited a moment longer, then stood and hastened after his friends and neighbors. They had a wearisome long and roundabout drive ahead of them, all the way back to Blanding by way of Land's End, Green River and Moab. (The shorter route, past Hite Marina over the Colorado, had been temporarily closed by the Highway Department for what were identified as "routine bridge repairs.") But Sam was feeling better, his stomach was feeling better, he felt the return of a healthy man's almost normal appetite. He and the lofty vulture, so high as to be nearly invisible, shared a common emotion:

Time to eat.

EPILOGUE

❧ ❧

The New Beginning

The lawyering was long and tedious. Seldom Seen Smith, having been captured in Wayne County, was jailed first in the county seat of Loa, then transferred after two days to the San Juan County Jail in the town of Monticello. Ms. Bonnie Abbzug and Dr. A. K. Sarvis were there waiting for him, right next door, in fact, in adjoining cells. Their patient, Bishop Love, was off the critical list, though recovering slowly.

Abbzug, Sarvis and Smith were arraigned in the County District Court on the following charges: assault with a deadly weapon, a felony; simple assault, a misdemeanor; obstructing justice, a misdemeanor; arson, a felony; aggravated arson, a felony; and conspiracy, a felony. Bail for each of the accused was set at $20,000, which Doc promptly arranged to have paid. After a few days of liberty the three were hailed into Federal District Court, Phoenix, Arizona, and charged with the following Federal offenses: conspiracy, arson and aggravated arson, unlawful transportation and use of explosives, and escape from official custody, all felonies, and interference with an arrest, a misdemeanor. Bail was $25,000; Doc paid the bonds.

After months of the usual delay the Federal court waived priority and allowed Utah to try the defendants first. The case of the State of Utah versus Abbzug, Sarvis and Smith came to trial in the District

Court of San Juan County, Monticello, Judge Melvin Frost presiding. The prosecutor was J. Bracken Dingledine (a distant cousin of Albuquerque's own W. W.), newly elected county attorney and a friend, associate and business partner of Bishop Love. A recovered but oddly modified Love, by the way. His convictions were no longer so clear, and his heart, under intensive care, had softened.

For the defense Doc retained two attorneys, the first a young graduate of Yale Law School with good family connections in both Arizona and Utah, and the second a native of San Juan County, the descendant of Mormon pioneers, an elderly, successful, highly esteemed and cool-mannered gentleman named Snow.

The first ploy of the defense was plea bargaining. All three defendants were willing to plead guilty to the misdemeanors if the felony charges were dropped. The prosecutor refused to bargain; he was determined to nail the defendants on all counts. Dingledine, like the former Bishop Love, had political ambitions. Doc's attorneys, therefore, worked carefully with the jury panel and succeeded in getting two closet Sierra Clubbers and one obvious crank (a retired Paiute and active wino from the village of Bluff) seated in the jury box. The trial began.

It quickly became evident that the prosecution did not have an airtight case. There was no hard evidence, such as fingerprints or eyewitnesses, to connect any of the defendants, beyond all reasonable doubt, with the crimes. The incriminating materials in Smith's truck and Hayduke's jeep were not in evidence, since neither of those vehicles could be found. Smith said his truck had been stolen. Although Bishop Love (summoned and under oath) and five of his Teammates testified that they had seen and pursued somebody driving Smith's truck on two separate occasions, none could positively assert that they had seen Smith himself or the other defendants in the truck at the time. The most powerful case against the defendants proved to be the fact that they had fled the scene of a crime at least twice, evading and apparently resisting arrest. All denied any knowledge of the rock-rolling incident north of Hite Marina and of the shooting that took place during the night along the jeep trail to the Maze, where, according to Doc, he and his friends had been enjoying a moonlight cross-country hike from Land's End to Lizard Rock. The defense attorneys furthermore pointed out that none of the defendants had a criminal record and that two had voluntarily come to the aid of the stricken Bishop Love at his time of direst need.

After three days all testimony was heard and arguments concluded. The jury retired to consider its verdict. They failed to agree. Two more days of sequestered wrangling could not produce a verdict, although the secret Sierra Club members later revealed that they both had voted for conviction on all charges. The jury was hung. A retrial was scheduled, to take place four months later.

Again Doc's attorneys attempted plea bargaining. This time they were successful. After weeks of private negotiations the following solution was reached: Doc took up serious study of *The Book of Mormon* and let it be known, through his lawyers, that he was preparing for conversion to membership in the Church of Jesus Christ of Latter-Day Saints; he and Ms. Abbzug were married by Bishop Love himself (a new man!) in a simple outdoor ceremony at Valley of the Gods, near Mexican Hat, Seldom Seen Smith acting as best man, Sam Love as a witness, and Smith's teenage daughter as bridesmaid; all three defendants pleaded guilty to the misdemeanors and to one felony each, the conspiracy to destroy public property.

They awaited sentencing, which had also been prearranged through Judge Frost. Here Abbzug and Smith created fresh difficulties by refusing, at the last hour, to completely recant their crimes, both of them grumbling that, in Smith's words, "Somebody has to do it." The probation officer assigned to the case to make a presentencing report to the judge was severely troubled. He consulted with Doc, the judge, and Doc's attorneys. Doc assumed full responsibility for the acts and attitudes of his co-defendants, insisting that he was the arch-conspirator, that he and he alone had influenced, indoctrinated and knowingly misled his younger colleagues; he guaranteed that he would retread their brains, socialize their hearts and bring them back to Christ. He also promised they would not do it again.

And he willingly agreed, at the judge's suggestion, to practice the art of medicine for at least the next ten years in a southeast Utah community of less than five thousand population. Settled. The judge pronounced his sentence.

Abbzug, Sarvis and Smith were sentenced each to concurrent terms of not less than one year and not more than five years, to be served in the Utah State Prison (where death by firing squad is still a feasible option). He then suspended the prison sentences, considering the defendants' records and other circumstances, but ordered all three to be confined for six months to the San Juan County Jail and thereafter to serve four and a half years each on probation, contingent upon good behavior and strict fulfillment of agreed-upon stipulations. In addition, Smith separately was fined the maximum (for a misdemeanor) of $299 for rolling rocks and ordered to make restitution to Bishop Love for the full value of the bishop's Chevrolet Blazer, which had been flattened, all agreed, flatter than a chinch bug. But the new Love forgave the debt.

The Federal District Court in Phoenix, taking note of the action of the Utah Seventh Judicial District Court and of Judge Frost's recommendations, tentatively dropped the charges against Abbzug, Sarvis and Smith for crimes allegedly committed in the State of Arizona, taking into account that the prime suspect involved in those matters, a Caucasian male identified only as one "Rudolf the Red" or "Herman Smith," was known to be dead.

County Attorney Dingledine, although privately if reluctantly acceding to this resolution of the affair, exhibited in public the symptoms of scornful indignation, as was only natural. Encouraged by many statements of outrage at the leniency of the courts, the coddling of criminals and the permissive attitude of society at large, Mr. Dingledine won a seat in the Utah State Senate on a program of rigorous law enforcement, expansion of the state prison system, Federal subsidies for the mining industry, completion of the Utah wilderness freeway system, tax relief for large families and fiscal responsibility in government. He was elected by an overwhelming plurality over his sole opponent, a retired Paiute whose entire political platform consisted of one plank: free peyote.

There were a few further ramifications. Both Love brothers quit the Search and Rescue Team. Poor Seldom Seen, already a convicted felon, was sued for divorce by his first wife and immediately after by his second; only Susan, the Green River girl, remained loyal. Upon receiving the news in the San Juan County Jail, Smith attempted to make light of this added batch of legal difficulties by saying, "Well, I hope both them gals get married again soon, because then I'll know there's gonna be at least two men sorry I got throwed in the slammer." A pause. "But what the hell should I do about them ambiguity charges? Doc?"

"Be of good cheer," said Doc. "Christ is the answer."

Dr. Sarvis sold his house in Albuquerque. He and Mrs. Sarvis selected the town of Green River (pop. 1200 counting dogs) as their new and legal residence. Doc bought a sixty-five-foot houseboat and moored it at the boat ramp on the shore of Smith's hay and melon ranch. He and Bonnie moved in within a week after completing their jail sentences. Bonnie cultivated a floating garden of marijuana, easily launched downriver, in case the need should arise, by casting off a single light line. Doc attended (for about a year) the Wednesday night meetings of the ward Mutual Improvement Society and went to church (for about a year and a half) each Sunday; he even tried wearing the official, sanctified, regulation Mormon undershirt, although his actual ambition was to grow up to be a jack Mormon, like Seldom. His wife refused to convert, preferring to retain her status as the only Jewish gentile in Green River. Doc rented an office in town, ten miles away, where he and Bonnie practiced medicine. He did the medicine; she practiced. Though the clientele was small and sometimes paid their bills in watermelons, Doc's services were much appreciated. His nearest medical competitor lived fifty miles away in Moab. He augmented his income, when necessary, by occasional knife jobs in Salt Lake, Denver and Albuquerque. They both liked life on the river and work in a small town, and enjoyed the company of their only neighbors, Mr. and Mrs. Seldom Smith. Doc even learned how to run a hay baler, though he refused to go near the tractor or drive a car. He and Bonnie always bicycled to the office anyway.

Here their story would happily have ended, except for a single and posthumous (out of the earth) detail.

It happens during the second year of probation. Five people sit around a hand-made pinewood table in the first-class salon of a large and comfortable custom-designed houseboat. The time is eleven o'clock at night. Illumination of the tables comes from two clear-burning, silent, shaded, kerosene-burning Aladdin lamps which dangle from iron hooks in the ceiling beam. The lamps swing a little, from time to time, as the houseboat rocks gently on the waves of the river. The table is covered by a green blanket. There are poker chips (sad to relate) in the center of the blanket and the game (dealer's choice) is five-card stud. The five players are Dr. and Mrs. Sarvis, Mr. and Mrs. Smith, and their communal probation officer, a young fellow named Greenspan, who is a relative newcomer to the state of Utah. (Newcomers are always welcome in the Beehive State but are advised to set their watches back fifty years when entering.) The conversation is mostly of a limited, practical nature:

"Pot's right. Here we go. Ten, no help. Seven, possible. Pair of deuces! Queen, no help, and—well, would you look at that, a pair of cowboys."

"How do you do that, Doc?"

"Control, friends, control."

"I mean, so often?"

"Nephi guides my hand. Make it ten on the kings."

"Jesus."

"Called."

"Called."

"No game for us shoe clerks but I guess I'll stay."

Pause. "And you?" says Doc.

"We only get one hole card in this game?"

"That is correct, my love."

"And nothing's wild?"

"Nothing."

"What a crooked, boring game."

Smith looks up from the table, hearing something. Doc hears it too. Not the wind coming up the river. Not the quiet creaking of the boat. Something else. He listens.

"All right, all right, I'm in, deal 'em. What're you gaping at?"

"Of course. In a moment. Seldom?"

"I'm out, pardners." Smith folds, not watching the game.

"Okay. Pot's right and here we go again." Doc deals the cards, laying them out one at a time, face up, the old old story. "Four, no help. Bonnie's deuce, sorry. Trey, no help. Ace, not much help. Kings bet ten more."

He listens, as the others call, fold, call. He hears the sound of—hoofbeats? Heartbeats? No, it really is the sound of a horse. Or maybe of two horses. Somebody or someone, riding up the dusty lane between the fields, under the glittering summer stars, toward the river, toward the houseboat. Not fast but easily, at a walking pace. The sound carries well in the stillness.

The game goes on. Doc rakes in the pot. The deal passes to Greenspan. He shuffles the deck. Doc glances at Bonnie, who is staring glumly at the table. Something is bothering that girl. Maybe it's her condition. Have to talk to her tonight. This game has gone on for four hours and we're only six dollars ahead. And Greenspan has to leave in half an hour. Can't make an honest living like this. He glances at her again; maybe it's something else. Must give her my ear tonight. Although there are some things, or there is one thing, which he and Bonnie never talk about.

The steady hoofbeats coming closer as Greenspan deals. Doc looks at Seldom, who is looking at him. Seldom shrugs. In a moment now they will hear the clumping and clattering of steel shoes on the old planks of the landing pier.

Greenspan looks at his watch. He has to drive all the way back to Price tonight. Seventy miles. Rather a dude, the young probation officer is wearing his new buckskin vest, the one with the mountain-man fringes and the silver conchos. "I'll open," he says. "Two beans."

Pushing two white chips into the middle of the blanket, where the ante lays.

Susan Smith is next. "I'll stay."

Bonnie's turn. "Raise you two," she says, staring with wonder at her hand. Good girl.

The houseboat rocks on the water, the lamps sway a bit. Wind coming up the river against the steady brown flow from Desolation Canyon. Little waves lap at the waterline outside, slapping against the Fiberglas-coated marine-plywood hull. (Doc had wanted an adobe houseboat, with projecting *vigas* of yellow pine on which to hang garlands of red chili peppers à la New Mexico. Not available, at any price. Even the Mexican navy, they say, has given up on adobe watercraft, except for submarines.)

The horses have stopped. Instead of shod hoofs he hears human feet in boots, with jingling spurs, step onto the planking. Doc stands up, letting his cards lie. He withdraws his cigar.

"What's wrong?" says Mrs. Smith.

"We have a visitor, I think." Doc feels a strong need to meet that visitor outside the door. Even before the knocking begins he has stepped away from the table. "Excuse me."

He goes to the door and opens it, barring the way with his bulk. At first he sees no one. Peering harder, he can make out a tall, thin figure backed off out of the lamplight.

"Yes?" says Doc. "Who is it?"

"You Doc Sarvis?"

"Yes."

"Got a friend of yours out here." The stranger's voice is soft and low but full of a practiced menace. "He needs some doctoring."

"A friend of mine?"

"Yeah."

Doc hesitates. *His* friends are all inside, around the table, looking at him. Facing them Doc says, "It's all right, I'll just be a few minutes. You go on without me."

He closes the door at his back and follows the stranger, who has retreated across the landing to the riverbank. A horse stands there, reins trailing on the ground. As his eyes adjust to the starlight Doc confirms his first impression of a tall but very skinny man, a total stranger, dressed in dusty Levi's, wearing a black hat, a bandanna over the nose and mouth. The man stares at him with one dark eye. The other, Doc notices, the left eye, is gone.

"Who the hell are you?" Doc says. He puffs on his cigar, making the red coal glow in the dark. The hex sign.

"You don't really want to know that, Doc. But"—a faint movement behind the mask, as of a smile—"some folks used to call me Kemosabe. Come on."

"Wait a minute." Doc has halted. "Where is this alleged friend of mine? Where's the patient?"

A pause. The wind sighs on the river.

The stranger says, "You believe in ghosts, Doc?"

The doctor thinks. "I believe in the ghosts that haunt the human mind."

"This one ain't that kind."

"No?"

"He's real. He's come a long way."

"Well," says Doc, a trifle shakily, "let's see him. Let's see this phenomenon. Where is he?"

Another moment of silence. The stranger nods toward the pathway on top of the riverbank.

"I'm right up here, Doc," says a familiar voice.

Doc feels the skin crawl on the back of his neck. He stares up through the darkness toward the voice and sees a second horseman silhouetted against the Milky Way, a stocky wide-shouldered brawny man with sombrero and a grin that shines even by starlight. He is mounted on a horse that must be seventeen hands high.

Good God, Doc thinks. And then realizes that he is not really surprised, that he has been expecting this apparition for two years. He sighs. Here we go again.

"George?"

"Yep."

"Is that you, George?"

"Fuck yes. Who the hell else?"

Doc sighs again. "They shot you to pieces at Lizard Rock."

"Not me. Rudolf."

"Rudolf?"

"A scarecrow. A fucking dummy."

"I don't understand."

"Well invite us in, for chrissake. I'll tell you all about it. It's a long story."

Doc looks back toward the houseboat. Through the light of the curtained window he sees Greenspan and the others at the table, cards in motion under the lamplight.

"George . . . our probation officer is in there."

"Oh. Well, shit, we'll get out of here. Get out of your hair."

"No, hold on a minute. He's a nice guy and I don't want to put him in a difficult position. You understand. He'll be leaving in half an hour. Why don't you and your friend here turn your horses out in the pasture and wait for us in Seldom's house? There's nobody there. You know where his house is?"

"We were there five minutes ago."

They stare at each other through the starlight. Doc is not quite convinced.

"George . . . is that *really* you?"

"No, it's Ichabod Ignatz. Come on up here and feel the wounds."

"I'm going to do that." Doc climbs the embankment.

The horse stirs nervously. "Whoa, you ignorant sombitch. Yeah. Give me some skin, Doc." Hayduke is smiling like a little boy.

They shake. They squeeze flesh. The apparition feels like the same smelly solid Hayduke of old. No improvement at all.

"My God. . . . It really is." The doctor finds himself blinking back tears. "Are you all right?"

"Fine. Got some old wounds acting up, that's all. And my friend here wanted to meet you. How's Seldom?"

"He's the same as ever. Still working on the dam plan."

"That's good." The horse stamps his feet. "Hold still, goddam-mit." A long pause. "How's Bonnie?"

"We're married."

"So I heard. How is she?"

"Four months pregnant."

"No shit." Pause. "Well I'll be fucked. Bonnie, knocked up. I'll be screwed, blued and tattooed. I didn't think it could be done."

"It happened."

"What's she going to do about it?"

"She's going to become a mother."

"I'll be goddamned." George smiles sadly and happily and fool-ishly, all at once, like a liberated lion. "You horny old fart. Doc, I want to see her."

"You will, you will."

Another pause.

"My name is Fred Goodsell now. I have a whole new ID." Hay-duke's smile grows wider. "And I got a job too. I start work as a night watchman next week. I'm going to be a regular fucking citizen, Doc, just like you and Seldom and Bonnie. For a while."

Doc looks back again at the houseboat. The front door is open-ing. Bonnie stands in the light, trying to see outside. "I'd better get back in there. You wait for us. I want to have a good look at you, and those wounds. So will Bonnie. And Seldom. Don't go away."

"Shit, Doc, we're tired and we're hungry. We ain't going *no-wheres* tonight."

Bonnie calls. "Doc . . . are you out there?"

"Be right down," he answers. "In a minute."

Hayduke chuckles. "Good old Doc. Say, that was a nice job you and Seldom did on that bridge."

"What are you talking about?"

"No? I mean the Glen Canyon bridge."

"That wasn't us. We were right here that day. We have witnesses to prove it." (Thank God.)

"Well I'll be fucked again," says Hayduke. Bemused, shaking his head, he ponders this information. "You hear that?" he says to his masked partner. The partner, who has remounted, nods. "Doc," says Hayduke, "You better get back to your spouse before she chews your ass off. Only there's one thing you got to ask me first."

"What?" Doc chews on the stub of his cigar, which has gone out. "What's that?"

"Aren't you going to ask me where my night watchman job is?" Hayduke is grinning at him again.

Now it is Doc's turn to ponder. Briefly. "No, George, I think I'd rather not know that."

Hayduke laughs and turns to his partner. "What'd I tell you?" To Doc he says, "You're right again. But you can guess, can't you?"

"Oh yes. I can guess."

"Seldom would like to know."

"You can tell him yourself."

"Right, you're the doctor. Okay, we'll be waiting for you. Let's go." Hayduke turns his giant horse away from Doc, touches it with his heels. The horse lunges forward, snorting with delight. "But don't keep us waiting too long," Hayduke yells, fading away.

The two riders vanish down the shadowy lane, loping off toward the pasture. Doc stares after them for a moment, then stumbles down the bank, regains his stability and walks nonchalantly into his floating home, puffing vigorously on a dead cigar. "What's the game?" he roars.

"Who was out there?" Bonnie asks.

"Nobody. Who's dealing?"

"This is the last hand," Greenspan says, shuffling the cards. "You in, Doc?"

"Deal me in." Doc winks at Bonnie and Seldom. "And don't forget to cut the fucking deck."

About the author

About the book

Read on

Insights,
Interviews
& More ...

Edward Abbey
The Free-Range Chronology

*The following timeline favors instances of
defiance and pure outlawry in the life of its
subject. As such, it makes no pretension to
wholeness; absent from its catalog are many
traces of Edward Abbey's everyday life—the
lovers and evictions, the wives, writings, and
jobs (ranger, bartender, painter of high-tension
towers, fire lookout, welfare caseworker, factory
worker, school-bus driver, college professor, etc.).
For a full portrait of the author, the reader is
directed to James M. Cahalan's* Edward Abbey:
A Life, *a fine biography upon which this
timeline heavily relies.*

Pete Dykinga

1927—Born January 29,
Indiana, Pennsylvania.

1928—Commences life of
wandering ("Goes everywhere
at thirteen months," his
mother records in diary).

1931—Protests to mother:
"I'm a big man and don't cry
when I get my head washed,
but I don't see why you have
to do these 'dumb' things
to me."

1937—Attempts to float
down creek in box used for
mixing cement; sinks.

1939 (circa)—"[S]tomp[s]
out of Sunday School . . .
after the teacher replied to his questions by
insisting that the parting of the Red Sea had

really happened" (*Edward Abbey: A Life*, James M. Cahalan).

1941—Moves with family to farm in Home, Pennsylvania; enjoys reading books while perched in apple tree; claims to have a bad heart when asked to help with farm chores.

1942—Writes letter to aunt, tells her he doesn't hunt—hunting being a senseless practice characterized by "dashing around in the rain, through swamp and swill, merely to make life miserable for the rabbits."

1943—Sets about hitchhiking cross-country; ends in Midwest.

1944—Flunks journalism class, junior year of high school.
—Hitchhikes to Seattle; is arrested for hoboing in Flagstaff, Arizona.

1945–47—Drafted into U.S. Army; serves as motorcycle policeman in Italy: "With the infantry in Italy I shot rats, bullied terrified chickens, ordered people around. Almost fell into Vesuvius. Got drunk in the Toledo area of Naples and made a big row. Went AWOL once, for two days, in Milan. Stole a .45 from the army. Rode a motorcycle. Once arrested a colonel" (*Confessions of a Barbarian: Selections from the Journals of Edward Abbey, 1951–1989*, Edward Abbey).

1947—Attends Indiana State Teachers College. "All of a sudden Ed Abbey came there in a blue workshirt, no necktie, jeans when it wasn't fashionable," recalls a classmate. "And you'd swear he'd just walked in off the farm and he didn't give a damn" (*Edward Abbey: A Life*).
—Posts public letter condemning the draft; FBI opens file on Abbey. ▶

Edward Abbey: The Free-Range Chronology
(*continued*)

1948—Enrolls at University of New Mexico, Albuquerque; explores desert in old Chevy.

1951—Edits school literary journal. During religious conference at the university, releases issue of journal with cover bearing the quotation "Man will never be free until the last king is strangled with the entrails of the last priest"—a Diderot quote he playfully ascribes to Louisa May Alcott. Abbey is dismissed as editor.
—Spends "last six weeks of the semester . . . living in a sleeping bag on top of a small hill in Tijeras Canyon."

1951–52—Attends Edinburgh University, Scotland, on Fulbright Scholarship; researches thesis, "A General Theory of Anarchism."

1953—Drops out of Yale graduate school after two weeks of class. "I had expected, somehow, so much more than is actually here, that the professors would be Platos, the students Aristotles. . . . [M]y calling and my study lie elsewhere, in the sweet air and under the open sky of the broad world . . ." (*Confessions of a Barbarian*).

1954—Assumes caretaking duties for owner of adobe mansion in Peralta, New Mexico; burns down mansion. "I built a wood fire . . . in the livingroom stove. That evening the place was a heap of smoking ash. Alas! No one knows. A superb, an excellent conflagration, a blazing spectacle. Sightseers came from far and wide, and the press too" (*Confessions of a Barbarian*).

1955—Sets fire to tires in "a crater west of Albuquerque and creat[es] quite a stir among people who thought it was a volcano erupting" (*Edward Abbey: A Life*).

1956—Writes "Rhapsody on Farts," an inspired journal entry about intestinal gas. "There are the honest manly unabashed farts of plumbers and locomotive engineers, the candid farts of farmers, the masculine and solitary farts of cowboys . . ." (*Confessions of a Barbarian*).

1959—Accidentally starts brush fire alongside San Juan River, Glen Canyon. "The fire spread into the dried brush, the ivy, the willow thickets. Billows of gray-yellow smoke gushed up, nearly filling the mouth of the canyon; the flames glowered at me, red and furious, thru the leaves and stems of the little jungle. I retreated . . . back to the boats . . ." (*Confessions of a Barbarian*).
—Saws down a dozen billboards with friends, Taos, New Mexico.

1960—Awarded master's degree from University of Mexico for thesis "Anarchism and the Morality of Violence."

1963—Burns furniture for fuel while house-sitting in Santa Fe.

1966—Attends antiwar rally, Washington, D.C.
—Takes LSD in Death Valley. "My one experiment with LSD was an uncomfortable and inconclusive failure: the stars quivered in a cloudy cobweb but the big spider-God failed to appear . . ." (*Confessions of a Barbarian*).

1968—Gives antiwar speech at the Rocky Mountain Book Festival; provokes some boos and some early departures. ▶

Edward Abbey: The Free-Range Chronology
(*continued*)

—Serves brief stint teaching English at Western Carolina University, in "dry" town of Cullowhee, North Carolina. "On wild, drunken, reckless drives through the countryside, Abbey thr[ows] his homebrew bottles out the window and rage[s] against the ugly billboards defacing the landscape" (*Edward Abbey: A Life*). Burns down billboard.

1969—Receives award from tourist bureau of hometown; uses occasion to scold civic leaders for adverse policies. "Get that goddamned traffic off Main Street and put in a parkway, benches, and trees."

1972—Writes Christmas letter to parents: "Merry Christmas and all that, but I must say that never has Christmas in America seemed to me so obscene as now—this national orgy of gluttony, fake religiosity, nauseating and hypocrite music, the cobweb of official lies, and deception while the B-52s are doing their shameful and cowardly work in Vietnam . . ." (*Confessions of a Barbarian*).

1973—Offends locals in Arizona's Aravaipa Canyon by skinny-dipping at the Whittell Nature Preserve—a preserve he is employed to patrol. "I'm as vain as Narcissus; I love mirrors and running around stark-raving naked. And I enjoy amazing success with girls . . ." (*Confessions of a Barbarian*).

1974—Takes poke at Tom Wolfe in letter to *Harper's;* calls him "a sycophant to the wealthy and powerful [who] has no peer but William Buckley."

1975—Sabotages bulldozers to protest construction of Route 95 in Utah.

1977—Gives reading at University of Arizona; his choice of material—poems rather than prose—incites small exodus and prompts ire of local newspaper: "Abbey should have stayed home . . . to preserve his image as the cactus jumping Henry David Thoreau. . . . Instead he came to Tucson to treat his audience to low-class erotic poetry."
—Publishes "The Right to Arms," a *Playboy* essay in which he declares: "I am opposed, absolutely, to every move the state makes to restrict my right to buy, own, possess, and carry a firearm. . . . The tank, the B-52, the fighter-bomber, the state-controlled police and military are the weapons of dictatorship. The rifle is the weapon of democracy" (*Abbey's Road*, Edward Abbey).

1978—Speaks at antinuclear rally on behalf of arrested activists, Boulder, Colorado; says nukes "take all the fun out of war."

1979 (ca.)—Is sent for groceries in Tucson by fourth wife; returns two days later.

1980—Writes article for *Running* magazine; says "I hate running, and most other forms of physical effort."
—Gives lecture to writing class at University of Arizona; tells students, "To avoid steady work for half a century, as I have done, requires talent."

1981—Funds and participates in Earth First! protest at Glen Canyon Dam, where activists unfurl a 300-foot plastic "crack" down face of dam.
—Writes "Before the Boom: A Last Look at the Towns and Trails in the Shadow of MX," a *Rolling Stone* essay condemning tests of nuclear missiles in desert. ▶

Edward Abbey: The Free-Range Chronology
(*continued*)

1983—Sends letter to be read at Earth First! event: "Climb those mountains, run those rivers, explore those forests, investigate those deserts, love the sun and the moon and the stars and we will outlive our enemies, we will piss on their graves, and we will love and nurture and who knows—even marry their children. . . ."

1984—Describes experience of writing for *National Geographic* as being "like trying to jerk off while wearing ski mitts."
—Gives interview to *Mother Earth News;* says: "I'm . . . something of an anarchist, because I learned long ago to distrust the government, and not only the government but all big institutions: big business, big military, big cities, big churches, big labor unions . . . any institution that grows so large that it's no longer under the control of its membership. My kind of anarchism is no more than democracy pushed as far as it can be pushed, government by the people, decentralized power in all its forms."

1985—Lays into cattle industry during controversial reading at University of Montana; waves pistol while uttering such vitriolic comments as: "Western cattlemen are nothing more than welfare parasites. They've been getting a free ride on the public lands for over a century. . . . We do not need cowboys or ranchers. We've carried them on our backs long enough." Describes audience response thus: "Sitting ovation. Gunfire in parking lot" (*One Life at a Time, Please,* Edward Abbey).

1987—Declines Irving Howe's invitation to event honoring his (Abbey's) induction into the American Academy of Arts and Letters:

"I appreciate the intended honor but will not be able to attend the awards ceremony on May 20th: I'm figuring on going down a river in Idaho that week. Besides, to tell the truth, I think that prizes are for little boys. You can give my $5,000 to somebody else. I don't need it or really want it" (*Edward Abbey: A Life*).
—Reviews John Updike novel *Roger's Version* in *The Nation;* calls Updike "the Engelbert Humperdinck of contemporary American Lit" and says, "[A]s in every work by Updike, the conclusion is crushing, satisfactory, and comes not a page too soon."

1988—Buys himself a red 1975 Cadillac convertible for his sixty-first birthday. "Finally bought my Pimpmobile," he notes in journal.
—Writes new preface for *Desert Solitaire,* saying "I did not mean to be mistaken for a *nature* writer. I never wanted to be anything but a writer, period. . . . I have never looked inside a book by Muir or Burroughs and don't intend to."

1989—Appears in public for last time, speaking at an Earth First! event in Tucson; dies ten days later, March 14, after bout of esophageal varices.
—Is buried by friends who, in accordance with Abbey's wishes, wrap him in his favorite sleeping bag and lay him to rest in the desert, illegally, beneath a humble gravestone:

Edward
Paul
Abbey
1927–1989
NO COMMENT

Jim Harrison Reviews
The Monkey Wrench Gang

The following review appeared in the New York Times, *November 14, 1976.*

Perhaps this is the only country where as violently a revolutionary novel as *The Monkey Wrench Gang* could be published with impunity to author and publisher. But not at all oddly, no particular attention was given the book when it first appeared a year ago. The novel is a long, extravagant, finely written tale of ecological sabotage in the American Southwest, and no small sabotage at that—great bridges, trains, mining, and road building equipment are destroyed.

Pete Dykinga

The irony is that Edward Abbey wrote this book in an atmosphere of political vacuum as a sort of solider of the void when the only possible audience the book could truly resonate against, the New Left, had largely turned to more refined dope, natural foods, weird exercises, mail order consciousness programs, boutiques, and Indians (jewelry). Surely a base of warhorses is left, a core of politically astute veterans who have changed their pace but not their intentions, but the sense of mass movement is deader than Janis Joplin.

In a society where the only interesting thing apparently is crime, the popular base

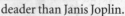

of the New Left, all the student children of orthodontists and that ilk ran off to Aspen and other lumpen-hip watering holes, far, far away from the creeps and ickies that end up in prison.

But the absolutely rejuvenating truth for the reader is that Abbey doesn't care any more than Thoreau cared. He writes about the Southwest with an almost sexual intimacy: passionate, knowledgeable, with all of the purity of anger owned by the betrayed lover. Abbey's fantasy of blowing up the Glen Canyon dam—an ecological disaster equal to a firebombing of the Louvre—appeared first more than a decade ago in *Desert Solitaire*. As everyone knows, Abbey's beloved desert country is fast becoming an industrial sump to feed the fast-buck tourist operators and the power hungers of Las Vegas and Los Angeles.

The Monkey Wrench Gang is a fantasia built on four people who try to stop the process of disintegration in the most uniquely beautiful part of the United States. There is the obligatory Vietnam Green Beret explosives expert, a girl from Brooklyn, a splendid Armenian M.D., and a river guide. They are all plausible, sympathetic in their sometimes comic torments, and Abbey renders them as convincingly as he does the landscape with all the breathless intensity of a true desolation angel. Abbey trips a bit over the question of violence to people but an ideological gaffe is easily forgivable contrasted to the heroics, the sense the reader has of wanting them to "get away with it." Everyone whose concern for the land extends beyond his own humble plot is at least secretly grieved when its beauty passes away permanently, like a race or species, and in the Southwest we have torn a hole in creation.

Reprinted by permission of the New York Times. ∾

" [Abbey] writes about the Southwest with an almost sexual intimacy: passionate, knowledgeable, with all of the purity of anger owned by the betrayed lover. "

The Desert Anarchist
An Essay by
Bill McKibben

Bill McKibben's essay—occasioned by the release of The Best of Edward Abbey (*Sierra Club Books*)—*appeared in* The New York Review of Books, *August 18, 1988.*

Early in his first collection of essays, *Desert Solitaire,* Edward Abbey describes a scene from a summer he spent as the ranger at the then-deserted Arches National Monument in southern Utah, his nearest neighbor twenty miles distant across the sand and the slickrock. Wishing one evening to write a letter, Abbey went outside and hooked up the four-cylinder gas engine that served as his generator. "The engine sputters, gasps, catches fire, gains momentum, winds up into a roar, valves popping, rockers thumping, pistons hissing up and down inside their oiled jackets." The lights go on—indeed,

> the lights are so bright I can't see a thing and have to shade my eyes as I stumble toward the open door of the trailer. Nor can I hear anything but the clatter of the generator. I am shut off from the natural world and sealed up, encapsulated, in a box of artificial light and tyrannical noise. . . . I have exchanged a great and unbounded world for a small, comparatively meager one.

Abbey has spent most of his life in the boundless American desert, occasionally coming in to write. His novels and essay collections (six of each) have found a devoted, even fanatic audience in the Western states, where he is the subject of critical studies and symposiums. Less well known in the East,

Abbey was born on a hardscrabble Pennsylvania farm just before the Depression. He hitchhiked to the canyon country as a teenager, and vowed to return as soon as he was out of the service—the great stone sculptures, the naked drops, had knocked from his heart the "fuzzy hills" of his Appalachian boyhood.

Of his forty years in the Southwest, a great many have been spent alone—not alone in a room, or alone in a crowd, but all by himself a dozen miles from the last pavement, in a fire tower or ranger shack or bedroll spread by a pool of water. For many years, until the movie option payments on his novel *The Monkey Wrench Gang* began to support his modest way of life, he worked as a seasonal employee of the Park Service or the Forest Service— at Arches, at Organ Pipe Cactus National Monument, on the empty North Rim of the Grand Canyon, at the Petrified Forest. And when he had a few days or a few months off, he would take a vacation deeper into the wilderness—a long, foolhardy solo hike, perhaps, trudging 120 miles from one dwindling, briny waterhole to the next. All in all, I would wager, he has spent more time alone than all but a few thousand Americans of his generation.

America, of course, has always been open to voices of solitude and of nature. Abbey argues in an essay from his 1982 collection *Down the River* that only specialists still find interest in William Ellery Channing or Dr. Holmes, and Emerson is more espoused than read, but "in the ultimate democracy of time," Thoreau, who died a minor writer, has outlived his contemporaries. Abbey fills Thoreau's ecological niche, I suppose— besides cantankerousness they share obsessions with the natural world as against human culture, and also with the duty and the methods of resistance.

But the differences are as distinct as the landscapes that inspired the two men— ▶

" For many years, until the movie option payments on his novel *The Monkey Wrench Gang* began to support his modest way of life, [Abbey] worked as a seasonal employee of the Park Service or the Forest Service. "

The Desert Anarchist: An Essay by Bill McKibben *(continued)*

actually, the landscapes probably account for many of the differences. Thoreau reveled in the profligate, fecund bounty of the Northeast—no need, he said, for a yard with "unfenced Nature reaching up to your very sills. A young forest growing up under your windows, and wild sumachs and blackberry vines breaking through into your cellar; sturdy pitch-pines rubbing and creaking against the shingles for want of room, their roots reaching quite under the house." Abbey chose to live in a region with much less rainfall and a higher mean temperature. The desert's main features—the canyons, mesas, buttes, reefs, spires—are the work of geologic time; even its stunted junipers are the slow, seemingly pointless (no saw-timber here) product of centuries. "Alone in the silence," he writes in *Desert Solitaire* of a hike to Rainbow Bridge,

> I understand for a moment the dread which many feel in the presence of primeval desert, the unconscious fear which compels them to tame, alter or destroy what they cannot understand, to reduce the wild and pre-human to human dimensions. Anything rather than confront directly the antehuman, that *other world* which frightens not through danger or hostility but in something far worse— its implacable indifference.

As a result, Abbey's thoughts echo those of the voice from the whirlwind, which asks Job if he knows why the rain falls in the wilderness, far from any human habitation. All creation is not for man, insist God and Abbey; the reasons for the desert, if reasons exist, are beyond our understanding. This thought injects a truly radical perspective into Abbey's nature writings—a perspective

66 Abbey's thoughts echo those of the voice from the whirlwind, which asks Job if he knows why the rain falls in the wilderness, far from any human habitation. All creation is not for man, insist God and Abbey; the reasons for the desert, if reasons exist, are beyond our understanding. 99

implicit in Thoreau, in John Muir, in Aldo Leopold, and in a hundred other unlikelier places, but a perspective still struggling to break into the culture.

The anthropocentric model remains as central as the idea, before Copernicus, that the earth stood at the hub of the universe. It is a comforting notion, the absolute primacy of man, and any attempt to break from it must disquiet us. In one essay, Abbey describes hiking in with a search party to Grandview Point, 2,700 feet above the Colorado, to find a missing tourist. The man is discovered, dead, "limbs extended rigidly from a body bloated like a balloon." Although the buzzards "for some reason have not discovered him, two other scavengers, ravens, rise heavily and awkwardly from the corpse as we approach." Eight men carry the body back to the road.

> Each man's death diminishes me? Not necessarily. Given this man's age, the inevitability and suitability of his death, and the essential nature of life on earth, there is in each of us the unspeakable conviction that we are well rid of him. His departure makes room for the living. Away with the old, in with the new. He is gone—we remain, others come. . . . A ruthless, brutal process—but clean and beautiful.

Perspective, though, differs from detachment. Abbey is firmly attached to the place he loves. He chose to live there because he found it so haunting and awesome. This attachment blazes again and again into anger, as he watches other people destroy what he adores. In one of his finest essays, "How It Was," from his 1971 collection, *Beyond the Wall,* he recollects a trip from Blanding to Green River across the Utah desert. With ▶

The Desert Anarchist: An Essay by Bill McKibben *(continued)*

three friends, he drove a pickup truck over 180 miles of unpaved jeep track past piñon pine and juniper, through the streamside cottonwoods "attended by a few buzzing flies and the songs of canyon wren," across the Colorado on a cable ferry, and up a side canyon, North Wash, where they camped by the bank of a flash flood. "Today the old North Wash trail is partly submerged by the reservoir, the rest obliterated." Utah has run a paved highway through the region, bridging the canyons. The Colorado River lies a hundred feet beneath Lake Powell.

All of this, the engineers and politicians and bankers will tell you, makes the region easily accessible to everybody, no matter how fat, feeble, or flaccid. That is a lie.

It is a lie. For those who go there now, smooth, comfortable, quick, and easy, sliding through as slick as grease, will never be able to see what we saw. They will never feel what we felt. They will never know what we knew, or understand what we cannot forget.

Over and over again the same sequence recurs. The Arches National Monument has been paved, with plenty of parking space and Coke machines. The air above the Grand Canyon is filled with the never-ending drone of sightseeing helicopters. The deep vistas are closed in by the smog from the Phelps-Dodge copper smelter.

Abbey does not consider such developments the sad byproducts of growth and progress, side effects to be ameliorated when possible and tolerated when not. He considers them—he speaks fairly crudely, on purpose—symptoms of the "madness," the "insanity," the "monster" that is "Industrial Civilization." And here he begins to tread on

66 The Arches National Monument has been paved, with plenty of parking space and Coke machines. The air above the Grand Canyon is filled with the never-ending drone of sightseeing helicopters. The deep vistas are closed in by the smog from the Phelps-Dodge copper smelter. 99

dangerous ground. We Americans can deal with someone who contends that he looks forward to the buzzards picking clean his bones; but what about someone who says, as Abbey does, that we must "curtail our gluttonous appetite for things, ever more things, learn to moderate our needs."

We don't worry, of course, that he threatens our standard of living. It is our peace of mind he disturbs, with the insidious idea that someone else might be leading a life with different means and ends, a fuller, more satisfying, life. (A life that, not coincidentally, does less harm to the planet.) Wouldn't *we* rather be floating down some canyon on a raft? Spending the night in Concord jail was not the most subversive thing Thoreau ever did; far worse was spending eight months living on $61.99 3/4. ("Poverty gave him all his wealth," wrote Van Wyck Brooks. "The leisure to spend a day, whenever he chose, walking twenty or thirty miles, or voyaging about the river in December, when the drops froze on his oars, pleased with the silvery chime of the icicles against the stem of his button-brushes.") Dangerous examples these, undercutting our consoling sense of the inevitability of our lives. For their power to disturb, they recall Muir's remark, after he climbed a pine tree in a gale to see what it would be like at the top: "Our own little journeys, away and back again, are only little more than tree-wavings—many of them not so much."

Abbey does not explicitly claim that the mass of us lead lives of quiet desperation, but he repeatedly advances examples that make the point. In his first book of essays, in 1968, he identified an enemy—"Industrial Tourism"—that he has been fighting ever since. Industrial Tourists, he explains, ▶

> " Abbey does not explicitly claim that the mass of us lead lives of quiet desperation, but he repeatedly advances examples that make the point. "

The Desert Anarchist: An Essay by Bill McKibben *(continued)*

work hard. . . . They roll up incredible mileages on their odometers, rack up state after state in two-week transcontinental motor marathons . . . and endure patiently the most prolonged discomforts: the tedious traffic jams, the awful food of park cafeterias, . . . the nocturnal search for a place to sleep or camp, . . . the ever-proliferating Rules & Regulations, the fees and the bills and the service charges,

and so on.

Look here, I want to say, for god-sake folks get out of them there machines. . . . Dig your toes in the hot sand, feel that raw and rugged earth, split a couple of big toenails, draw blood! Why not? Jesus Christ, lady, roll that window down! You can't see the desert if you can't smell it. Dusty? Of course it's dusty—this is Utah!

Though it's obviously not his doing, in the two decades since Abbey wrote that passage, more people have begun to explore, to hike beyond the parking lot. At least his crankiness wasn't entirely eccentric.

He's had considerably more effect in spreading another idea, one that found in his writing its most eloquent expression—the idea of personal direct action to protect the environment. Vandalism, some might say, though Abbey would probably call it counter-vandalism. As early as his college days he was knocking over billboards. In *Desert Solitaire* he describes pulling up the survey stakes laid out by the crew planning the paved road through the Arches, forcing surveyors to do their work over—"a futile effort, in the long run, but it made me feel good." During the years that followed, working by night he poured sand or sugar in the fuel tanks of a "goodly number of earthmovers, ore trucks, front-end loaders, and Caterpillar bulldozers," anything that spent the days ripping up his desert.

Finally he wrote *The Monkey Wrench Gang,* an adventure story about a team of four people—Hayduke, a Vietnam vet; Seldom Seen, a jack Mormon outfitter; Doc Sarvis, a Tucson physician; and Bonnie Abbzug, Sarvis's girlfriend—who set out across the canyon country, doing their best to wreck bridge after mine after road, a spree of merry ecological sabotage. The book, while not as carefully written as his other novels, has much beer-drinking in it, as well as car chases and pickup chases and four-wheel-drive jeep chases through towering scenery, as angry developers and rednecks less enlightened than Abbey's rednecks pursue the quartet. Abbey also provides a large supply of very American technical details about how to damage machinery ("Now we select our operating speed. We have five speeds forward, four in reverse. . . . Now we engage the flywheel clutch." The bulldozer lurches forward, over a cliff, never to build another road.) Unlike his other books, *The Monkey Wrench Gang* sold half a million copies, and provided the ready-made legend for a radical environmental organization, Earth First!, that was formed a few years later, adopting Abbey as its patron saint.

Dave Foreman, who founded Earth First!, resigned as chief Washington lobbyist for the Wilderness Society in the late 1970s after becoming convinced that the mainstream environmental organizations were compromising too often, surrendering too much of the remaining American wilderness to miners, ranchers, and oil interests. Foreman, who organized the loosely knit ▶

> [*The Monkey Wrench Gang,*] while not as carefully written as his other novels, has much beer-drinking in it, as well as car chases and pickup chases and four-wheel-drive jeep chases through towering scenery.

The Desert Anarchist: An Essay by Bill McKibben (*continued*)

and fast-growing group as a "tribe," and who speaks nostalgically of a return to a hunter-gatherer society, still spends most of his time arguing for increased wilderness tracts. But along with letter writing, civil disobedience, and guerrilla theater, Earth First! members engage in fairly wide-spread "ecotage." The group took as its emblem the monkey wrench, and as one of its chief slogans "Hayduke Lives!" (As indeed, at the book's end, he does—Abbey is writing a sequel.) They have dreamed up new techniques Abbey didn't consider (putting spikes in old-growth Douglas firs and redwoods to keep loggers from felling them, for instance) and they have refined others. *Ecodefense,* a handbook of sabotage tips culled from the advice column of the Earth First! journal, has already gone through two editions. But the soul of the enterprise is still *The Monkey Wrench Gang* and Abbey's blend of Thoreau and Ned Ludd.[1]

In his latest essay collection, *One Life at a Time, Please,* Abbey argues his view in three short pieces. The first, "Arizona: How Big Is Big Enough?," asks if increasing the population of Tucson and Phoenix is really a laudable goal: "Where, when, and how is this spiraling process supposed to reach a rational end—a state of stability, sanity, and equilibrium? . . . Growth for the sake of growth is the ideology of the cancer cell." In "Eco-Defense," where he instructs readers on the proper size nails to use in spiking trees (60-penny) he argues in the simplest terms the right to resist—if an Englishman's home is his castle, "the American's home is his favorite forest, river, fishing stream, her favorite mountain or desert canyon, his favorite swamp or woods or lake." Finally, in three pages on anarchy—the most insistently

> 66 The soul of the [Earth First!] enterprise is still *The Monkey Wrench Gang* and Abbey's blend of Thoreau and Ned Ludd. 99

political essay of his career, written for the Earth First! journal—he predicts our civilization will not last a century more before an environmental crisis will force a return to a higher civilization: scattered human populations modest in number that live by fishing, hunting, food gathering, small-scale farming, and ranching, that gather once a year in the ruins of abandoned cities for great festivals of moral, spiritual, artistic, and intellectual renewal, a people for whom the wilderness is not a playground but their natural native home.

His idiosyncratic anarchic vision exalts human dependence on the natural world at least as much as human freedom. Freedom, he implies, involves fitting back into our proper place, "remaining loyal to our basic animal nature."

One could argue with all this, of course. Monkey-wrenching costs time and money to people whose only crime is that they grew up to be loggers or surveyors. It bypasses, in the fashion of the Old West, the democratic process of discussion and compromise. It probably makes life harder for more conventional environmentalists. The saboteurs give traditional answers, too— that it's the huge mining corporations and the powerful timber lobbyists that override democracy. Or that wilderness gone is gone forever, so the stakes are high. Or that a clearcut hillside is the real destruction, and a spike in a tree merely a "vaccination." Or that the radicals can act as Malcolm X to the Sierra Club's Martin Luther King, Jr., making the mainstream conservationists look more reasonable. Or that conscience leaves them no choice. In any event, Earth First! members seem more and more inclined to protest peacefully, sitting down in the path of roads ▶

> " Freedom, [Abbey] implies, involves fitting back into our proper place, 'remaining loyal to our basic animal nature.' "

The Desert Anarchist: An Essay by Bill McKibben (continued)

or camping high in trees slated for felling or hanging banners off the side of Mt. Rushmore, rather than risk muddying their message with debates about "terrorism."

For even the most radical tactics mask the true extremism, which is in ends, not means. Virtually every act of a normal modern life argues with Abbey's premises. Most of us do not really believe that we need to fit back into nature, to dramatically temper our ambitions as individuals or as a species. Sometimes, amid the oil crisis of the 1970s, scientists or politicians would argue that we lived in an "age of limits," a very mild form of the radical ecological argument. Ronald Reagan successfully attacked this line of reasoning as the pitiful, whining surrender of men unwilling to push forward and seize their destiny—of men who didn't understand that it was morning in America. Of weak men, like Jimmy Carter. And Abbey—with his vision of a nomadic society, of Tucson buried under sand dunes over which "blue-eyed Navajo bedouin will herd their sheep and horses, following the river in winter, the mountains in summer"—goes farther than Jimmy Carter.

Abbey, though, has a natural advantage. His gruff pronouncements have an almost unfair power to persuade because they come from a leathery cowboy-without-cattle, a loner, and because they echo up from the canyons of the arid West, the landscape where our idea of ourselves has traditionally been formed. Hayduke is a sort of Henry David Wayne. And Abbey's argument is the argument of a confident man who poses a dare. Man's special gift is reason, as a bird's is flight. His highest calling, then, is to overcome his biological instinct to breed in great numbers and to extend his range of

> " [Abbey's] gruff pronouncements have an almost unfair power to persuade because they come from a leathery cowboy-without-cattle, a loner, and because they echo up from the canyons of the arid West, the landscape where our idea of ourselves has traditionally been formed. "

habitation—to use reason to do the one thing no other animal can do, that is, limit himself voluntarily. Not to build more dams and use more power and grow genetically "improved" mice, but to use less power and tear down dams and leave mice the way we found them.

Perhaps the premise is utterly wrong—the advantages of industrial civilization hardly need listing, and maybe man's happiness does lie in growing in numbers and in power, using his technical ability to stave off disaster. (The oil crisis, after all, went away.) Or perhaps the premise is half-right, and Abbey and others like him will help move us toward a balance somewhere between the Santa Ana Freeway and the state of nature. But the ozone hole above the Antarctic widens each year and the global temperature climbs with each decade and a radical analysis becomes at least a little plausible.

The ultimate goal of the Monkey Wrench Gang is to destroy Glen Canyon Dam, which backs up the Colorado River into "Lake" Powell. Glen Canyon stands with Muir's drowned Hetch Hetchy atop the list of places mourned by American environmentalists. Smaller and more intimate than its downstream neighbor the Grand Canyon—but what, on earth, isn't? —Glen Canyon disappeared before all but a few thousand had the chance to float down it. Abbey was one of the lucky ones, making the trip while construction on the dam was in progress. Abbey called the canyon "paradise," and the descriptions of his trip in *Desert Solitaire* make the term sound technical, precise. From an anthropocentric point of view, the great concrete plug made a certain sense, providing light and power to the expanding Southwest, and helping to water the region even during ▶

The Desert Anarchist: An Essay by
Bill McKibben (*continued*)

this year's drought. But Glen Canyon is the navel of Abbey's universe—its degradation stands for all human folly and arrogance, and its salvation would be the sign that man had turned the corner, begun the trek back toward his proper station. Abbey has not figured out in any systematic way what his ideal, ecologically sound, world would look like. It is safe to say, though, that in it Glen Canyon would be a canyon again, not a dead reservoir.

When Earth First! formed, its initial major action was the symbolic destruction of the dam. Standing on top of the giant structure, members unfurled a black plastic crack that, filmed from a distance, looked astonishingly like the real thing. If the dam ever does go, Abbey once wrote,

> [It] will no doubt expose a drear and hideous scene: immense mud flats and whole plateaus of sodden garbage strewn with dead trees, sunken boats, the skeletons of long-forgotten, decomposing water-skiers. But to those who find the prospect too appalling, I say give nature a little time. In five years, at most in ten, the sun and wind and storms will cleanse and sterilize the repellent mess. The inevitable floods will soon remove all that does not belong within the canyons. Fresh green willow, box elder, and redbud will reappear; and the ancient drowned cottonwoods (noble monuments to themselves) will be replaced by young of their own kind. . . . Within a generation—thirty years—I predict the river and canyons will bear a decent resemblance to their former selves. Within the lifetime of our children Glen Canyon and the living river, heart of the canyonlands, will be restored to us. The

wilderness will again belong to God, the people, and the wild things that call it home.

[1] *Selections from* The Monkey Wrench Gang *and the other books discussed in this essay appear in* The Best of Edward Abbey *(Sierra Club Books, 1988).*

Reprinted by permission of Bill McKibben.

❝ Glen Canyon is the navel of Abbey's universe—its degradation stands for all human folly and arrogance, and its salvation would be the sign that man had turned the corner, begun the trek back toward his proper station. ❞

Have You Read?
More by Edward Abbey

BRAVE COWBOY

Jack Burnes is a loner at odds with modern civilization. A man out of time, he rides a feisty chestnut mare across the New West—a once beautiful land smothered beneath airstrips and superhighways. And he lives by a personal code of ethics that sets him on a collision course with the keepers of law and order. Now he has stepped over the line by breaking one too many of society's rules. The hounds of justice are hot in his trail. But Burnes would rather die than spend even a single night behind bars. And they have to catch him first.

"Abbey writes with fierce eloquence of landscape and city, of stunted souls and drunken despair; he can be funny and poignant at once."   —*Publishers Weekly*

FIRE ON THE MOUNTAIN

Grandfather John Vogelin's land is his life— a barren stretch of New Mexican wilderness, mercifully bypassed by civilization. Then the government moves in. And suddenly the elderly, mule-stubborn rancher is confronting the combined land-grabbing greed of the county sheriff, the Department of the Interior, the Atomic Energy Commission, and the U.S. Air Force. But a tough old man is like a mountain lion: If you back him into a corner, he'll come out fighting.

"[Abbey] states his case with a lyricism that is highly persuasive."   —*New York Times*

Don't miss the next book by your favorite author. Sign up now for AuthorTracker by visiting www.AuthorTracker.com.